LU MIN was born in Jiangsu, China. She has received numerous awards in China including, in 2009, the highly prestigious Lu Xun Literary Prize. Her novel *This Love Could Not be Delivered* has been translated into English, as have several of her short stories and essays, including 'Paradise Temple', 'Hidden Diseases', 'Xie Bomao R.I.P.', and 'The Banquet'.

NICKY HARMAN lives in the UK and is a full-time translator of Chinese literary works. She has won several awards, including the 2020 Special Book Award, China, the 2015 Mao Tai Cup People's Literature Chinese-English translation prize, and the 2013 China International Translation Contest, Chinese-to-English section. When not translating, she promotes contemporary Chinese fiction through teaching, blogs, talks and her work on Paper-Republic.org.

HELEN WANG is a UK-based literary translator. In 2017 she won the Marsh Award for Children's Literature in Translation (UK) for her translation of Cao Wenxuan's novel *Bronze and Sunflower*, and the Chen Bochui Special Award (China). She has previously translated 'Xie Bomao, R.I.P.' and 'A Second Pregnancy, 1980', both by Lu Min.

Lu Min

DINNER FOR SIX

A Novel

Translated from the Chinese by

Nicky Harman and Helen Wang

BALESTIER PRESS
LONDON · SINGAPORE

Balestier Press
Centurion House, London TW18 4AX
www.balestier.com

Dinner for Six
Original title: 六人晚餐
Copyright © Lu Min, 2013
English translation copyright © Nicky Harman and Helen Wang, 2022

First published by Balestier Press in 2022
Published by arrangement with People's Literature Publishing House and
Yilin Press Ltd through Beijing Gliese Culture and Media Co Ltd

A CIP catalogue record for this book is available from the British Library.

ISBN 978 1 913891 32 9

This book is a work of fiction. The literary perceptions and
insights are based on experience, all names, characters, places,
and incidents either are products of the author's imagination
or are used fictitiously.

Contents

DINNER FOR SIX

Prologue

MARINA WALKED THROUGH the air of the old factory zone. With every step she took, time groaned and creaked backwards, the leaves grew back on the trees, the road became muddy again, and tears streaked her cheeks.

In fourteen years, Crossroads had changed beyond recognition: the shop signs, the interiors, the shopkeepers, Marina's own reflection in the glass as she walked past. Everything was different; it was a completely new era. There was new life in those shops, just as there was new life in her belly – the baby that would never know its father. But all she could think about was getting to the other end of Crossroads where she knew Victor would be waiting for her.

She hadn't told him she was coming. Of course not. In all the time they'd known each other, they had never arranged to meet. Their relationship was nothing more than an unreliable accumulation of memories, like the grapes that took so long to ripen on the Crossroads vines. But that would change soon – today, she hoped, in a few minutes' time, in The Glass House, when she and Victor would finally taste their sweet bunch of grapes.

Marina smiled as she walked through the air of the old factory zone. Although eight months pregnant, she felt as light as a cloud. The closer she got to Victor's glass workshop, the more she felt like a little bird about to take flight. She was giddily oblivious to everything else, even failing to notice the unusual smell, the pungent aroma that was drifting in the air, like a vat of rich soup bubbling away, with a handful of black pepper tossed in for seasoning.

It was strange that she didn't notice it. After the explosion, everyone on Crossroads – indeed, everyone who'd been outside at the time – was clamouring to give evidence, almost drooling over their descriptions of the arresting smell that had tickled their nostrils and made them stop whatever they were doing to look up at the grimy sky. They'd sniffed the air greedily, which had set off a chorus of sneezing, and, after the sneezing subsided, there'd been the commotion as they tried to identify it. They'd speculated and argued passionately and loudly, drawing analogies from their individual life experiences, exercising their imaginations. A dealer in fake artwork elegantly likened it to fresh acrylic on an unfinished painting. A burly dealer of second-hand motorbikes (mostly of dubious origin), rubbing his belly, bizarrely declared it a combination of synthetic diesel oil, insecticide and Six Gods toilet water. A tramp who hung around Crossroads by day and occupied the ATM cabin of the Agricultural Bank by night lewdly declared it had the milky pong of the bathwater that a woman with enormous breasts and an angelic face had just finished scrubbing herself in.

But Marina smelled nothing. Her state of mind was far more complex than the smell in the air. She was completely enveloped and overwhelmed by her yearnings.

Even her silk scarf, previously unworn though she'd had it for years, seemed to sense danger lying ahead. It slithered anxiously around her neck, hissing warnings like a snake. But Marina and her bump continued walking through the vivid air of Crossroads, on that axle of time, eager to reach that sweet bunch of grapes.

She had yet to learn that life rarely goes according to plan, that the river doesn't wait till you're thirsty, that fruit doesn't wait to be picked.

As Marina walked through the air of the old factory zone, time flowed in two directions. It crept slowly, with trepidation, towards 2:42 in the afternoon of 13th April 2006. And it raced backwards, like a shadow running back up a tree, to that moment in 1992, when it all began for her and Victor, for all of them.

I

The Exercise Books

1

THE AIR IN the factory zone was where it all began. It was the starter, the yeast, that brewed up all the emotions. It was also the pigment and preservative that would pickle the past.

The factory zone was in the northernmost outskirts of the city, like an enclave that has been flung out into the open. But the air itself was anything but open; it was heavy and close, with a tendency to wrap itself around everything, to embrace with passion, and inveigle its way into your nostrils and throat and down into your lungs. Sometimes it stank of hydrogen sulphide, as though a clutch of rotten eggs had taken to the sky. Or the cloying smell of rust. Or the rotten fish stench of nitrogen. Or, worst of all, xylene, which has that hard burnt-oil smell that makes your throat feel tight, as though someone has grabbed your neck from behind. Depending on which way the wind was blowing, and which factory was upwind, there might be one smell in the morning and another in the evening, or a combination of two or more smells, as though an engineer was being slapdash with the chemicals.

When a strong wind blew, the fulsome air of the factory zone would journey into town, where its passion and devotion were unrequited. And when the city people had to venture out into the sprawling factory zone in the back of beyond for work, the all-embracing smell turned their stomachs. They cursed in silent disgust, held their breath, and hoped they could make a quick getaway. They couldn't bear to see children playing in the dirt at Crossroads, or the fried snacks and steamed buns set out in front of the shops exposed to the wind. To them, that was living like animals.

When the cars came to take them back to the city centre, they couldn't get in fast enough. Their pale, frowning faces were a blur in the car windows as they sped away. The factory zone people saw them off, quietly relieved and reassured. The air in the factory zone was like your parents: you can't leave them or hate them, so you find a way to get along.

Young Ash couldn't find a way to get along with other people. It was probably because he was obese.

Everyone in the factory zone knew the fat boy. It was a label that stayed with him all his life. Even years later, in the humid tropical climate of the South, standing in front of the mirror as a tall, slim adult in a black T-shirt and close-fitting jacket, it was his childhood self that he saw in his reflection.

He had a triple chin and no neck to speak of, his eyes were reduced to small slits, he had rolls of fat around his middle, and his chubby thighs rubbed together, which meant that he walked with a waddle. He'd never had a school uniform that fitted properly, and even the longest watch-strap was too short for his wrist. Whenever the local radio station organised sports events, the teacher would tell him to take the day off. His classmates didn't want to be seen with him.

Fate had cruelly assigned a mediocre script to this sensitive and precocious boy, whose thought processes were as intricate as the twists and turns of an art-house film. But Ash himself would direct that script, his experiences in life shaping his mind as much as his body. I should go back a little – to his father's death, three years before the start of this story. The traffic signal was unmistakeable. The Almighty stood there waving his arms like a white-gloved traffic policeman. That was the moment Ash's destiny began to unravel – when he was eight, and his sister Marina was twelve.

I won't go into detail about their father, but after he died, eight-year-old Ash became a poor little thing. The news spread in hushed whispers. Human kindness is like shit and spit, it has to come out. Compassion, nobility and kindness have a positive physical effect, like an appetite stimulant or a detox. That was important in a place like the factory zone, where you felt the lack of family, where you were always meeting new people, and you had to be familiar with unfamiliarity. Everyone in the factory zone became family: you could be as rude as only close friends and family can be, you could snoop into someone's fertility problems, you could laugh out loud at people's physical defects. Such rich vulgarity complemented the air in the factory zone perfectly.

Compassion requires an object, and the women in the factory zone went out of their way to look after the poor little thing. The moment they spotted him, their hands shot out, jostling to stroke his head, his ears, his skinny little arms, his back, right down to his little bottom and his thighs. If they could, they would have taken off his shoes and nibbled his toes.

"Such a poor little thing, losing his father so young."

"His skin is so soft!"

Their hearts went out to him as they caressed him. At that point, Ash was only a tiny bit plumper than other children. While the women in the factory zone drooled over his peachy skin and dimples, his cute little tummy and bum cheeks, his mother, the newly-widowed Mrs Su, was expected to look fragile and hesitant. She would stand there, squeezing her hands together, looking forward to the future when their intense interest in her family's well-being, and their charity, would cease.

The women's hands, overly familiar and unrestrained, left indelible imprints on Ash. Long after the physical sensations creeping up and down his body had faded, they sent octopus-like tentacles deep into his brain that were knobbly, sticky, and impossible to shake off. This unpleasant feeling grew like a mould on his childhood, silently permeating his entire youth. Even when he took the overnight train to a city in the South, it went with him as a recurrent nightmare in the early days of that unfamiliar place. It would develop into a lifelong wariness of the female of his species.

Later, in the South, each time Ash sat in one of those consulting rooms with the blinds pulled shut and miserably recalled those details, the drowsy psychologists would spring to life, and exclaim, "That's it!" followed by something incomprehensible in English. With a look of relief, they'd scribble a few words in their notebooks, circling them a few times, as if to justify their hefty fee.

Shortly after his father died, Ash started to hang his head on his chest like a rotten gourd. He became very proficient at this submissive gesture. Indeed, it was the bowed head that Lao Shan would spot in the crowd some years later in the city in the South, that would draw him to the twenty-year-old Ash and be the cause of a beautiful misunderstanding.

Ash's childhood experiences shaped him, but they did not nourish him. As I said at the beginning, it was the unique air of the factory zone that nourished eleven-year-old Ash.

Imagine the fat boy on his way home from school, the book bag banging on his buttocks his only companion, going home to a broken and dysfunctional family. He had no father, a mother who was always out, and a sister who kept her head buried in her books. So Ash looked around, swivelling his head on his invisible neck. He felt incomplete, as though he was missing an arm or a leg. He looked out of the window and saw black smoke curling from the chimney in the distance. It was next to the long stretch of rusty iron buildings and the grey giant that was the electricity substation. A little closer, a heavy goods truck crawled along the road, ugly and proud, emitting exhaust fumes that smelled of diesel oil about to ignite. He felt lonelier than a bedbug, more abandoned than an orphan. Why, when there were so many people in the factory zone and so many families in the world, was he so alone?

He stared anxiously at the horizon, wishing that someone would appear. Someone he could rely on, someone strong, whose role was to protect him. But no one came. The air laughed raucously around him, baring its fangs and extending its claws. Each time the wind changed direction, the air somersaulted and mocked this forlorn, lonely figure. Ash decided to make the air his companion and protector, and to write about it every day in his journal in as much detail as he could.

Friday, 31st May 1991

Marina ignored me all day, as though I didn't exist. She was in a bad mood because I deliberately threw away one of her workbooks. She doesn't love me at all. I only did it to get some attention, but I won't do it again. It's not worth it.

The air was good. It smelled like rubber boots and plastic washbasins were cooking in a massive wok with someone stirring in sugar and perhaps some vinegar, and making a thick liquid like tar or dark honey that might drip from the sky at any time, like milk dripping from a breast, not that I remember.

Wednesday, 11th September 1991

Mum is so mean. She never buys prawns. Every now and then she buys fish, but they're always tiny ones that are about to go off. She's a terrible cook. She's always forgetting to add salt, or burning things.

Today the air smelled like dead fish, or rather dead prawns, dead squid, dead blue whale, dead swordfish and dead ambergris humpback whale (I saw a photo of one in Marina's encyclopaedia and they're really ugly). It smelled like our factory zone was at the bottom of the Pacific Ocean and all the water had gone. The teacher told us that the Pacific Ocean is the biggest ocean in the world.

I'm walking about in the biggest ocean in the world, and there are dead fish all around me.

Thursday 12th March 1992

The teacher took us to plant trees. I'm strong, so I dug holes for all the girls in the class, and planted the trees. They ignored me like they always do. So, I went back after school and pulled them all out again. That made me feel better, though I scratched my hand on one of the tree trunks and it hurts.

Today the air smelled really strong, like the smelly water we poured on the trees, or bits of tofu that have been sitting around for a week. It was like having a wet dishcloth shoved in your face all the time.

After school the wind changed direction, and the air smelled of the electron tube factory next door, which was nice. It was like that lovely warm feeling of being next to a very hot TV, like someone was holding my willy. I get that nice tight feeling in my willy every time the wind blows in this direction.

~

The air in the factory zone had a big influence on Ash, affecting his mood and giving him ideas which, although they appeared to be harmless, would have an impact as colossal as a nuclear blast.

In 2004, Ash, now twenty-four, returned from the South to the factory zone he had left ten years earlier. As the train approached the station, he opened the window and took a deep breath of the outside air. The smell brought hot tears to his eyes, and he recalled every single word of those journal entries steeped in loneliness that he'd written a decade ago.

When the girl beside him poked him to check if he was all right, he sniffed a couple of times and mumbled vaguely, by way of explanation, "It's just that I did something bad when I was about your age."

"Are you crying because people were angry with you?"

"No . . . I'm crying because they still don't know about it."

2

ASH'S JOURNALS WERE actually maths exercise books, the kind with a pink cover and green-lined paper inside. A neighbour who was a teacher had given them to him, a stack of twenty to thirty books that she didn't have any use for. They were faded and limp with age, and if you wrote in them with a fountain pen, the ink always smudged.

After his father died, the neighbours kept gifting Ash and his mother things that were well-intentioned but turned out to be useless. His mother had thanked the neighbour and accepted the exercise books, but tossed them to Ash as soon as she'd gone.

"Use them as scrap paper, or throw them away if they're no good," she said coldly as though the neighbour had offended her. But that was as far as she went. She was still dealing with the situation as best she could. Since her husband's death, she'd become an outsider. Men greeted her more briefly than before, whereas women greeted her at length. It seemed very difficult to have a natural relationship with anyone.

Ash didn't throw them away. The ugly, floppy exercise books reminded him of himself. He decided to use them as his journal.

One night after Ash returned from the South, he had a long conversation with Marina, now pregnant but separated from her husband. He told her about Lao Shan and brought out the old exercise books that he'd taken with him to the South and brought back again. It was the first time he had shown them to anyone.

Marina was gobsmacked to see Ash's journals. After sixteen years, they were battered and yellowing with age. She found his old handwriting difficult to read, but discovered that his journal about the air was, shall we say, very dramatic: sometimes vicious, foul-mouthed and sarcastic; sometimes affectionate (with long strings of metaphors about the spring wind slapping his face); sometimes anthropomorphic (with a lot of exaggerated accounts of him grappling for power). Marina tried to laugh about it with Ash, to mask how sad it made her. If he had continued to write about the air in the factory zone like that, who knows what might have happened – sooner or later he would have gone crazy. Fortunately, a few months after he started the journal, the air was replaced by something else. A real protagonist appeared on the scene: Over There.

When Marina saw those two words, she cracked. The tears she'd held back all those years, tears hardened with resolve, came flooding out. She sobbed so hard that the baby inside her started kicking, as if in sympathy.

"Over There" was an interesting way of putting it. It was a simple descriptor, and Ash had probably not given it a second thought, but the euphemism was just as loaded as "doing it", "that kind of money", "that kind of place" and "that kind of woman".

It had all happened so quickly. Suddenly, there was Over There, and Mum had a man. For Ash, preoccupied by his weight and the air in the factory zone, it came like a bolt from the blue.

The first Ash knew of the man's existence was when they were on their way Over There to meet him, he on the back of Mum's bike, and Marina riding her own. He had tried to hold Marina's hand in the dark, but she'd brushed him away. He had looked to her for reassurance, but she was sixteen and thought she was an adult. She had totally ignored him.

Once again, Ash was left to his own devices. Why couldn't anyone be patient with him, or kind? Going Over There was another mountain he had to climb on his own.

Viewed from above, Over There wasn't that far. It was within the perimeter of the factory zone. From Ash's home by the alkylbenzene factory, they went around the L-shaped plastic chemical factory as far as the back gate and turned right to where the electron tube factory workers lived. The factories were like neighbours, sharing facilities like the bathhouse, shops, employees' cinema, canteen, clinic, and primary school. These essential components were like drawing pins stuck on a map in no apparent order. Together, Ash, his mother and his sister wove their way through these random drawing pins, twisting and turning for about twenty minutes.

Ash soon realised that Mum knew this route very well. In an instant the penny dropped. Mum had been going out in the evening for a while now. She'd been vague about where she was headed, then had started staying out all night. She must have been going Over There, which meant that Over There wasn't a bolt out of the blue, it was a great big cloud that had been floating overhead for some time.

When they reached the building, Mum fussed like she had when they set out.

"Remember to say hello to everyone. Manners are important," she told Ash again. Then she turned to Marina, and said, "Please be polite." Why had she repeated herself? Once would have been enough. And why had she said these things in that strange tone of voice, which suggested there might be a reason for them not to be polite?

They went up the stairs and stood in front of the door. Mum gave them the once-over, but there was no life in her eyes, as though she was only doing all this because she thought she had to. Finally, she knocked on the door.

The door was opened by a coarse-looking man in the factory zone's standard navy-blue overalls. He rubbed his hands together and grinned. His bald head shone like a yellow lightbulb and his red nose lit up in front of them. It was clear to Ash that he was a drinker. He was shocked.

"Say hello to Uncle Ding," Mum said.

In the living room, there was a two-seater imitation leather sofa that was splitting at the seams. On it sat a good-looking boy (though his overgrown fringe covered half his face and any expression that might have been on it) and an unattractive girl (whose over-wide grin made her jaw look enormous). They stood up awkwardly out of sync with each other.

"Hello, Auntie Su," they said as their eyes shifted robotically from Ash to Marina and back. In return, Ash and Marina scrutinised the brother and sister as much as they dared without being rude. Then Ash spotted a photograph draped in black gauze: it was the siblings' late mother, peering at the guests from behind the glass frame.

Moving her hand, Mum directed Ash's attention to the sofa, and told him to say hello to his big brother, Victor, and his big sister Pearl. Ash did as he was told. Marina said hello to Uncle Ding and brother Victor, but couldn't bring herself to call Pearl her big sister. As Marina's lips twisted defiantly, Mum had a flash of inspiration. She laughed and started discussing the ages of the two girls with Uncle Ding. They worked out the month and year each girl was born, in the solar calendar and the lunar calendar. After exploring every possibility, they finally established that Pearl was older by three and a half months, and concluded that Marina should call Pearl her "big sister". Then they laughed in satisfaction, as though they had just worked out an extremely complicated mathematical problem.

Mum asked Marina to say hello to Pearl again. This time, Marina turned her head to one side, her lips pursed as if she was trying to hold too many sweets in her mouth, and blurted, "Hello, big sister Pearl." Her words received a simple acknowledgement, tinged with a small sense of victory. Pearl would enjoy that feeling of elevated status again, in the future, under very different circumstances for all of them.

Time is like sugarcane: sweet on one end, bitter on the other, and you never know which it will be. In that moment, in that apartment, when those two adults and four children from two different families came together, not one of them had any idea that with these introductions the tracks for the future would be laid. All they would remember from that awkward first meeting was that until the introductions and greetings were over, they had all stood as stiff as tree stumps in their predetermined spots in a predetermined circle with varying degrees of rigidity.

That night, Ash stroked his floppy exercise book, then rolled it into a tube, flattened it out, and rolled it up again. His brain felt like a blocked drain. He couldn't figure it out. What did Over There mean to him?

He pondered the conundrum every which way, then quietly wrote down some of the set phrases he'd learned at school that week to shift the troublesome thoughts that were weighing so heavily on him: Devote yourself to your country. Pure in blood, pure in heart. Care for the country, care for the people. A mighty spirit lasts an eternity. He wrote each one three times, and by the time he was finished, he had forgotten his troubles and felt much better. Ash loved set phrases. Literary writers might think they were common and restrictive, but to Ash they were amazingly accurate and full of potential, the perfect way to pour his heart out to the world.

As soon as he put down his pen, something went "ping" in his head: every day on his way home from school he had wished for a lovely warm home and a lovely warm family, and now his wish had come true. Of course, Uncle Ding's bald head and red face were awful. And Pearl was just like Mum and Marina. But in Victor he saw a brother, a big brother, a firstborn, a guardian he could rely on, someone who would look out for him. He could stop hanging his head like a gourd on the vine.

Although he was a big, heavy boy, he felt like a soft, mushy fruit, like a willow trembling in the wind. His thoughts about support and protection at that moment would have set the psychologists' pens wagging.

Ash felt hopeful as he closed his journal, but deep in the creases of his triple chin something niggled at him. After the introductions, his "big brother Vic" had gone to his bedroom and stayed there.

He'd shown his face for only a few minutes. His indifference was painfully obvious.

3

FROM THAT POINT ON, Ash switched his attention from the air in the factory zone to finding a guardian-protector and building a happy family. His aim was to turn the six petals into a big flower, to stitch the two pieces of cotton wadding into one cosy quilt. Years later, recalling his original intention, he still felt it had been a good idea, and that it could have gone smoothly. It was just that his emotional investment had gone too far. He hadn't had any objection at all to a stepfather, or a new brother and sister, even if they weren't real ones.

Ash kept a close eye on Mum. He needed to figure out her relationship with Over There, the pros and cons and the prospects for the future.

But it was so hard to see into her mind. She was the epitome of the impenetrable mountain fortress he had read about in school. Ash had always wondered about the change in Mum. His father's death had been a watershed moment, and she'd been a different person ever since. Sometimes, she didn't feel well and wouldn't cook for days. She'd just buy some sesame flatbread, shaobing, for him and Marina, and lie on her bed staring at the ceiling. Then, a couple of hours later, she'd spring to life, jump up and start cleaning vigorously. She even got their winter boots out of the back of the cupboard, cleaned them and put them back again. But one thing was for sure, she didn't talk much anymore, and when she did say something, it sounded insincere. In a matter of months, Ash learned the meaning of the expression "the walking dead" just by observing his mother.

Then she started going Over There. Those evenings began like all their boring evenings, with Ash and Marina at the table doing their homework under the fluorescent strip that buzzed like a fly, and Mum on the sofa. But on those evenings, Mum couldn't settle. She got up and walked about, touching this and that for no particular reason. They watched from the table, Ash scratching his head and Marina chewing her pen, as Mum tried to hide her restless fingers that seemed to be moving beads up and down an invisible abacus. Well, she was an accountant in a subsidiary of the alkylbenzene factory.

They carried on doing their homework, and Mum poured another glass of water for each of them. Finally she shut up shop, so to speak. Frowning as though she was doing something against her will, she said, "I'm going Over There. I'll be back in the morning to make breakfast. Ash, do as your sister tells you."

Ash kept his head down, as though keen to finish his homework. Marina got to her feet and politely said goodnight.

As soon as the door shut, Ash put down his pen and started pacing about like a fat little pony. The small room felt even more cramped with him walking up and down like a philosopher preoccupied with some complex hypothesis.

Marina's good manners didn't last, and she yelled impatiently at him. "Can you stop that? I can't learn my vocabulary with you walking up and down. If you've finished your homework, go and get ready for bed."

The two of them never talked about Mum or Over There. Ash didn't mind Mum going Over There and believed Marina felt the same way. It wasn't an issue, and given her situation, why shouldn't she be "seeing someone"? (Ash had overheard the neighbours gossiping about his mother and her weekly rendezvous.)

The problem was they weren't a good match.

First of all, that Ding fellow, Ding Bogang, was, frankly, common. He was bald on top, had a drinker's nose, a grubby way of rubbing his hands together, navy-blue overalls that stank of rust, and a dodgy look in his eyes. And you could hardly say the factory zone was a small place and there weren't many men around. There was nothing special about Uncle Ding, you could bump into someone like him with your eyes closed. Ash knew he shouldn't judge people by their appearance, but Ding Bogang was so different from his father, who spoke Russian like a foreigner, wore a beige trench coat, and polished his leather shoes every night.

What on earth is Mum thinking? Ash often wondered.

Which led to another question that was even more unsettling. Mum had thrown herself into this relationship with Uncle Ding, yet she never went public about it and avoided mentioning it to anyone outside the family. She had naïvely tried to keep it secret, as though her neighbours, colleagues and acquaintances were even more foolish than she was, as though all the members of the factory zone family, especially the women, were blind, deaf and mute.

It made Ash feel anxious. Mum's refusal to say a word about it meant there was always a possibility that she might, at any moment, deny having anything to do with Over There. Like a gambler walking away from the game.

Why did life always feel so wobbly and precarious?

4

Mum went Over There most Wednesdays. On those days, Marina read through the night and Ash's journal entries were sketchy. Sometimes he didn't write anything at all, just doodled a bit, or drew a few spindly plants which he covered with thorns, jabbing ink marks into the faded pages of the tatty old exercise books.

Why Wednesday? There was an easy answer. Pearl had passed the entrance exams for technical college that year and was living on campus. Victor had failed the gaokao, the national college entrance exam, so there was no university place for him. He was looking for work but living at home, and had signed up for a night class which took place every Wednesday. The class ended too late to catch the last bus home, so he stayed with a classmate. On Wednesday nights, Uncle Ding had the nest to himself. In other words, Mum could sleep over, and they could all pretend there was nothing untoward going on.

When Ash realised this, he breathed a sigh of relief but then immediately felt annoyed. You see, it gave Victor a reason to look down on him. Ash had been hoping to establish a straightforward relationship with him, brother-to-brother, loyal and noble. He also wanted to construct his own big family, one that was respectable. Why did the grown-ups have to go sneaking around, doing disgusting things on Wednesday nights? It was practically written all over their faces.

They had ruined Wednesdays. Now once a week, every week, Ash felt a deep pain. It wasn't a physical pain, but it still hurt every inch of his body. Throughout the week, Wednesdays preyed on his mind. So he pretended that Wednesdays didn't exist, that he didn't have a mother, that he wasn't her son, and that all of this could be flushed down the toilet, without a trace.

One Wednesday, Ash drew a black window across two open pages of his exercise book, with an outstretched hand in the middle. It was a horrifying image that compelled you to look at the hand. There is a story behind it, but first I need to tell you about the layout of their apartment.

Ash would never forget their little apartment. It was at the end of the alkylbenzene factory workers' housing block, right next to a narrow alley. They lived on the ground floor, with their windows opening into the alley. Marina's bed was below the window, and he and Mum shared the double bed by the internal wall. If his father had lived another year and a half, or had been good at currying favour with his bosses, they would probably have been able to transfer from this basic apartment to a slightly bigger one. Of course, there was no point thinking about the what-ifs. Life is harsh, and, like an arrow, only goes forward. In life, there is no time for idle speculation.

I should also say more about Marina. His sister was pretty, even Ash acknowledged that. In factory zone parlance, she was "a pretty girl", just as he was "the fat boy". In fact, there were a lot of pretty fifteen- and sixteen-year-old girls in the factory zone, but when Ash heard people talking about his sister, it was her enigmatic spirit they remarked on, not her looks. She was very determined and self-possessed. Everyone who met her had an opinion, and their opinion was always the same: they didn't know what to make of her.

If that sounds a bit strange, well, it wasn't. Marina was a bit strange. She couldn't stand people saying she was pretty, as if she was an embroidered cushion to be gawked at! She deliberately dressed down, wearing Mum's cast-offs, or the neighbours', without caring how old and unfashionable they were. But her school grades were excellent. She was patient and determined, and she was ambitious. The way she devoured the world classics and learned every word in the dictionary one by one, it seemed she was destined for a great future.

On the surface, there was one word that described her perfectly, and that was "proper". Words like "excellent", "pure" and "diligent" also came to mind, but seemed ridiculous in the shabby context of the factory zone. Who did she think she was? Did she really think she could emerge lily-white from the mud, or grab fate by the throat? She was so proper that it wasn't natural, it was a refusal to acknowledge her fate. There was something deep in her eyes, or in the ends of her hair, or in the hems of her clothes, something that didn't ring true, something that niggled and scared Ash.

On that fateful Wednesday when Ash drew the hand, he'd gone to bed while Marina was still reading. It was a hot summer night, the window was open, and the curtains hadn't been drawn. Years later Ash realised how much of a bookworm she was. If she'd had an ounce of common sense, she would have known that a bright light on a dark night might attract the wrong sort of person, the kind who would quickly suss that only a stupid fat boy and his pretty sister were at home. Marina had spent the evening slogging through her homework, then sat on her bed, relaxing by the window, enjoying the light cool breeze. Feeling a sense of achievement, she fell asleep almost immediately.

Ash had been asleep for a while. At some point, he woke with a start, as though someone had pinched him. He lay on his side without moving, and stared into the dark. Right in front of him was Marina's bed, and, no mistaking it, there was a big black hand reaching in through the window, groping around, searching patiently, stopping and starting, moving and pausing, like an explorer trying to find their bearings. Slowly, the hand felt its way over her shoulder, veering onto her chest, where it stopped, having found what it wanted, then moved extra cautiously. Ash's mouth fell open. He was sure he was screaming, but strangely enough, no sound would come out.

Marina didn't move, she was dead to the world. After what

seemed a long time, she moaned, and rolled from her side on to her back. By this time the buttons on her pyjama top were undone, and the top fell open, revealing her chest. The fingers splayed out, touching her all over. Then the face and upper body that the hand belonged to appeared, the shoulders leaning over the window, the black silhouette looming larger and larger. Ash wanted to sit up, to hide under the bed, to push away that hand and the person it belonged to, but his arms and legs wouldn't move. Then the hand joyfully moved down, deftly rolling back the top of her pants, and sneaking its way inside.

"Victor, Victor!" Ash finally shrieked, not entirely sure why he'd called for Vic's help. Then he curled up as small as he could, wrapping his arms around his head, squeezed his eyes closed and kicked his feet about in the air, like a giant new-born baby.

Marina woke with a start, sat bolt upright, then got out of bed, and staggered over to Ash's bed. "What's the matter? Are you okay?"

She was completely oblivious to what had just happened. She didn't even notice that her top was undone.

Ash pointed at her, then at the window. "Hand, hand," he said, like a child learning to talk that only knew one word. Of course, by then the hand had vanished, and the square wooden frames of the window in the dark looked back at them innocuously.

Suddenly Marina was wide-awake. She looked down at herself, then, using both hands, she pulled the two sides of her top together, held it in place with her left hand, and quickly used her right hand to pull up her pants. Clutching her top and her pants, she started shaking her head, then, keeping her back to the window she scurried around the room like a little white mouse that's been given a lethal shot, trying desperately to find a corner where she could curl up and die.

Neither of them could go back to sleep.

Needless to say, they bolted the window and drew the curtains. They also stitched the bottom corners of the curtains together, not very neatly, but at least they were secured. In front of the curtain they stacked up a stool, some coathangers, a washbasin, an empty pencil box, and a kettle. It was a simple but effective construction that would come clattering down with a terrific noise if anyone tried to push the window open from outside.

But they still couldn't sleep. They sat together on the edge of Mum and Ash's double bed, as though watching a movie, staring at the window, terrified that the hand might reappear.

Mum came home at about five o'clock. She always came back this early, before the neighbours were up. She would creep around like a thief in the night, slipping her bike quietly into the rack, opening the door without making a sound, and while it was still dark, somehow manage to put the kettle on and start making breakfast. She would wait until it was light outside, then tweak Ash's nose with fingers smelling of soap.

"Time to get up! Egg-fried rice for breakfast!"

Ash loved this time of the day, and before opening his eyes he'd repeat to himself, Mum's clean, she smells nice, and she's happy. Time to get up. The embarrassment of another Wednesday was over.

But that morning, when Mum pushed the bedroom door open as gently as a shadow, she jumped back, as if someone had flicked dishwater at her. Her daughter had dark rings around her eyes and sat motionless on the bed, staring at the window and the anti-intruder devices. The whole room was gloomy and stuffy, with the sour smell of sweat.

Ash and Marina snapped out of their stupor and got up to say good morning. Marina did her best to be polite as she greeted Mum, but Ash, instead of stammering as normal, related what had happened during the night with unusual fluency but with an oddly babyish vernacular ("the handy-wandy at the window"), which made it even more horrific. While Mum was Over There, a scandal of unimaginable proportions had taken place at home.

But Ash's storytelling backfired. Mum watched him carefully as he wittered on, looking thoughtful. She tried to pull her trembling daughter towards her, but Marina pulled away, wiped the tears that were brimming in her eyes and marched off to brush her teeth.

Mum went silent. Her hands dropped to her sides. Ash was keen to continue talking, but Mum looked at him, her eyes dull and lifeless.

"You're not a little boy any more. You need to grow up."

Ash had expected tears of guilt and comfort from his mother. Instead, it felt as though she blamed it all on him. Surely she didn't think he was making it up? But I didn't. I didn't. Deep inside, he started bawling like an infant. It's true. I was terrified. I need someone to be kind to me and protect me.

If only he had a big brother, none of this would have happened. A big brother would have taken care of everything for him. Please help me, God, I beg you, I need a big brother.

Exhausted after recounting it in great detail, Ash sat down, dejected. In the early morning light, he grabbed his exercise book with his chubby hands, slammed it open, and very carefully drew the window he had stared at all night. In the middle of that black window he drew a hand with its fingers spread, fingers that Marina would see again many years later, with hot tears in her eyes and a lump in her throat, wishing she could turn back the clock and return to that night, put her arms around her poor little brother and wipe away his horrified tears.

That wasn't the end of the window story. The ending was one of extreme realism. In typical Ding Bogang-style, the window was fitted with an anti-theft barrier within the week.

Ash came home from school to find a wire mesh over the window, made of brand-new five-strand steel wires woven into a grid. It was beautifully made, and glinted like a fishing net in the slanting rays of the sun.

It was brilliant. None of the neighbours had one. Probably no one else in the whole factory zone had one. This unique, ingenious contraption was like a flag of shame flapping innocently in the breeze.

"Uncle Ding brought some scrap metal from the factory. He put it together during his lunch breaks this week and took the day off to fit it," Mum explained, glancing at Marina.

Marina tried poking her hand into the squares of the wire mesh. "Well, it's too small to put my hand through, but big enough to let the breeze in, which means we can still open the window," she concluded. Since it met his sister's approval, Ash decided that the extra layer of protection was a good thing. Marina's so much smarter than me. She's objective and fair, he thought.

Even so, they never opened the window again, not even when Mum was at home or on the hottest days of summer. Marina refused to have the window or curtains open. She refused to talk about it for a whole week. The three of them were trapped in a suffocating, unhealthy space, sweating profusely as they struggled to sleep.

Ash wrote about the new wire mesh in his exercise book with the kind of details you find in an instruction manual. He used an expression he'd recently learned, "Heaven casts its net wide; though the mesh is loose, it lets nothing through." It was a perfect description. One net, two little fish.

Thirteen years later, on an unusually hot and sticky day in late summer just before the workers' housing at the alkylbenzene factory was demolished, Ash and Marina stood outside the window and said goodbye to their old apartment. At noon, the heavens opened and rain poured into the alley. They had not forgotten the hurt and hard times of their childhood, but they looked back on it as passers-by observing from a distance. With determined optimism, they ditched their umbrellas, and got soaked in the rain. The shiny mesh grille that Ash had written about in his exercise book had rusted a long time ago, and stained the rainwater that ran down the walls like an opera singer's painted-on tears.

5

IN HIS LAST YEAR in the South, at Lao Shan's expense, Ash had gone from clinic to clinic, trying to let go of the past and embrace the new. When psychologists asked him to fill in a form for an initial diagnosis, he skipped over the box asking for his age at puberty, as though he didn't know what it meant.

In fact, Ash had invested great hope in puberty, with its strong odours and awakening of masculinity. Not that anyone had ever told him the facts of life (how could they when they never went near him?), but he'd seen it happen to people of his age, and he'd been very optimistic. He'd have a growth spurt and slim down, he was sure of it.

But the reality didn't match up. Years had passed, and there'd been none of the usual signs: no Adam's apple, no voice breaking, no acne, no broadening of the shoulders. If you looked hard enough, you might find an Adam's apple the size of a peanut buried deep in his fleshy neck. As for his voice, well, that was a joke: it had gone higher rather than lower! Even more ridiculous, when you saw him from behind, it wasn't his shoulders that broadened, it was his backside. I mean, his buttocks grew bigger and rounder than watermelons. And, thrown in for free, he got man boobs. Unsupported, they sagged limply, and when summer came, his thin T-shirt skimmed the contours of his chest, highlighting curves that were the envy of flat-chested girls. The thought of Ash wearing a backpack, or running, or sweating, or going to the public baths was enough to make people laugh.

Whatever Ash felt about his ever-expanding body – self-pity, self-loathing or indifference – was taboo. He never discussed it in his exercise book. Like an evasive historian, he found another way of recording it: through Saturday dinners Over There. Every meal he wrote about was like a little commentary on his tendency to put on weight, and lent substance to the journal entries. Those greasy lists recorded the 1000 to 2000 calories that invaded and occupied Ash's body, and turned him into what can only be described as a very fat boy.

After that first meeting, Mum took Ash and Marina Over There every Saturday night, and the two families would eat dinner together.

Mum always made them wait until dark before setting off, which meant eating much later than they were used to, and their stomachs would be rumbling. She wanted to be sure that they wouldn't bump into anyone they knew. But then they'd bump into the neighbours Over There in the stairwell, who'd stop and press their backs against the wall, politely letting them pass. But their eyes said it all: Hey, the widow's here again, and she's dragged her two kids along with her. Ash felt as though a bucket of water had been thrown in his face. He wished he could shrink his huge body to the size of a fly. He didn't dare look at Marina or Mum, because then he'd feel doubly ashamed, whether they'd gone red or not.

After the baptism of stares came the dull, boring evening. Over There were the hosts but let's just say they hosted it in their own way.

Perhaps it was down to shyness that Victor, meeting the "guests" for the first time, had stared at the floor, most of his face hidden behind his hair. He'd uttered a vague greeting in what may or may not have been their direction, and then, without engaging at all, had slunk back to his den – the bedroom they had made for him by enclosing the balcony. Ash had watched the old-fashioned sheet metal door quiver, his mouth wide open, captivated by what he had seen. Pearl had sidled up behind him with a big grin and slapped him on the shoulder.

"Don't look," she whispered, "he's like a guard dog in there, no one's allowed in, not even me."

Ash had reluctantly turned away and sat down like a polite guest. Pearl was watching him. She was so close she was almost touching his face, and kept smacking her lips as she spoke. "Look at you. Your skin's so white! And your eyelashes are so long!"

Ash wanted to shrink back into his chair, but the armrests were digging into his flesh, so he'd pretended not to care as she passed judgement on the other parts of his body. He tried his best to behave well. As for Marina, she'd picked a chair on the other side of the room and quietly opened the book she'd brought with her, lowering the temperature ever so slightly in the tiny space where she sat looking so proper. Mum, on the other hand, put on the face of virtue the moment she stepped through the door: she assumed the role of hostess, and headed straight to the kitchen.

Uncle Ding always wore that horrible brown wipe-down apron that had a greasy shine and made him look like a butcher. Not that it cramped his style. Every inch of that tiny kitchen was carefully put to use, their dinner-to-be laid out like a model landscape – the raw and the cooked, the greens and the whites, the meats and the vegetables, the main ingredients and the seasonings – everything had its place and its role, and they were all chopped and sliced by Uncle Ding. He would spend the entire evening in the kitchen, joined by Mum when she arrived, the two of them working together in clouds of cooking smoke, like slaves to the stove, which gave them an excuse to avoid each other's children.

That's right, neither of them were comfortable talking with the other's children. If there was anything that needed to be discussed they would leave it hanging in the air or change the subject. Many years later, when Ash brought up Ding Bogang with Marina, the man was a faint figure from the past. Thinking back carefully, Ash reckoned that in the two and a half years that they'd been a part-time family, the entirety of what Ding Bogang had said to Marina and himself – just the words, not the pauses and ellipses – would fill less than a page in his exercise book. Mum had done slightly better:

her conversations with Victor and Pearl would probably fill a page and a half. Eighty to ninety percent of all those conversations had taken place at the dinner table.

Saturday dinners were like formal but fruitless diplomatic occasions.

In the awkward time while they waited for dinner, Ash sat in the living room with only Pearl to talk to.

Pearl was neither tactful nor subtle. She grinned pretty much all the time, and made no attempt to hide the fact she was watching him and Marina, measuring them up, alternating between them. She watched them like a dog, staring at the two of them so keenly it was embarrassing. And she kept asking questions, despite their perfunctory answers.

It's worth saying a few words about her appearance as well. Although she didn't look very girly, this didn't stop her from following the latest fashion trends. This may have had something to do with the school she went to, which had pretty relaxed rules about school attire. Every weekend, the attentive Ash would notice something new about her: perhaps she'd curled her eyelashes, or painted her nails a different colour, or had her ears pierced, or switched from big curls to little curls. These things made her seem older than she was.

Pearl took great pleasure in these changes. She would sit at an angle on the sofa, beaming as she examined her nails, or fiddled with her sparkly gold polyurethane belt. It was obvious that she was waiting for Marina to initiate a conversation, preferably about her clothes and accessories, even a few words of criticism would do. Her wide-set eyes sparkled.

But she didn't know Marina at all. Clothes and makeup were the last things Marina was interested in. Marina sat there, absolutely still, as though tied to her book.

With some difficulty, Ash shuffled his backside into the chair, and kindly tried to give Pearl a way out. "Hey, what do you write about every day?" he blurted, shocking himself with the question.

Why on earth had he asked that?

Pearl's eyes widened in surprise and she burst out laughing, "Do you mean a diary? Oh, I can't stand the things. Having to find something to write about every day. Although there is something I do every day. Can you guess what it is?"

"I don't know."

"I look in the mirror. Every girl does!" She laughed again, revealing her pink gums.

There was a loud slap as Marina suddenly closed her book, and a whooshing noise as she stood up. Then she quickly sat down again and yanked open her book once more.

Pearl smiled and shook her head, then, like a magician, pulled a little mirror out of her pocket. With a small and very feminine movement she held it up at an angle in front of her and peered round at Ash at the same time.

Ash caught a glimpse of himself: of his fat, sweaty face, and great big smile. A surge of anxiety rushed through him. Stop wasting time, he told himself. He had to do something to bring these two lumps of clay together as one. Like in the movie *Light of a Million Hopes*, where two families come together and the carefree children laugh and chat in the hazy lamplight. Ash had been moved by that scene. He stopped thinking about Pearl, staggered to his feet, and began to walk about purposefully, like a sentinel striking out for the front line.

Ash went into the bathroom. A bathroom can tell you more about a family than anything else. This one had an old-fashioned toilet that stank of urine and a stained washbasin full of dirty clothes. There was a black terrapin trying to crawl out of an earthenware pot. A metal shelf had been installed across the window, and there were a few empty bird cages hanging from it, and a row of plant pots and bowls, in which garlic, onion and other plants were growing. The whole bathroom was so full of life and so masculine. The opposite of their horrible bathroom at home, that was so feminine, and smelled of shampoo, face cream, cologne, menstrual blood and old lip balm.

Ash squatted for a long time, pretending he needed the toilet. He felt the cold air on his backside, and looked through his long eyelashes at the half-dozen towels that hung opposite. They were dry and hard and grey with age, marked with map-like stains. Ash studied them, then suddenly had a weird idea: if he could work out which ones were Victor's, he could rub his hands, neck, face, mouth and thighs with them, until the hard little bobbles hurt his skin.

Back in the living room, Ash glanced around. The Dings' shelves had no ornaments on display, just untidy piles of old mimeographed factory newspapers. When they needed to wrap something, or put something under a hot dish, or go to the toilet, they just came and took a sheet. There was a small bookcase as well, but that was where they put things like out-of-date desk calendars, cotton work gloves, playing-cards, and bottles of alcohol. Marina had already given her opinion, "I bet you won't find a single book Over There, it doesn't seem like any one of them can read. Bizarre!" At the time, she was sorting through some of Dad's old dictionaries and engineering drawing paper. She had tried to sound fair, but Ash hadn't responded. She was so annoying, he thought, why couldn't she just ignore their differences?

Of course, the two families did have one thing in common: a photo of the deceased. During the boring wait for dinner, Ash's eyes often landed on the mother's photo. She had a curious look of understanding, her fixed gaze fell like a ray of light on Ash, a level of intimacy that gave him the illusion of both warmth and fear. She understood his loneliness better than his own mother, better than any living person around him. It was as though she was still alive, and had just popped out to see a neighbour. When she came back, she would chat with him about the idea of "the big happy family", and paint a picture of warmth and affection, a happy and busy scene.

When the dinner was finally ready, Mum poked her head round the door, and told him in that fake virtuous voice of hers to call

Victor to come and eat. In fact, she spoke loudly enough for all of them to have heard. But he still had to knock on Victor's door for ages.

"Victor. Brother," he shouted in the high-pitched voice that he hated. Eventually, Victor opened the door very slightly, squeezed through the gap, and quickly closed the door behind him, not wanting anyone to catch a glimpse inside.

Victor was tall and thin. Short, fat Ash looked up and saw a forehead covered in acne under Victor's scruffy hair. He felt the pain of envy: He has everything I haven't got.

"Don't call me Brother. It freaks me out. Call me Victor, or Vic." His Adam's apple moved when he spoke, and he had a deep voice.

He doesn't want me to call him Brother? Ash's heart sank. Then he persuaded himself that Victor was right. It's not that simple for him – taking me on as a brother implies additional cost and responsibility. Becoming a family is complicated.

Ash looked over at the dinner table. His dashed hopes transformed into a ravenous appetite.

They always sat in the same places at the dinner table. Although it was a round table, they sat in two camps, the two sets of children down the sides, facing each other across a dividing line, and the adults at the ends.

Those Saturday dinners were lavish beyond belief. As a factory fitter, Uncle Ding wasn't well off, but, as Mum explained while looking straight at Marina to make sure she was listening, Uncle Ding was only extravagant like that when the two families ate together.

Years later, when Ash and Marina talked about those weekend dinners, Marina brought up Engel's coefficient, or how much of a person's (or family's) income is spent on food and drink. The higher the ratio, the worse the quality of life. She implied they lived like pigs and dogs. But Ash wasn't happy with this theory – eating and drinking were an important part of life, especially for those who lived on their own or didn't know other people. It was like huddling together for warmth.

With so many people and so many dishes, everything in the Dings' kitchen came together in a cheerfully haphazard way. The glazed yellow bowl, the little aluminium pan, the stainless steel lunch box, the plastic bowl and lid with a printed flower pattern on it, and the chipped porcelain bowl . . . All of these items brought a kind of vigour and energy to the crowded table. And the wonderful colours of the food seemed especially welcoming, "Come and eat. It doesn't matter what we're served in. Come on. Eat me. Eat me. Drink me. Drink me."

It was probably in response to that primal call that when they ate, they ate with silent gusto. There was no conversation or laughter, just the clicking of chopsticks and sounds of munching as they huddled round the table and focused on the food. Oh, those dinners for six, those churning bellies, the greasy tabletop, and chopsticks clinking against the rice bowls were reminiscent of Van Gogh's The Potato Eaters where the people around the table look terminally poor despite their best efforts. This scene was repeated almost every Saturday night for more than two years, until this makeshift family split up.

Fourteen years later, there would be an echo of those nights, when the two families sat down together on a tablecloth spread on a grassy embankment of the Yangtze, with the newly deceased and the newly born. Dusk would hide their crisscrossing shadows and their faces drained of any expression, and they would avoid any mention of those crowded dinners of the past, or the disaster that had just occurred.

For most of the time he was in the South (except for the short period he knew Lao Shan), Ash ate by himself, a single person with a single pair of chopsticks. It became a conditioned reflex to think back on the Saturday dinners Over There. Lots of people, lots of food – it was the closest he got to his perfect family. Even if it only appeared so on the surface and there was no interaction, it was quite understandable to remember those times with fondness, Ash reflected.

Uncle Ding wouldn't have said anything because the main thing for him was to have a couple of drinks. He had a special cup that was rough to the touch and had a dark green glaze, which matched his liquor perfectly. He only drank Yanghe – the plain bottles with the flying fairy in the green dress on the red label. His one-bottle, one-cup drinking set was a permanent fixture on the dining table. When he came to the table, he would strike his macho pre-drinking pose, then tenderly pour himself a drink, filling his cup to the brim, then sip at it leisurely. He didn't have time to talk.

And of course Ash could understand that Victor would want to keep a distance, only emerging from his den and honouring them with his presence when it was time to eat. His lips were for eating, not talking.

As for Pearl, it was best not to think about her, although that was easier said than done. At the dinner table, she was larger than life: eating noisily as if she was on her own, picking bits of vegetable from her teeth, spilling soup down her front, pursing her lips as she tried to pick up a chestnut that kept slipping from her chopsticks.

Fortunately, in contrast to the dearth of words and enthusiasm, there was a lot of lively eye contact across the table. In his exercise book, Ash likened it to the draw-a-line-to-match-the-words puzzles he was always doing.

For example, Ash himself watched Uncle Ding's cup obsessively. He kept count of how many cups he had drunk, how many he drank in total, and how many it took for him to keel over. He noticed that Pearl watched Marina and copied her every move. When Marina elegantly took the tiniest morsel, Pearl would do exactly the same. Victor would occasionally glance in a random direction through a gap in his fringe. True to form, Marina ignored everyone and stared at the bottom of her bowl as though praying to God to forgive everyone at this mistake of a dinner.

Ding Bogang's gaze was the widest. Steeped in liquor, he transformed from General Butcher (as Ash secretly called him) to a gentle drunk, his eyes like a radar benevolently sweeping the scene after each lip-smacking mouthful, then returning to the table for a little something to help the alcohol go down. It was the same every weekend. He'd keep going until he finally collapsed, as predictable as a runner flopping at the finishing line.

Mum didn't bat an eyelid. She looked as though she'd lived all her life with this boozy mechanic sat across the table from her and had never been an accountant married to an engineer. But there was no warmth in the sunny gaze she cast on the four children as she moved the dishes around the table, or in the way she leapt to her feet to serve them more rice.

In addition to all this, Ash spotted something unusual. It was the eye contact between Victor and Marina, or rather, I should say, the complete lack of eye contact between them. There was nothing, absolutely nothing. But Ash knew that they irritated each other, and were somehow keeping an eye on each other. Honestly, hand on his well-developed chest, he'd swear he wasn't making it up or imagining it: they were definitely watching each other.

There was something going on! Ash felt a frisson of excitement run through him, as though a fluffy-eared rabbit had just tickled him.

In that invisible web of eye contact and non-eye contact, Ash enjoyed his food. Each dish was delicious. His chopsticks and the serving spoons flew back and forth, and the mechanical movement of his teeth and cheeks stimulated and indulged his appetite. By the end of the meal he needed to lean back and spread his legs. His T-shirt clung to the rolls of fat around his middle, and made him look even more like a big-bellied Maitreya Buddha.

When Uncle Ding's boozy radar caught Ash enjoying his food, he would raise his cup and take a gratified gulp. Encouraged, Ash would tuck in again. He wondered if he was eating to please or just doing what a fat boy does best at a dysfunctional dinner: stuffing it in.

But it was too late to stop or change the situation, and after the others had more or less put down their bowls and chopsticks,

Ash would launch another round of attack, happily picking up several pieces of red-cooked pork at a time, drowning his rice in sauce, turning the fish over and picking the bones clean, and hoovering up what the others had been unable to finish. Finally, having polished off the remaining food, he'd survey the damage and let out a magnificent burp, fully aware that everyone at the table, including Ding Bogang, was watching him, their eyes wide in amazement at this human dustbin.

On the way home from Over There, Ash sat on the back of Mum's bike as usual. The tiniest bumps made his stomach lurch, like it does on a swing, when you've swung as high as you can and your stomach drops when you swing down. By the time they got home, he was really suffering. Mum went to boil some water, she said she'd make him a cup of tea, but the thought of drinking tea made him want to clutch his stomach and roll about on the floor.

Marina glared at him, then had an idea. She fetched a toothbrush, and mercilessly poked it down the back of his throat. The bristles made him gag and throw up – all kinds of foods and flavours came out, mixed up together. The smell was horrendous – he was spewing up the entire dinner. Ash watched the vile sticky vomit coming out of his mouth and felt a strange sense of relief.

Marina held her book over her nose and patted his back, his flabby flesh shifting like a hessian sack. She was disgusted.

"Why do you do this? It's such a waste." She didn't understand.

Mum gave him some water to rinse out his mouth. She wasn't sympathetic either, as though it was all down to a change of season, as though there was a frozen river ahead and they each had to decide for themselves how to get across.

When Ash recovered, he would sit down, open his exercise book and quietly make a list of all the food he had eaten: Five-Spice Peanuts, Tiger-skin Green Peppers Stuffed with Mince, Diced Chicken and Soya Beans, Fried Sliced Aubergine Stuffed with Mince, Stir-Fry Loofah-gourd and Youtiao, Duck-blood and Chives, Red-cooked Pig's Trotters, Wafer-thin Tofu Skin Tossed with Bean Sprouts . . .

After that, whenever Ash felt sad or angry about the past, all he had to do was flip through these exercise books. Even when he was at his belly-grumbling hungriest, the carefully catalogued menus brought back those distant Saturday nights and the combinations of delicious aromas reached into the deepest folds of his stomach.

6

Q ING MING IS A festival devoted to one's ancestors, observed by tending to the graves of loved ones and making food offerings. For families without local roots, tidying up the graves at Qing Ming marks the passing of each year with a special poignancy, perhaps more so than New Year. It's quite understandable. In Ash's exercise books, Qing Ming always started on a new page.

Every year, he would recall the Qing Mings of the past in fine detail. In fact, he wrote the same things every year, and in doing so had unconsciously discovered a truth – that life is endless repetition. Having conversations we have had before, filling stomachs we have filled before, yearning for things we have yearned for before . . . Human life is a never-ending cycle of death and rebirth, decay and regrowth.

After Dad died, the Qing Ming they repeated every year involved setting out from the factory zone which was north of the city, taking three buses on the slow suburban public transport system, through the city centre where everyone was burning joss paper for the deceased, to a place in the outskirts far south of the city. Burial plots were expensive, so Mum had arranged to keep Dad's ashes there, for a five-yearly fee, for twenty years.

"What happens after twenty years?" Mum had asked when she was doing the paperwork. The attendant looked at Mum, then at lanky Marina and dumpy Ash.

"Twenty years? That's about right."

Dad had a proper mailing address, for adverts and invoices: Number 64503, Room 8, Floor 5, Runyang District.

Ash had recorded this precise earthly location in detail on the green lines in his exercise book:

Runyang District: the third block in Shigang Memorial Park, looks like an apartment block from outside. Floor 5: Dad's floor, looks like student dorms, with a corridor that has 23 big rooms. The room number is written in black above each door. Dad's in Room 8. There's no door though (perhaps there really wasn't a door, or perhaps he didn't remember seeing it, but rooms containing ashes were supposed to have doors). Inside there are about ten stacks of shelves, like the ones at the supermarket. 64 is Dad's stack number, 5 is his shelf number, 3 means he's the third one back.

Dad occupied a space that was about the size of two glossy magazines and about four or five pencil boxes high. He was at the end of the stack, and when the weather was good, the sun would shine on him. The attendant had pointed this out to Mum as if it was a bonus.

But Ash found the sunshine in there upsetting. For him, stepping inside Room 8 was like falling into an underground river, with no gravity to keep his feet on the floor. He longed to hold Marina's hand but didn't want to admit his terror. She was the opposite. For her, these visits were empowering. She went in without any hesitation, and walked slowly up and down the stacks as if she was visiting a museum. When she reached the end, she started from the beginning again.

She read the plaque on the front of each casket, enthusiastically calculated the age of the deceased, compared it with their photograph, and whispered their names. If someone had left a small offering or something personal, she dragged Ash to go and see it. Ash turned to Mum for help, but she seemed to have disappeared.

Mum repeated what she did every year. She had a very simple ritual: she brought a cloth with her, gave the shelf a thorough clean, from front to back, and to the immediate left and right. When she cleaned Dad's neighbours, she muttered mechanically, "Look after each other now, look after each other." Then she lit a couple of cigarettes for Dad. Pursing her lips, she inhaled, held the smoke in her mouth, then slowly released it. In the time it took for the two cigarettes to burn out, she calmly reported Ash and Marina's school grades and rankings in class over the last year. After a long string of numbers, she stared silently at the cigarette ends as, agonisingly slowly, they burned to ash.

Meanwhile, Ash stood on his own, trying to avoid looking at Dad's photo. Like all the photos in the room, Dad was a stranger to him. How tall was he? Was he fat or thin? What did his voice sound like? What was his favourite food? No matter how hard he tried, he couldn't remember his father. How was he supposed to feel sad when he came to this place? Bored, he watched his fat shadow, and Mum's tall, slim shadow, and Marina's shadow flitting about. He had a vague sensation of floating in mid-air, above this monument that was deathly quiet, which was kind of appropriate for a giant tomb. He drifted about on his own, trying not to think about Dad, which was like trying to scratch an itch through your boot, and in his despondency searched for shadows on the ground below.

Walking through the memorial hall on their way out, they would pass small groups of people who'd just been to a funeral: wailing family members with their heads respectfully covered, and colleagues, talking in hushed voices, each wearing a white remembrance flower on their chest. Marina would always grip Ash's hand as she watched them, straining to catch their conversations, glancing back at the mourners as they dragged themselves sadly away.

Marina would talk about it all the way home, and keep on about it for the next few weeks. She had a unique memory and could remember the dead people she'd rubbed shoulders with. She'd just randomly start talking about one of them. It was like those dead souls from all walks of life were passing through the apartment.

Mum put up with it for ages, then finally had a word with her.

"But death is so interesting," said Marina, with a big smile on her face. "My classmates love to hear me talking about it. I feel sorry for them, because they've never thought about death, or seen death. Their lives are so superficial." There was a superior tone in the way she talked, as though she'd started a new field of study and was way ahead of everyone else.

As Qing Ming drew close in the year they started going Over There, Ash hinted at his unease in his exercise book. This time, when Mum went to see Dad, when she lit the incense and joss paper, and reported their grades, would she mention Over There? Surely that would be more important to Dad than their school grades?

But he needn't have worried, because Over There brought it up first, and invited them all to go to their tomb to introduce them.

"What do you mean, introduce us? Introduce us to whom?" Marina's eyes were almost popping out of her head, the white parts flashing like a dove's wing. Ash shook his head, secretly pleased. That was Over There's style – to do things their way, nicely. Ash thought about the woman in the photo with her delicate features and kind, understanding smile. He wanted to be introduced.

Mum was obviously very uncomfortable. She couldn't make up her mind what to wear, whether or not to buy joss paper to burn as an offering and other minor details.

Marina didn't mess about. She took control of the situation, applying her sense of what was right and proper, "It'll be more respectful if you dress smartly." And as for joss paper, "You don't need it."

The six of them met outside the Dings' building. Victor, who hadn't been out of the house for a long time, had shaved off his hair and moustache, and looked a shadow of his former self. He was carrying a hoe, and looked so different he could have been his own non-identical twin. Pearl was carrying a basket, which must have been heavy because she was bent over like an old farmer's wife.

There was a slightly awkward moment when they met, as though they were all surprised by each other's appearance and attitude. It was the first time they had met in daytime, or outside the home, and, of course, it was their first outing together. There was a little tussle when Pearl refused to let Mum take the basket from her. Pearl looked enviously at Marina and Mum's outfits.

"We can't go by bus, so we'll walk. It's not far." Uncle Ding quickly took the lead, his small team meandering behind him. Ash barely recognised him without his apron tied around his waist and his drinking cup in his hand. It was a good job he was still bald and had a red nose.

It turned out to be a pleasant walk. It was a bright spring day, and as they gradually headed north into the outskirts, the asphalt road turned into concrete slabs, then into flat bare earth, then into a not-so-flat dirt road. The air began to clear, and through the acrid smell of burnt plastic came the smell of cauliflower and wind-dried dung, and as they neared a small river, the smell of foul water. The spring sun innocently stirred up these smells, which sneaked inside nostrils and sleeves, clinging like prolific but benign bacteria. Gradually, the initial feeling of unfamiliarity was blown away by the breeze.

Mum walked with Uncle Ding, and they chatted about the weather: how spring was such a short season, about last spring, the spring before, and the spring before that.

Victor was easy company that day and taught Ash how to use the hoe. Ash twisted his mouth, tightened his fat jaw, and followed Victor's instructions, "Lift it up in the air", "Use your left hand", and, "Bring it down again. Make a bigger gap between your thumb and your index finger." Ash listened carefully. It was a sign, wasn't it? They were going to be brothers. The six of them were going to be a real family.

Marina and Pearl didn't talk to each other, but carried the heavy basket between them, walking with a good rhythm, as though towards a common goal. Marina's lilac skirt floated in the breeze, revealing her slim knees.

This warm, almost perfect, scene delighted Ash. It was a proper family outing. He would never forget it as long as he lived.

They started to see graves dotted about by the roadside. Some were overgrown with weeds, others were small stacks of bricks, and some more elaborate ones had concrete around them.

The grave they had come to see was on the other side of the garbage mountain. Ash had heard of the garbage mountain, but he was overwhelmed by what he saw: it towered above him, the entire city's waste concentrated in one place. A battered truck that had just emptied its load whooshed past them, rudely leaving a trail of dust and smoke roiling behind it. The garbage mountain was alive with flies, and even from a distance they could see the mounds of black insects crawling all over it.

Ash and Marina dragged their feet. Whereas Pearl, suddenly invigorated, dropped the basket, leaving it for her father, and ran lithely through the graves, watching where she put her feet, and disappeared into the scrub and grass beyond.

"After we chose this place, a lot of people in the factory zone came here too. It's convenient and economical," said Uncle Ding, making a sweeping gesture in the air, proud to be able to show his authority on the subject, then cheerfully pointed out key sites on the mountain: where X from Y factory, that produced Z, was buried, having died of A cancer, or B cancer, or an accident, and how old they were when they died.

There were more and more graves, like a crowd of faces rushing to greet them. Marina refused to step over a single grave, and started to lag behind the others. She looked pale, one leg wavering in the air, unsure where to put her foot down. She was obviously more comfortable observing and discussing the funeral home with its plastic flowers. Ash saw Victor glance at Marina and instinctively slow down. Then he took Ash's hand and led the two of them on a roundabout route, avoiding the graves as best he could.

So he did care about Ash! He was holding his hand! And it felt so intimate! Ash felt a rush of gratitude to Victor, and immediately took Marina's hand in a way that said he'd look after her. The three of them walked together, their arms forming a Z-shape that stretched and squashed as they moved through the graves.

They finally stopped at a rough concrete headstone. Carved into it in straggly writing was "Beloved Wife, Huang Mingxiu".

Uncle Ding stroked the headstone, "I poured the concrete and wrote the characters myself with a chopstick. I forgot to write the dates, and by the time I remembered, the concrete was almost dry. Never mind, I won't forget them."

The grass had grown nicely over the grave and where a few strands of white plastic landed on the green, Uncle Ding brushed them off tenderly, as gently as he might remove a stray thread from someone's hair. Ash noticed that he looked different from usual.

By then, Victor had made a start with the hoe on a patch of earth close to the grave. He had a practised touch, and lumps of black soil rolled over, crushing the grass. Their family ritual was to add a layer of earth to the grave and gradually make it bigger. Ash, Marina and Mum stood and watched, the wind whistling in their ears.

Perhaps it was his age, or being immersed in physical labour for a change, but Victor looked good working that hoe. Very soon, he grew hot and stripped down to his vest. He had always looked so long and lanky that it was a surprise to see such a toned body. When he raised the hoe, the muscles in his chest and arms bulged and rolled.

Ash's eyes burned with envy as he thought painfully of his own big girl's chest. Victor looked like a real man, something he would never be. Ash inadvertently glanced at Marina, and was surprised to see her face was bright red. She had turned away and was staring uncomfortably at the headstone. Was she really so terrified by all these graves?

Ash felt another frisson, the same soft tickling of the rabbit's ear. What was that about?

When they'd finished adding earth to the grave, they started with the offerings. The heavy basket took centre stage as one after another, dishes were taken out and laid on the ground. There wasn't much of each one, but there was an astonishing variety of sweet, spicy, stir-fried and braised food, as well as rice, steamed buns and noodles. It was even more of a feast than their weekly Saturday dinners.

Ash suddenly felt vaguely annoyed and resentful. He couldn't help thinking about the funeral home – that tiny space at 64503, Room 8, Floor 5, Runyang District, the miserly two cigarettes that Mum lit in front of Dad's casket, and how she watched the ash drop with no expression at all. Ash glanced at her now. She was standing to one side, her eyes closed, completely still, as though her thoughts were elsewhere.

When the food was laid out, they started burning the joss paper. The basket was like a magician's box – out came the ready-folded ingots and long banners, and the squares of red paper with charms written on them. The coarse yellow paper burned hungrily and the flames flickered in the air, then the ash drifted and settled on the food. It seemed they really were communicating with the deceased.

Uncle Ding found a space to sit down between two graves, and gazed at the food with a look of satisfaction, "I do this every year. I don't cut corners. She had stomach cancer, it was in the cardia. In the end she couldn't eat anything, and she literally starved to death. So every year, I make a proper feast for her."

"It hurt when she swallowed, so she used to stretch her neck and make it as long as she could," Pearl chipped in. And in case Ash didn't believe her, she demonstrated with her own neck. "She had to, even to swallow water and saliva."

Ash nodded solemnly. It was a good topic of conversation. He reeled off what he'd remembered hearing about his father's illness. "With my dad, it was his liver. Can you imagine, at the end his liver was rock-hard, but the rest of his body was soft and swollen. If you pinched his skin, it left a big dent."

"He used to have very pale skin, much paler than all of you. But it went so dark that at the end I didn't recognise him," Marina added unexpectedly, then quickly squeezed her lips tight, shocked by what she'd just said.

Uncle Ding nodded knowingly. "That's what happens with the liver. You know, these past few years, I've heard so much about different kinds of cancer. But cancer in the cardia, at the entrance to the stomach? I can't get my head around it. I mean, how on earth did she get that? We'd never even heard of the cardia before."

Pearl joked affectionately, "Oh, you made such a fuss about that word! You were furious, you were ready to tear that word to pieces. The doctors had no patience with you, they said you get lots of unusual diseases in the factory zone, you shouldn't be making such a fuss about it."

Mum joined in too, but her voice kept cracking. "In our case the liver disease was contagious. Every time I came home from the hospital I was so scared of bringing something in on the soles of my shoes, of not being able to get rid of it, in case one of the children touched it. In the end, I took all the towels, water bottles, washbasins, fans and thermoses and threw them in the hospital bins. It was so sad."

Victor ran his hand over his head, and said unexpectedly, "I can still remember those big pills Mum took. They came in hollow plastic balls, sealed with wax, in boxes of six, all nicely packaged."

By this time, Marina was completely relaxed. "My dad's medicine came in exquisite packaging. Each dose came in its own bowl with a lid, a porcelain one with a pattern on it; the kind that people used to drink tea from in ancient times, the ones that had a saucer and a lid. They were so pretty that we kept them. We couldn't bear to throw them away. In the end, we had them everywhere: under the beds, under the sofa, under the TV cabinet, on top of the fridge . . ."

"Porcelain bowls with lids. That's stylish!" said Pearl, laughing and clapping. Her laughter was infectious, and the others couldn't help joining in. The atmosphere between them had never been so natural. Ash was more optimistic than ever now. He had every confidence about the relationship between the two families. From that moment on, they'd be as thick as thieves, part of each others' lives.

Ash suddenly noticed that Victor was staring at Marina, apparently unable to take his eyes off her, transfixed by her beautiful smile. She almost never smiled when they went Over There, and he'd never seen her chatting so animatedly.

Those little rabbit's ears were tickling Ash again, for the third time. Something had touched a nerve and a shiver ran through him. His heart started racing. He knew in an instant what he could do for Victor, and for the whole family, how he could make the glue that would bond them together. The situation couldn't be more perfect! It was as though an extensible ladder had been set up in front of him, and all he had to do was start climbing.

A soft spring breeze blew by, bringing the stench of the garbage mountain with it. The gravestones all around them were like an understanding audience listening patiently to their conversation, the grass around the stones nodding in sympathy. The discomforts of the deceased, and the circumstances of their demise, all the images and details that the families couldn't forget, came flooding out. Once they started there was no holding back, as though they were bringing out the family jewels to admire. It wasn't like anyone would be envious or begrudging of the deceased. They brought everything out into the open and shared it all freely, as they sat facing the fetid garbage mountain and the fragrant offerings, spring burgeoning around them. By now, there was not only ash on the food, there were fat-bellied bugs and ants crawling all over it, savouring the tasty dishes on behalf of the deceased.

It had been a lively, fun Qing Ming. Fourteen years later, things were very different. Other people had died and gone to the otherworld, and those left behind came together to mourn them. But there were no graves to sweep. Instead, they took their loved ones' ashes to the river in packages wrapped in red cloth and scattered them in the murky water. It was during those funeral rites by the river that something touched Ash's heart, and he mentioned that first picnic. Of all the vivid memories he could be having at that moment, it was the Qing Ming outing that suddenly came to mind.

Finally, when their muscles were aching and their mouths were parched with thirst, they left the jumble of gravestones and headed home. As they reached the door, the colour drained from Ash's face.

"Uncle Ding, you forgot to introduce us to her."

From the tone of his voice you'd think he was talking about a new friend.

"That was the introduction. I'm sure she'll have told your dad about us already, which means that everyone's been introduced." Uncle Ding's answer was straightforward, spoken with dignity and authority.

What Uncle Ding said made sense to Ash. From that moment on, he took Uncle Ding seriously. He made a mental note to write those great words in his exercise book, exactly as Uncle Ding had said them. He was convinced that the people in the otherworld were friendly, that they talked in whispers and worked together to look after everyone in this world.

7

YEARS LATER, at the insistence of the psychologists, Ash tried to think back to the moment he came of age. Sweating profusely, he searched for the imaginary oasis in the desert of his memory.

"I don't think there was a particular moment . . ." he said, wringing his hands.

"Ok, forget that. What about sex? When did you first show an interest in sex?" The doctor tapped on his notebook and asked more directly.

"Well . . ." Ash looked down and squeezed his fingers. Between examining the whorls on his finger pads and his nails, he went back to when he was fourteen. That's what he needed to examine in detail.

By then, Mum had been going Over There for a year and a half. The time had flown past, but there were two things that Ash was anxious about. First, the relationship between the two families wasn't going anywhere. None of them had come out of their shells, especially Victor, who had never taken much notice of him. Ash still felt all alone in the world. Nothing had changed there. Second, how shall I put it, he had become very interested in a particular word.

This brand-new keyword raged like a tiger inside his head. But Ash had backbone, and was doing his best to kill it off silently in his exercise book, no matter how relentlessly it came roaring back at him.

I won't spell it out, suffice it to say that it was associated with another word: "bed".

That's right: bed. The place where you snuggle up after taking your clothes off in the dark. As for who sleeps there, and with whom, and how – he could write a long essay about it. He had the structure all planned out: the introduction, elucidation, transition and conclusion, the gist of each paragraph, the central idea. Most adolescents muddle through puberty, but Ash wasn't one to muddle through. His mind was as sharp as his belly was flabby, and it was in his nature to take the bull by its horns.

Frustrated, he looked at the beds at home: Marina's bed, and the bed he shared with Mum.

There wasn't room for a third bed, so he'd cautiously suggested to Mum, "I'd like to have my own bed. Perhaps Marina could sleep in your bed? You're both female after all."

"What? What did you say?" Mum squeaked, like Ash had said something dirty, something taboo. She stared at him accusingly. "You're too young to be talking about male and female! I don't want to hear another word!"

It was as if Mum and Marina had completely forgotten his age and his gender. They got dressed, washed and did this and that right in front of him, and he had to turn a blind eye to all their stuff: their underwear, their toilet paper, their combs, their floaty scarves, their facial scrub. He knew their bodies and idiosyncrasies, he recognised their particular smell and irritability for a few days each month. The dried blood he occasionally happened to see made him go limp as candy floss, and prompted him to check inside his own underpants for blood.

You think that's weird? Not at all. Take a look at this freakish hulk of a boy. When he looked in the mirror, he saw a fat white backside, and a chest with real breasts. Ash was disgusted and confused: What on earth was he? Were men and women really so different? He often thought about the hand in the window. It had come in through the window in the middle of the night. It had crept inside Marina's clothes, and into his journal. It had even crept into Ash's hormones. That groping hand came to him in flashbacks. Like a filthy laugh, it whispered in his ear, "See? That's what men and women are like. Which one are you? A big girl with breasts and a big backside, or a hand in the dark?" No, he couldn't possibly belong with the hand, could he?

No! I don't want this! I'm so confused. In his head, Ash begged for help from his father, whose face he could no longer see; from his calm-faced mother, and from Marina, who was rote-learning English. But they all turned away. In the end, Ash collapsed into his lonely exercise book, where, on pages damp and crinkled from spittle, he was impressed to find he had made a very realistic drawing of a vulva.

OMG! Ash was shocked at what he had drawn. It was gross. He scratched at it furiously with his pen, tore out the page, shut the exercise book and hit it as hard as he could. Not that it did any good. He had already made that mark on the world – years later, he could still see the outline of the drawing on the page beneath the one he'd torn out. The dust of years had accumulated in the shallow grooves and made the very concrete image of the vulva look like a teenager's face. Even more intriguing were the strings of letters that Ash had written next to it in his dream: AABB, ABB in higgledy-piggledy letters, some fine and wispy, some fat and splodgy.

Finally, having investigated the hand incident from top to bottom without result, our rascally philosopher decided to extend his exploration of the subject to Over There.

His focus was Uncle Ding's bed. To Ash, it was like a sinister fishing line, rising slowly, then falling, hooking a certain part of Ash's anatomy, and painfully reeling him in. That bed had all the essential components: a man, a woman, the night, the closed door ... Ash had a superficial understanding of what went on, but it was all in abstract, which made his thirst burn even stronger. He had to be there at the scene on Wednesday night, he had to be there in person. Ash tried to stifle this weird idea, but he couldn't. It was like the sun at the equator, blinding him, burning him up.

Poor, foolish Ash. But we should cut him some slack. He was a lonely young boy, with a fat baby's body, faltering towards sexual awareness.

That Wednesday evening, after Mum left, Ash finished his homework, washed and got ready for bed. He suddenly felt faint, his face turned bright red (perhaps that evil idea was roasting him alive), and the wet cloth he pressed to his face was like ice touching fire.

When Marina heard him groaning, she went to put her hand on his forehead. "You've got a temperature," she said, annoyed.

"A temperature?" Ash wasn't sure whether to believe her or not, but it had given him a brand new idea.

"Drink some water. And keep the wet towel on your forehead," Marina told him. She was in the middle of a physics question and not taking Ash very seriously.

"I don't want any water. It hurts . . . here," Ash pointed to the pit of his stomach, and pulled a face to show that it was more than a temperature. He tried to stand up, but his legs trembled scarily, his massive body flopped into the chair and his eyes rolled upwards, showing the whites. He'd rehearsed this action on his own many times before.

"Ash!" Marina exclaimed, frightened. "I don't know where the nearest hospital is. And I don't know where Mum keeps her cash. We can't go and ask a neighbour, because they'll make some joke about Mum not being at home at night." She was on the verge of tears, as though he was really about to drop dead.

Worried about his sister's inability to think on her feet, Ash half-closed his eyes and mumbled, "Let's go and find Mum."

"You'll have to hold on," said Marina, flustered. She put on a jacket, pulled him to his feet, and together they staggered out of the door.

It was late and the sun had long since set, but the moon was bright, a willing and canny accomplice, shining cooperatively over them. Of course, Ash was strong enough to "hold on", though he slumped like a sack of flour on the back of Marina's bike. She pedalled hard, struggling to remember the way as they passed ugly heaps of building material by the side of the road. Lanes that in daylight were full of people coming and going were now dark and confusing. They took a wrong turn, but were able to get their bearings from the lights at a shaobing shop. What should have been a twenty-minute ride took them almost an hour.

Ash didn't mind how long it took them, the longer the better as far as he was concerned. Then he'd see Mum in Uncle Ding's bed. Just one look, that was all he needed.

Uncle Ding opened the door. No doubt startled to see them, he immediately called out to Mum in the bedroom. She answered but didn't appear. Marina was exhausted. She leant against the shoe cupboard and shouted across the apartment, "Mum, he's got a temperature and a stomach ache."

Ash didn't care anymore. He seized his chance.

He wrenched his hand from Marina's and burst into the bedroom. Mum was sitting on the edge of the bed, putting on her slippers. When she saw Ash, she impatiently put her hands out to stop him, then calmly touched her forehead to his. Ash quickly took a deep breath. He was surprised to pick up the smell of alcohol in the bedroom. It was a warm, heady odour, and made his legs turn to jelly.

He forced himself to stay calm and, like a puppy nuzzling its mother, he sniffed Mum and scanned her from top to bottom: her collar, the buttons down her front and the waistband of her trousers. Everything except her bare feet and loose hair was normal. Disappointed, and reluctant to give up, Ash turned and looked at the head of the bed. There were two pillows side by side, and the sides of the quilt were folded under to make a tube-shape, like normal. There was nothing remarkable at all. The most unusual thing he saw was a roll of Golden Lotus toilet paper, its wrapper removed, so just the pink crepe paper remained. Uncle Ding came in, rubbing his hands, wearing a pair of knee-length pyjamas that showed surprisingly hairy legs. He gave Ash an unnaturally wide berth.

Ash was still surveying the room, not quite sure what he was looking for. Mum watched him and asked nonchalantly, "Shall we go to the hospital?"

Ash froze for a moment. "Hos . . . hospital?" he stuttered.

"Marina," Mum suddenly raised her voice, "he doesn't have a temperature."

Ash panicked and felt his forehead, which seemed normal now. He was in trouble. That stupid temperature must have gone down. He changed track, and quickly huddled up in his clothes. "I'm feeling cold now . . ."

Marina tried to work it out, "But the whites of his eyes were showing, and he was wailing?"

Mum didn't take it any further. She looked down as she put on her socks, "Come on, let's go home." She looked round at Uncle Ding and explained, "I expect his temperature went down in the night breeze on the way here."

Mum cycled fast. Ash hung his head as he sat dejectedly on the back of her bike. He didn't dare hold on to her waist. He knew she'd seen through him. But that wasn't what bothered him, because Marina could vouch for him. He really did have a headache, and what kind of mother would argue with a sick child?

What bothered him was what he had seen that evening. Had he seen something? Or not? What was he supposed to have seen? He'd gone to all that trouble, and was still none the wiser. He had no idea. Ash suddenly felt twice as sad. Would he ever find out, or would he always be so obscenely confused? He needed guidance, the kind of enlightenment you get from an older brother.

That day, he didn't record his temperature in his exercise book. Nor did he write about the moonlit outing, or what he had seen, or how alone he felt. He wrote a single kindergarten-grade sentence in wonky characters that ached with sadness: I want a big brother.

And guess what? Heaven took pity on him! It turned out that night hadn't been in vain after all.

The following Saturday night, as usual, Uncle Ding fell asleep, drunk as a lord, and Mum was busy cleaning up the aftermath.

Victor, who usually went back to his den, banging the door behind him, unexpectedly stayed at the dinner table. Out of the blue, he blurted, "I heard what you did in the middle of the night. Good on you, guys. Now this is interesting. They think we don't know." As he spoke, his eyes kept wandering in Marina's direction. But her eyelids were down, and she made no comment.

Ash couldn't believe it. His ears pricked up, and he cocked his head at Vic like a puppy that's just been stroked. So he wasn't such a klutz after all? Vic thought it was interesting!

Victor lowered his voice, and said knowingly, "Let's wait and see what happens next." He wiggled his wrists, then after doing nothing for a while, he perked up again. "Pearl, we could learn a thing or two from these guys."

Marina's eyes were still lowered, but it was clear as day to Ash: they were doing it again, pretending they weren't watching each other.

Pearl moved closer. "Sure. I'm up for it," she said. "Hey, Ash, looks like I could learn a thing or two from you, fat boy," she teased, slapping him hard on the shoulder.

There was a rare feeling of collaboration and intimacy in the air that evening, as the four of them formed the Wednesday Alliance. When Mum came in to wipe the table, they each responded as they should have, including Pearl, although she probably didn't know what was really going on.

Ash didn't move at all. He knew what Victor had in mind, though he'd not actually said it, and could envisage an awful scene. He sat there feeling like an idiot, sweat beading on his back, not daring to look at Mum. He had instigated all this. He couldn't back out, nor did he want to. You see, this Wednesday Alliance was the first time they'd been so close. Like real brothers and sisters. He loved it.

There were two weeks of seemingly impossible calm. But Ash sensed that trouble was brewing.

He had almost forgotten it was Wednesday again. Mum went Over There, but this time she said she wouldn't stay long, "Pearl's brought some classmates home. She says they need to rehearse for a show, and they're going to be up late." Feeling the colour rising on her face, Mum turned around and, with her back to Marina and Ash, straightened the quilt. At that moment, Ash couldn't help thinking about Uncle Ding's bed and his quilt-tube, lying there with its mouth gaping and empty.

The following Wednesday, Mum came home just after two in the morning. She was very careful not to make a noise as she turned the key in the lock and pushed open the door. It took her a full five minutes to come in. She didn't made a sound, but Ash woke nevertheless. It was as though he'd been waiting for her to come back. He closed his eyes, and tried not to blink.

Mum came in and sat down on the edge of the bed. Ash stole a glance at her. In a corner of the light from the table lamp, he could see her hair and face, damp from the night dew. There was no expression on her face, no sign of strain. With the tiniest movement, she unrolled her quilt.

Who was it this time? Ash reckoned it must have been Victor. Had he come back from night school? And brought some friends home? Were they playing cards all night?

He could imagine that sooner or later Victor and Pearl would get tired of arranging these random counterattacks, and without any explanation or reason, would just knock on the door in the middle of the night, which would be like lifting the cover in public and then these secret sleepovers would be dangling out in the open. Then they'd really know embarrassment. But it had all started with Ash, and it would be his neck that was on the line. His conscience was like an onion, and as he peeled off the layers to the guilt in the middle, tears fell in the dark. He felt a reckless urge to confess to Mum and promise it would never happen again. He would find an opportunity to talk to Victor, man to man, and put an end to it. The Wednesday Alliance would fold. But there was one question he didn't dare ask: was he really willing to break that fine red thread of friendship?

In the middle of all these what-ifs and maybes, Ash fell asleep. When he woke up, his eyes popped open with a range of new possibilities: Pearl going home to fetch something, and having to rummage through cupboards and boxes in Ding Bogang's bedroom; Victor saying night school had finished, and slobbing out in front of the TV in the main bedroom; Ash accidentally cutting his foot on a knife, and Marina dutifully taking him Over There and pounding on the door . . . Staying Over There would become a nightmare for Mum: she'd think twice about going out, then decide not to go, then toss and turn all night, and hold out till dawn when she'd get up, with dark circles under her eyes, as though she'd been at a vigil.

The Saturday dinners continued, as did Uncle Ding's drunken scanning of the table and Mum's determined virtuousness. The Wednesday Alliance didn't fold, but kept a low profile. The four of them hadn't lost their spirit. If anything, their apparent indifference confirmed their membership of an underground organisation, their guiding principle being to do what they could when they could.

When the four of them eventually came of age, they would see their parents' relationship from an adult's perspective. Like the time Victor and Marina met to talk about Marina's application for an MA course. For some reason, the Wednesday night pranks had come up. After an awkward silence, Victor swallowed loudly and acknowledged how destructive the Wednesday Alliance had been.

"We really shouldn't have done it, but I thought you enjoyed it. I did it for you."

Marina looked away, at some place far in the distance, as though she could see her father as a young man wearing a beige coat. "You're right, I did enjoy it."

"Then it was worth it," said Victor, with a hint of mischief.

They didn't mention Ash. They always underestimated his role in their relationship.

8

TWO MONTHS LATER, the impact of the Wednesday Alliance was felt in a new way. Ash came home from school to find a brand new bicycle in the middle of the living room. A twenty-six-inch blue bike.

Mum stood beside it, waiting for him. "Do you like it? It's for you."

Ash had mixed feelings about bikes. He'd always wanted one, that was for sure, but at the same time he felt embarrassed and scared. He was so big and heavy, he couldn't imagine himself riding a bike. What if he crushed it flat as a pancake? He pictured himself hurtling to the ground on the corner of the street, the bicycle a twisted wreck, while he himself lay on his back like a turtle with its feet in the air unable to turn over, and people standing around, pointing and laughing at him.

Ash crouched down and turned the pedal. The bike was on its stand and the back wheel started spinning. It whirred as it churned the air. It was brilliant. Ash was determined to try it. He forgot the turgid air of the factory zone; he knew that these wheels would buoy him up and carry him along. He would never have to sit on the back of Mum's bike again, like a fat girl with his legs hanging down. He thought he might write a long piece about the bike in his exercise book, with a scented ball-point pen in his neatest handwriting.

A childish smile spread across Ash's broad face. He was so excited.

"Uncle Ding bought it for you," Mum added, in the same tone of voice. Ash didn't look at her, he could imagine her face from her voice.

He felt completely deflated, like a punctured balloon. He

continued turning the pedal, spinning it faster and faster, as if he were a martial arts expert wielding a wind-and-fire wheel that would carry him away from this suddenly-thick air.

So, it wasn't a bike, it was a message – a bribe perhaps? Would he accept it? Why couldn't they have some fun and games together? He made himself get angry. Dammit, he'd rather not have the bike, he'd rather sit on the back of Mum's bike like a fat girl.

No! He would ride the bike and to hell with it! It was retribution. And compensation. Let him swap one horrible thing for something even worse.

Ash grabbed the bike and pushed it outside. He'd never learned to ride a bike, but he was going to start now. He was like a clumsy bear rolling over and over. Sometimes he landed on the bike; sometimes the bike landed on him. The more he fell, the bigger the grin on his face. He didn't mind the bruises, scrapes and bumped elbows – he was happy! Was anyone watching? Well, they were welcome to come and laugh as much as they liked and call him a Fat Pig or a Stupid Donkey and ask what a big oaf like him was doing riding such a lovely new bike. And how did you get it? he said to himself, by selling someone down the river, and being bought yourself. It stank!

Marina came running out. When she finally managed to grab the bike, Ash simply let go and threw himself to the ground, face down, as though trying to disappear into the earth. Marina didn't try to pull him up, but clattered to the ground beside him. "What's with the temper tantrum? They gave me a present too, an Oxford English-Chinese Dictionary. Starting today, I'm going to look up the words I don't know."

His sister had no conscience at all! Ash was even less willing to get up now. He studied the pits and cracks in the concrete road surface, which were even bigger and clearer close up. So what had these clever grown-ups given Victor and Pearl in this generous round of gift-giving? Just like that, their precious alliance ended. Their comrade-in-arms spirit vanished. Which meant he was back to being on his own again, doomed to be cold and lonely forever.

Ash felt wretched. He was filled with a sadness and a disgust he'd never known before, for the four of them and the two adults. If only he could lie there forever and sink deeper and deeper into the mud until he reached Dad and the mother from Over There. It seemed they were the only ones who could truly understand his sorrow.

What's more, Mum punished Ash. It was like she had him on the end of a kite string and wouldn't let him go. She kept hauling him in over the smallest incidents until everyone had pretty much forgotten about the matter.

Like the time he got a tiny spatter of ink on a white shirt. Mum hit him, something she'd never done before, and she did it when Marina was home, right in front of her. She hit him hard, without saying a word. Ash didn't yowl in pain or beg her to stop. Marina tried to ignore them and kept her head down and focused on memorising vocab. She didn't watch or try to stop them. So Mum gritted her teeth and continued hitting him.

The silence between the three of them left a deeper impression on Ash than the bruises on his buttocks and back. It hung over the apartment like a thick mist all night. Perhaps the three of them needed some kind of physical break from the past. Perhaps this was their way of creating an indelible memory of their relationship with Over There.

Ash woke in the middle of the night, or maybe he hadn't slept at all, because of the pain. Either way, the pain was so bad he couldn't write about it in his journal. What use was writing a journal anyway?

He was damned if he was going to write any more.

He limped to the bathroom. He peed, and looked in the mirror at the fat boy with messy hair and lifeless eyes. He looked for a long time, trying to think what to do.

What should he do?

He picked up the three toothbrush mugs, took out the toothbrushes and toothpaste, and filled them with water. Then he took the lids off the two soap boxes – facial-soap and laundry-soap – and filled them with water. He did the same with the various washbasins in the bathroom, all the different ones they used to wash their faces, feet and laundry. Then he did the same in the kitchen, with all the rice-bowls, serving bowls and plates, and all the glasses too (there were quite a lot of them), and the little bowls for condiments. Very patiently, he emptied out all the contents, then took his time filling them with water.

But that wasn't enough. Ash grinned, waddled to the bedroom, felt around for his school bag and found his box of twelve watercolour paints. He went back to the containers of water, carefully distinguishing between warm and cool colours, and squeezed different colours into the water and let them slowly mix together. He stepped back and enjoyed the beautiful swirls: the colours of the changing seasons, the rainbow high in the clouds, the fireworks bursting in the sky.

He wanted the whole sleeping world to see it in their dreams, this kaleidoscope of colours swaying like waterweeds in the bowls. The lightbulb shed a yellow glow from above, beaming warmly and lovingly at Ash. The lights and colours loved him like members of a happy family. He wasn't all on his own. This was the best dream of all.

But Ash's joy was tinged with regret. You see, to forge a new way for the two families to be close, there had to be another couple, not just Uncle Ding and Mum's relationship. If he could bring Victor and Marina together, he would bring the families closer as well.

Of course, Ash didn't really want them to fall in love, that would have been off the scale. He wasn't that naïve. He could see from Marina's character and ambition that it would be completely impossible. His aim was to make them feel good together, to have more of a bond, so that the family he had created in his imagination could stand on a firmer footing. It was a simple idea, it just needed a little push. And then Victor would take him more seriously.

Ash squeezed the paint into the water, a drop at a time. That was all he needed for Marina and Victor's relationship, a couple of drops to sow a seed in their hearts. This would guarantee a heaven-sent harvest, and it would be entirely of their own making.

9

But there would be no harvest. A mere six months later, and without any warning at all, the two families suddenly broke up. Ash's painstaking efforts were for nothing.

Ash could remember every conversation that took place on the day of the breakup, because it was as abrupt as their very first meeting. It was like an internal appointment, or a hike in the price of sugar, or someone suddenly receiving a promotion, where everyone hears the news through mysterious channels, through whispers and glances, and those in the know keep their lips tightly sealed as though it had nothing whatsoever to do with them. Ash was the last one to know about it.

All six of them were there for the last Saturday dinner. For the previous six months, the two girls had often been absent, with Marina revising for the gaokao and Pearl doing extra shifts at the small hotel where she was now a trainee.

For this last Saturday together, Pearl had changed out of her ill-fitting maroon uniform and dressed for a banquet, her big earrings dazzling in the light like another pair of eyes, looking left and right, giddy with excitement.

Ash tried to persuade himself there was a reason to celebrate. Piecing together a family was like herding cats. Only a fool would think otherwise. The most appropriate thing to do was to give a long sigh and enjoy it.

Pearl and her earrings were staring at Marina. Perhaps because she hadn't seen her for ages, or because she'd never have to see her again. Tall, thin Marina, who'd brought her revision with her, was slightly more polite than before. She leaned back in her chair, her textbook opened on her lap. She wore the expression of someone who was about to set off on a long voyage, patiently waiting out the tides.

"Are you doing humanities or sciences?" Pearl asked tentatively. It had clearly taken her some time to come up with this question.

Marina held up her book so she could see.

"Oh, humanities, yes, that's what girls usually do," Pearl said knowingly. "Three of the hotel staff on our floor failed the gaokao, and they were all doing humanities."

The girl didn't know when to stop talking.

Marina gave a meaningless smile. She was confident that she would perform well in the exam.

"Are you all female in your team?"

It was a ridiculous question: they were hotel staff, so of course they were female.

"Yes, my team's all female. And the other team is all female too. And the two team leaders are female as well. I'm not a team leader though." Pearl racked her brain for another question, and asked, "Are all of you girls too, in your humanities course?"

"No, but there are more girls than boys. There are fewer girls doing sciences."

The conversation was limited and boring, and went round and round on the subject of girls and humanities. To put it bluntly, it showed how little they had in common.

The conversation staggered on. They were struggling to keep it alive when Victor came home from work. (He had finally found a job as a factory glassblower. Ash didn't know it at the time, but this was one of the reasons why the family was breaking up.) Marina immediately stopped talking and started reading her book. She didn't say another word all evening. Having sown the seeds, Ash was watching. It was such a pity, and so mean of her, when he'd put so much thought and effort into it.

Victor was holding a birdcage. It was strange that he'd chosen that day of all days to buy a bird. It certainly provided him with an excuse to avoid everyone: with the bike-key in his mouth, the factory newspaper in one hand, and the bird-cage in the other, he couldn't talk to anyone. He went straight to the bathroom, hung the birdcage in front of the window and started whistling to the little bird. The short whistles behind the closed bathroom door sounded like he was addressing it with a speech that no one could understand.

What kind of bird was it? A huamei? Ash suddenly thought to ask, thinking of a little brown songbird with white circles around its eyes. But he didn't ask. His voice had recently started to change, breaking at last, and it was at that horrible stage when it sounded awful. He didn't want to say anything anyway – from the looks of things, it seemed that he was the only person there who was shocked and upset that this was suddenly their last dinner together. They didn't seem to care. They were too lazy and mean to show even the slightest emotion.

Ash bit his lip. He hated being the age he was. From twelve to fourteen and a half, however much he'd grown up, he was still a kid. The others had exit routes: Victor was an amazing glassblower, Pearl put pristine sheets on hotel beds, Marina was going to get into an amazing university. Ash didn't. He was the only one who yearned for this "family", even if it was lukewarm. He adored Victor, he tolerated Pearl, he sucked up to Marina, he hadn't made a fuss about Ding Bogang, and he hadn't borne any grudges against Mum. He had done all that compromising and flattering to make this messy situation work, and they were going to throw it all away in the blink of an eye.

Nothing unusual happened for the rest of the dinner. They all talked about the bird. It was seemingly the one topic of conversation that could get them through the evening. It was so engrossing you'd think they were watching a ship about to sink beneath the waves.

"What kind of bird is it?"

"It's a waxbill, see its orange beak?"

"It's so brightly coloured. Can it sing?"

"Is it a kind of sparrow? Is it related to the canary?"

"Someone was selling them by the side of the road. This was the last one. The man was keen to go home, that's why it was so cheap."

"Can I go and feed it some rice?"

"Not today. It prefers hard food. Things like corn, millet, and sunflower seeds."

"What about vegetables? Do you have to change the water every day?"

Ash was astonished that at this last dinner, they were talking about something as insignificant and ordinary as a waxbill. It seemed as though they'd all become bird-lovers and this bird was of the highest importance. They were all competing to express their opinions about it, opinions that were so ordinary and superficial. They were doing their best to make their last night together a hasty affair devoid of any emotion.

Ash had yet to learn that people don't take things to heart, and that they are right not to, that life is a series of ambiguous periods of time. You spend some days with some people in one place and other days with other people in another place. One way or another, there are always people leaving and people being left behind. Too much emotion is excessive, and inappropriate.

"Come to our little hotel, I can give you a staff discount," Pearl said with a burp as Ash followed Marina out of the apartment. This odd invitation was the closest any of them came to a decent goodbye. Ash forced a nod, and glanced back at Ding Bogang who was asleep on the table with the leftover food. Victor had gone to the bathroom again, and was whistling tunelessly to the little waxbill.

The series of exchanges devoid of all meaning and emotion left Ash with a feeling of ice-cold despondency. He sat on the back of his mother's bike, while she and his sister chatted with fake enthusiasm about tomorrow's weather. They were in a good mood. How many times had the three of them done this, cycled this same route Over There and back again. He'd come to like the rhythm and the relationship, and the relative stability of it. And now, just as he was beginning to get into his stride, the banks of the river had collapsed. He'd known for a long time that his moody mother might throw in her cards at any moment.

As the bicycle swerved gently from side to side, rising up and down over bumps in the road, Ash realised sadly that the greatest damage humans do to each other is not done with sharp things like hatred and revenge. No, it was done with soft, fluffy indifference. It was in this moment of sadness that the idea of making a long journey was born. Ash was in third grade, and could apply to go to school in another city the following year. The further away the better. Ash resolved to be ruthless when he left, so ruthless that he would shock them all, to show them what he was made of.

This new thought felt like compensation to Ash. He sat patiently on the back of his mother's bike without saying a word, his legs dangling, looking like a great pale lump of a girl.

10

IN LATE AUGUST the following year, Ash's wish came true. He clambered aboard a dark green train with a beige suitcase and headed off to the far distant South.

The secondary technical college that Ash went to was a surveying and mapping school. It's hard to explain why he went for surveying and mapping, perhaps from some romantic notion that he might use his fat body to measure the rivers and roads in unfamiliar places? Or perhaps because there were tangible benefits: a guaranteed job, good conditions? No, none of those were important. He didn't give a toss about them. Romance or reality – he hated them both. In fact, the only thing he wanted was to move away. As far away as possible. Those cold-blooded creatures could stay right where they were. He was going to leave it all behind and never think about it again.

But Ash knew, deep in his heart, that he had never shaken off his longing for a family and affection. From Dad's death to the women's octopus-like hands, to the Saturday dinners, to the waxbill on that last evening, six years had passed. He was like a tree that had grown crooked. He felt an incompleteness and a hunger that could never be satisfied.

The long whistle of the train sounded. Ash was determined not to look back. There was nothing to look back at. The only things here were his father's ashes (he couldn't remember what he looked like, only what the woman from Over There looked like); the air that assaults your senses, the cold and indifferent brother that he'd once tried so hard to befriend. The brother-who-never-was wouldn't know that he'd left the factory zone. What a worthless relationship that had been! All he had were his beloved, old exercise books. He was determined to bring them all with him, even though he had to remove a couple of sweaters to make room in his suitcase.

Why on earth was he taking sweaters anyway? It was always springtime in the South, and who knew, perhaps there might be a little love as well.

II

The Drinking Cup

1

THE SMALL POTTERY CUP that Ding Bogang used for drinking his booze was virtually indestructible. On the afternoon of 13th April 2006, when almost everything else was reduced to smithereens, it spun through the air, landed on a pavement covered in debris, rolled over a few times, and survived the explosion without so much as a scratch. If you were a Buddhist, you might explain this strange fact by saying that with Ding Bogang's death, the cup had attained immortal life as its owner's sole relict. As a drinking cup, it had probably already seen its best days. Like Ding Bogang, it was crude and quite smelly.

Our memories can be strangely selective. Analyse the memories of most people, and you'll wonder why they remember this but not that. It's so random that you'd think they just picked their recollections out of a hat. In fact, it's because the brain is choosy. It decides for you what remains vivid and what fades to nothing. Ding Bogang's memories were really not bad at all.

Just four years after the two families separated, when he was fifty-five, his head had become a veritable wine bladder, spurting and splattering booze, until it gradually drained and held nothing but air. One year after the breakup, however, he was still in good shape. He used to sit holding his cup in both hands turning things over in his mind. The alcohol fuelled his temper and made him aggressive. Polite society and all its pettifogging rules and regulations annoyed the hell out of him. For instance, his short-lived relationship with Su Qin (a mere two years and seven months), he thought of as just a little jaunt. He saw the six of them, the two families, as a group of tourists taking a brief rest at the foot of a boulder before getting up, patting the dirt off their bottoms and going their separate ways. It was that simple.

Ding Bogang was unable to explain the reason for the break up of their relationship. After all, they had not quarrelled or come to blows. If he was pressed to find a reason, he supposed there might have been a couple of things. Ding Bogang counted them on the fingers of one hand. Let's see . . . The thumb, that must be Vic's job. The index finger might be Pearl wanting them to apply for a marriage certificate. The middle finger? The little lass's moodiness. The ring finger and the little finger . . . Well, if they were reasons, they must be down to him and his cup. And he laughed without resentment.

Ding Bogang didn't mind admitting it: he was a dyed-in-the-wool drunkard.

It was traditional for a factory man to drink, it was even considered a sign of manliness. And he was a factory fitter whose wife had died, leaving him to bring up two children on his own. What else was he supposed to do to while away the time? You couldn't expect him to doze off in his chair like an old man, or go and hang around in Crossroads like a youth.

Ding Bogang had a pure, ardent love for the booze. The stash of bottles under his bed board proved that.

I mentioned his bed earlier. Ash had only grasped one function of the bed. In fact, compared to what went on under the quilt on top of the bed, the underside of that bed was pretty decent. If we could lift up every bed board the way we lift up quilts, just think what a cornucopia of odds and ends we would find, some of them quite disreputable. Sad little love tokens, hidden poison or stolen goods . . . Not under Ding Bogang's bed! His bed board was completely innocent. It concealed nothing but genuine, top-quality liquor: Fenjiu, Luzhou Laoyao, Xifeng, Jian Nanchun brand bottles. You will recall the Wednesday night when Ash burst into the bedroom. The first thing he smelled was the fragrant fumes from those liquors.

Yes, Ding Bogang was convinced that the best place to store liquor was under the bed. Hardly any light got to the bottles, plus he could lay his hands on them at any time of the night.

It had taken Ding Bogang a lot of effort to build up such a collection. There was a lot of scrimping and saving, but he had the patience and ambition of a true connoisseur. His customary tipple was a few cups of whatever came to hand, it could be Maohuaxiang, or Yanghe would do. But the really good stuff he treasured like his best clothes, they were what made him who he was. Sure, they were expensive, but if you spread the costs out thin, like a flatbread, it was not a problem. He would buy two bottles every Ghost Festival, two bottles at the Dragon Boat Festival, and two bottles when he got a factory bonus. Ding Bogang had a map of China which he was slowly filling in with distilled spirits from Sichuan, Anhui, and Jiangsu. He even had a treasured bottle of Maotai from the east bank of the Qingshui River. No one knew about that one, and he wasn't telling. It lived in its box hidden away under the bed, among a jumble of old shoe boxes.

Why did he buy all this liquor? Even Ding Bogang was not sure. He felt something approaching reverence for his collection. Of course, he craved his drink, but still he stashed those bottles there, gloating over them as if they were gold bars. They were assets intended to tide him over in the event of a crisis, for when he really needed them.

However, there's a cruel proverb which decrees that when someone is prudent enough to stockpile assets for a rainy day, then that rainy day will surely come. And when that happened to Ding Bogang, his bottles were indeed liquidated.

In the meantime, completely unawares, he carried on knocking back the booze. Day after day, he performed the same ritual: raising his cup to his chapped lips, pressing the rim against his stained red gums, tilting it slightly until the smooth, fiery liquor slipped past his teeth and into his mouth. There was no rush to swallow it. You held it in your mouth as long as you could, swilled it around, left and right, up and down, so that the liquid caressed the biggest possible area; the inside of the cheeks and top and bottom jaws. Of course, you couldn't be too greedy, otherwise the sides of your mouth would go numb. You had to keep this alcoholic experience under strict control. You couldn't hesitate as you guided the liquor into your throat with your tongue and dispatched it to the darkness of your belly. Then your mouth, teeth and lips, empty once more, immediately parted again in expectation of the next intimate encounter.

That was the right way to drink booze. Ding Bogang never bothered with the customary snacks. He found peanuts, pig ears and beef jerky unnecessary, even vulgar. Instead, he accompanied his drinking with intangibles: vague, half-conscious thoughts. How a person's gloom could be lightened by liquor. How dry wood could be lit with liquor. How a field could be irrigated with liquor.

Most recently, however, Ding Bogang had only one thought to accompany his drinking, and that was getting his son, Victor, a job. This unattainable goal hung like a millstone around his neck, weighing him down wherever he went.

Ding Bogang had such high expectations of his son – even though he himself was only a fitter, even though everyone in the factory, male and female alike, was either a worker or an apprentice or a retired worker. That was what the factory produced – workers! But he wanted more for Victor. His son, after all, had once been a genuine prodigy.

Ding Bogang never spoke to Su Qin about this. It was something he only shared with his late wife. The promise they saw in their son, the hopes they harboured for his future, these were the focus of their lives together. He remembered with crystal clarity the moment when they chose to name their son Victor. It was at the baby's first-month celebration. Ding Bogang had downed his last bottle and was staggering around the house, his thoughts as cockeyed as his gait, when inspiration struck. The name came to him effortlessly, as if he were an intellectual. It sounded so damned ambitious and grand. His son would be a golden phoenix flying from the hen coop, he would have a meteoric rise, he would live the good life, eating and drinking to his heart's content. He might even land himself a high-level government job, and then the whole family could ride on his coattails!

But it didn't quite turn out like that. Victor went and failed the gaokao, and hadn't even landed himself a job! After two years of hanging around with nothing to do, he was as thin as a drill bit. His hands and feet had gone rusty, and he couldn't even be bothered to use his eyes. He would fix them on something trivial for an interminable time, focusing all his energy on a task that served no purpose. For instance, he would hunker down for a couple of hours and count how many times the tortoise stretched its head out of its shell. When he wiped the table, he used to spend a quarter of an hour studying the stripes on the cloth.

One evening, Ding Bogang saw Vic at the window, pouring over an old factory newspaper from a few years ago. He read for an hour until it got too dark to read. Then he reluctantly looked up and set about methodically tearing the paper to bits. He had an unusual modus operandi. He tore each character out individually: the large-type headlines into bigger pieces, the characters in the articles into tiny squares. Patiently, he accumulated the fragments in the palm of his hand until he had torn up a whole article. Then he reached out and flung them up into the air. They cascaded down as if a constipated sky had suddenly released a diarrhoea of snowflakes.

Ding Bogang watched his son in utter exasperation. He almost wished that he were one of those scraps of newspaper, torn to pieces and thrown out of the window. They could not go on like this. Ding Bogang sat down at the dinner table. It was not time for dinner yet, but he found himself reaching for his cup and the bottle of Yanghe. He needed a drink.

Ding Bogang had only had a small sip when it suddenly hit him that those damned bottles of spirits stored under the bed that he had never touched had a purpose, and that was to get his son a job.

The heavens weren't going to drop a job into the boy's lap, so he had better call in some favours. The only hard currency of any use in the factory was a bottle of liquor. No one would be able to resist. Even those with a heart of stone would know that giving up one of his bottles was like cutting off an arm and a leg.

Of course, when it came down to it, Ding Bogang could not bear to give away the bottles himself. It would have been heart-rending, like selling a son or a daughter. His lips and tongue would have cramped up at the words, his red nose would have gone redder. He might have even humiliated himself by snatching the bottle back and drinking it. Ding Bogang was acutely aware that his feelings about liquor were an unstoppable force.

2

So Ding Bogang asked Su Qin to do the deed. He and Su Qin had been together for almost a year by then. Getting her to pass out the gift-bottles seemed like an ideal solution. It would be less distressing for him. Besides, she was the only respectable person he knew. Everyone would give her the time of day with the way she looked and presented herself. She and her late husband, an engineer, were quite different from most of the factory folk. They knew how to approach the higher-ups in the factory.

Then Ding Bogang hesitated; his old anxieties re-surfaced. The problem was that he still did not know why Su Qin had got together with him, given that they were polar opposites. He had never figured it out. He still remembered the time they were first introduced. She had not even waited for the introductions to be completed before nodding. Ding Bogang had been taken aback by her casual agreement. All the same, he realised he had landed a very good deal. She wanted a face, a body, a chest, a back and a neck and he had all of them. His two children were neither here nor there. Anyone could have two kids. Feeling like he had gone shopping and found a bargain that might slip away from him, Ding Bogang had wasted no time in nodding either.

Then he began to wonder. In fact, he often took his puzzlement out and mulled over it. But he did not dare confront Su Qin and ask her point-blank. Who knew what she might say? Su Qin was an enigma of a woman. Completely po-faced, but very good in bed. Ding Bogang allowed himself to dream. She must like him, at least a bit, otherwise she wouldn't enjoy it so much, would she?

That's enough of that! he told himself. He'd only been in it for the sex, why should he expect her to get serious about him? Ding Bogang shook his head and, in his drunken stupor, came to an illogical conclusion: Su Qin was the ideal person to find his son a job. He could almost say it was her duty. She acted so classy, she should show what she could do.

One Thursday, as Su Qin got her bicycle out, ready to go back home after spending the night with him, Ding Bogang threw his clothes on and chased after her, carrying a heavy bag in one hand. He might have had gold bars in it, the way he hissed in her ear: "This is Fenjiu liquor. This is Xifeng. This is Jian Nanchun."

As he spoke, one hand reached out blindly and caressed the bag, though he could not bring himself to look at it.

"What's this all about?" Su Qin asked, completely flummoxed.

"Eh? It's to get Vic a job!" Ding Bogang seemed to think it was quite obvious. "Those people I mentioned to you last night, why don't you drop in on them?" he went on casually, avoiding the words "and give them a bottle". He squinted at her through drink-sodden eyes, still stroking the bag affectionately.

"Why are you asking me? I can't do it!" Su Qin shook her head in disbelief. In bed last night, he had mumbled a few names, but never explained what they had to do with her.

Ding Bogang acted as if he and Su Qin had already come to an agreement. "It's common courtesy to give them something," he said. "Here, take it! Look what fine liquor this is!" Then he threw down his trump card, Vic's brain power: "Remember, you've got to tell them that my son used to be a child prodigy, he deserves a good job! Really, he was a child prodigy! His late mother and me, we both knew that. It's no word of a lie!"

In the faint morning light, it was as if Ding Bogang was seeing a golden dawn galloping towards them like a horse, its hooves raising the dust. His teeth flashed white as he revived and embellished long-gone memories.

"He could count at the age of one, recite pi at the age of two, memorise Tang poems by the age of three, read newspapers at the age of four, and in the third year of primary school, he could read fourth grade books. In the first year of junior high school, he passed the second year exams. So you see, he's an outstanding kid. He has great prospects! He'll have a meteoric rise! The Ding family depends on him." Ding Bogang paused for breath, then added: "His mother was unlucky, that's true. But you, Marina and Ash, will all be able to depend on him too. As long as we give him a leg-up, he'll be able to pull our two families along behind him. Trust me."

Su Qin stood holding the bicycle, one foot spinning the pedal back and forth. She was not really taking his words in. All she wanted to do was to get moving. He was talking nonsense. Vic, a child prodigy? There was no such thing. She started to push her bicycle in the direction of home.

But Ding Bogang stumbled along behind her, puffing out alcohol fumes into the night air.

"The thing is, it all started when his mother died. He just went downhill, and now he's useless. I feel so bad about his mother, I promised her I'd give him a good start in life. So you see, he absolutely needs a decent job. Don't you think? You have to talk to them!"

Who were "they"? Su Qin tried her best to recall the names Ding Bogang had mentioned the night before, and their jobs. But this was a fantasy. Would "they" really do anything to help Victor on the basis of a bottle of spirits in a dog-eared old box? Besides, she could not, would not, breeze in and demand a job for a boy who'd flunked all his exams. It would mean admitting her relationship with Ding Bogang and there was no way she would do that.

She looked him in the eye as he carried on mumbling, and suddenly understood that he was still drunk, this whole performance was a necessary part of his hangover. It would not have mattered who was standing in front of him, he just needed to show he was making an effort. Giving away his beloved liquor was his way of being a father. At this point, Su Qin decided to compromise so that she could make a quick getaway. She took the liquor, got on her bike and pedalled off.

Ding Bogang ran behind her for a little. His laggard figure, like the shadow of a wall, expanded in the morning light, becoming thin then wide, spreading infinitely to one side, stretching upwards in time and space. He was grandly, and illogically, convinced that these bottles would get his son an amazing job, that in the interval between sobering up and getting drunk again, the problem would be solved. His prodigy-of-a-son had a brilliant future. He would never be like those youths he saw hanging around in Crossroads, who were just factory fodder and lived worse than pigs and dogs.

Ding Bogang smiled. His confidence in this matter was equal to his confidence in the power of alcohol in its pungent mystery to guide him through life.

However, this immense mystery was only good in and of itself. It was ineffective in finding a job for his son. He never foresaw the blow that finally fell. At dinner one Saturday, Victor ran his fingers through his hair and suddenly announced with steel in his voice: "I've found a job. It's at the electron tube factory."

Ding Bogang stared at Victor's mouth, as if he was looking at a bomb, and croaked, "Meaning what, exactly?"

"Workshop number eleven. It's new. I'll be a glassblower on a three-month apprenticeship. I have to report to the Personnel Department next Monday."

Victor glanced around the table, perhaps at Su Qin, or perhaps at everyone except Su Qin. Of course, it was no secret that Ding Bogang's under-bed liquor stocks had been run down to zero in the past few months in aid of getting Victor a job. And they all knew that Ding Bogang's losses had made the old man depressed and irritable.

"How . . . How did you find that job?" Ding Bogang blurted out, hoping against hope that his son was joking. "You're going to blow glass? What kind of a shit job is that?"

"It was posted at the factory gate, two weeks ago. Nobody applied, so I did," Victor replied coldly. He had no idea what a glassblower did, but so what? He could choose his own job.

Ding Bogang jerked his head back as if he had been punched. He held his cup in a trembling hand and, strangely enough, found himself raising it to Su Qin. "Come on, let's drink to it! Now you can relax. He found a job by himself! You heard, he's going to be a glassblower!"

Su Qin got to her feet, accidentally knocking her stool over. She hesitated, then said, "Actually . . ."

Ding Bogang was not listening. He jerked his chin up to drink, missing his mouth and spilling the contents of his cup all down the front of his shirt. Then the corners of his mouth turned down and he burst into terrible sobs. Everyone at the table was overcome with dismay. Pearl clapped her hands twice, whether it was to applaud her brother for his job, or her father for crying, no one knew. Ash felt ashamed. Marina just closed her eyes tight, and wondered what else she could close too.

After his tears, Ding Bogang pulled himself together and glared at his empty cup. He felt a violent surge of emotion, and bravely acknowledged a new feeling: he was beginning to detest Su Qin.

He was loath to admit it, but he had always been insecure about their relationship. She had been so offhanded when she accepted him. She had absolutely refused to acknowledge him publicly, on the pretext of protecting her reputation, but it was really because she despised him. He had been looking for a reason to hate her, and now he had found one.

His real outburst came later. It happened when his bottles of liquor queued up to come home, looking exactly the same as when they had left, their tatty old packaging as intact as a virgin's hymen, and their alcoholic odour wafted gently over him once more. He almost wept.

"But why?" he demanded, sounding as angry as someone rescued in the act of committing suicide. Then he waited for Su Qin to explain, his heart thumping in his chest.

"Well, actually . . . I never gave any of the bottles to 'them', I didn't give them to anyone," Su Qin admitted, dropping her gaze but sounding stubborn. She obviously had no idea of the consequences of her words. "I knew they wouldn't be able to help!" she went on, "I knew they'd say right back, 'He's only a high school student, how can he expect anything more than a worker's job?' You were throwing the liquor away on them. Besides," Su Qin looked respectfully at Ding Bogang, whose eyes were protruding like glass balls, "I know how much you like your liquor!"

For heaven's sake, just listen to her, he thought. I told her to give the bottles away but she didn't! She made absolutely no effort to approach "them". She didn't even try, she just ignored me! She let my son drift into a piffling, worthless job and become a glassblower!

And as for that "I know how much you like your liquor". It showed she didn't understand a damned thing.

Ding Bogang's heart rolled and bounced like a dice thrown onto a concrete floor. She had ruined Victor's life! His whole family's life! It made his blood boil to think about it. His son had had such potential, he had been a prodigy. His dying wife had entrusted Vic's future to him. He wasn't like Pearl, a fool of a girl with no expectations at all. What a good thing his wife was no longer alive to see this day.

Well, that was that. He shouldn't have pinned his hopes on her successor. He had forgotten the most basic truth, that nothing could match the original. You got a new plug on any electrical appliance, or a new tray for the tea set, or sewed a new button on a garment, and no matter how new and modern the replacement was, it was never as good as the original. He should not have expected Su Qin to be a replacement, and he wouldn't any longer. Should he break up with her? No, that would be letting her off too lightly. Instead, he would carry on stuffing her kids' mouths with food and he'd carry on taking her to bed and screwing her every which way. Let her think he was grateful to her! It would add a bit of excitement to nurture his grievance.

As for those fucking expensive bottles of booze, they had been resurrected from the dead. Their return was an added perk, and he could drink to his heart's content.

Ding Bogang smiled lazily and decided to turn himself into a connoisseur of spirits. He would lavish kisses on those bottles, drink them to the dregs, and transform them into piss!

Once he had made up his mind, he took this new idea by the scruff of the neck and gave it a shake. Graciously receiving the bottles back from Su Qin, he opened one and sat at the table, as immovable as a nail. Then he began to drink, remorselessly, recklessly, unhurriedly nurturing his dark resentment of her.

Six cups later, he leered at Su Qin, who was lying on the bed. He turned into a raging madman, his eyes blood-shot, the alcohol surging in him. He was going to give Su Qin the kind of going-over she had never had before.

Su Qin had her eyes closed, as if meekly accepting her punishment, but her limbs seemed to express a deep contempt, as if she was far superior to this madman.

He sighed. This woman would never belong to him. The part of his life that he had shared with her was like food that had gone off and sooner or later would end up in the bin.

Ding Bogang threw his cup down in despair. It was curiously sturdy – it rolled on the table a few times, as if this was all part of its training for the stormy times that would surely follow.

3

THERE WAS ONE drinking session that Ding Bogang never forgot. Firstly, because it triggered his breakup with Su Qin. Secondly, it transformed him from a mawkish drunk into one that was quick with his fists. Drunks can be separated into categories just like other people.

He had been drinking liquor from Suixi county, Huaibei city, Anhui province. Ding Bogang had done his research into Suixi, just like he did his research into the places of origin of all the liquor he bought. Suixi was unusual, in that it was a coal-mining area. Chairman Mao had once ordered that the Huai River should be brought under control, and so it was dammed and divided into many small tributaries. In winter, these almost dried up, but the water quality was good. It contained sulphates and, like all such bitter-tasting water, was known to produce good liquor. Its claim to fame was the Shilixiang brand. The area had produced two famous drunks in history: Ji Kang and Liu Ling. Of course, Ding Bogang did not know these two people – he was only vaguely familiar with their names – but as far as he was concerned, if they were fellow drinkers, they were his brothers. He followed their example and chose the local grain spirit, Kouziyao. The first mouthful numbed his tongue, teeth and jaws. He swallowed, and the liquor tingled in his mouth as if he had rinsed it with mouthwash. He opened his mouth again and an astringent aroma rushed out of it and invaded the room, starting from the top of the dining table and spreading to the door, the windows and the cracks in the wall.

Ding Bogang drank three cups straight off. His snack du jour, funnily enough, was a marriage certificate.

It was Pearl who brought up this very ordinary topic of conversation. That Saturday, the girl skipped her usual stint at the hotel and hurried home for dinner. They were all enjoying their food when suddenly something seemed to occur to her. With a completely straight face, she said, "You know, you two, why don't you get married? You don't need to have a big banquet, just make it official!"

This happened just after the four kids started the Wednesday Alliance, and her words were like a clear admission that the two of them were a couple. Everyone at the table froze. No one said anything. The only sound to be heard was the smacking of lips.

Pearl sipped her soup and carried on regardless.

"In our hotel, almost every week there are people having a wedding. It's very lively. Even an ugly bride looks pretty in a wedding dress."

Still no one spoke.

Pearl burbled on.

"The thing is, I've never seen a middle-aged couple having a wedding party. So it wouldn't matter whether you do that or not. But a certificate, that's so simple, I think you should get one. None of us children have any objections."

She spoke as if Victor, Ash, and Marina had agreed on all of this and put her in charge. It was hard to imagine what was going through her head.

Luckily they were almost at the end of the meal and everyone soon left. Su Qin went to do the washing up as usual, but she made it quick, because she wanted to take the leftovers while they were still warm so that Marina, who was doing some last-minute revision at home, could have some. Ding Bogang knew quite well that he wouldn't get any gratitude from the girl, but all the same, he had set aside a portion of each dish for her – a nuisance for Su Qin to carry.

Ding Bogang allowed himself to doze off, thinking that everything was the same as it was every Saturday. No one took

Pearl's words seriously.

However, just as Su Qin was putting on her shoes at the door and about to open the door to leave, Ding Bogang's eyes snapped open and he looked at Su Qin. Completely alert, he issued what was partly a challenge, but also an invitation.

"What do you think then? Shall we get married?"

He saw Su Qin's leg twitch in a peculiar way, and suddenly felt uneasy. He had a premonition that very soon everything was going to fall apart.

He looked at his son's bedroom door, but there was no sound from within. Then he looked at the photo in the living room, but his dead wife looked back with her usual indifference. While he waited for Su Qin's response, Ding Bogang admitted to himself that in his heart of hearts, he rather liked Pearl's proposition. Wouldn't it be a good idea to make things formal, put the seal on it? He'd feel much better if they were official.

But Su Qin's leg jerked again. She lined up the slippers she had taken off neatly and said laconically, "Do you really think so? Us two?"

Then, without further ado, she shut the door and left.

As Ding Bogang chewed over her words, he was reminded of the taste of raw peanuts – a little bit tart, sort of like uncooked beans, with an aftertaste of peanut oil. He drank another three full cups. He knew quite well what she was getting at. He happened to agreed with her that they weren't well-matched. But did he care? He could get rid of her just like that! Tomorrow, if necessary! Honestly, he'd never miss her!

The Kouzijiao began to lash him tenderly, as its flame slid down his throat and gullet and into his stomach and intestines. When he next pissed, he was sure his pee would burn and crackle like flaming straw. A blast of hot air surged upwards, all the way to his eyes, turning them scarlet. He glanced at the picture of his wife, thought of the times they had shared together, as a family of four, and of the strange times they were living through now. Life was so difficult.

Don't be such an idiot, he chided himself. With a fine bottle like this, you should be in a good mood! Ding Bogang refused to feel sorry for himself. He decided to drink another three cups, and each time he filled his cup, the liquor caught the light and demonstrated the precision with which he had measured it out.

Then, he stood up, steadying himself on the table and chair. He felt like all his internal organs were churning. His whole body seemed to have become one big drinking vessel.

This man-shaped vessel swayed over to the small living room window. Through it, he could see an utterly familiar scene, as familiar to him as the booze he drank every day: two tall chimneys and a water tower sitting alongside like an obtuse-angle triangle. The short, dumpy water tower was built of bricks, a dark red colour, like an old woman's face, that dominated his field of vision. The two chimneys had markedly different personalities, as could be seen from the smoke they expelled. The shorter one belonged to the cement factory. It emitted a light haze all day which, when the sun was out, was almost invisible. The haze was actually a fine soot which permeated everyone's homes and seeped into every corner, patiently laying down layers through the day. When the workers came home from work and brushed their hands over the table, brought indoors the quilts they had hung out to air that morning, or lifted up a porcelain jar, they saw the fine chiffon-like layer of dirt that covered everything, like a veil draped over a blushing bride. The other chimney, scorching hot, only came on duty in the evening, just as Ding Bogang got off work. Its charcoal-coloured smoke rose into the air and fanned out into the shape of a woman's willowy waist and hips. He found it fascinating.

Ding Bogang gazed abstractedly out. He loved the view of the factory zone at dusk. Whenever he heard young people complaining that the factories and workshops were old-fashioned and backward-thinking, it made him angry. Why were they picking on them? This great, sprawling factory zone had never done any harm to anyone. What was there not to love about it? He knew what he was talking about too. Think of the number of workers just like him who had given their best years to this place, who had thrown themselves into production. They never forgot how many miracles they had created, how full of life the place was.

At dusk, the sky darkened and the charcoal-grey smoke and the dark-red water tower vanished from view, replaced by a burst of red and blue flames. These were from the petrochemical plant; it had been discharging industrial waste for many years, burning pointlessly, month after month. It reminded Ding Bogang of someone holding a torch, condemned to carry it aloft forever because that was what they had been paid to do. Ding Bogang stared at it unblinkingly. The red and blue torch flared ever brighter, as if it had become the burning heart of the whole factory. He imagined his fellow old gits staring out of their windows at it, rubbing red eyes and transfixed at the sight. He refused to believe he was the only one.

As Ding Bogang stared at the scene beyond his window, a familiar sorrow overwhelmed him. The torch reminded him of Victor – a majestic flame suddenly reduced to a little wildfire in the glassblowing workshop. He could picture his son, his arms bare, blowing into the glass-making tube, he could see the soft molten glass. He felt sick. He saw him blowing his life away, as he progressed from apprentice to master, to old git, his clothes grease-stained, his whiskers straggly, slowly getting paunchy and going bald, taking to the booze, just like his father, drunkenly standing at the window and looking out at a miasma of black smoke and exhaust gas.

Ding Bogang tried to drive the image out of his head. It was as if he was standing in front of a mirror, looking at his son twenty years from now. Ding Bogang felt like an awl was piercing his heart. He could accept that his own image was a disappointment, but he couldn't bear to see his son that way – his son, the child prodigy, should have had a rosy future.

Frantic, Ding Bogang turned around and pounced on the cup

that sat on the table. He proceeded to fill and empty it over and over, in a kind of feverish desperation.

It was that bottle of Kouziyao that started Ding Bogang beating his son. In all fairness, he was not entirely to blame. The violence was an unfortunate by-product that came with the drink.

As is usual with such gifts, it came as a package delivered the next day: headache, puffed-up eyes, sour taste on the tongue and toothache – nothing special about any of those. The weird thing for Ding Bogang was what happened to his arms and legs. They got bigger and longer. They felt stiff and awkward. They trembled like a baby's and everything felt difficult, even something as simple as squeezing toothpaste on his toothbrush was a challenge. It took a lot of time and effort to gather himself together. Well, he had only himself to blame. Did he think he was drinking fucking fruit juice? Dammit, the booze was a wonderful thing! It had its own temperament and style. It deserved to be welcomed with a fanfare at the dinner table, and sent on its way afterwards with wailing and puking. What was there to complain about? Ding Bogang was resigned to the hangovers. At least the bottle could help him transcend the endless grumblings and grievances of ordinary folk.

When he was hungover, Ding Bogang was like a priceless porcelain vase, teetering dangerously in position. His innards changed colour like a chameleon as they cramped and flopped and lurched desperately from side to side.

Just now, Pearl was putting clean sheets on the beds and scrubbing the toilet. The house was quiet, with nothing to distract him or draw his attention, except for the closed balcony door behind which his wretched son slept.

Ding Bogang stared at the door as intently as if it were a TV screen broadcasting some particularly violent and blood-thirsty Hong Kong kung fu film. The longer he watched, the angrier he got. Why in hell's name was life so meaningless! It must be because of the brat behind the door. If it weren't for him, he wouldn't be so desperate, he wouldn't feel he had let down the boy's mother, he wouldn't be so resentful of Su Qin. The boy was at the root of it all.

"Come out here!" he yelled at the closed door.

The door remained infuriatingly, stubbornly, shut. Ding Bogang got to his feet, galvanised with energy, and aimed a mighty kick at the balcony door.

It swung open as if it were mechanically controlled, on silent hinges. Ding Bogang almost fell over. Victor poked out a bald pate. When did he shave his head? It was razor-cut! His father thought. He never told me. He looks like a prisoner! The bald head didn't speak, just stared at his father. If Ding Bogang was right (and he was, there was no doubt about it), it was a look full of pity and contempt.

"What are you doing in there? Get out! I want to go and sit in the sun!"

Victor smiled, came out, closed the door behind him and stood in front of it. Over my dead body, he seemed to be saying.

"Disobedient brat!" Ding Bogang transferred his strength from his toes to the palm of one hand, and performed an arc with it that was a little clumsy but nevertheless conformed to the principles of mechanics. Wham! He whacked Victor across the face, almost scaring himself in the process.

A red mark appeared on his son's pale face, and a trickle of blood oozed from the corner of his mouth, as if he was now in the kung fu film he had imagined. Victor wiped his cheek, looked curiously at the blood on his hands, and nodded at Ding Bogang with a faint smile.

"You must be really drunk. But, fine, if there's more, bring it on," he challenged.

It seemed perfectly appropriate to Ding Bogang that his son should comment, calmly and sarcastically, on his drunkenness. He had every reason to be drunk, after all.

And so the first beating began. Ding Bogang didn't beat him very hard, because he was new to this game. He just banged away monotonously and silently, not even swearing. He steadied himself before each blow, as if he was discussing it with his son every time he took aim. Here? There? One more time on the left?

Victor wrapped his hands around his head to protect it and stooped, guarding his poor little balcony like a faithful door god, sometimes going side-on or turning his back to parry Ding Bogang's inexorable fists.

The intermittent thud of fist on flesh was like some weird ritual being played out, embodying the enduring, intimate relationship between father and son.

Eventually Victor staggered away from the door. Ding Bogang poked out his stiff tongue and gave his swollen fist a lick. He grimaced sideways at the picture of his wife and pulled an ugly face. That thug who had just beaten up his son, was that really him? Why on earth had he wanted to do that? He was happy to beat up anyone else. He shouldn't have touched his beloved child prodigy though.

So that was the night when the drink first aroused a little demon in Ding Bogang's body. Eventually, it would fall asleep and Ding Bogang would be overwhelmed by a wave of numb sadness, which would give him a terrible night. That particular night marked a turning point, after which the verbal communication between Ding Bogang and his son plummeted to a new low, replaced by physical movements, which increased year-on-year, until they became the main way in which the pair communicated. There was never a reason why one beat and the other got beaten, it was like the way people greet each other, chat, and eat. No whys or wherefores.

Years later, when Ding Bogang was dead and gone, his son used to feel an itch on his back whenever he thought of him. He longed to reach out through time and space to grab his father's hand again and move it onto his back. How he wished that Ding Bogang would give him another pounding with his fists! This was not just nostalgia; it was gratitude, too. If his old man hadn't beaten him, he wouldn't have run off to Crossroads, he would never have met Marina on her way home after a tutoring session, and nothing after that would have happened. He would never have known what true love was, in all its sweetness and sorrow. He was especially grateful for the beatings when he and Marina had their secret meetings, because she liked to make a careful inspection of his injuries (though they were only minor) and treat them. Every time that happened, he was able to reassure himself that Marina cared about him. What a shame that Ding Bogang never knew he had played Cupid, albeit unwittingly.

After the explosion at Crossroads, everyone was desperately keen to tell and retell their story and say how sorry they were. But Ding Bogang was already dead by then, and could claim that Vic and Marina's relationship had nothing to do with him.

In any case, even if Ding Bogang had been alive and did know, he would simply choose to forget it. That was how he handled things – with unexpected delicacy.

4

TAKE HIS BREAKUP with Su Qin. The scene – every minute and every second of it – had been as clear as an HD video, but he immediately decided to start over and forget all about it.

It had begun unremarkably enough. She arrived late that Wednesday night, unhurriedly took off her clothes and announced, "This is the last time we're screwing."

Ding Bogang closed his eyes.

"The last time we're screwing?" he repeated, before he suddenly understood: she was breaking up with him. Who would have thought that such a posh woman could be so crude?

"Yup," Su Qin nodded calmly, as if this had all been rehearsed well in advance, perhaps since she first met him.

"I was expecting this. About time!" Ding Bogang forced his puffy red eyes open. They watered as if the wind was blowing into them.

"You were expecting it?" Su Qin repeated, a little surprised.

"Sure! By the way, if ever something in your house breaks down, or you've got a heavy job you need doing or anything, just ask me and I'll lend a hand," said Ding Bogang generously, suddenly remembering his strengths. He got up heavily, re-filled his cup, then sat down again. He raised his cup so that light shone on the brimming liquid. "As the old saying goes, happy days for happy couples. It's true we're not a couple, but we had plenty of days, right?"

It wasn't well expressed, but Su Qin looked touched. "Don't you want to know why?" she said gently.

But he shot back, "Don't get all touchy-feely with me! It really winds me up." Ding Bogang was talking rough, which was just the way he liked it. Besides, she was never going to tell him the truth. "Happy days for happy couples," he repeated, his voice squeaking ever so slightly.

Su Qin looked at Ding Bogang. If he waited, he knew, she might just tell him the reason. But he didn't want to hear it.

"Let's have a good screw tonight. Then, on Saturday, we'll get the children together and have a proper last supper," said Ding Bogang, sounding very organised. "You go and sort out the bed. Let's have an early night."

He grimaced at Su Qin.

The only word to describe their last night together was "abandoned". In the darkness, thick with the miasma of alcohol, their flesh glistened and they slithered in each other's bodily fluids. Ding Bogang used up all the obscenities he had ever heard on the factory floor to insult every bit of Su Qin. He squeezed, he rubbed, he lashed out, he dug in, and his eyes flashed murderously. Su Qin's cries were heart-breaking. As she accepted every humiliation he meted out, she wept floods of tears, and no one could tell if these were sobs of joy or grief.

As he rolled off her for the last time, almost winded by his efforts, Ding Bogang seemed bashful. He let go of Su Qin's bruised nipples and complained, "I knew, the first time I saw you, that you looked down on me. You randy bitch! You just wanted me for my body, isn't that right?"

Su Qin didn't speak. She felt rather dizzy. In the darkness, she asked a very stupid question, and as soon as she said it, she wanted to take it back: "Will you remember me?"

Ding Bogang was already dozing off. He grunted impatiently and pushed her arm off.

"No, I won't remember, I've drunk too much and my memory's shot. I'll have forgotten by tomorrow."

Then he fell fast asleep. He had no idea that in the darkness beside him, Su Qin was smiling broadly. This was the right answer, the best possible answer. This was how she wanted to say goodbye, not only to Ding Bogang, but also to sex and the pleasures of the flesh. This would be the last sex she would ever have in her life. When the first ray of sunshine shone on the churned-up bedding and she got up the next morning, she would be an old woman, bereft of all physical desire.

Ding Bogang was speaking the truth. Under the tutelage of the God of Sleep and the bottle, he would suffer complete amnesia. All self-awareness would wither as the most joyous and peaceful stage of his life was ushered in.

5

In the eyes of Ding Bogang's factory mates and others, his amnesia started with the restructuring of the factory, the influence of state power being greater than that of the soft flesh of a woman.

By 1999, asset liquidation was in full swing. This didn't just include the material assets, of course, but the human assets as well. The assembly lines of lathes and furnaces were sold off, accompanied by cries of despair from the workers who were being made redundant. The massive cut-backs swept from the workshops to the cafeterias and the kiosks. In fact, there had been hints that restructuring might be on the cards almost ten years earlier, in the form of the Contract Responsibility System and by way of a dress rehearsal five or six years ago, when a policy called "Grasp the Big and Let Go Of the Small" kicked in. However, these particular factories and workshops were remote and unimportant, and it was not until the turn of the century that the larger workforce felt the full impact of the offensive. In a devastating sweep, workers were forced to take early retirement and the most senior ones were all culled. Experienced asset-strippers stripped the human assets down to their underwear, until they were naked and cowering in a corner, their hands clasped over their private parts like virtuous women resisting rape and pillage.

The unhappy workers crawled around like ants. As they packed up their pitiful belongings and faced destitution in their old age, they bemoaned the fact that they had not been born as directors or deputy directors, or even managers or deputy managers, whose shares had made them rich overnight. Some were shrewd enough to go around all the local factories examining the severance offers made to senior workers who were getting the chop and comparing the fine print in voluntary redundancy terms, searching for any differences. The devil was in the detail: it was like putting yourself on a scale to see if you could raise your price by a couple of yuan. There was also some industrial unrest: people organised petitions, demanding discussions with the factory manager – or rather, the CEO. The managers were supposed to be the workers' brothers, weren't they? How could they throw them on the rubbish heap like this? These officials were all corrupt, they were attacking the working class, root and branch! The workers had given the factory their youth, their blood, their lives, and now they were unceremoniously being swept out of the door.

Ding Bogang steered clear of all the fuss. He took nothing in the way of countermeasures except to drink. As the endgame played out, he sat like a theatre-goer in the back row, watching the hysteria and panic of his old factory mates. It gave him a dull pain, as if he was watching a big ship taking in water and sinking beneath the waves. One more kick and they'd all be goners.

What was that word again? He couldn't remember it but he knew he liked it, his new status. The thing was, the word would come to him, and the next second it was gone. He would grab hold of the nearest person and ask them frantically, "Say it again, what am I called now? I know I'm not a worker anymore. I have a new title."

"Ding, old man, I told you just now, you're a laid-off worker, what's up with you? If you start getting confused, you better be careful, 'cause no one's gonna pay your medical expenses."

And the other person would say to anyone else who would listen, "See what this restructuring has done? It's made an old man like Ding so upset that he's lost his memory!" There was a certain glee in the sympathetic words.

His family saw it differently. Pearl and Victor figured that their father's memory loss, the time when his memory slip-ups really got creative, began on the night that Pearl and Heipi went to Heipi's place and did it.

Heipi was Pearl's boyfriend. (He was a swarthy lad, hence the nickname, Dark Skin, he'd acquired.) It hadn't been going on long between them when she brought him home for the first time. She'd spent about half an hour telling her father about him, while Ding Bogang sat at the table, bored stiff. He looked like some sort of booze-sodden clay figure, blurring at the edges, and apparently incapable of taking in what they were saying. Eventually something penetrated: The boy was a sales rep, he sold . . . He rubbed the boogers from his eyes and opened them wide. This boy sold Walk-on-Water shoes? Never heard of them! Two years of hard graft and Heipi was still broke. And now Pearl had taken him on.

Ding Bogang was completely useless as an ordinary sort of dad. But a boozy Ding Bogang was something else. He acted refined, far-sighted, and his mental agility knew no bounds. He was like the traffic at the crossroads, stuck in a jam then suddenly moving again.

His face flushed red, he gave a gigantic belch and exclaimed, "What kind of fucking rubbish is that? What a con! Do you really want to make a living? Do you really want to marry my daughter? Do you? Listen to me! The whole factory compound is like a pot of gold at the end of the rainbow. You want to get your hands on it, you've just got to get them dirty! Forget being respectable!"

Before Heipi had time to confess that he actually had no respectability to forget, Ding Bogang grabbed his cup and pointed with it. But he did it with too much force and his whole body jerked forward, shooting half the contents out of the cup. Undeterred, he exclaimed, "It's simple! You go to each of the factories one by one and collect the scrap they've left behind. I tell you, that's real money, what they call scrap. You go and crawl around on all-fours, have a good sniff, like a dog, and then you dig. You'll get iron filings, scrap steel wire, spare parts. You just go and collect it all. You'll make a fine living that way!"

Ding Bogang pointed, the way those giant figures on propaganda posters did. He pointed to the future, to the scrap, and to real money.

Heipi's dark skin grew darker as he listened, and his mouth gaped, showing startlingly white teeth.

Ding Bogang pointing the way with his drinking cup led Heipi to make a very good living. His words really were a bright light shining in the darkness – the darkness being the old factories, the bright light being the money that Heipi began to make from collecting and selling scrap. Sure, it was lowly, dirty work, and he was at the beck and call of the factory reformers desperate to junk the old production lines, but as the important folk carved their steaks with their knives and forks, Heipi was under the table, picking over their discarded scraps like a dog, and he made plenty to sustain himself.

In less than a year, Heipi was ready to go back to Ding Bogang, to ask for his daughter's hand in marriage.

Heipi rested both hands on the table top. His nails were black with grime, but a large gold ring on one finger covered the grease and dirt. He placed another, equally shiny, gold ring to one side, ready to slip onto Pearl's finger. Heipi was laying out all his possessions on the table, making it clear that he was expecting something in return.

Ding Bogang stared at these two alien rings and carried on drinking. He took a look, he saw two, then another look, and saw four, then six rings. This was no drunken buffoonery, but a well-founded expectation that the king of scrap with the dirty nails in front of him was certain to earn more rings for Pearl.

However, and heaven only knows why, Ding Bogang was not pleased. Not to put too fine a point on it, Heipi frightened him. It was the speed and scale of his success. Heipi was fattening up like the gadfly feeding off some scrawny nag and the stronger he got, the more Ding Bogang felt a deep sense of guilt. It was as if Heipi's work was actually hastening the factory's demise. He could see with his own eyes how more and more workshops were shutting down.

Their doors were sealed, and people with southern accents prowled the factory compound, briefcases tucked under their arms, sizing everything up, ruthlessly working out the value of the remaining assets. Soon, more useless old gits like him would be chucked into far corners like pebbles and end up living out the rest of their lives on a bit of booze.

"You want me to make more?" Heipi filled Ding Bogang's cup for him and placed it behind the ring on the table. If Ding Bogang wanted more to drink, he had to go around the ring to reach his cup.

He pulled himself together. This young man was still waiting for his reply.

Not that his words were going to make any difference. Pearl had obviously decided on Heipi. With him, her future would be rosy. There was no need to worry about her. It was Victor he should be worrying about. Ding Bogang scowled at his son, who was dozing in a chair, and felt doubly depressed.

At the beginning of that year, Victor got a lucky break and was seconded to work in the trade union office. This should have been great news – moving from manual to clerical work was a big step up – but his father had hardly had time to feel good about it when some of his old work mates turned up to harangue him. Did he have any idea what that wonderful son of his was doing in the trade union office? they asked angrily. He had turned into the bosses' lackey, he spent all his time handing out layoff and severance letters to the employees.

It was a crazy world. Ding Bogang's kids had both been blessed as a result of the restructuring, while other luckless families suffered even more bad luck.

Ding Bogang looked at Heipi and sniggered. He ran one finger around his thumb, then his index finger, then spread out his middle finger, ring finger and little finger, and drawled, "Oh-kay!"

It was his only English word, picked up from the TV. He had never had a chance to use it, until now. On this occasion, as he settled his daughter's marriage, a happy union entirely based on the demise of the factory, what could be more appropriate? He gave his agreement.

Heipi was delighted and put away the ring. Naturally, he and Pearl went out for the evening. Where did they go? No one asked. At least, Ding Bogang didn't.

He carried on boozing until late at night, then climbed into bed. On this first night that Pearl did not come home, he snored even louder than usual. Then at one o'clock in the morning, he woke up. He pricked up his ears, stretched to ease his stiff muscles, and wondered suspiciously what was going on in his almost empty home. Suddenly seized with anxiety, he went to look for Victor.

Compared with the silent beatings he had become accustomed to inflicting on his son, his performance this time was remarkably polite. Ever so gently, he knocked on the door to the balcony where Victor slept, until the latter opened up, still neatly dressed. He didn't notice that Victor had clearly not been in bed.

"Where's Pearl?" he asked.

Victor stared at his father. He could imagine exactly where Pearl was now. She'd be lying naked in Heipi's bed, spreading her legs, submitting willingly as Heipi pawed at her. The image flashed through his mind and was gone. He could not pursue it any further, not only because she was his sister, but because of his own lack of experience, a regret that made it hard for him to find the words as he thought of his own situation.

After a brief silence, he said vaguely, "Didn't you agree she could marry Heipi?"

"Of course I did, and I'll keep my word. But has he taken her away?" Ding Bogang blinked and nodded as if he understood. But now, new doubts assailed him. He put a second question to Victor, with great earnestness: "Then, can you tell me, where's your mother?"

Victor was not used to Ding Bogang being so polite. In fact, he found it irritating. Besides, the night was his time for thinking.

He had his own stuff to work out, as we will soon find out: that very day, four years after his father and Su Qin broke up, Su Qin's daughter, Marina, had come looking for him. So, somewhat preoccupied, Victor snapped back, jerking his chin in the direction of the photo in the living room, "She's still there, isn't she?" Then he shut his door.

Ding Bogang turned his head and stared at the photo of his deceased wife in shock. Suddenly the tears began to roll down his cheeks. "When did that happen? Are you really dead?" He was as grief-stricken as if she had just passed away. He rested his head on his arms at the dining table, holding her photo, and wept like a tired old plough ox. It was a haunting scene, the first of many that became part of Ding Bogang's repertoire. His deceased wife constantly came back to life in his imagination, only to die once more, leaving him in bleak despair. He was heartbroken every night, as he lifted his cup and drank tearfully to her photo.

You could trace Ding Bogang's ever-increasing eccentricities back to that day.

To start with, he gave up on numbers. He forgot to keep an account of his severance pay, his age or the number of years since his wife's death. Then he forgot new words, such as the name of the new company after the restructuring, and the alley where he had lived for decades. Gradually, he forgot things that had happened a week ago, two days ago, the night before, or even a few minutes ago. The food he cooked was inedible or over-salted, or he forgot to turn down the flame and dinner was burned to a crisp.

It got to the point where if he met Victor brushing his teeth in the bathroom in the morning, he would ask in wary surprise, "Who are you? What are you doing in my house?"

"I'm your son," Victor would say dispiritedly.

"You can't be! My son's a child prodigy. He's going up in the world. Look at you!"

6

IN TIME, everyone accepted Ding Bogang's amnesia, although they were surprised to note certain details. There was a definite possibility that Ding Bogang was intentionally cultivating his memory loss. He was playing a private game with himself: deliberately stirring the past, as if stirring his favourite cold dish around and around until the taste became muddied, and truth and falsehood were thoroughly mixed.

However, even if he was doing it knowingly, it would hardly be right to denounce him. He was, after all, bearing the weight of past memories, keeping them safe from squalls and traumas; suffering in silence, and that was impressive. Maybe his endless troubles in the past had been magnified because his memory was too sharp, and by letting his memories fade, he would be much happier. And so it happened that as Ding Bogang's memory faded, he became less angry at his son, at his failure to fulfil his promise as a child prodigy. Eventually, the daily beatings he inflicted on him were a mere formality.

But, every now and then, Ding Bogang's amnesia game let the occasional troublesome truth slip through. I can give you two pieces of evidence. Somehow, about two years after Victor and Marina secretly got back in touch, Ding Bogang smelled a rat. The boy went to bed very late every night and seemed to be in a dream world at dinner time or other times when he spoke to him. You could never tell what mood he was going to be in. Sometimes he took refuge in the bathroom and whispered to the waxbill in its cage.

One day, fortified by the booze, Ding Bogang swiped his son

brusquely across the shoulder and asked, "Tell me, boy, how old are you?"

"Twenty-seven."

"Twenty-seven? You're a bit old to be a scrounger!" He rapped him on the head. "And how old am I?"

"Fifty-six."

"Dammit, I've got old." Ding Bogang exclaimed cheerfully as he leaned close to Victor. "Well, if you're twenty-seven, shouldn't you be looking for a woman?"

By this stage, Victor had a steady, if secret, relationship with Marina. He was desperately, deeply, in love. Be that as it may, he never thought of her as his woman and Ding Bogang's words made him go scarlet. Mortified, he turned his head mutely away.

Ding Bogang looked pleased with himself and pushed his face closer, "Ah, you've already got one, have you? I know some of the factory girls know their own minds and do what they want!"

Victor stood up and said, "I'm going to bed!" Then he pushed through the door and slammed it hard behind him.

It was then that Ding Bogang made a big mistake. He went to the door, and stood before it, solid as a tree. There was no sound from the other side. He stood there silently as time passed into the small hours. When he reckoned that his son must be asleep and no one in the whole wide world would hear him, he muttered dully, "Right from the get-go, I saw you drooling over that damned girl. I don't know what you see in her, she goes around poker-faced all day long, as if the world owes her a living. Well, you just go ahead then, if you really want her! But the thing is, that'll make Su Qin and me into fellow in-laws. Awkward, if we're sleeping together. It would look a bit off . . ."

Suddenly, the balcony door was flung open, and Victor poked his head out, his expression contorted in despair.

"Shut up!" he pleaded.

This gave Ding Bogang a fright. Then he was humiliated and angry. His fury gave him the agility of an ape. He grabbed hold of Victor and punched him viciously to the ground, then laid into him with his feet too.

"You little fucker, pretending to be asleep, you overheard everything I said! You're fucking useless, you can't even get yourself a girl! You want me to pee so you can see your face in my piss? What kind of a boy are you? Just a useless scrounger. I don't know why I don't beat you to death. At least then you can go and join your mother!"

Ding Bogang carried on beating and kicking Vic until eventually, exhaustion, or something else, slowed him down. A few tears rolled down his cheeks and he wiped them roughly away. When Victor finally succeeded in getting to his feet, his father played the tired old amnesia trick again and said to him, "Hey, who are you? What are you doing in my house?"

The second piece of evidence that his selective memory was deliberate has to do with his late wife's grave. It was 2001. By then, the factory zone, once a byword for industrial filth, had been thoroughly restructured and reorganised, smartened up so much that it was positively elegant. It had emerged from the back of beyond where it had been virtually abandoned, and had undergone the largest demolition and reconstruction in history. The property market was booming, its progress unstoppable. The smallest plots of land in and around the factory zone were snapped up by insatiable developers, promising that the old factory buildings, idle warehouses, public baths, training workshops and work clinics would soon be transformed into high-end office buildings that would house software developers, hotel chains, industrial parks, fitness clubs and the like. But what about the latecomers, the developers who were left hungry for land? They had to settle for second best, on the periphery of the zone proper. And so it was that they set their sights on the infamous mountain of rubbish and the neglected cemetery area. Who in heaven's name could have foreseen that the developers would be fighting to pour money into buying up dreadful places like that? But they did, and they promised to build fine, new high-rise buildings. It was all very exciting.

But let's not get ahead of ourselves. Behind the outpouring of excitement, there were still a few problems to be ironed out. Some people were getting their toes trodden on. Ding Bogang, for instance. Not once, but twice.

The first thing that happened was that the workers' accommodation where he lived had the words "For demolition" daubed in wonky writing over its gate. Fortunately, the developer got into trouble and the demolition was suspended, so they were able to struggle on. But the second time, they were not so lucky. Each household received a written notice instructing them to move any family graves from the cemetery within three months. If they missed the deadline, any remaining graves would be regarded as unclaimed and would be dealt with accordingly by the authorities.

They were telling him to disturb his wife's old bones and move her somewhere else! Ding Bogang pored over this notice for hours, as if he were illiterate. He looked like he was trying to work out the best plan of action. Two months went by and the paper was beginning to look a little frayed at the edges. Victor tried several times to take over and deal with it but his father refused to let him. However, whenever Victor asked what he was going to do, Ding Bogang refused to give a straight answer. He gripped his cup, banged the table with his fists, and complained loudly.

"What kind of world is this where even the dead can't be left in peace?" he cried, tears pouring down his face. "It's monstrous to dig them up like this! It's indecent. It's an age-old tradition that we lay our dead to rest, what possible reason could there be for putting them in the earth, then taking them out again? I've always known my place, I've given my life to being a good worker, I've never done anything wrong. What did I do to deserve this? I'd rather die than disturb her! Kill me! Kill me if you've got the balls to!"

But half a minute later, his face still tear-streaked and his nose running, he would change his tune. "Your mother's blessed, you know. Think about it, it's like she's hopping from the chaff to the rice basket. She was always going to lie on the edge of the rubbish mountain in that terrible stink but now, they might build it up into a city centre. How amazing is that? Do you know what that means? The land will be worth tens of thousands per square metre! If I hadn't taken the trouble to choose a place with such good feng shui for her when she was buried, she could never have ended up in a city centre, and without me spending another cent. Too bad she's the only one of us who's lucky enough to get such a great deal. It won't happen to me."

In the last week before the deadline, Victor decided he could wait no longer. He would have to sort it out himself on the quiet. He found two guys who specialised in moving graves, and they collected spades and shovels and set off. But incredibly, the cemetery he knew so well, the place they went to once or twice every year, was unrecognisable! Most of the old graves had been moved, and the holes in the ground left behind were filled with rainwater and rubbish. A large quantity of broken bricks, cement boards and rotting wood had been turned up in the process, and then been collected by scavengers. All that was left of the ground was a maze of weird lumps and bumps.

Victor stood rooted to the spot. He was dumbfounded and also a little embarrassed. Finally the two diggers told him impatiently to get a move on and find the grave. Victor leapt into action, but to his astonishment, his mother's grave marker was nowhere to be found. The diggers, worried that they might lose the business, started looking too, expanding their search to the edge of the rubbish mountain, muttering to themselves, "Huang Mingxiu, Huang Mingxiu." It was as if the grave had come to life and grown legs and was playing hide-and-seek with them.

After two hours of futile searching, they were forced to accept that something decidedly odd had happened: Huang Mingxiu's grave had gone.

Victor paid them a bit of cash and sent them on their way. The midday sun shone down on the tangle of grass and weeds, and the water-logged holes in the ground shone back like unseeing eyes. Victor sat there and smoked a cigarette. He felt dismayed. Maybe my dad was right, he thought. Mum really will find a forever home here in this future city centre.

He looked up and blew out smoke rings – and realised that his father was standing silently not far away from him. How long had he been there? He was looking at him with a smug smile on his face. That disingenuous expression full of guile certainly did not suggest an old git with severe memory loss, not at all.

Before Victor could say anything, Ding Bogang put on his lunatic act. "Ah, I know why you're here," he said. "You came to see your mother! You've been lying to me all this time. She never died. She's just hiding somewhere nearby, right? Mind you, she shouldn't be roaming around here, the factory's been turned upside down a few times now, she'll get lost! By the way, did you tell her that you're working for the workers in a trade union job and you get to wear a clean white shirt all day long? That would make her happy for sure!"

Victor didn't answer, he just threw down his cigarette butt and stood up. Then he led the way home without saying a word. If Dad didn't want to tell him what had really happened, then so be it.

Ding Bogang trailed behind for a little while, and then suddenly seemed to realise that this time he had gone too far. He caught up with Victor, and looked searchingly at him as if begging for forgiveness. Then he bent his head close to his son's ear and in a low voice (in case someone else in the cemetery might hear his great secret, worthless though it was), he confided, "I fixed her grave. I didn't want to dig your mother up. I wanted her to stay there forever, like the stone in a fruit. Think about it, even if we did find a new place for her, she'd get turfed out again! Everything gets demolished, the houses of the living and the dead. If not this time, then next time. Just you wait and see."

He paused, then said with an air of embarrassment: "I want to ask you something."

Victor halted, but was afraid to look his father in the eye. If he misspoke, his old man might retreat into himself again. He had never heard him express himself with such awkward sensitivity. He was overwhelmed with sadness.

"I want to ask you to do something for me. Whatever you do, don't put me in the earth. It scares the hell out of me. I've worked in this factory all my life, I've lived in our house all this time, your mother's been buried in the earth here for half of her life. And the whole bang lot of it is going to be pulled down, moved, and dug up. If you put me here, I'll never be at peace. I'll tell you when I think of a good place. Just don't put me in the ground here."

This was Ding Bogang's last major achievement: stopping his late wife's grave being moved. After that, he fine-tuned his amnesia and began to put on strange performances in Crossroads. Every morning, as punctual as the street cleaners, he would leave the house and creep around, making a circuit of the shopping street with its shiny storefronts, passing the large supermarket, the leisure centre and swimming pool, the lobster restaurant and mobile phone store, all still firmly shut. He seemed blind and deaf to his surroundings. He saw only what was in his mind's eye – the old days, the old scenes. With the utmost seriousness, he passed the non-existent shaobing stall, the hardware shop, the table tennis area, the bicycle repair place, pausing to greet and chat to non-existent passers-by of his acquaintance. There was a place where he used to turn a corner, only now a cake shop had been built over it, and he took little steps on the spot to pretend he was turning.

When he reached the point where the subway construction works were fenced off, he stopped and laughed loudly. In his mind's eye, there was the big tree providing ample shade, the old table where he used to sit, and around it the same four or five old guys playing cards. Except that two of them had passed away by now.

Ding Bogang would keep walking until he reached a building where a signboard reading "Luo's World Resources Company" hung outside. This was his son-in-law's company. Sometimes he looked up at the signboard and the scales seemed to fall from his eyes. He would look anxiously back down the street, and the illusion of his walk would crumble like a demolished building. The bubble burst, and his sight and memory returned: the factory zone had been transformed. The alkylbenzene factory, the electron tube factory, the plastic chemical factory, the petrochemical plant, the cement plant, and all the other damned factories that belched filth into the air – they were all gone. He and his fellow workers, who had come here as youths and knew the trades and skills inside out, had all been kicked out.

Each time, the realisation made Ding Bogang's legs buckle under him and he collapsed onto the curb. All those distressing memories that he had pushed to the back of his mind came flooding back again: his late wife's grave, the booze and Su Qin, Pearl marrying the king of scrap, and his son, the child prodigy, who had left his white-collar job to open a glass workshop. Ding Bogang's display of emotion at such times was embarrassing: he moaned, he mussed up his hair, his nose ran, tears streamed down his cheeks, and he mumbled indistinctly, "I don't remember what I had before, I don't know what I'm missing now . . ."

No one knows, except his drinking cup, that around this time he met Su Qin a few more times, as I will describe later. It is worth noting here that during all these meetings with Su Qin, he was impressive: with a couple of exceptions, he maintained an absolutely authentic air of aloofness, ignoring the tears in her eyes and her sad words. When he said goodbye for the third time, he reminded her a little shyly, "Next time, don't forget to bring some booze."

But this woman, whom he had been treating as a stranger, shook her head firmly despite the tears in her eyes and declared, "I won't come again."

We have excellent records of this classic case of amnesia right up until his death.

Ding Bogang's death came so suddenly that it seemed like another trick he was playing.

~

It was 2004, the last year of his life. His various mishaps were quite creative. He once went to the Crossroads general store three times in an hour to buy the same thing. It was a run-down old shop that was about to close, selling out-of-date and dust-covered goods. But he did not like supermarkets, even though they were bright and clean. For nearly twenty years, he had been buying his cheap booze, vests and Golden Lotus-brand toilet paper here. On this occasion, he went in three times, giving the same greeting like an actor forced to rehearse a scene over and over. He handed the shop owner ten yuan and asked for a bottle of Red Star Erguotou in exactly the same tone. While waiting for his change, he made exactly the same small talk, and as he left, he turned his head at the same angle and shouted cheerfully but obscurely at the owner, "Watch out it doesn't catch alight!"

He became obsessed with going to the toilet. He went more often than he drank water. Then he began to spend more time in the toilet than outside it. He was convinced that he hadn't done a crap today, or that he hadn't had the pee just now, even if he had. He ignored what his body was telling him, preferring to play hide and seek with his memory.

The worst thing was that his drinking got completely out of hand. He had gone from being a functional drunk to a deplorable one. He drank throughout the day, on an empty stomach in the morning, or the middle of the night. He drank when he woke from a nap, swigging the booze as if it were water, tea, or soup. His alcoholism landed him in the nearby emergency room on many occasions. His arms were like a drug addict's, needle-marked all over, sometimes with the plasters left on from his previous visit.

Every time he lost consciousness and was taken to the emergency room in the middle of the night, it would be the same procedure: stomach pump, IV drip, sleep it off, discharge from hospital. This was repeated over and over, in the same way he'd gone three times in an hour to buy his Red Star Erguotou.

On the very last occasion, Ding Bogang made a mess of it. He fell unconscious, was taken to the emergency room, came around, had his stomach pumped, was put on an IV drip and fell asleep, all exactly as before. It was just that he forgot to wake up. In the early hours, the nurse went to take his temperature and could not rouse her regular customer.

Five years after his memory started to go, the alcohol finally killed Ding Bogang. He was sixty-one.

Because his death was so sudden, neither Victor nor Pearl had the time to think of a place where he could be laid to rest with the cast-iron assurance that he would not be dug up again when the cemetery was to be demolished. In order to fulfil Ding Bogang's capricious, mule-headed wish, they were forced to leave his ashes, alongside his drinking cup, in his rickety old home, even though it was marked for demolition.

III

The Matchmaker

1

WHEN THE TERRIFIC EXPLOSION at the crossroads happened, everyone, including the tramp who'd been squatting for years in the ATM cabin of the Agricultural Bank, had the shock of their lives – second only to birth – with the exception of Pearl, who, as usual, only realised its impact in hindsight. At the time, she was crawling about in the dimly-lit loft, covered in sweat, going out of her mind as she searched through their stuff. Her lips were turned down and she was on the verge of tears. The love of her life, her wonderful husband, her Heipi, had been gone all night, a full fifteen hours, which might not seem like a long time, but all the signs showed, especially the list of urgent calls on his mobile (he hadn't taken it with him) that he'd probably disappeared. Pearl had started to worry, not about the main issue, but about little things: whether he'd taken his toothbrush, a change of clothes, a big bag or a little one. If he'd gone, he'd have taken something with him, wouldn't he? She'd turned their apartment upside down, emptying wardrobes and cases, with the sole purpose of checking what he'd taken with him. The result left her both worried and secretly relieved – nothing was missing. It looked to all extents and purposes as though Heipi had simply gone out for a walk, swinging his arms, and might come through the door at any moment, saying he was starving.

She'd been buzzing about like a headless fly and eventually remembered the loft. It was only a metre high, too low to stand up in and stuffed with old things they'd never use again but couldn't bear to throw away. She crawled around, covered in dust, her backside in the air, coughing when the dust caught in her throat.

In the furthest corner she stopped coughing, shocked to discover that something was missing – the only thing missing from the whole apartment. When she first met Heipi, he'd been trying to sell Walk-On-Water shoes, and he'd kept a sample pair.

She remembered them very clearly; those big plastic foam Walk-on-Water shoes took up so much space, she'd always wanted to get rid of them. But Heipi insisted on keeping them. He said with a cheeky smile, "Leave them! If things don't work out and I have to start from scratch again, I can go back to my old business."

Pearl's lips opened wide. She was about to cry. Heipi hadn't gone for a walk, he'd gone for good.

Dammit, she'd only been pretending to be pregnant. And he'd believed her, and now he was furious. Pearl burst into tears at exactly the same time as the earth-shattering explosion, which drowned out her howls.

Pearl continued crying regardless, and stayed in role for a good length of time. Then it suddenly occurred to her that no one would be able to hear her with all the commotion that was going on outside. There was nothing for it, she'd have to go outside and wail like a poor, abandoned woman, go and writhe on the ground in Crossroads. She wiped her dirty hands on her face, hurried down from the loft, messed up her hair, and made herself look desperate with grief.

When she reached the main road, she couldn't believe her eyes. The whole street looked as though it had been turned inside out, just like her apartment. There were other people with dirty faces and messed up hair, all looking desperate with grief. And there were already people writhing on the road!

Shocked and disappointed, she told herself to get a grip: something big must have happened. Something as major as Heipi disappearing. Her knee-jerk reaction was to go and check Dad's place. There was nothing important there, of course, just some old family stuff, and it had nothing to do with what had just happened. It was simply the first thought that came into her mind.

She tore down the main road, past everyone else who was tearing down the street, all the way to the electron tube factory housing. The forty-year-old buildings had been badly shaken, but were still standing. Most of the windows had been shattered, like eyes suddenly blinded, and seemed to stare at her in terror. Without a second thought, she ran up the stairs, past those running down. They were yelling furiously.

"It's the fucking demolition! The fucking underground pipes have exploded! They can take bribes, but they can't read the fucking plans!"

A peculiar feeling came over Pearl when she heard the words "plans" and "underground pipes". A few minutes earlier, when she'd been checking the calls on Heipi's phone, hadn't all those urgent calls, those different voices and different accents, said the same words? They must have foreseen what was going to happen. How clever was that!

But she chose not to pursue that line of thinking. No, no, forget it. She was the silly girl, everyone knew that: her mother, who'd been dead a long time; Dad, who'd died more recently; her perpetually depressed brother, all the neighbours, school teachers, colleagues at the hotel – everyone who knew her. She could only do useless and trivial things, like going to check Dad's place when something much bigger was happening.

The door hung askew. Pearl forced it open and wandered around the wreckage, randomly surveying the place. The photos of her parents were still there, though there was a crack in the glass in Mum's frame. But something was not right, something was missing – she stared at the photos and thought hard, but couldn't work out what it might be. Then, she charged down the stairs without looking where she was going and walked around the building, her feet sinking into the uneven ground. At one point, the toe of her shoe sent something flying. Oh, Thank God! It was Dad's cup, the one that stood in front of his photo. It was still in one piece, there wasn't even a crack, and it had rolled right under her feet.

With a gasp, she squatted down, and very carefully, lifted it up, checked no one was watching, and whispered to it: "Oh, Dad, it's a good job you're dead and can't see what a mess your beloved Crossroads is in."

Pearl was happily holding up the cup when it occurred to her that she should go and check on her brother and his glass workshop. In all that commotion, his workshop was bound to have been hit.

She staggered back towards the end of Crossroads, but even from a distance what she saw made her gasp. Shit, what had happened to The Glass House? It used to tower in the sky. Now she had to look down to see it. The two-storey building looked like a hamburger minus the filling and bottom bun, with just the top bun squashed flat and tilting like a boat stuck in the mud. All the glass had been blown out. Pearl imagined the glass exploding, bursting into the sky like the National Day fireworks she'd seen on TV, shooting high then trickling down, creating this uneven sharp surface of glass – frosted, embossed, threaded, hollow and coloured glass, it was all there.

Pearl clutched the cup in horror. The ground gave way underfoot and she didn't dare take another step forward. She didn't dare go and see how her poor brother was. There was only one thought in her head. She had to hide, anywhere!

Panicking, she ran back the way she had come, turned left at the corner and straight into the ATM cabin of the Agricultural Bank. This was the homeless man's patch. She knew that because she'd often bought bao buns for him. Thank goodness he wasn't there. Pearl crouched in the farthest corner of the ATM cabin, and for a moment felt much better. It was a blind spot, where she could see out, but people couldn't really see in. She watched people running about and flashing lights whizzing past, but kept perfectly still, curled up in the corner like a hibernating bear. She tried to reassure Dad's cup, and herself: It was a joke, I only did it to cheer him up! Why did he have to run off like that? Just when all hell is breaking loose in Crossroads. Why is all this happening?

2

PEARL WAS BORN, how shall I put it, from Ding Bogang's liquor-infused sperm to play a happy-go-lucky supporting role. Unlike some people, she didn't want much – her only extravagance was her flashy clothes. An easy life with enough to live on suited her just fine.

And her life was easy. After the internship, the little hotel had kept her on. The hotel itself was nothing special, but it was full all year round, and so she continued the unglamorous work of folding sheets and cleaning toilets, enthusing to Dad, "It's a great place! They give us food and refreshments! And tights! And lipstick!"

Having got herself a job and regular wages, Pearl felt herself grow in every respect. Her life had come together as the two families were splitting up. Pearl felt a bit guilty about that – if only she hadn't mentioned the stupid marriage certificate, the breakup might never have happened. She'd been horrified to discover that her throwaway remark had grown out of all proportion, the proverbial sesame seed turning into a watermelon. She felt she had to do something. As the only woman in the family, she had to rise to the occasion and be the responsible one.

Of course, this wildly ambitious task was beyond her strength and capability, but that didn't stop her shouldering the yoke without knowing what she was getting into. She'd certainly given it her all.

Take Ding Bogang's drinking, for example. And that time she'd cleared up after him, not long after the breakup.

Victor had been working overtime that night, so there were just the two of them at home. After the third or fourth cup, Ding

Bogang held his cup out for a refill. Pearl shook her head at him.

"Starting today, no more than three cups at mealtimes." She spoke assertively, not just for his benefit, but to reassure herself that she was making things better.

Hadn't the silly girl done enough already? Over the past few days, Ding Bogang had been getting quite irritated with her and he was ready to burst. He frowned at her.

"And what if I want another one?"

Pearl took the cup, and said with a wry smile, "Pour another one and see."

Ding Bogang had never taken Pearl seriously. He poured another cup.

Before he could put the bottle down, Pearl grabbed the cup, threw back her head, downed it in one and held it out again, "Would you like another?"

Ding Bogang was stunned. The girl had form. He poured another cup, and Pearl downed that too.

And so it went on, like a river flowing, like a video tape on a loop, for five or six cups. I'm afraid that cup held about eighty millilitres. Pearl was practically breathing out baijiu and her brain was burning. Her eyes lit up and moved back and forth, like a searchlight scanning the sky.

Ding Bogang stopped. He knew she was doing it for real, and that on that dull evening, with nothing to look forward to again (like there used to be in the past), no one was going to come and stop her – not unless the dead came back to life. He felt a sudden burst of sadness. Who'd have thought that this wretched girl that he'd never had any time for would stand up to him? Right now, she was the only person in the world who cared about him, who wanted to pull him back from the brink.

Ding Bogang grunted as he shook the bottle. "This is good stuff, and it's wasted on you. I can't bear to see you gulp it down like that!" He screwed the lid tightly back on the bottle. Pearl smiled as she picked up her bowl again, ate a couple of pieces of meat that had gone cold and drank half a bowl of cold vegetable broth. The scene at the table was looking more or less normal when she suddenly turned around, and unable to make it to the kitchen sink in time, threw up violently on the leg of her stool.

Vomit-induced tears of apology and shock filled her eyes, and waving her hands in front of her, she mumbled, "I'll mop it up, good and proper; I'm good at cleaning, it's what I do every day at the hotel."

Having started with trying to control Ding Bogang's drinking (it didn't work, he got round it by pouring himself a drink before she got home), Pearl felt herself increasingly taking on the role of the woman of the family, not just managing her father, but also taking care of her brother.

She adored that brother of hers. Of course, she was the kind of girl who adored lots of people, because she felt they were stronger and smarter than her and understood things that she couldn't. Take her brother: he'd always been clever, and he was so good-looking, just like the boys who went to university. Actually, she thought Dad had a point. Why did you have to go to university if you already looked the part? No one was going to run after you asking to see a certificate, were they?

Her brother was blessed with both brains and good looks, but she'd noticed he'd been very down recently. Of course, the poor thing had fallen to pieces when Mum died. He hadn't been the same since, and it had been a real struggle for him to get a job (though it was a much better one than Heipi's scrap business). And Dad was violent with him, hitting him when he was drunk. Pearl truly felt for him!

But, his current unhappiness was different from his usual don't-care-if-I-live-or-die attitude: when he ate, it was like the food was eating him; when he watched TV, it was like the TV was watching him. He went to and from work like a block of wood.

What was going on? She wanted the two men at home to be normal again. She was the one sorting everything out, pulling them back from the abyss. She was the strong one.

Pearl tried to figure it out, but she lacked the emotional intelligence to do so. No matter how hard she tried, she'd never be able to see what was going on in Victor's mind. But God must have been watching, because it was at that point that she fell in love.

3

YOU MIGHT THINK that romance for a chambermaid in a small hotel was nothing special. But, how shall I put it, there is no absolute logic in the relationship between ambition and class background, and one's social progress and quality of life.

For example, even in a small hotel you can still meet important guests, like company bosses from Suzhou, Yangzhou, Wenzhou and all other -zhous. They need their shirts washed and ironed, they order food to their rooms and they pay the girls a bit extra to go and send faxes and so on (the hotel was too small to have a business centre). Of course, most of the guests were lower-class, with grimy faces and strong accents. They only stayed a night or two, but still dirtied all the towels, took all the disposable items and left the quilts and blankets all over the place.

With guests like that who flew in and out like birds, you might think there was no point in learning more about them. But there was! Oh, yes there was. All service staff, from the moment they came into the industry, were familiar with the story of the top hotel in town. Over eighty percent of the first intake of employees at that hotel, thanks to connections and introductions from guests from all over the world (and relationships with the guests themselves, of course), had married wealthy men, with many of them going to Hong Kong! Or Taiwan! Or Singapore! Or America!

Yes, that was the great myth of this industry; it had the seductive power of a pyramid scheme. As long as you weren't hideous and had some initiative, all you needed was a bit of luck and you could find a way to move up in life. Girls need an incentive like that – a little bit of hope.

So, as far as Pearl's colleagues were concerned, when out-of-towners didn't approve of the services they offered they were just being snobbish and failed to appreciate their ingenuity. Let's not go into detail though, and focus on Pearl's love interest instead.

He was dark-skinned, so the girls nicknamed him Heipi – black skin. He had a northern accent and a small-town stubbornness. None of the girls were remotely interested in him. They thought he was ridiculous, trying to sell those dumb Walk-on-Water things! They were giant feet made of plastic foam that you had to strap to your own feet, so you could keep afloat and waddle like a duck on the water. To think that the idiot who invented them had applied for a patent for such a ridiculous idea! They couldn't see the point of it, or how he was going to make any money from it.

But Heipi could. He was patiently travelling around China, going to any city that appeared developed enough to have residents with exotic tastes to push his Walk-on-Water shoes. The first thing he did on arrival in a new place was find a small, cheap hotel with good transport links. Then he visited all the parks and tried to persuade the management that buying a few pairs of his big foam feet for their tiny artificial lakes would attract more tourists.

Heipi had high hopes for this river-side city at the centre of the map. It had a long traditional-style waterfront, and with his limited romanticism, he imagined an endless stream of tourists queuing to strap on his plastic foam feet and float on the water between the pretty white walls and black eaves of the kind of houses you see in paintings in art galleries. He pictured them following the gentle current, pointing here and there, leaning back, peering forward, perfectly demonstrating the magic of his Walk-on-Water shoes. He was convinced this was the place he would find his first pot of gold and turn the tide of his long history of failure.

Full of hope, Heipi had booked into Pearl's hotel for three nights: Friday, Saturday and Sunday. He spent three days visiting all the parks in the city, said all the positive things he could think of and exhausted his enthusiasm and passion. But to no avail. He shrank from a puffed-up foam foot to a three-inch golden lotus shrivelled with humiliation.

The girls in the hotel saw a lot of this kind of thing. They watched his face grow darker and longer by the day. Poor guy, we see it all the time – you go into business, think you're gonna get rich . . . In your dreams, it takes more than a yawn or a fart, you know.

On his last night, Heipi bought some baijiu to drink in his room. But he didn't buy any food, and his only company was that big bag of Walk-on-Water shoes, still unopened. He'd brought a lot of them with him this time. He had been worried he hadn't brought enough, and now look!

Within half an hour, Heipi was well and truly drunk. His batteries recharged, he danced around the cramped single room, ripping everything around him, then throwing up everything inside him like a flower girl throwing petals at a wedding. By the time he'd finished, his room was like a wild animal's cage, and the stench was even worse. Finally, the beast fell asleep in his own vomit. He woke at four in the morning, desperately thirsty, feeling as though he'd been trussed up and tossed into a deep hole. He phoned the front desk and asked for some water.

Pearl's colleague picked up the phone. She'd been dozing and thought the caller might be a young company boss from one of the -zhous. An order for water at this hour was an opportunity, right? When she established it was Heipi, she was furious. He didn't have the money to get water delivered to his room! She shook Pearl, who was snoring beside her, "You take this one, I'll take the next one."

It was as simple as that. Pearl went to Heipi's room.

The moment she stepped inside, the smell hit her and she put two and two together. She had plenty of experience with people falling asleep drunk. How many times had she seen to Dad after one of his drunken episodes? She immediately dropped into that role, without passing judgement the way the other girls did when they were trying to work out whether a guest was worth the effort or not.

Methodically, Pearl drew back the curtains and opened the window to let in the cold early-morning air. She poured half a glass of cold water and told Heipi to rinse his mouth out and wash his numb, furry tongue, then poured him some warm water and sprinkled some sugar in it to take the edge off the alcohol. While Heipi was glugging it down, she gathered up the dirty sheets and pillow covers and cleaned the dried vomit from his bedside cabinet, chair and armchair, and from inside his shoes.

During the whole of this process, Heipi lay motionless on the bed, sweaty hair covering his face, eyes half-closed, trying hard to keep one of them open to follow Pearl's every move. She moved briskly on her strangely sturdy legs in the knee-length maroon uniform. Whenever she leaned forward, her hand would brush over her ear (where there was a little mole) and tuck a stray wisp of hair behind it. Her disapproval was apparent, but she was determined to show that she could make the place clean and tidy. In the dark hours before dawn, mired in anxiety and self-abandonment, the horribly hung-over small-town man stared at Pearl's arse as she bent over, feeling a rush of physical and emotional submission run through him. He would gladly spend the rest of his life as a dog and trot along beside this girl's heels.

Pearl worked fast. With big flick-flack movements, she soon put the room back to rights. She was about to leave when Heipi said, "Hey,... whazz... your... name?" His tongue was numb and swollen, and he had to concentrate on every word he said.

"What?" said Pearl, getting cross. WTF! Is he going to complain?

"I... I'll azzk for you nezzt time I come. Thank you."

Heipi struggled to sit up, then suddenly found himself crying. God knows why, he just wanted to cry. He remembered the other places he'd been, those snobby places further down the map, all those long days, late nights and early hours. Each day started in much the same way: running around the city, his cap dripping with sweat, sheltering under the eaves like a chick keeping out of the rain, walking back and forth on the lakes like a clown demonstrating his hopeless foam feet. Sometimes he tried to act like a dick, but he got waved off and told to move on. Then there was the night-time performance: drinking in his room, retching in the early hours, feeling like he was dying of thirst. It was always the same. But this time things had turned out differently. The girl who'd knocked and come in hadn't put her hand over her mouth and walked away in disgust, or called the fierce duty manager, or demanded he pay some service charge or compensation for damaging hotel property.

Look at her! She was an angel the world has never seen, with a heart of gold, 99.99% pure gold. And he was a useless lump who couldn't even stand up, let alone pick up his chopsticks. She was out of his league!

When Pearl saw his booze-infused tears, she knew exactly what they were. Her father often had hot tears spilling sideways when he was beginning to sober up. To her, they were a bodily function like sweating and pissing. She thought for a moment before answering.

"My employee number is 9617."

She was pleased with her answer: a four digit employee number that he was guaranteed to forget as soon as she walked out the door.

"9-6-1-7," Heipi drawled with his engorged tongue, as he tried to write the digits in his mind. He opened his eyes as wide as he could, engraving her face on his blurry retina, so that he would never forget her, even if he went to the end of the world. Pearl was stunned, and in that moment of panic, she felt her heart skip a beat.

Oh shit, what was happening? She felt as though a certain part of her body had been, well, turned on! So that's what it was like. She almost laughed out loud.

4

A NEW PEARL reconsidered Victor's troubles from a new perspective. He was lovesick! She clapped her hands, and without stopping to think if she was right or not, pursued this thought until she reached a dead end. Who had he been meeting? Did she know any girls who were about the right age? Pearl laid out the evidence like a police officer. And there it was, right in front of her eyes, like a louse on a bald head. Pearl immediately thought of Marina, revisiting old memories to look for more evidence.

She tilted her head one way, then the other, sucking her teeth as she thought hard. Yes, yes, she remembered that time when the two families were still getting on well, and the four young people had gone shopping in the night market. It was the only time they'd done anything together, but they did buy a lot of bargains. Pearl had always loved bargains, so she remembered it very clearly.

It was a Saturday in late spring. It was still light after dinner, and the foul-smelling air outside the window was swirling about invitingly, tempting them outside to enjoy the warm evening.

Pearl blew impatiently on a cup of hot water as she walked up and down the room, unable to take her eyes off Marina, who was fanning herself with a book. Why did people have to be so different? Marina looked great in that ordinary round-necked T-shirt. Just look at her long neck! And her thick, black hair that flowed like ink. And it was all real! No wonder no one wanted to talk to her, Pearl told herself, when Marina was like a juicy bao bun, a ripe peach, a honeydew melon. She was such a catch, why weren't the boys drooling over her? Pearl looked at Ash – the fat boy was only interested in tucking into his food. But what about Victor?

Victor was sitting at the table. For some reason, he looked more tense than usual that day. Since he started working, he'd been a lot more relaxed, chatting with everyone, which he hadn't done before. He'd started lighting up too. After dinner, as naturally as though he'd been smoking for a hundred years, he'd take out a cigarette. The cigarettes were probably awful, but the way he lit up was so cool: his face in profile, his hands cupped around the cigarette, the tiny flames in the air, its glow flickering on his dark stubble. Pearl was spellbound, like an idiot or a drunk. The way her brother smoked was one of the most awesome things she'd ever seen.

Victor stood up, put his hands in his pockets, took a couple of steps, then suddenly suggested to Ash, "How about some ice cream or a cold drink at Crossroads? My treat!"

"Really!" Ash looked up in surprise, and almost knocked over the chair as he leaped to his feet. You only had to mention food and that fat boy got all excited.

"I want to go too! We could go to the night market as well!" Not wanting to miss out, Pearl plonked her cup down, and rushed to her room to get changed. She could see the fat boy twisting his lip. Well, too bad, he's not your brother, you can't have him all to yourself.

Pearl put on a short denim skirt and touched up her makeup till she was happy with the black, red and white on her face. When she came out of her room, she immediately noticed Victor looking straight at Marina. Dammit, she'd never seen that look on his face before. She suspected that Dad, now slumped to one side, and their poor old mum in her frame, hadn't seen it either. He looked so pathetic, so unsure, so limp. It was obvious he wanted to invite her too.

"Would you come with us? Just this once? My treat."

Pearl saw how Marina's cheeks had immediately gone red, but somehow she'd kept her cool and turned to Ash.

"Mum worries about you going off on your own, and I'm supposed to keep an eye on you. I'll go and have a word with her."

Well, well, she'd accepted!

Victor didn't seem as pleased as he might. He kept his head down, and pulled the sleeves of his jacket straight.

Pearl took out a pocket mirror and checked her appearance. She was delighted with her big red lips, but not at all happy with Victor's deceit. Why invite Ash for ice cream when it was obvious he wanted to ask Marina out! And he hadn't even thought to ask his own sister! Never mind, don't make a fuss, let's just go and have a good time!

Crossroads in the evening had recently become one of Pearl's favourite places. It was so lively, with all those makeshift stalls cramped together by the side of the road, and the sound of torn plastic sheeting flapping in the wind. Beneath the coloured fairy lights and the tangle of cables, the stall holders cheerfully laid out their goods: socks and underwear, hair clips and lipstick, torches and batteries, kids' shoes, digital weighing scales, three-minute pain-free ear-piercing, deep-fried stinky tofu . . . It was exciting and chaotic, as though the whole factory area had been blended together and spread out here. In an instant, they were engulfed in this great mishmash of colours and smells.

Victor stopped at one of the stalls, greeted the stall holder with a look that suggested he knew him, and, snapping his fingers, asked for three ice cream sandwiches. He pursed his lips as he took out his packet of cigarettes and casually lit up, then stood there at ease in the twilight, one hand in his pocket, staring nonchalantly at the hustle and bustle on the main road. They looked good together, Victor and this street! Pearl watched him as she licked her ice cream. He was so cool, in a bad-boy kind of way, completely different from how he was at home.

"If you see anything you like today, you can have it. My treat! I've got enough cash. If not, I'll go play a couple of rounds and double my money!" Victor said with a bit of a swagger. Pearl knew he was talking about snooker. He always won, that's where he got his money for cigarettes.

Pearl finished her ice cream in a few mouthfuls. She looked at Marina impatiently. But Marina was pulling a face as though forcing herself to take medicine. That girl! She didn't like anything.

Victor led them down the road, commenting as they passed by the air rifle stall, the little video rental stall, the hoopla stall, the buy-one-get-one-free stall, a group of youths standing at the roadside, a parked three-wheel police-car with its lights flashing and so on. He knew it all.

"They'll cheat you if they can! The guys in uniform know what's going on, but don't do anything about it. Serves people right if they get cheated. See over there? They're taking bets on the snooker, every fucking cue is a money-spinner. You can bet with cigarettes or video tickets, or late night snacks, if you want. I only play for cash though."

After marching them around for a while, Victor seemed to have had enough of playing the tough guy. He slowed down and became his gentle self again. With some embarrassment he shook his head.

"This is the video hall, but I can't take you in, it's not safe. Have you seen *Casablanca*, or *The Thirty Nine Steps*? Or *The Last Metro*? Someone in my class at night school took me to see them."

Pearl didn't want to hear this, she knew it was all for Marina's benefit. But the more they walked, the stiffer and – dare I say it – uglier Marina's expression became, as though someone was watching her, as though she'd sworn to herself that she never wanted anything to do with the place. It made Pearl angry, honestly, no matter how good your grades were or how pretty you were, you couldn't behave like that.

But before Pearl could get really cross, their attention was drawn to a fight on the street corner ahead of them. There were often fights in Crossroads – you could see two or three a day, if you were lucky. A crowd had gathered round, their mouths hanging open.

Victor stood and watched for a couple of minutes as he worked out from the unintelligible shouting what it was about. Then, all of a sudden he tore off his shirt and stormed in bare-chested to defend a short man who'd taken such a beating he hardly knew where he was any more. Victor paid for his efforts with a couple of vicious punches in the back. Then the short guy kicked him as well.

"I can fight my own bloody battles!" he said through gritted teeth.

"Well, now you won't have to, kid," said Victor, patting him on the back.

The whole scene took no more than two minutes from start to finish. Once the fight was over, the crowd lost interest and dispersed. When Victor put his shirt back on, Pearl made a startling discovery. As he took his shirt from Marina's hands, he said a quiet thank you, then, as he did up his buttons, he said solemnly, as though teaching Ash a secret move, "I always take off my shirt when I fight, sometimes my trousers too, in case they get damaged or torn. Better to take it on the flesh."

Pearl saw Marina's eyes light up for a moment, her mood suddenly improving. Ash gasped and ran his cowardly hands over his flabby body.

The four of them walked on. At night markets like this, fancy things weren't what they seemed, and low-grade things even less so. But they were cheap, and this was the only place where you could splash the cash and show off. And they were certainly on a spending spree that night: ice cream, nine lamb kebabs, turns on the weighing scales (Ash had refused), on the air rifle (Marina hadn't had a go), and on the hoopla stall (Victor hadn't had a go). Pearl chose a four-colour palette of eyeshadow and a gold belt, Ash chose a Rubik's Cube and two packets of crispy coated peanuts, and Marina accepted a little green torch. She had gone bright red trying to refuse it, but Victor insisted, eventually pressing it into Ash's hand, cheerily exclaiming, "It'll be handy if there's a power cut, or you have to get up in the night!"

As the evening drew to a close, they got back on their bikes, laden with their gifts, and headed home. Crossroads felt emptier now, the shops were closing and the stall holders were walking away, dragging heavy jumbo zip storage bags behind them. The ground was covered in scraps of paper and torn plastic bags, while the neon lights of the dubious shampoo parlours and small hotels struggled on, spelling errors and all.

Victor rang his bicycle bell all the way back, patrolling this ravaged and dilapidated territory. Ash sat on the back of Victor's bike, his feet curled up off the ground. Marina was silent as always, the little green torch wrapped in a red plastic bag and tossed into her basket, trembling in the night breeze.

As she remembered that cut-price shopping spree in Crossroads, Pearl felt she was back in her too-tight denim skirt again, wiggling her backside as she struggled to keep up with the others. Only now she could see things more clearly. Those little details and glances were all coming back, she could see the connections, and some of them were important. She slapped her thigh. She could see it now, it was there all along!

When Pearl finally worked out what was wrong with her brother her whole body tingled with excitement, then abruptly stopped. Her poor brother, why did it have to be Marina, of all people? Pearl had always been wary of her. She was so aloof, she'd got into university, she was going to be a bright star in the sky. Reaching for a star sounds wonderful, but Pearl didn't want her brother to do that. If he couldn't reach his star, then he'd fall, and get hurt. There was only one thing for it. She'd have to step in.

Pearl was anxious. She had to sort it out. She didn't stop to think whether it was a smart thing to do, or whether it would be effective. Just like she hadn't planned how she'd sort out Dad's drinking. She just knew she had to do it.

She was mulling this over as she walked past one of the most expensive shopping centres in the city. It wasn't somewhere she went, as she did all her shopping at the night market in Crossroads or the wholesale market and couldn't see why anyone would pay those outrageously high prices. But this time, she did go in. She went to the accessories counter, boldly pointed to a hand-embroidered, pure silk scarf and said she'd take it. As the sales assistant wrote out the sales ticket, Pearl pretended not to see the price. In a split second, she had devised a plan: she would go and have a little chat with her brother's "star" and ask what her intentions were. If he had a chance, she wouldn't stand in his way. But if he didn't, she would nip it in the bud. She planned to take the scarf to Marina and pretend it was a gift from him.

5

PEARL PUT HER PLAN into action with lightning speed. Marina was one of the few youngsters in the factory zone with potential, and it was easy to track her down. Too excited to change out of her maroon uniform, she went straight to the teacher training university. She'd never been to such a cultured place before, but as she was doing it for her brother, she did not feel daunted at all.

In 1997 the university campus was still a pure and innocent place. She sat in the beautiful spring breeze near the girls' dorms and waited. She saw so many girls walk past, some in trousers, some in skirts, their books and notebooks tucked under their arms; some with long hair, some with short hair, some in small groups, some alone. You could tell they were university students just by looking at them. Pearl watched them keenly, taking stock for her brother. He certainly had a good eye! But it wouldn't be easy for him. On the other hand, he could blow glass, he knew everything there was to know about glass. There wasn't a single person in the entire university who knew more about glass than he did. That was his strong point. And he was good at snooker as well. You could sit on one of the folding seats in Crossroads and see him beat the shit out of anyone there. Pearl couldn't help smiling, and almost missed Marina in the group of girls that walked past.

She hadn't seen Marina for three years, and she was even prettier than before. She looked so relaxed walking with her friends. There wasn't a hint of Crossroads about her. If you'd said she was from Shanghai or Beijing, Pearl would have believed it.

It was only when the group was about to go into the girls' block that Pearl came to her senses. She was in such a hurry to catch

Marina's attention that when she called out her name it sounded angry. All eyes turned to Marina as she stopped, shocked and confused, and told her friends to go on ahead.

In her tight maroon uniform, Pearl hurried over to Marina. "I have something for you," she said breathlessly, ignoring the curious eyes that were peering out of the windows of the girls' dorm, and the staff and students who were walking past. With a big gesture and much rustling, she pulled out a paper bag, enthusiastically ripped open the packaging, and with the flourish of a magician, whipped out a long, thin, white scarf covered in bright embroidery, reminiscent of a Tibetan hada, and presented it with both hands to Marina.

"The hotel kept me on, you know, I've been on the payroll for a month now!" Pearl beamed. After this gift, everything was bound to go smoothly.

There was a flash of recognition in Marina's eyes, a memory of the distant past, and she recalled the tedious conversation about women and the humanities that she'd had with this girl at their last dinner. She put out her hand, but stopped halfway, and greeted her with a twist of her lips instead.

Pearl drew back her hands and wrapped the scarf around her own neck, like an enthusiastic hawker trying to push a sale: "See, it looks lovely on, it's so white! And it's pure silk, embroidered on both sides! It'll look even better on you. If you don't believe me, try it on and see!"

She presented it to Marina again.

Marina felt embarrassed, but had to take it, and did her best to fold it neatly as it fluttered in the breeze. "It must have cost you a fortune."

"I don't want to take up your time, I know you're busy with coursework. I'll be off in a minute. There's just one thing I want to talk to you about." Pearl bit her lower lip, and gripped the hem of her uniform tightly.

Years later, when Marina was watching the American drama

series *Lie to Me* online, which relies on inference and analysis of facial expressions and body language, she suddenly recalled very precisely Pearl's small movements that day. The way she bit her lip and twitched fit the most basic patterns of anxiety and uncertainty.

But, at the time, Marina didn't know about compassion. She was angry, and she didn't like Pearl's barefaced logic. Did she really think that silk scarf would give her some special power? And that embroidery was so tacky.

Her tone of voice was not very friendly. "What is it?"

"Er, it's about Victor and you . . ." Pearl was clearly nervous about bringing it up. She was garbling the words, and looking down and to the left, lips curling, which, according to *Lie to Me*, meant avoidance and reluctance. But Pearl forced herself to speak: "I'm sure you know . . ."

"What? I don't know what you're talking about." Marina was even angrier now. What was she supposed to admit to knowing? There was nothing to say about Victor and her. How could there be?

"You don't know!" A stack of faint lines appeared on Pearl's forehead and her eyes widened – expressions that meant "unbelievable" and "this is serious". She looked gleefully at Marina, and then out it poured, like a big bowl of water: "Then no wonder! If you don't know, then I'll tell you straight out. My brother loves you. He loves the bones of you! The poor thing is in a bad way since our families split, he's hit rock bottom. He never smiles. Honestly, I can't bear to see him like this! So I've come to find you, and talk to you about it."

By the time she got to the crunch, her spit was almost flying out of her mouth.

Marina checked all around her, and covered her ears. "That's enough!"

Pearl was confused. She waited until Marina had taken her hands from her ears, then got straight to the point: "So I'd like to ask . . . I mean, it's not like we don't know each other, I'd like to know if you'd be friends with him again! Otherwise, I can't see him getting over it. What do you say? Oh yes, he's working for the trade union now, he's a worker-cadre! He's stopped glassblowing. What do you say?"

Pearl pushed her chin forward, in that hopeful way, just like she did when she bought lipstick at the wholesale market, when she was trying to haggle down the price.

Marina was so angry she didn't know where to start. "Did he ask you to come and talk to me?"

"Of course not," said Pearl, beating her chest like a woman warrior. "It was my idea. I wanted to sort this out for him, without any fuss. He's not the tough guy he pretends to be in Crossroads, he's not as thick-skinned as he makes out! So, he needed someone to do it for him. What do you say?"

Marina had suddenly had enough.

"I'm not going to beat about the bush. It's not going to happen."

She said her piece and walked away. She didn't realise that the way she touched her ear when she answered was a classic sign of lying.

"Why not? You got into university, so it wouldn't be a big deal any more." Pearl hurried after her, sounding puzzled.

"Getting into university's just the first step! I want to keep on studying, do a Masters, a PhD, then a postdoc. So there's no way I'm going to get in a relationship with anyone, least of all your brother."

Marina marched off. She didn't go into the dorm building, but hurried down the path towards the baths, leaving Pearl in her tight uniform in the distance. Marina walked quite a long way before she realised that she was still holding the scarf that Pearl had given her. She swivelled round and waved to Pearl to say she wanted to give it back, but Pearl was so scared that she turned and ran.

Pearl didn't slow down until she was on the other side of the university gates. Her legs felt like jelly and she could barely feel the ground beneath her feet.

It wasn't desperation she felt, but awe. Marina was so focused, so strong-willed. When she said she wasn't looking for love, she meant it – even if the heir to the throne turned up, she still wouldn't be interested. She had set her sights high, and she was going to achieve them. She had it all planned out, like a set of steps leading straight to the top. She was amazing!

Poor Victor, there's nothing more I can do. I could give her a hundred silk scarves, and it still wouldn't work! Oh, who do I think I am? Pearl gave a long sigh, and let her drive, determination, willingness and affection disappear into thin air. Let's face it, she couldn't help anyone.

She was still feeling deflated when she returned to the hotel and stepped inside the reception area with its grubby peach blossom ceiling lamp. She saw Heipi coming towards her, but didn't recognise him, or the grin on his face.

"Ah, 9617, I've come to see you, but my bag was stolen!" he said, patting his ribs with his empty hands.

"Why are you looking for me?"

As she caught sight of those white teeth against the dark skin, she began to recall the drunk who'd once cried in front of her in the early hours of the morning. He looked a lot better now, in a new coat with creases down the back, the kind you get on a long distance bus ride.

"I came to thank you! But I've lost my bag. And now I have nothing to thank you with," Heipi gave an embarrassed laugh, like someone finally making their stage debut only to have the lights come on and find the most important props have gone missing.

Pearl smiled, and suddenly felt a sense of relief. He was just her type! He'd lost his bag and had nothing but the clothes he was standing up in. Well, she could help this one. And that made her feel good. The poor man's bag had been stolen, but it had nothing to do with her. And he'd come all this way just to thank her!

Pearl's heart sang for joy. Feeling cheerful and bright, she walked over to him, "So you've not come to sell your Walk-on-Water shoes this time?"

Her cheeky question set Heipi's heart racing. Inside, he was slapping his face, yanking his ears and yelling, "I want 9617!"

This hadn't been part of his original plan. The trip was not just to thank Pearl, but to go back to those parks where he had failed and climb back up again. Only he wasn't going to be climbing anywhere now he'd lost his bag! So he'd had to think on his feet.

"I've come back to thank you, 9617!"

But losing his bag turned out to be a good thing. Otherwise he wouldn't have met Ding Bogang, and he wouldn't have made his fortune. Every time Heipi remembered the story of how his marriage came to be and how he got rich, he sighed at his good luck and thanked the thief that ran off with his suitcase from the bottom of his heart. Thanks to his scrap business, he'd got out of poverty faster than he'd ever expected, but he would never forget the look on Pearl's face when she asked him about those ridiculous foam feet.

6

THAT EVENING, Heipi followed Pearl home like a big black tail. Her heart had softened, and she decided to invite him home for dinner. It was a spur of the moment idea. If she hadn't taken him home, none of this would have happened. Her heart softening at that precise moment had a profound impact on both their futures; it lit the fuse that would slowly fizzle away until the explosion.

Of course, this wasn't a calculated move, Pearl was just being her usual self. On the way home, she naively asked, "So if you hadn't lost your bag, how were you planning to thank me?"

Heipi carried her shopping for her. Inside the clear bag were pastries that the hotel sold to the staff at a discounted rate. They were a bit squashed, but Heipi didn't mind. From that moment on until he made his first fortune, even when he was seeing other women – in fact, right up until he left home – Heipi was always respectful to Pearl.

"I . . ." Heipi looked around, scanning Crossroads. He could have grinned, showing his big white teeth, and spun her a fancy, heart-rending tale. But he didn't want to. Instead, he shook his head, "I didn't bring you anything. Because I wanted to ask what you liked first."

"Really? If I said I liked something, you'd buy it?" Pearl was astonished. Nobody had ever thought to ask for her opinion. The limited love she'd known had gone to her brother, the child prodigy, so Heipi's response, however brief, had her floating on cloud nine.

"Well, I like ice-cream cones, I can't get enough of them! And I like makeup, you could buy anything in the shop, I like it all! Or a belt, a bag, or stockings, a pretty little umbrella, deep-fried stinky tofu strips, I like all these things! I've shocked you, haven't I, with all the things I like?"

Pearl pointed here, there and everywhere. Not a single thing would have cost more than fifty yuan, but you'd think she was in heaven, the way she talked about them. She didn't know that she had already fallen head over heels for Heipi, that this was exactly what being in love was like.

Heipi followed Pearl's finger wherever she pointed. It took him right back to the first time they'd met in the early hours a month earlier. He said solemnly: "I'll buy them all for you!" It was the second time he'd promised her that. She trembled and looked at him with disbelief – how amazing would that be!

After his future father-in-law had drunkenly pointed him in the direction of the scrap-to-riches route, and driven by love as well as survival, Heipi's potential grew exponentially. He was made of the perfect material to be a King of Scrap, particularly suited to the murky, devious world of the factory zone. As workers fought for their lives amid the turbulent waters of layoffs and buyouts, he dived into the corners of the factory zone with chutzpah and sensitivity, pleading poverty to the rich, being generous to the poor, using whatever methods he could to sort out the obstacles created by workshop deputy directors, boiler operators, warehouse security men's wives and guards' drinking mates. He turned these obstacles into super-fast shortcuts, the links in a chain, and took possession of all the scrapped assets: lathe frames, metal cabinets, files piled up to the ceiling, water pipes, bundles and bundles of protective gloves, spare tyres, water pumps, coal, offcuts and so on.

He spent all day covered in filth. And he stank. He'd come home in the evening and shower, wash his hair, and change into clean clothes, but the stubborn smell of scrap clung to him. It was hard to say where it came from – it seemed to be in his voice, his sweat and saliva, in the gaps between his teeth, his bones and his flesh.

But Pearl loved it! Cleaning dirty places and people was her strong point. Whenever she saw him climbing out of that pile of dirt, she'd delight in telling him off, shoo him into the cramped little bathroom and tell him to scrub himself all over with the hot water she'd boiled earlier and the two bars of soap – one that smelled awful, the other fragrant. When he finally came out squeaky clean, she'd march straight into the bathroom and complain about the black handprints on the tiles, the soap and towels, and the layer of grime floating in the wash basin. How much pleasure there was in all her grumbling!

By the end of that year, the failed Walk-on-Water plastic foam feet salesman had gradually become known to people of all ranks in the factory zone as the King of Scrap and was making a small fortune. He left the small room he'd been renting (it was like kicking off an old shoe) and bought a place facing the street in Crossroads, in between the hardware store and the oily car repair shop. He bullishly hung up a sign saying "Luo's World Resources Company" and moved in above the shop. Until then, people didn't know his name was Luo, and the sign amused them. World Resources Company? The man was just a scrap dealer!

The best time of Pearl's life was just around the corner, in the murky air around the King of Scrap. We have to believe that every living creature has a high point in their life, no matter how ugly or destitute or wretched they may be. Even an ant will have its sweetest moment, the biggest grain of sugar in its lifetime of heavy manoeuvring. Pearl's sweetest moment lay somewhere in Heipi's old scrap.

On the night he took the gold ring to Ding Bogang and received his approval, Heipi invited Pearl to go out with him. They went to Crossroads and stood in exactly the same place as they had that first night she had taken him home, when Pearl had pointed all over the place, almost drooling as she enthusiastically listed all the things she liked.

Heipi stood in that very same spot and took the greatest pleasure in declaring his love for her: "How about ten ice creams? Five to eat now, and five to let melt! Makeup? Just go into the shop and pick the most expensive things they have. You can have whatever you like! You wanted an umbrella – let's get a variety: an umbrella and a parasol for you, and a big one for the two of us. And tights, of course. I know they don't last long, so we'll buy a hundred pairs, enough to last you all year! What else was there? Oh yes, deep-fried stinky tofu strips, I know you love those, so tonight I'll pay the stall-holder to cook stinky tofu just for you!"

In fact, that was just about as much as Heipi could afford, but to Pearl it seemed like a lot. You could hear in their voices how giddy with happiness they were.

Pearl could barely breathe. Had she died and gone to heaven? She wanted to go down on her knees and bang her head on the ground to see if she was still alive!

That night, when Pearl rolled into bed with Heipi, she had no idea how distraught her father was at the thought of her leaving home. That was the night he finally succumbed to the amnesia that had been brewing for a long time. But how could she not go with Heipi? She had to, he had moved her to tears. Heipi could have his way and dump her the second it was over and she'd still feel the same.

Of course, Heipi didn't dump her the second it was over. It would take him another eight years to do that, in a more tactful way, by going missing. But, as Pearl herself would acknowledge, it was her fault to start with. She'd taken the joke too far. On the other hand, as she knew only too well, he could have dumped at her any second during those eight years.

7

EIGHT YEARS LATER, Pearl sat in the corner of the ATM cabin hazily thinking over her life, and came to the rather serious conclusion that she should be grateful to Heipi for not dumping her already. There was just one thing that puzzled her: she knew from her attempts to curb Dad's drinking and help her brother reach for his star that she was useless at taking the initiative. But she had never been unfaithful in any way to Heipi, so why had things gone wrong again?

It was all because of that stupid bump. Pearl wrapped her arms around it. She might look like eight months pregnant, but it had been an empty pouch all that time.

How she hated that empty pouch! Some people had babies as easily as farting or sneezing, but not Pearl. Meanwhile, Heipi was waiting desperately for a son, for reasons that were practical, but annoying: "I crawl about in the trash all the time, and what for? I don't eat out, and I don't need anything, I'm just waiting for a little person to spend it on. I want him to have imported milk powder, go to an international kindergarten and bilingual primary and middle schools, then straight on to university abroad. They say it takes three generations to make a gentleman. Well, we're the first, our son will be the second and our grandson will be the third. Perfect! So Pearl, we need to get a move on, have that son, and turn our lives around."

He had no idea where he had heard about this grand lifestyle, but he rattled it off like he was an expert.

By then, they'd been married for over two years and there was still no joy in that regard. Heipi's frustration was starting to show, and not just on his face. He went out drinking and playing cards, often staying out all night. The situation became a vicious cycle. Pearl could hardly go out and face the world on her own. Except that's what she did. She painted her face and powdered her nose, took a deep breath and put on the biggest act of all.

I should mention at this point Pearl's chance encounter with Su Qin, whom she hadn't seen for a long time, and who indirectly contributed to Pearl's bellyful of air.

This apparently minor episode occurred on the day Pearl had gone to see the Crossroads neighbourhood committee about her father. They had been giving him grief.

As she drew near, Pearl caught sight of someone she knew at the front desk and her face broke into a smile.

"I didn't expect to see you here, Auntie Su! I thought you were an accountant in the branch factory? Have you been laid off? Or promoted? Or rehired? And now you're in charge of the whole of Crossroads and have so much power, that's wonderful!" Pearl rambled, her voice rising and falling enthusiastically. Su Qin stared at her in silence; she did not look welcoming.

"Hey, it's me, Pearl! Don't you recognise me? It's been, what, seven or eight years now? I got married the year before last. I've put on a bit of weight since you last saw me!"

"Oh, yes. I remember," Su Qin said cautiously, looking around to make sure that there was no one in earshot.

"I heard that you . . . I mean, the neighbourhood committee, that is, has said my dad should go into a care home. We couldn't do that, could we?" said Pearl, almost grovelling. "His memory's not so good, and he likes a drink or two, but that's all. You know what he's like."

"We're trying to attract investors to the new development area and he's giving a bad impression. The way he lives in the past, out on the main road every day weeping and wailing, swearing left, right and centre . . . We've had letters of complaint. I hope your family . . ." Su Qin spoke very fast.

"Yes, I understand. Our Heipi told me to come and ask, er, how much are you, the neighbourhood committee, prepared to pay?"

"How much?" Su Qin asked, confused.

"Yes, our Heipi said if the neighbourhood committee's paying, he can go to the best mental hospital right away. But if you're not paying then the old man can weep and wail all the way to Beijing, as far as we're concerned – that's what Heipi said, anyway, I'm just the messenger. You know how men like to talk big."

Pearl laughed innocently at Su Qin when she said "talk big".

Su Qin looked at Pearl, and said in a strange tone of voice, "Your Heipi . . . Does he treat you well?"

"That goes without saying! See this ring, and this necklace, they're 99.99% pure gold," Pearl waved her hands in the air.

"Last month, when we raided the area with Public Security, we found your Heipi in a private room in the karaoke hall."

"Gosh, how did you know it was our Heipi?" Pearl wondered out loud.

"I've . . ." Su Qin hesitated, then reluctantly explained, "I've been to your old place a couple of times. The neighbourhood committee needed to understand the situation. I saw your wedding photo."

"Really! How did it go, did my dad recognise you? What did you talk about?" Pearl avoided, or missed, the issue, but was keen to know more about her father and Su Qin.

"Did you hear what I just said? Heipi is seeing other women!" Su Qin pressed, her face still fixed with the same expression.

Pearl went quiet. The colour drained from her face. After a while, she said, with textbook composure, "I know, I've known about it for a long time. It's no secret here in Crossroads, the shops and neighbours, just about everyone knows. So please, Auntie Su, the next time you bump into him, please be kind, and don't embarrass him, there's no need to make things difficult."

"Why do you put up with it? Why let him get away with it? It's so immoral!" Su Qin demanded angrily, her rage bursting out of nowhere. "Female comrades need to remember 'The Three Selfs:

Stand Up for Yourself. Make Yourself Strong. Love Yourself.' Do you understand?"

Pearl responded with a dry laugh, "Ha, that's easier said than done. In fact, he puts up with me! And this." She poked her belly, "Not even a twitch! I can hardly complain about him looking elsewhere! He hasn't been near me for almost two years. Well, at least I know why I'm not getting pregnant and that cheers me up."

"What? Almost two years?" Su Qin looked as though she was about to explode.

"Auntie Su, please hear me out. Don't make things difficult for him, just leave him alone. That way, at least I can relax."

Before Su Qin could get another word in, Pearl changed the subject, "How are your children? Is Ash still in the South? Has he got a girlfriend? Is Marina married? Does she have a child? She's only three and half months younger than me!"

Pearl genuinely wanted to know about Marina, she needed to know, because her hopeless brother was still single and living on his own. Who could have known that such ordinary questions would cause so much offence?

Su Qin's voice caught in her throat, and when Pearl pushed, Su Qin raised her hand and said, "Go home and ask your dad. I told him everything."

"Oh, don't tease, Auntie Su, he can't remember a thing!" Pearl protested, and then suddenly laughed again, "Every time I go, he asks 'What? Still no baby?' and I give him the same answer every time, 'I only just got married!' And he believes me and nods!"

Su Qin rubbed her face, as though rubbing away any visible traces of hurt, and in a semi-official tone of voice brought the conversation to a close, "Let's leave it there for today. Regarding Ding Bogang's situation, the neighbourhood committee has made the suggestion that a care home might be a more suitable place for your father, and at the end of the year we can consider the question of compassionate funds. Meanwhile he must do his best to behave appropriately in public. As for having a baby, don't worry, you look in good health, and it seems that all you need is to plant the seed! I'll try and have another chat with Heipi, but you mustn't let him bully you. We women . . . We have to think of ourselves, OK?"

Pearl looked at Su Qin, and wept unashamedly.

As Pearl was heading out of the door, Su Qin looked down to attend to something else. But instead of going away, Pearl came back, and, squirming a little, said, "Auntie Su, I've been wanting to come and see you for a while. When I suggested you and Dad should get married, I never meant to cause problems. I wish our families hadn't split up."

Su Qin looked at her, and rather than responding to Pearl's confession, said, "I believe that you'll have a baby soon."

8

PEARL NEVER KNEW IF Su Qin managed to have another chat with Heipi or not. However, it wasn't long before the two women met again to arrange Ding Bogang's funeral together. This time, Su Qin took the initiative and went to see Pearl. For her, it was like being widowed for a second time. Not that anyone was interested in her feelings on the matter.

Anyway, not long after Ding Bogang's funeral, Heipi started being nice to Pearl again, or to put it more bluntly, he started "taking care" of Pearl on a more or less daily basis.

After well over a month of grunting and groaning in the dark, Heipi released a long sigh and asked, "Have you been counting?"

"Counting what?" asked Pearl. She was worried now. There had been so many opportunities recently that it was getting concerning. What if she still wasn't pregnant?

"How many times I've slept with you!" said Heipi. He stuck three fingers up in the dark, "Thirty times. That was the plan I set for myself. Someone told me I had to guarantee quality and quantity right here with you. And that fucking made sense to me. I've done my bit, now it's your turn."

Pearl didn't make a sound. She knew this was Su Qin's doing. Oh God, where on earth had she cornered him and managed to tell him? She'd given him very precise instructions and he'd followed them to the letter for a month! Yes, good old Auntie Su had kept her word, and good old Heipi had stuck to his plan. Now it was her turn.

Naked from the waist down, she felt she was on the executioner's block, close enough to smell the rust on the blade.

"Wife, I'm waiting. I'll wait until a month from today. Yes or no, you'll hear me scream. But, it can't be a no, do you understand?" Heipi muttered before turning over and going to sleep.

At this moment of heightened emotion and panic Pearl became pregnant. In the beat of silence between his voice fading to nothing and his first snore, Pearl hugged her belly, and truly and honestly believed that something was happening inside her. That the sperm were swimming vigorously and the egg was ready to select. She could feel it happening. Then, bang! The sperm and the egg became one, the Great Divide started, and began to make her little treasure. In the middle of the night, Pearl cradled her belly with the utmost care.

From the beginning of the second month, Pearl was busy. Methodically and patiently, she made an appointment at the city's Mother and Baby Hospital to register her pregnancy, discuss her condition and ask about the precautions she should take. She also put up with a series of physical discomforts (the usual ones of early pregnancy: nausea, loss of appetite, dizziness, drowsiness), and, clutching the rather nice wad of cash that Heipi had given her, went shopping for baby clothes, baby toys and bath items, and also meticulously compiled a long list of things she'd need for her month of confinement: brown sugar, soft-soled shoes, head-scarves, long-sleeved nighties, nursing bras, waterproof bedsheets, and so on and so forth. Everyone is talented in their own way, and Pearl was surprised to discover she had a gift for being pregnant.

Heipi was almost paralysed with joy. It was a wonder he even managed to smile. Pearl was finally going to give him the son he'd been waiting for, the son that would have a better life than his own, a life that he would pay for. What a beautiful thought! He couldn't wait to share the good news. He splashed out on a pile of gifts and dragged Pearl along to go and thank Su Qin.

"You know, your dad's old ... What shall I call her, his old flame, his lover? Anyway, the old lady's the key to this marvellous result."

Pearl could have come clean at any point until then, but once they'd been to see Su Qin, who'd dropped her usual reserve as though she'd been awarded a special medal for exceptional service, honesty was no longer an option. Su Qin was excited beyond belief.

"What wonderful news! Absolutely wonderful! I've been useful for once! Heipi, you must promise to treat Pearl well for the rest of her life! And Pearl, you must promise to produce a beautiful chubby baby!"

Su Qin went on and on. Even as they were walking out of the door, she was falling over herself to tell Pearl how relieved she was at their news, albeit with an odd tinge of bitterness in her voice.

"You see, I can be useful, and I do get some things right. It's me who should be thanking you! Anyway, you've made me very happy!"

Pearl was mystified by Su Qin's emotional response. She longed to ask about Marina and Ash, but remembering how Su Qin had reacted the last time, kept her questions to herself. She was sad to say goodbye to Auntie Su. Unless she really did get pregnant, she couldn't go and see her again. She wouldn't have the nerve or the guts to face her otherwise.

As for Marina's news, Pearl would discover it by herself soon enough. And her subsequent meetings with Marina would bring added colour to her fake pregnancy. Pearl drew her eyebrows, put blusher on her cheeks, wore brightly coloured clothes and took her crazy pregnancy scheme to the next level.

9

O N THE DAY OF her appointment at the hospital, Pearl bumped into Marina in the waiting room, where they were both waiting for the nurse to call them.

Among the women with bellies like watermelons, pumpkins and winter melons, Pearl immediately noticed a belly as unimpressive as her own. It belonged to a stick-thin woman with a sallow complexion. Pearl recognised her instantly. Well, if it isn't Victor's star! She gulped in surprise. There was a large group of plump faces between them. Pearl wove her way through the pairs of swollen legs as though striding through a field of tall wheat searching for a lost member of the family.

"Oh my goodness, what a coincidence, are you expecting too? I've only just found out as well. Er, let me see, I'm fifty-eight days along! What about you? You look terrible though! Are you throwing up too? Can't stand the smell of fried food? Low blood sugar?"

Marina completely ignored this cosy human charcoal stove that had plonked itself in front of her. Two people had just vacated their seats by the wall, and Pearl claimed them with the same agility she used to get seats on the bus, beckoning Marina to come and sit next to her. She looked Marina up and down, then sighed with total sincerity.

"Oh my goodness, you're so thin! This won't do! When the time comes you're not going to have enough energy. You have to eat like a trooper, even if you're throwing up. Look at me, I'm eating loads!" She pointed to her flushed face and the spare tyres around her middle.

Marina was clearly not in a good mood, and seemed to be

harbouring some kind of resentment. She looked away, pulled her hand from Pearl's and gave her a forced smile, "I just found out, and came to have it confirmed."

Marina was a shadow of her former self: she wasn't just thin, she had lost a lot of her drive as well. She was like a flag that had been flying proudly until the wind suddenly stopped, causing her to droop sadly. Pearl was appalled, and kept sighing as they waited in the long queue.

"You look terrible! Did something happen? Do you remember when I went to the university to give you the silk scarf? You were amazing then, like you were in heaven! If it wasn't for my brother I wouldn't have dared go and talk to you. And now look at you! Where's your husband? Who did you marry? Wasn't he worried about you coming here on your own in your condition?"

Marina was pale to start with, and the more Pearl talked, the worse she looked. She bit her tongue and waited for Pearl to finish. Not that Pearl noticed.

"Have you told Auntie Su? She'll look after you properly!" Pearl declared, staring straight at Marina.

Marina shook her head and looked even more uncomfortable.

"I went to see her a couple of days ago, to tell her I was expecting. No wonder she didn't say anything if she didn't know anything about it! But what are you waiting for? She's your mum! If my mum was alive, she'd be the first person I'd tell."

Pearl could see Marina was about to get up and go, but couldn't stop talking.

"I'm so pleased we met! Don't worry, I know what it's like, right now the only thing I can think about is this baby! So maybe we can be there for each other!"

Pearl grinned as she offered her help, though she didn't know how Marina might help her, or what that help might entail.

"Thanks, but no thanks. I mean, I don't want to have a child," Marina somehow managed to get a word in, and hoped it would get Pearl off her back.

"What?"

Pearl stared at Marina in disbelief. She felt a mixture of pain and admiration: apart from being so thin and pale, this was the same elusive Marina as before. Pearl would never be able to understand her! What planet is she on? Why doesn't she want a child? She has a real live baby growing inside her and she doesn't even want it! God almighty, she doesn't know how lucky she is. How can she be like that!

Pearl felt her shoulders slump, then all of a sudden, her quixotic enthusiasm lit up like a beacon. She had a fake baby in her belly, and Marina had the real thing in hers. No matter how, she had to stop Marina!

And that marked the start of Pearl and Marina's incongruous relationship, which can only be described as the pair of them singing two completely different songs at the same time.

From then on, Pearl looked to Marina as the most authentic reference on the physiological details of pregnancy and its manifestations. She religiously followed her every move, just as she had copied the way Marina ate at the Saturday dinners all those years ago, even if it looked ridiculous. Even at home, without her model to guide her, Pearl played the role remarkably well, like a bit-part actor with an acceptable level of exaggeration in her limbs and her expression – for an audience of one.

Heipi was a straightforward man, and like any straightforward man who knew Pearl, he would never suspect her of twisting the truth. Or, maybe, in eager anticipation of his son's arrival, he was willing to believe anything. In any case, he was working twice as hard for his son, crawling all over the demolition sites in the factory zone. On the rare occasions that he did have spare time, he'd stroll proudly around Crossroads with Pearl and go over the plans for their son's luxury education. They'd do the same if they had a girl, as through her they would gain a son-in-law. Their grandson would still have his name, and their plan to have a gentleman in three generations would still work out! Heipi grandly declared as he swaggered along feeling magnanimous.

Pearl hugged her belly solemnly and calmly, and ate non-stop (she was eating for two, after all) with breath-taking results. Her breasts and belly filled out nicely, and when she was out with Marina, everyone thought she was four months at least and Marina was keeping her company. It was an incredible result! Pearl proudly refused to sleep with Heipi. She wouldn't let him in the bedroom, never mind the bed, and relayed the gynaecologist's words with authority: she needed absolute rest, her umbilical vein was delicate, and for the child's sake, she wasn't to let a man anywhere near her. Besides, Heipi stank of scrap, and she didn't want to scare the child.

The nonsense about the umbilical vein was inspired by Marina's condition. About three weeks earlier, Pearl had gone to the clinic with her. The doctor had looked at Marina's beansprout of a body and pulled a long face, as though her lack of maternal form offended him.

"The foetus's heartbeat is weak. If you're going to have this baby, you need to rest and look after it, preferably in a hospital bed where you can have nutrients on a drip."

Marina had left the clinic with a blank face. "You see, it's God's will, I'm not cut out to be a mother, so what's the point? Because it's expected of women? You can't force life, I should know, I've spent all these years trying . . ."

Pearl didn't catch the last bit, but she heard the message loud and clear: Marina still didn't want the baby!

For Pearl this was a call to arms. Her knee-jerk reaction was to pack up her medical notes, water bottle, egg, milk and apple (the nutritional supplements she brought with her), and insist Marina eat with her. In future she'd bring double. She took Marina to a quietish corner, where she tried her powers of persuasion. In an instant, she had transformed into an eloquent speaker with a unique oratorical style, employing her raw talent for mixing metaphors, curses, philosophy and rhapsody.

"What do you mean, God's will? If God's will got you pregnant, it's God's will you should have the baby, no matter how hard it is! Do you have any idea how many people would love to be in your position? There are women weeping and wailing, at their wit's end, because they can't get pregnant!"

At that point, the edges of her smile turned down, as though she pitied those unfortunate women. Then she continued, her eyes widening, almost threatening, "Honestly, if you really don't want it, then it's not just me you'll have to answer to, but all those other women as well. Who knows, we might even get violent!"

She paused, then said with worldly solemnity, "What are women for? Giving birth is the one special thing about women, right? Think about it, where did we come from? If our mothers hadn't given birth, where would you or I be? Or Victor? Or Ash? If there were no women, there'd be no people. It's our job. Every woman should give birth if she can. It's non-negotiable!

"And then there's the most important thing. You know, everyone's going to die one day, but if you have a child, there'll always be a part of you alive somewhere. There'll always be someone who remembers you, and the shape of your eyes and your favourite foods, and you'll live on from generation to generation! For example, my mum loved persimmons, and guess what? I'm the same, I love them! And I reckon the child inside me will love them as well, and will pass that on to the next generation. Anyway, every winter when I eat dried persimmons, I always put a few out for my mum, because I know she'd enjoy them. And my future child will probably do the same for me. So you see, you'll not only break even, you could even make a profit – nine months of torture and you get to live forever!"

Pearl didn't miss a trick, and while she was talking, pushed the milk, hard-boiled egg and other things in front of Marina. She shut her eyes reverently and drank in the moment.

"A baby is part of our own flesh and blood, it's the only thing that truly belongs to us. Think about it, what do you have in this world that is truly yours? Your man? Your home? Money? The books you read? The stinky tofu I love? No, none of them! That's all fake and empty, and has nothing to do with you! There's only that little bit of your own flesh and blood that really, truly belongs to you!"

She sucked in her saliva as she spoke, which sounded crude and greedy, but the unusually tender way her hand patted Marina's sad little belly as though it contained the most precious treasure in the world spoke more than words could ever articulate.

Something in Pearl's boundless rambling touched Marina, or perhaps it made her head spin. Marina pushed away her half-drunk carton of milk, and forced out the words, "You're right. The baby's not the problem, it's me."

Pearl had been waiting for her to spit it out, and eagerly moved closer until their knees were touching.

"You? What is it?" asked Pearl. "Heart disease? A blood disorder? Are you sure about the diagnosis?"

She stared at Marina with cow-like eyes, full of loyal devotion.

"It's not that," said Marina. She pointed to her chest, and said through gritted teeth, "I've been unfaithful."

In an instant, Pearl's eyes narrowed to barely a slit. She relaxed her shoulders and gave a crooked smile, "Oh, you should have said! So it's not your husband's? Who'd have thought it?!"

"No, no, it's not that. Of course the child's his. I've never been with anyone else," Marina said, waving her hand in exasperation. "I mean here, in my heart. I love someone else!"

"In your heart!"

Pearl pointed to Marina, then threw her head back and roared with laughter. Marina had read all those books, yet was so naïve and narrow-minded.

"In that case, I've been unfaithful too, with a hundred people! There's Andy Lau and Jay Chou, then there's Liu Dehua, and Zhou Jielun, and Huang Xiaoming, and Liu Hua. You're such a joker, Marina! Oh, I mustn't laugh any more or I'll lose the baby!"

With uncharacteristic patience, Marina put up with Pearl's outburst. She waited for her to calm down, then explained her dilemma. "I knew when I married my husband that it was a mistake, and I've regretted it ever since. The past four years, not a single day's gone by that I haven't thought about the other man, the one I truly love. It's been so hard, you know. When I found out I was pregnant, my resolve strengthened. I had to take action. My husband and I are separated now, and I haven't told him yet. I need to get my head round it first. I have to do something. This half-dead life isn't fair on Huang Xin – that's my husband – and it won't be fair on the child either."

"Oh, don't be silly!" Pearl interrupted her. "Our Heipi – you haven't met him, my old man who stinks to high heaven – do you want to know how he treats me? Look, I'll show you!"

Pearl rolled up her sleeves, loosened her collar, spread out fingers, and revealed her ankle. There were bruises everywhere.

"Even a good man like him goes looking for wild flowers," she said, choosing a more elegant literary expression, perhaps because she could see that Marina was rolling her eyes. "Haha, I don't care! People are more open-minded these days. You're worrying about nothing! Being unfaithful doesn't mean anything. Nothing at all! Neither does sleeping with someone. Unfaithful – that word isn't in the dictionary these days, you know. And you're telling me you don't want a baby because of a stupid word that isn't in the dictionary anymore? You're hilarious!"

Marina's tortured way of thinking had been dismantled by Pearl in an instant. She felt cornered, and unsettled.

"Aren't you going to ask who it is?" she said a little crossly.

But Pearl wasn't listening. She seemed to have lost interest in the conversation. With quick hands, she washed the fruit knife she'd brought with her in some mineral water, took out a paper plate, peeled the apple and cut it into slices. She'd even brought some toothpicks with her. The entire series of movements was executed with efficiency, as though she wasn't in a corner of a busy hospital but in her own little kitchen. She carried on talking throughout.

"You know, when you're pregnant, your gums bleed easily, so

you have to cut fruit, not bite into it."

Marina's voice suddenly changed. She spoke very slowly, but her words were like thunder in Pearl's ear, "Why don't you ask who he is? It all started with that silk scarf you gave me. I continued seeing him until I married Huang Xin. From my third year at university, through graduation, work, finding a boyfriend, right up until the day of the wedding, we hid our relationship from everyone else."

Marina's voice was shaking with resentment and courage, and a girlish wilfulness, "And you started it all, when you gave me that ugly scarf! I just wanted to give it back to him."

Pearl's hands stopped in mid-air. She swallowed thickly, then swallowed again. She felt a bitter taste in her mouth. She quickly started to eat a slice of apple and kept crunching until the last slice on the plate in front of her had gone, simultaneously eating away her energy and courage. Then, timid as a mouse, her eyes darting about, she said vaguely, "I never expected you'd take it seriously, that you'd both take it seriously. No wonder my brother . . . Oh, what a mess."

Pearl was so confused and emotional she didn't know what to say. She simply picked up the plate of apple she'd peeled and sliced for Marina and started to eat her way through that too.

"I wish I had taken it seriously! But I was just playing, teasing your brother, and myself. And then, as I'd always planned, I went and married someone else," Marina laughed dryly. "And sleepwalked into getting pregnant."

"Shh, don't bring the baby into it! It hasn't done anything wrong. Weren't you listening to what I just said? Vic . . ." Pearl stopped short of saying his name, and stared at Marina as though in a trance.

"If you'd been serious about my brother, you'd be my sister-in-law now, and I . . . Oh, it doesn't bear thinking about! But you married that whats-his-name, Huang Xin, and your life must have been good! And our Victor, do you know what his life's been like these past few years? He quit his job and opened a glass workshop

– nice to look at but useless. He basically earns nothing. If you'd stayed here with him, you'd be living on air, you'd be worse off than ever. Oh, what am I like? I shouldn't say things like that. Anyway, he's been single all this time."

"I know about his situation from Ash. He went to the glass workshop when he came back from the South. You might not know, but he's a bit of a gossip, and likes to spice things up a bit. He always has," Marina said with a wry smile.

"So, what's your plan?" Pearl looked straight at Marina. Was she really going to give up her good life and go back to Victor?

"I don't have a plan! You couldn't have imagined it, could you? Your dad and my mum together, then me moving away and still getting together with your brother? It's a joke! And all because our families split up because my mum didn't want me anywhere near your brother. Do you remember how strict she was? She refused to let me have anything to do with him."

"What? I thought it was because I'd mentioned the marriage certificate!" Pearl gasped, with relief or disappointment, it's hard to say. "I've lugged that burden around for years, like a heavy wok on my back. Dad was furious with me over that!"

Marina waited for her to finish, then calmly filled her in: "When Ash came home, he had so much unfinished business. Neither of us were settled and Mum couldn't stand that. To cut a long story short, I can't go and see your brother again. I can't turn the clock back, but I can't go forward either, not with a baby!"

Marina laughed at herself and at the mess she'd made.

"And you keep urging me to keep it!"

Pearl didn't know what Ash's "unfinished business" was, but she needed to stop Marina from thinking about not having the baby. Suddenly, she had a light-bulb moment, and, as though presenting Marina with a most precious gift, said, "Look, I'll be frank, I've got a problem too, and it's a big one, potentially bigger than yours!"

She peered around furtively, then went up to Marina, took her hand and placed it on her belly.

"There's nothing here. I'm not pregnant at all, I was just winding Heipi up! He's always wanted a son. He has this thing about wanting a gentleman in three generations. I only wanted to make him happy."

Marina pulled her hand back in shock. There was a look of horror on her face. Before she could say anything, Pearl had narrowed her eyes, and her plump face was flushed bright red. Strangely excited, she went on, "Look, sooner or later this massive lie is going to come out, and I'm not scared at all! You don't have to hurry, take your time, think it over, we've got lots of time, at least eight months. If we put our heads together, I'm sure we'll be able to work out the best solution – in your case, whether to go backwards or forwards, and in my case, how to deal with my big fat lie. In any case, no matter what, the die has been cast: you are going to have this child. You and I are not going to end up with nothing."

10

DURING THEIR LONG PREGNANCIES, carrying their real and fake foetuses, Pearl and Marina had all kinds of counterproductive discussions, going from one extreme to the other in their debates, and, using their previous mistakes as bargaining chips, tried to play with and against God.

During this period, Marina made a trip back to the factory zone because the alkylbenzene factory workers' housing was due for demolition. Pearl didn't know if anything had happened on that trip or not, but she could certainly sense a change in Marina's attitude. Within her fierce aloofness there were now flashes of silken softness. Pearl didn't dare ask too many questions, but was pleased to note that Marina had stopped talking about getting rid of the baby.

Nevertheless, things were getting a bit too close for comfort. The women they'd seen at the prenatal check-ups, with their everexpanding medical files, and indeed Marina herself, had less than two months to go until the physical ordeal of labour, at the end of which they'd give birth to their little treasures. Pearl couldn't keep up her charade for much longer. When her time came, it would be like handing in a blank sheet of paper in an exam. She'd been playing with fire, and it wasn't just her eyebrows that were going to get singed – she was in for a roasting.

Marina was waiting for her moment to come. In her last discussion with Pearl she had sighed and seemed almost relaxed.

"Actually, these past few days I've been thinking, the simplest solution is the best. Let's trust in God, and let him decide. Let's not complicate things, just let him decide."

She glanced at Pearl, looking ready for action.

"You go and tell Heipi, and I'll go to the glass workshop and talk to your brother. Honestly, I'm not scared of anything anymore. I don't care what my mum thinks. Let's just come clean and tell the truth. What do you think? Are you up for it?"

The sudden gleam in her eyes caught Pearl completely by surprise.

"Yes! Yes! That's what I've wanted to do all along! And what I wanted you to do too!"

Pearl clapped her hands in delight. Marina was being straightforward, they were on the same page! Not that they had any alternative.

Thinking back on that conversation, Pearl remembered that they were still in the Outpatients Department at the Mother and Baby Hospital, and that they went their separate ways as usual. Marina was in an excellent mood, her cheeks rosy and pink, and she smiled as she said quietly, "Can you believe it? I'm going to wear the silk scarf you gave me when I go to The Glass House tomorrow. It's hideous, but I'm still going to wear it. I remember the first time I went to see him, when I intended to give it back to him."

Pearl stood and watched as Marina walked away. She was eight months' pregnant now, and her upper back seemed broader as well. In her loose-fitting clothes, she looked like a duck waddling along. It was so good, so touching to see a real pregnant woman walking down the road. Pearl was surprised to find hot tears rolling down her face. It was so sad that she couldn't waddle down the road like that too.

But she pushed the sadness down, and tried to think positively: just think how happy Marina was going to make her brother tomorrow!

An irrepressible thought popped into Pearl's mind, like an unstoppable magpie (they're not called birds of joy for nothing). She could go first, and tell him the happy news now!

It wasn't much of an idea, but it was good news, and if she told him, he'd be happier sooner. Poor Victor had been so lonely. Telling him in advance was a good thing to do, right? I mean, what if he wasn't sure if it was good news or not? Marina meant what she said. Pearl had been a go-between before, when she'd found her way to the teacher training college. And she would do it again now, for her brother.

This time was bound to be much more successful than the last. She'd go and put her brother in a good mood, then there'd be love, and a baby as well. A wife and a child, how good was that!

Pearl shot off to the glass workshop like a blazing arrow, the hair on her forehead soaked with sweat. A happy thought ran through her mind: the river was flowing backwards, and they were all going to be family, Su Qin and Ash included. Dad would never have imagined it could turn out like this.

She remembered jogging all the way there, excitedly bursting into the shop, and being too out of breath to utter a word, all the things she had to say piling up behind her teeth, straining to burst out. Victor was cleaning the workshop, and when Pearl finally managed to compose herself enough to speak she snatched the cloth from his hand and exclaimed, "You're going to be a dad, to a ready-made baby! Marina's going to give you a baby! The three of you will be a family! She's going to come and see you, she gave her word, tomorrow at the latest! You're going to be so happy!"

She remembered Victor's deadpan expression, and his silence as he'd let her explain enthusiastically: Marina's regret, her getting pregnant, then separating from her husband. She'd gone through it all, step by step, but he didn't appear to have taken it in. He was quiet the whole time Pearl rushed to get her words out, as though he was not listening at all. After a while, he put his head in his hands.

Pearl stood there, open-mouthed. She didn't understand. After a beat of silence, she panicked and hit him on the arm.

"Why aren't you saying anything? Surely the baby's not a problem? Are you really so old-fashioned? I tell you, that baby, when that gorgeous little baby pops out, it's going to call you Daddy. You don't know how lucky you are!"

She stressed the bit about the baby, saying almost exactly the same encouraging things she'd said to Marina a few months earlier, only changing a few words here and there.

Victor shook his head vigorously. He finally took his hand away from his face and continued cleaning. The light bounced off the sea of glass all around him onto his face, but his expression was still opaque.

"I can't accept this. I won't let it happen."

Victor poured Pearl some water and moved a stool to a place in the shade for her, then got on with what he was doing before her interruption.

Pearl's mouth went dry. She had a sinking feeling that she might have made another mistake. She grabbed the paper cup in a panic, threw her head back and drank the water in one big gulp. For some reason, she thought about Dad. No wonder he liked to have two cups. She felt so sorry for Marina. She was still in her dream, believing that Victor would welcome her with open arms, looking forward to a beautiful springtime.

Pearl lost her temper. She hurled the empty cup at Victor as hard as she could. What was wrong with him, for God's sake? She'd brought him good news and he wouldn't even reach out and take it. Was he always going to be as cold and stand-offish as this? If Dad was still alive, she'd ask him to carry on beating him.

Victor dodged. The paper cup landed softly on the floor and rolled over a couple of times. He calmly poured her a new cup, filling it halfway with hot water, then topping it up with cold water, so that the temperature was just right. He passed the cup to Pearl, and in a kind but bleak tone of voice, asked her not to be angry. She needed to look after her health for the sake of her baby, so that it would be a clever, healthy baby, preferably a child prodigy, who'd be able to count at the age of one, recite pi at the age of two, memorise Tang poems by the age of three, read newspapers at the age of four, and in the third year of primary, read fourth grade books, just like he had when he was a little boy.

Pearl couldn't contain herself. She was laughing so much she was crying. He sounded just like Dad!

In a composed, measured way, Victor told her that he'd been back to their old place not so long ago. He had heard it was due for demolition, so he'd gone to pour a cup of baijiu for Dad. Just now, he was repeating what Dad always used to say about him. They were Dad's words, not his.

As he was speaking, Pearl bit her lip in shame to stop herself from blurting out the rest. She'd vaguely thought about dropping her fake pregnancy into the conversation as well, but she could see it wasn't the right time to do so. What Victor said made her feel anxious and she started sweating again. She felt like the proverbial clay bodhisattva crossing the river, not able to save anyone, let alone herself. Indeed, she hadn't fixed her own problem yet.

No, one thing at a time for now. She'd said what she came to say. Marina would come tomorrow and explain to Victor for herself. She had to go home and see Heipi now. It was getting late, and today was the day she was going to lay her cards on the table.

Pearl remembered watching Victor wave her off as she left The Glass House. Through the layers of transparent material, she could see multiple images of her brother in profile, moving in perfect unison, dusting and pausing – that movement, that image, seemed eternal, as though he would continue dusting for the rest of his life.

Pearl felt an inexplicable sadness. She turned around and started to run. Pearl was a good girl with a good heart, but she had no idea that her running would light the fuse that would change things forever.

IV

Su Qin's Way of Virtue, Her Daodejing

1

THE MATERNAL INSTINCT is like a crouching lioness, ready to leap out with a roar at any moment to ward off impending danger. A well-worn cliché, but true nonetheless. Case in point, Su Qin had a premonition that something terrible was going to happen on that fateful day, 13th April 2006, when so many people were blown to pieces in the street.

That afternoon, she had gone to the wholesale market to pick up some bags of craft supplies to make sparkling Korean barrettes and headbands for Ash. Ash's return from the South had coincided with the boom in online retail and he'd jumped on the bandwagon because he was bored, and because it enabled him to conceal that problematic body of his behind the online storefront he had created for himself, like a silkworm spinning its own cocoon. He sold anything and everything. In spring, it was cut-price skincare products and cosmetics; when the weather got hotter, water pillows and sexy underwear; in winter, his-n-hers scarves and stick-on heat pads. Business was quite good. Su Qin was wholly in favour of Ash's new enterprise and came up with a promotional idea of her own: giving each buyer a free hair accessory. She took it upon herself to buy the materials in the wholesale market and make the ornaments at home. It cost them almost nothing.

On that memorable afternoon, she was at a particularly cheap-and-cheerful wholesale market in the factory zone when she suddenly felt a terrible pain in her chest. Thinking it was because the place was too crowded, she hurriedly bought two bags of craft materials and left. But she only felt worse once she got outside. Her heart was palpitating so wildly that she had to stop in the middle of the street. She began to sway on her feet and the bags felt like they were pulling her down. She had had moments of panic like this before, and now, as she did back then, she thought of Marina, even though she was married and hadn't been home for ages.

When she finally got her legs to move again, an uneasy feeling in her gut compelled Su Qin to take a different route home. She staggered along, instinctively making for Crossroads. She had an irrational feeling that Marina was there today, walking down the street at that very moment. She wanted to stop her daughter and have a nice quiet chat with her. They had not exchanged a single word since that flaming row in the rainswept street outside her home.

She didn't get very far. All of a sudden, blasts of air and spurts of flame erupted from a subterranean pipeline at her feet, relieving her of the two big bags and tossing them high into the air. The shiny Korean hair accessories and colourful wrapping paper rained down on her like confetti. Unfortunately, the beauty of the spectacle was lost on Su Qin, who went pale with horror. Now she was certain that something terrible had happened to Marina and her baby. Motherly instinct kicked in, and with some kind of inbuilt compass, she cut through an alley, then turned right at a T-junction and found Marina lying on the kerb, her eyes closed, her hair falling over her face, a nasty wound on her left cheek and her hands tightly clasped over her belly. Blood was pooling between her legs.

Su Qin slumped to the ground and gently put her arms around her daughter. She laid Marina across her lap, as she used to when she was a child, resting her head in the crook of her arm. Someone nearby was calling for an ambulance, so she sat there and waited. She cherished these few precious minutes, because she hadn't been so close to her daughter in a very long time. The wait also gave her the time to repent. All of this, she acknowledged, was her fault.

Right from the start, she hadn't been a good mother. But she didn't hate herself – instead, what she hated was this crazy body of hers, and her conflicting emotional obsessions. Her body and feelings were constantly at war, and her immorality had brought the wrath of heaven down on her head.

2

S U QIN HAD BEEN widowed at thirty-nine, after which the devil possessed her. This devil caused her no end of trouble. It left her alone during the day, and she could get on with her work, endlessly checking the company accounts, income and expenditure, over and over again. (She was so meticulous that even if she had added something up correctly a hundred times, she would still check again one more time.) It was in the evening that the devil made its presence felt. Su Qin was astonished to find herself so enslaved to her body. She couldn't bear to look at her bed, quilt, pillow, pyjamas or anything else that had to do with the night. Even darkness, the moon or electric lights caused her distress. Her cravings visited her every night, dragging her down into the swamp before spitting her out again. She stretched out every limb of her body, she wrapped her arms around herself, she arched her back, but nothing made any difference.

Su Qin did not take the devil seriously at first. She sneered as she recalled the old joke about the lonely widow who could not sleep. In the story, the widow got up, threw a handful of beans on the ground, and spent the night groping in the dark for them and picking them up one by one. When someone suggested that it would be easier if she turned on a light, she replied, "But what else am I going to do all night?!"

Su Qin wasn't going to spend her nights scrabbling around for a handful of beans. After all, this was the '90s. There was nothing to stop her getting married again. She could start a new relationship, start a new life. In fact, people were falling over themselves to give her advice. Was there any point in staying faithful to a man who had died? It was much easier to go and find a new partner. Except that it wasn't. Su Qin soon discovered she was unwilling to take the easy route.

She was still emotionally attached to her late husband. Her grief was real, and the reality of her loss weighed heavily: the bookcases with his large dictionaries, five or six thick photograph albums and stamp albums, the witty things he said, and the watch he had chosen for her. Nevertheless, she was not one to indulge in overt displays of grief. She kept her desolation hidden inside her, even on Qing Ming or the anniversary of his death. No one could believe how deeply she grieved for him; she could barely believe it herself.

But life as a single parent was challenging. She had to do everything for her small family: taking down the ceiling fan to wash it, fixing a dripping tap, changing the filter in the cooker hood. And on birthdays and holidays, she found herself even more anxious when she looked at Marina and Ash. The children had not been the same since the death of their father. They looked through her, sometimes with hostility. She had fallen in their estimation and they had lost faith in her. That made her feel doubly lonely.

When Su Qin looked in the mirror, the woman who looked back at her was dignified, with calm eyes and mouth firmly closed. She was putting up with things as they were, with life like a river, pitilessly blocking her way. There were no bridges or boats to help her across, and if she wanted things to change, she would have to get her feet wet and wade across. That meant finding a man to deal with her demons and bring a bit of welcome warmth to her life.

She got a friend to make enquiries for her. Ding Bogang was not her first choice. The frontrunners had stronger personalities. They bore certain similarities to her late husband, though it may have been that Su Qin was subconsciously looking for a likeness in the plaid scarves and trench coats they wore, the way they talked about photography, hummed Russian folk songs, collected stamps and told jokes. There was no way she would choose them. Just the sight of them reminded her painfully of her husband. Her memory of him was still so vivid, sometimes she could still feel his eyes on her.

So one after another, she turned them down. Her matchmaker was growing increasingly frustrated, and Su Qin struggled to explain her rather peculiar requirements: she wanted a man who differed from her husband as much as possible.

The matchmaking friend obviously thought that Su Qin had it all wrong and was annoyed by Su Qin's pickiness. In a final half-hearted effort, she introduced Su Qin to Ding Bogang. He was bald and had a red nose, thought books were a pile of shit, went around in blue or grey overalls, wasn't a great talker though could swear fluently, and was always drunk as a skunk. Well, so be it, she thought, and accepted this final offering. With a man like that, they could jump into bed and fuck the living daylights out of each other, and there was absolutely no danger that she would become fond of him.

Su Qin never told anyone the whole story. Who could she tell? Where would she start? It all sounded so bizarre – no one would believe her. Besides, everyone has a right to privacy. It was nobody else's business, and she didn't need their approval. Deep down, Su Qin was a proud woman. Wherever she went, she held her head high. She had her own way of remembering her husband, and still regarded herself as loyal to him. She decided that she would never acknowledge her relationship with Ding Bogang to anyone outside the family, and neither would she bestow true friendship on him. She would rather be a recluse for the rest of her life.

How little Su Qin understood the ways of the world! She had no idea that she had crossed a line. Her secrecy invited suspicion, and what she did – more importantly, what she failed to do – deeply offended the open and upfront kind of attitudes maintained by residents of the factory zone. This was a community, after all. Its residents cared about the relationships between the men and women who lived there, especially the ones who were on their own. The more hopeless, the more rough and ready these people were, the more people encouraged them to be bold and go after what they wanted, even if it meant behaving badly. There was only one stipulation. The men and women involved had to be open about what they were doing. They couldn't hold anything back. Anyone who assumed the moral high ground was not tolerated. Su Qin's deliberate aloofness and refusal to admit what she was doing simply drew more attention to her. People would not stop gossiping, following her as she went about her day, trying to ferret out her secrets. Ugly rumours swirled around her and she became increasingly isolated.

But Su Qin didn't care. Her desperation made her fearless. When her clandestine visits on Wednesdays and Saturdays were noticed, she simply ignored the pointing fingers. Privacy was privacy, loyalty was loyalty, and she had no intention of sharing or explaining anything to anyone. That was the end of the matter as far as she was concerned. She had given up all hopes of living a decent life as a decent woman.

However, she soon realised that the shadow that had fallen on her had enveloped Marina and Ash as well. The more this business went on, the more harm it caused her children. She feared it might even destroy them.

Su Qin turned a mocking smile on herself. You shameless bitch, what was all this nonsense about loyalty to your beloved husband? Open your eyes – can't you see the price you've paid? The price your children have paid?

Right now, Su Qin was sitting in Crossroads, cradling her limp daughter. Even though Marina was a grown woman, pregnant with a child of her own, she was still her mother's precious little girl. Su Qin tried to work out when their relationship had begun to go awry.

Perhaps it was because of those Wednesday visits. To a girl like Marina, who had the stern puritanism of youth and was intolerant of even the slightest wrinkle in the fabric of life, those nights must have been an ineradicable stain on her mother's character. How could Su Qin expect her to understand?

Su Qin had nothing but exhausted, stormy memories of those

times. Every Wednesday, the shame would creep up on her from midday and extend into the night. I won't go, she would tell herself, but her urges were like a ball bobbing on the surface of the water, she could not keep them down. She would resist until about nine o'clock in the evening, then she would hurriedly sort the kids out, and, nursing her fury, she would get out her bike and steal away to Ding Bogang's flat, and to his bed. At five thirty the next morning, even if she felt like death, and however cold it was outside, she would hurry back home and sneak indoors, hoping that she had not disturbed the neighbours. She could never admit what she was doing in these few hours of darkness. And Marina could not understand the agonies she suffered. Neither of the children understood. They ganged up against her, taking it in turns to make trouble on Wednesdays. Eventually the feeling of them metaphorically spitting in her face was too much to bear. It made her feel like a bitch fleeing through the rainstorm from the stones that pelted her. No one respected her, she didn't even respect herself. A woman obsessed with privacy was a mud-splattered figure, the lowest of the low.

She deserved it, and bore it with as much dignity as she could muster. The only thing she could not bear was the thought that Marina and Victor had struck up a romance. Heaven knows she shouldn't say things like this, but that boy, even though he was perfectly polite and respectful to her, spent his days bare-chested in a workshop blowing glass and his nights playing billiards and spending his winnings on cigarettes. He reeked all over just like all the other Crossroads yobs. Su Qin simply could not believe that Marina had really fallen in love with him. She must be doing it just to annoy her mother!

Of course, if Marina was just messing around then there was nothing to worry about. But they did seem to be serious.

Su Qin still shuddered at the memory of that appalling night.

Marina was eighteen and in her third year at senior high school. She was taking extra classes after school and never came home before 8:30pm. Then one night, it got to 9:30pm, then 10:00pm, and there was still no sign of Marina.

Su Qin was terrified for her daughter. There were always stories going around about the things the local youths got up to. If anything happened to Marina, Su Qin knew it would be her punishment for being immoral. Late that night, when she couldn't bear to sit around waiting anymore, she slipped out and cycled around Crossroads. The area was all but deserted, and with tears running down her cheeks, Su Qin muttered wild prayers to God and Guanyin, the Goddess of Mercy. Please don't let Marina come to any harm, I'll do anything if she's all right. I'll stand in the middle of Crossroads with a megaphone and apologise to the whole factory zone, admit what I've done, and never see Ding Bogang again. I'll live on my own for the rest of my life! Anything, I'll do anything, just so long as nothing's happened to my precious girl!

But hang on a minute, what on earth was that? Coming towards her along the dark street, in and out of the pools of light cast by the street lamps, she saw something decidedly odd: it was Victor, and he looked like he was doing circus tricks. He was riding along, steering his bike with one hand and pushing another bike with the other. There was someone else, sitting behind him on his bike – her daughter, Marina, the pair of them flying along like birds. There was something rather beautiful about it.

Su Qin's despair turned to fury in an instant. She found herself hoping that Marina would fall off. Why did it have to be this yob picking her up? And what were the two of them doing together so late at night? Was he spiriting her away somewhere?

Su Qin rode straight up to them without saying a word. The closer she got, the harder her expression became. The gods were making sport of her, and it felt like torture.

Su Qin noticed that Victor's face was bleeding and bruised. Well, of course, it was only to be expected with a street kid like that. These hooligans were always fighting and messing around, regularly ending up hurt. No doubt he'd soon be pickled in booze, too. Like father, like son. As she met them head-on, Victor put his foot to the ground, and Marina hastily jumped down. It was hard to interpret her expression – she was shocked to see her mother, of course, but there was something challenging in it too. She sidled close to Victor, holding his left arm, and ignoring the way he suddenly tensed up.

Su Qin dropped her bicycle, threw herself at Marina and boxed her ears. Two satisfyingly hard slaps echoed in the empty street, the first she had ever inflicted on her daughter.

"You little slut!" she raged. But no sooner had her palm landed on her daughter's flesh than Su Qin realised she'd done the wrong thing. She would only push Marina farther away from her.

Marina did not flinch. She glanced at the boy beside her and nodded slightly as if to say, You see? My mum hit me because of you, Victor. As if the slap meant that their fates would be forever intertwined. Her eyes were bloodshot and her expression thoroughly mutinous, and she gripped Victor's hand tightly. Marina burned as hot as the sun bursting through clouds.

Years later, as they kept watch over Ding Bogang's coffin, Victor confessed to Su Qin that before that evening, even though he knew he liked Marina, his feelings were still unformed. It was those two slaps that made him fall genuinely, stubbornly, in love with her.

By the time Su Qin got Marina home, it was nearly eleven o'clock. Since Ash was in bed and sound asleep, Su Qin decided to take the opportunity to see if she could remedy the situation.

"Victor can't be your dream man, can he?" she began.

"And is Ding Bogang your dream man?" Marina shot back.

"I'll break it off with him next week," Su Qin found herself saying flippantly. It sounded as though she was going to cancel a haircut.

Marina didn't answer immediately. After a pause, she said, "That's not what I meant."

"I'm not doing it because of you," Su Qin replied, strangely calm. She felt that she was telling the truth. This was an opportunity to free herself from her troublesome physical urges and become an upright citizen again. She had had enough of being an outsider. She remembered the promises she had made when she went out to search for Marina. This might be what the Almighty wanted of her.

"I wasn't trying to wind you up by going out with Vic," said Marina. Su Qin was puzzled. Was her daughter being conciliatory or hypocritical?

Many years later, Marina told Victor sadly of that brief, impulsive conversation. She still felt guilty. She shouldn't have used him as a bargaining chip to threaten Su Qin. If she hadn't pushed her mother so hard, the two families might have stayed together. Victor reacted very calmly.

"But it was never going to last," he said. "The very first day you three came to our house, I knew we'd never be a family."

Su Qin ignored her daughter and silently got on with clearing up. Marina was still insisting: "Do you think I don't know what Victor's like? But I'm not going to drop him because of the relationship between our two families. I don't look down on him because he hasn't got a proper job. We're equal and we're free."

She made it sound like the Declaration of Human Rights.

Su Qin's reaction showed her lack of experience as a negotiator. "That's enough of that," she said. "I'm breaking it off with Ding Bogang next week. But I want you to swear you'll never see Vic again."

"Mum, don't be stupid, I never said I wanted a relationship with Victor!" Marina insisted. "You're worrying about nothing. Why would I want to stay around here?"

As Marina carried her heavy schoolbag to the table, and prepared to get on with her homework, she glanced around the cramped flat with disdain.

"I've got big ideas! Didn't you always say I had a career ahead of me, like Dad?"

Marina suddenly reached out her hand, little finger extended, to pinkie-promise with her Mum, as if she was five years old again. She seemed totally sincere, and Su Qin was overcome with emotion.

She relaxed. She knew that Marina meant what she said, that was why she relied so heavily on her. Her daughter had always been ambitious. The decision she had just taken to ditch Ding Bogang felt right. She should be like her daughter – a sunflower, working hard towards a bright future.

3

BEFORE SU QIN told Ding Bogang that she was breaking up with him, she stared at him for a long time. The light bulb above them cast red and yellow rays unevenly over his face, throwing into relief the corrugated lines across his cheeks, his thinning eyebrows, the flaky skin at the corners of his mouth, and of course, the blackheads scattered over the tip of his red nose like sesame seeds. Just looking at him left her lost for words. Had she really been sleeping with this repulsive man for the past two years and seven months?

That evening, Ding Bogang drank too much as always. His eyes were puffy and red, as if he was leaning into a gale-force wind and could not open them. She could not make out any expression on his face. Maybe there had been one, but the alcohol had erased it.

Eventually, he squinted at her and said, "What's up? Why are you looking at me like that?"

She remembered blurting out crudely: "This is the last time we're screwing."

She was quite upfront about it. She knew just how long they had been doing this: two years and seven months, 132 weeks, minus those two or three Wednesdays when the kids put a spanner in the works, or it was a public holiday, or she had her period. In total, she and Ding Bogang had slept together about eighty times.

Was that all she had with this man? Yes, there was nothing more. She had felt nothing but her body's primal urges, like a bitch in heat, and that was fine by her. She couldn't expect affection as well. She wasn't going to humiliate herself anymore. It had to stop.

Afterwards, Su Qin felt that she had made a big mistake in her relationship with Ding Bogang, but convinced herself that she was back on the right track now she had broken up with him. Especially when Marina got a place at teacher training college not long after. That was a huge relief, and Su Qin felt satisfied with her decision. If she hadn't broken up with Ding Bogang, Marina would have surely hooked up with Victor, and what a disaster that would have been!

She remembered the day when the offer letter arrived. When the good news reached Su Qin, she hurried home on her bike, overwhelmed with emotions. After all those dark winter Wednesday nights when she had made her humiliating ride to Ding Bogang's house, she could finally hold her head up high and cycle in the noonday sun that blazed so bright it burned her skin. Not that she cared. She was blissfully happy for the first time since the death of her husband. Word spread quickly, and people took it upon themselves to greet her along the way. She stopped and exchanged a few quick words with each and every one of them. Time after time, she got off her bike to accept their congratulations with modesty and gratitude.

The locals stared after her, watching the subtle twist of her buttocks as she pressed one foot down on the pedal, then the other, and instantly they forgave her former secrecy.

"Well, it's never easy bringing up two kids on your own," they murmured. "But now she's almost made it! Her girl's going to do well, and her old mum won't have to worry!"

This was a happy new beginning in Su Qin's life. There were no more slurs on her reputation as a mother; in fact, she took on a new job and became a guardian of social morality. Of course, she had to admit that in her new job, she took the opportunity to take care of some private matters too. For instance, that business with Pearl and Heipi.

4

By 2001, Su Qin was no longer known as a woman ceaselessly tormented by insatiable lust, having moved into a highly symbolic role in the forefront of public life: that of a mature woman and a respected member of the neighbourhood committee.

It was quite a transformation. It is possible that the uncompromising way she ditched Ding Bogang gained her brownie points in the Crossroads community. Moral judgments, for ordinary folk, are arrived at rather scientifically. The past and the present are combined horizontally and vertically and considered in conjunction with each other. Having observed Su Qin, people concluded that she was a woman with a mind of her own. If she wanted to be your friend, she would. If she wanted to be alone, she would be alone. She knew her own mind and made no bones about what she was going to do. The factory folk liked and respected that more than anything. Besides, look at her daughter, now at college; and look at her son, working in the South! This was a hard-working woman, a woman who no longer had anything to do with sex and other vulgar activities. And when the layoffs came, she had it just as hard as everyone else. So they came to respect her and her methodical way of doing things.

As hints of this new positive view of herself were fed back to her, Su Qin felt that she had finally turned the page on the whole Ding Bogang affair. In fact, she had ripped the page out of her life, crumpled it up and thrown it in the rubbish bin. She had regained a little of her lost dignity. At the very least, however vulnerable she felt inside, she was able to take on some of the neighbourhood committee's vital work: mediating between mothers-in-law and daughters-in-law, sweeping graves in preparation for the Qing Ming festival, checking up on the health of unemployed women, preventing pet diseases, doling out advice to the sick and the disabled, family planning, participating in Public Security Joint Defence Patrols, carrying out Transient Population Surveys, keeping local bulletin boards up-to-date, organising flags, slogans and banners for public holidays, volunteering in local clinics, registering Subsistence Allowance Households, keeping an eye on street peddlers, as well as working with Overseas Chinese Affairs and United Front organisations, and managing elections for the District People's Congress. You could say that every task she performed had come down to the neighbourhood committee all the way from the Central Government in Beijing and was vital to the national economy and people's livelihoods. Su Qin's desk was stacked high with files. Every month, she had to register twelve ledgers, submit twenty-three forms and affix more than sixty official seals onto as many reports.

However, what was special about the work of the neighbourhood committee was not that it was important and kept her busy, it was the pervasive moral influence which made it unique. The committee had the privilege of sticking its nose into people's private lives. For example, in order to manage the transient population, she had to take the wives of migrant workers for medical examinations to have them fitted with IUDs and provide condoms to them (after asking: "What size? Medium or small?"). In order to mediate family conflicts, she had to go into someone's house, sit on their squeaky bed, and probe in detail to identify the root cause. ("How is your sex life? Do you do it every night or every few nights?") When she went out with the Public Security Officers on a mission to crack down on pornography, gambling and drugs, they had to venture into dingy basements plastered wall to wall with risqué advertisements or strange-smelling massage rooms, even bursting in on couples wrestling naked in bed.

Can you imagine the impact these things had on Su Qin? She

was a fifty-two-year-old woman, once a social outcast but now a reformed character. You might imagine that she'd be implacable in the face of such immorality. Rather like the stern "aunties" of the city neighbourhoods, whose job it was to put a stop to jaywalking.

But no, the opposite was true. Su Qin simply got on with her work and never let on how shocked she was, or how she had lived her whole life without even knowing such things existed. What a range of physical desires and longings were revealed to her! They drove people to set up a new family with a mistress, to elope, to commit adultery, to get involved in same-sex relationships, sex with multiple partners, with children, with siblings . . . Compared to them, she had to admit she had been an amateur. This was quite comforting, but she felt oppressed too: so many years had gone by and yet little had changed – people's intimate secrets were still being attacked by the guardians of social morality. The miscreants suffered the full glare of publicity and were then severely punished. She felt great sympathy, but she was also on high alert for her own children. She desperately hoped that they would be upright and honest, that they would not be seduced by darker desires best left suppressed. She was very aware that living a moral life was hard work – it was like a rubber band, apparently elastic, but in fact capable of tightening around your neck until you choked to death.

Apart from meddling in public morals and intruding on people's privacy, her new job had another surprise in store: It put her back in contact with Ding Bogang.

She came across his name when she was handed a stack of citizens' letters addressed to city government offices and was instructed to deal with the complaints. She took off her glasses and peered at the paper. She could hardly believe what she was reading – and at that very moment, her memory unashamedly dredged up lurid details of her last night with Ding Bogang. She also remembered his parting words before he fell asleep: "I have a terrible memory, I'll probably have forgotten everything by tomorrow morning."

Oh my god, this letter really is about him, she thought. And he really has lost his memory!

The letter from the veteran cadre read like a newspaper report, and Su Qin had to read it three times. The disgruntled citizen who had written it was filled with indignation. In neat and precise handwriting, he described the dramatic scene that Ding Bogang put on around the factories every morning. In a drunken stupor, he brought the glorious past and its inhabitants back to life, he wept as he bewailed the demise of the old factory zone, his old worker friends, and everything that had belonged to the working class.

"They've been reformed out of existence! They're the unpalatable face of the past, they can't be allowed to disfigure the beautiful face of our new factories!" Ding Bogang was quoted as saying. The powers-that-be had passed the letter down to the neighbourhood committee, with instructions to "promote social harmony" between Ding Bogang (who was now labelled as one of the "poor, sick, or disabled members of society") and his neighbours.

Without a moment's hesitation, Su Qin bought a bottle of Yanghe and headed for Ding Bogang's home. It was six years since they had split up.

As she arrived at the entrance of the building, her eyes were drawn to the single word "Demolition" painted on the wall inside a big circle. Her gaze swept over the familiar cracks on the concrete stairs where the same dim light bulb hung from its truncated cable as she turned the corner. She wondered if those Wednesdays and Saturdays they had spent together would come back to life. Would it be embarrassing and emotional to meet again? She told herself firmly to put it all out of her mind and continue to walk with the sturdy tread of a neighbourhood committee representative. She was a middle-aged woman with a middle-aged mind and a middle-aged body. Who cared how she felt? It was her job to speak on behalf of the local community. She marched up to the door and knocked.

When he answered the door, Su Qin was struck by how much Ding Bogang seemed to have mellowed.

Nodding politely to her, he said, "I'm sorry, there's no one at home," as if he himself were not a human being. He looked behind him, frowned, then added: "My child prodigy son has gone to take an exam. I've got a daughter, but she and her husband are out looking for scrap."

By now, Heipi was running the fine-sounding Luo's World Resources, but Ding Bogang always called him a scrap dealer.

"There's no one at home," he smiled apologetically and said again.

Su Qin stood in the doorway, peering at Ding Bogang and concluded that he really didn't recognise her. It was like a one-way mirror, she could see him, but he could not see her. As far as she was concerned, that was fine.

He invited Su Qin to sit on the sofa. It was the same one as before, just that the springs were looser and it was a lot grimier. Then he ignored her and carried on with what he was doing. The table was covered in photos, which he was picking up methodically one by one. Every time he raised one up to his face, he reacted as joyfully as if he were looking at them for the first time.

"See?"

He looked up shyly at Su Qin, presenting her with a black and white photo of a woman in a bulky cotton-padded coat and her hair blowing over her face. The Yangtze River Bridge loomed grey and majestic in the background.

"This is my wife, soon after she got here. She was just a village lass."

Another one showed Ding Bogang in his twenties, with a group of his mates in crumpled workers' overalls. They were standing crowded together in front of a window with the light shining on their faces, smiling stiffly, clutching work gloves, screwdrivers and hacksaws in their grease-stained hands. The composition of the photo was strange: they were standing side-on, craning their necks to read a newspaper.

"We were studying the New China Daily," he explained. "'In agriculture, learn from Dazhai; in industry learn from Daqing.'

That was what we were reading."

As he reminisced, there was something sweet in his expression that surprised Su Qin. He had been in his prime back then. The factory too.

Then there was a family photo with everyone beaming, while firecrackers were going off in the background in swirling red ribbons. A swarthy young man stood next to Pearl, the pair of them grinning from ear to ear. Above their heads, you could just see half of a signboard which read "Luo's World Resources". As he showed Su Qin that particular photo, Ding Bogang hesitated and his smile stiffened. He hurriedly tried to turn it over, but Su Qin reached out to take it and examined it carefully. She peered at Heipi. The colour photo made him look very dark. She couldn't help comparing her own daughter unfavourably with Pearl. Marina had failed to get accepted into a Masters programme and things hadn't worked out on the job front either. She had been assigned to a third-rate middle school with hopeless students, but her outlook was as positive as ever. She lived in the staff dormitory, volunteered to teach extra lessons and diligently did home visits where she spoke to the parents with assurance, even when they mocked her. Su Qin was worried about her not having a boyfriend, but Marina, half-joking and half-serious, declared, "Stop fussing! Don't you want me to catch the biggest, fattest fish? I haven't baited my hook yet!"

But Pearl had landed one easily. Maybe Marina wasn't as good as her . . . Su Qin fixed her eyes on Heipi, unaware that she looked as if she was trying to fix him in her sights and take a pot shot at him. Ding Bogang was getting impatient. He reached out and snatched the photo from Su Qin's hands and, peace of mind restored, carried on going through his collection.

By now, Su Qin was in a sour mood. She couldn't hang around forever, she had to get the job done.

"Ding Bogang," she shouted impatiently. It felt strange and sad to say his name. Life really was like playing badminton, you never knew where the shuttlecock was going to go next.

Ding Bogang looked up in surprise, as if wondering how the woman who had knocked on the door knew his name.

"That's me. What do you want?" He stammered a little, eyeing her unblinkingly like a child.

"From now on, you're not to go out in the street alone. No more sitting outside and crying. You're embarrassing people!"

Su Qin's tone softened. It occurred to her at this moment that in all the time they were together, she had never shown him any affection. In fact, she had made a point of showing that she despised him. She sighed. If he behaved well today, she could make up for it and have a good chat with him. She could not believe that he had lost his marbles.

"On behalf of the neighbourhood committee, I'm formally telling you that you're not to go out and roam around in the morning. What if you get lost? In fact, we're suggesting to your family that they put you in a care home," Su Qin stated with authority. Ding Bogang looked confused.

"But . . . But what am I to do all morning when I get up?"

"You can look at your photos," Su Qin suggested.

"But I look at them in the afternoon. Like now. It's the afternoon now."

It was clear that Ding Bogang had his routine and was reluctant to alter it.

"And I have a drop to drink in the evening. In the morning, I just get up and walk around the factory zone."

"Alright, well, in the morning, you could . . ." Su Qin came to a halt. Actually, what could Ding Bogang do, the way he was now?

"You come up with an idea and I'll do what you say," said Ding Bogang with a confident smile, and looked down again to flip through his album.

He picked up a photo of Victor, standing in front of a rusty old steel structure, wearing a suit with a lanyard hanging around his neck, smiling at the camera. He looked drunk with happiness. Su Qin knew that kind of smile. She had taken pictures of her husband once and he had been smiling the same way, not looking at the camera, but at the person holding the camera. Su Qin was moved, and a bit jealous too. That ne'er-do-well, that glass-blower, Victor, was in love. And now he really was doing well!

She looked more closely and suddenly screwed up her eyes, trying to focus. There was no mistake, down by the foot of the iron girder, she could see half of a brown and green checked canvas bag. She knew that bag only too well. It was Marina's. She had bought it out of her wages and brought it with her whenever she came home for the weekend.

Su Qin's heart beat fast.

"When was this taken?" she demanded. What was going on? So Vic was Marina's big, fat fish! No wonder she was always so averse to talk of boyfriends. So had the two of them just been pigheaded and got together, even though Su Qin had broken up with Ding Bogang? Oh God, she'd been blind!

Ding Bogang misunderstood her question and happily replied, "That's right, that's my prodigy of a son! He could count at the age of one, recite pi at the age of two, memorise Tang poems by the age of three, read newspapers at the age of four, and in the third year of primary, he could read fourth grade books. In the first year of high school, he passed the second year exams."

He reeled it all off just like the first time. Then he added: "See? He's wearing a suit. They promoted him to a trade union job without him even asking. He'll never have to blow glass again! That's what happens when you've got talent!"

Suddenly, Ding Bogang's gaze landed on Su Qin's face, and he seemed confused. He stared at her, and the words dried up. Su Qin remained still and let him stare. If he really recognised her, she could ask about this photo and talk about Victor.

There was a long pause, then he asked very politely, "Next time you come, will you bring a bottle?"

5

ABOUT SIX MONTHS LATER, Su Qin did go back again, but instead of taking a bottle, she took a person – Heipi. She had dragged him out of the back door of a karaoke hall and frogmarched him to Ding Bogang's.

Su Qin had not realised it was Heipi at first. This was not surprising, since he had no clothes on.

She had not been able to stop thinking about the photo of Victor and Marina's checked canvas bag. She was worried sick, constantly in turmoil. No matter how hard she tried, she simply couldn't get her head around it. It was seven or eight years since she had broken it off with Ding Bogang, so how come these two young ones were back together again? Everything she'd done had been for nothing. What should she do this time? The situation had changed. She couldn't break up with Ding Bogang again, and she couldn't appeal to her daughter's ambitions – she didn't have any anymore, they'd all fallen by the wayside. It seemed so desperate, an act of despair, for her to have got together with Victor. And now Su Qin was doubtful that she could talk to Marina about the photo. She'd have to explain where she saw it and what she was doing with Ding Bogang. It would all be far too complicated, she couldn't face it.

Su Qin sighed. She always had to give in when it came to Marina, regardless of what it was.

The day she met Heipi, she had been doing an extra shift for the neighbourhood committee. As part of a campaign to crack down on pornography and suppress illegal publications, they had teamed up with the Public Security officers, with the neighbourhood ladies patrolling the local hotels, hair salons and massage parlours, intent on catching hookers and their clients. The neighbourhood committee and their superiors took their work very seriously, probably because they were rewarded with a percentage of the fines they levied. When the joint patrol team kicked open a cubbyhole at the far end of the corridor at the karaoke club, they were able to catch a couple in flagrante delicto. As the man and woman leapt apart, they each reacted differently: the woman covered her body, and the man covered his face. The patrol whooped in delight. They separated their quarry and asked each of them for their name, work unit and age. If the couple were simply engaging in fornication, then they would be allowed to carry on. But if money had changed hands, it was: "Sorry, you'll have to come with us."

Heipi first covered his face, then tried to shield his crotch as well. But all he had was his trousers, and they couldn't do both jobs at once. Su Qin realised she knew this man's face. She gave a little cough and went up to him. He was still bollock-naked and intent on hiding his face from view. She peered at him, racking her brains . . .

Just then, Heipi pulled himself together. He grinned at the team and tried to reason, "Okay, no need to make a fuss, I'll pay up. No need to take it any further."

Suddenly light dawned. This was the King of Scrap – Pearl's husband.

Heipi was quite unconcerned, talking figures with the patrol team. Su Qin was torn: Should she tell Pearl? Or Ding Bogang, or Victor? Someone needed to sort this man out! He was clearly an old hand at this game. It seemed like Pearl's marriage was not all it was cracked up to be. Still unsure, she decided to take the initiative. She stepped forward and whispered to her two companions, "You levy the fine, then I'll take over."

They looked slightly surprised, but didn't question it. It would, after all, save them a lot of trouble. Heipi was counting out his money. He had pockets full of cash, it was no problem paying for his night of sex. He was also keeping an eye on Su Qin, no doubt casually wondering if the old bag wanted to squeeze him for some of his fortune as well. Not that he was bothered. As long as there was scrap to be collected, he'd always be ahead of the game.

Su Qin had taken possession of Heipi's ID card. The card was like a leash which she could use to tug Heipi along with until they reached the road. She still hadn't made up her mind what to do next. However, the more she thought about it, the more she felt it wasn't right. She had always felt stuff like this was private business. Why should she make a big fuss about what Heipi was doing? Then it occurred to her that that policy only worked with people she had nothing to do with. Let them have their fun, she would give them her blessing. But this business affected Pearl, a girl who had once been almost-family, and she couldn't let it go. There was one thing that Su Qin was crystal clear on: she wanted to help Pearl.

As she led him out of the building and along the road, Heipi realised where they were headed and came to a halt by a telegraph pole, just like a dog, and refused to take another step. Su Qin brandished his ID card at him, but he still didn't budge.

"What are you up to?" he asked cautiously.

"I'm taking you to see someone."

"She hasn't lived here for ages. She moved to my flat above the business as soon as we got married. Over the shop front. I didn't want her to have to work."

Heipi had figured that this woman might be one of his wife's former neighbours and was taking him back to Pearl.

"We're not going to see her," said Su Qin, and she carried on walking without waiting for Heipi to follow.

So Heipi had to follow. It seemed as if he was being taken to his drunken washout of a father-in-law's place. He really had no idea what this weird old woman had in mind, but whatever tricks she had up her sleeve, he was suddenly incredibly irritated. He was not afraid of Ding Bogang, but the thought of the man and his booze reminded him of the first time he met Pearl. She had been cleaning up his room in that seedy hotel, and his mind conjured up the image of vomit-covered walls and Walk-on-Water shoes. Heipi almost burst into tears, something he hadn't done in a very long time.

"Er, Auntie . . ." Heipi began. He didn't know how to continue, but eventually slipped back into that truculent small-town attitude of his from four years earlier.

"OK, I made a mistake, but show me a man who doesn't want to play the field, all my mates are the same. I just got unlucky today!"

So that was what popular morality meant. Su Qin understood perfectly well, and she was not happy. She carried on walking right up to Ding Bogang's door. She knocked on the door, and, without even glancing at Heipi, simply said, "Don't worry, I won't tell him. I just want you to see him."

When Ding Bogang finally appeared, he looked at Su Qin, then glanced sideways at Heipi. His forehead beaded with sweat and he looked worried. He closed his eyes momentarily and opened them again. He focussed on Su Qin, and addressed a tentative question to her: "I know you. You know me and my son Victor, don't you? Do you know my poor little Pearl as well? I just can't remember what she looks like! I'm so worried about her, I want her to come home, there are too many bad people out there, I miss her, I worry about her. And I don't remember where I put her photo, I can't find it . . ."

Su Qin gave him a reassuring smile. "Don't worry, she'll be back to see you. And I'll come tomorrow to help you find your photo."

"What photo?" Ding Bogang asked, looking bemused, and Su Qin had to accept that it was pointless coming here.

Heipi was silent as Su Qin took him back downstairs. Ding Bogang called after her ingratiatingly, "Er . . . You, thingummy, don't bring any strangers next time. Just bring me a bottle!"

The old rascal never forgot his booze.

"This has nothing to do with how I treat Pearl," Heipi said huskily as Su Qin gave him back his ID card. "I still treat her well."

"I really don't care. You can go now."

"Who . . . Who are you?"

"Me? Didn't you see? I'm with the neighbourhood committee."

6

Su Qin failed to keep her promise – she didn't go and help Ding Bogang look for his photo the next day. It was a long time before she went there again. Her chief concern right now was, of course, Marina. Luckily, she soon stopped worrying about the photo of Victor and the checked canvas bag, and she never did get to use the various conversation strategies she had devised to broach the matter with her daughter. Because not long before Marina's twenty-sixth birthday, things took a completely different turn: Marina brought her a son-in-law.

His name was Huang Xin and he seemed very respectable – he said he was an architect and had his own company. He was satisfactory in every way, he was the "big fish" both Marina and she herself had been waiting so patiently for. Marina announced with a smile that she was going to marry him. They weren't planning on a big wedding banquet and wanted to go straight to Southeast Asia for their honeymoon.

The effect of this news on Su Qin was akin to a tropical cloudburst. On the one hand, it extinguished the smouldering anxieties she had been harbouring for some time, but on the other, it chilled her to the bone. She felt as if Marina was treating her with contempt. This had come like a bolt out of the blue. Huang Xin seemed to have popped up out of nowhere. No matter, Su Qin swallowed her misgivings without complaint. After all, the man Marina had brought home seemed decent and reliable. At the very least he wasn't Victor.

Once she thought about it that way, Su Qin ceased to be upset. She pretended to be thoroughly open-minded and greeted the stranger as if they were old friends. She tried to corner Marina for a tête-à-tête, but her daughter wasn't having any of it. Instead, she was full of bright chatter about their new flat in the city centre. It was as if she were teasing Su Qin. She might as well have said to her directly, "You wanted me to land a good one, and now look, I've done it, haven't I? This is what you always wanted for me, I hope you're satisfied. Life's going to be lovely!"

On that first visit, Marina threw together the last few bits and pieces she had left at home in such a hurry that Su Qin felt like her daughter was worried that she might be tempted to back out of this dubious marriage contract at any moment. She held up the Oxford English-Chinese dictionary with a beaming smile on her face. This was the bribe Ding Bogang had given her after the Wednesday Alliance.

"This dictionary's too heavy to take, so I'm leaving it. You don't mind, do you?"

Su Qin closed her eyes and didn't reply. Some things were better left unsaid. At least her daughter's life was looking up. She had been so worried about Marina for so long. Surely she could rest easy now.

A few months later, a report arrived from the local tax office, and Su Qin discovered that a new premises had been registered in Crossroads. It was a glass blower's workshop. As was her usual practice, she checked to see who the owner was and was surprised to see Victor's name. Had he resigned from the factory? Hadn't they given him a job in the union? Where did he get the money from to quit his job? She looked at the date he had registered his business – it was almost exactly when Marina went on honeymoon.

What a coincidence! She couldn't put her finger on why, but Su Qin felt very uneasy.

On her frequent trips out into the neighbourhood, she found herself, whether she meant to or not, prowling around the strange-looking workshop, eyeing it from a distance. She had to admit that he seemed to have very few customers. All she ever saw was the young man himself sitting at the back, or sometimes walking around with a large white cloth, wiping the surfaces down. It was as if he wasn't looking after the shop, but time itself. Seeing him through the layers of glass, she was reminded of a young monk. It was an ominous thought, one that Su Qin did not dare pursue, let alone tell Marina. She kept her confusion and remorse to herself until Ding Bogang died, when she got the chance to talk face-to-face with Victor at the funeral.

7

AFTER MARINA MARRIED, Su Qin was lonely but tranquil, at least for a while. Although Marina came home less and less, the bits and bobs she did for the neighbourhood committee sustained her. However, the peace did not last long. Three years later, she went to the bus station to pick up Ash who had come back from the South. He had stubbornly refused to return for ten years and, when she saw him, Su Qin was in turmoil once more. Clearly, she was never destined to find real peace.

Ash had lost weight and was smartly dressed. His speech sounded garbled, his words mixed with southern dialect. Yet he looked as restless and boyish as he always did, and Su Qin felt a sudden urge to throw her arms around him. She decided not to. He might find it awkward, and so might she – it had been so long. She was keenly aware that in Ash's eyes, she was a bad mother. She felt the same way about herself.

She still remembered how her son's third-year class teacher had looked at her. The woman had once summoned Su Qin and pointed out to her that there was a problem with Ash's personal statement. She knew that Ash's father had passed away and felt obliged to keep an eye on her unfortunate student. She regarded Su Qin fiercely, as if trying to judge whether she was a competent mother, and asked curtly, "Have you asked him what he wants to do? Why doesn't he want to apply for senior high school? He's not going to have great prospects if he goes to a vocational school. And even then, why choose some mediocre, out-of-the-way school no one's ever heard of that offers courses in animal husbandry, forest safety, or maps and surveying? What a waste!"

"Yes, I tried to persuade him. I'll talk to him again when I go home," said Su Qin, fixing a determined smile on her face and pretending she had always known her son's peculiar aspirations. She said goodbye to the teacher and walked home wearily, thinking glumly that she had no chance of persuading Ash to change his mind. Was it really worth talking to him about it?

He was being deliberately provocative, wasn't he? It was teenage rebellion. She had not seen it coming. She had spent years worrying about Marina's future, thinking that her son was still a kid and too fat to get up to any mischief. She really didn't have the energy to do anything but cook his meals for him. But it seemed that the warning signs had always been there. She remembered him telling stories about seeing hands at the window, and pretending to have a fever and bursting in on her and Ding Bogang. Once, she had hit him and he got in such a temper that he filled all the pots and bowls in the bathroom and kitchen with water and paint. She should have paid him more attention. Anyway, he had grown up an introverted, weepy child, teased by all and sundry for being fat. It seemed impossible he was ever going to leave home.

Su Qin's pace slowed. She felt utterly dispirited.

This business with Ash happened six months after she broke up with Ding Bogang. For six months, she had repeated to herself like a mantra: "I was right to break it off, for Marina's sake, and for my own good – and of course, for Ash's sake too."

But she had to admit there was something up with Ash. He had been very silent since their last Saturday dinner. Even when Marina got into university, he had seemed indifferent.

Su Qin remembered Marina's last evening before she left for university. She had wandered around the flat, her eyes gleaming with excitement, looking like she was about to take off and fly up to heaven.

"I'm never coming back to live here again. I'm going to knuckle down and study, I'll spend weekends and holidays in the college library, I'm going to win a scholarship, I'm going to sit the College

English Test, and maybe the TOEFL too. And now I'm going, Ash can have my bed."

Su Qin was startled. Marina seemed so adamant that she was going to sever her family ties. She felt a bit like she and Ash had been abandoned. But she told herself she was being over-sensitive. Her daughter had great prospects.

Su Qin pulled herself together. She ran her hands over the clothes that Marina had laid out on the bed and agreed solemnly, "I know, this is all very exciting. But if you have time, come back and see us. You need to take Ash with you on your journey."

Su Qin remembered the strange expression on Ash's face. He had looked at the bed that had just been bestowed on him, then looked at Marina and said something rather odd: "Sure, you just wave us goodbye. You're so all-powerful, both of you, you can do whatever you want, break up a relationship, swan off into the world! But just so as you know, I don't care what you do! And thanks very much, but I don't need a helping hand, I'll go my own way from now on."

It seemed like he had made up his mind then and there. So when the time came, she had let him go – not that she could stop him. She was completely on her own now. She had to admit that she rather missed Ding Bogang, both then and later. Probably because she had too much time on her hands and was feeling lonely.

That evening, as Su Qin went over the personal targets he had set for himself, she made sure to look pleased.

"I never knew you had such big ideas. That's good, a man should spread his wings and see the world. You know I'll support you, you can do anything you put your mind to."

Ash seemed relieved at first, but then she suddenly saw his face fill with misery. He was struggling to hold back the tears. He had probably taken it for granted that she would be full of remorse and beg him to change his mind and stay, promising to treat him better.

Su Qin had looked at Ash's eyes shining with tears and felt her own cold indifference. After he left, she often recalled this scene. This had been the moment when, as a mother, she felt utterly defeated. She had given up Ding Bogang because of Marina, and her daughter had shut her out of her new life. Now she had as good as abandoned Ash to his fate. When he sent out a distress signal, she had not thrown him a lifeline; she had pushed him further out to sea.

She was keenly aware that, as a mother, she had short-changed her son.

Still, on the day she went to pick him up from the station, she did not put her arms around him. The complex emotions she felt as she set eyes on him were immediately replaced by shock when she looked again.

There seemed to be something wrong with him.

Tugging his purple suitcase behind him, he cautiously made his way along the shiny streets of Crossroads. He looked like he was teetering over a slippery suspension bridge high above the ground and might topple over at any moment. He looked around him in horror, closing and then opening his eyes again. Crossroads had been transformed beyond all recognition. The factory zone was not there anymore – the warehouses he used to pass on his way to school with their red tin roofs, the giant grey transformer substations, the long lines of juggernauts parked one after another, the drains in the road blocked by old shoes and plastic bags – they had simply vanished.

"Yes," said Su Qin with forced light-heartedness, "They've all gone, just like your spare tyres. You're so thin now!"

She was dismayed to realise that her voice sounded accusing even to her own ears, as if she preferred her son fat.

It wasn't just that he was thinner. She found the way he walked quite off-putting. He always used to waddle, but now he walked with his legs clamped together. And when he was sitting, he jammed his hands between his thighs. When he smiled, he kept covering his mouth, and sometimes stuck his tongue out too. And he kept looking around and blinking, craning his scrawny neck.

Su Qin felt a headache coming on. Her temples hurt. First the left, then the right, and then her whole head felt like a band had tightened around it and the muscles began to twitch. Fragments of memories from her years of work with the neighbourhood patrol team flickered through her mind, flashes she had seen in the light of their torches. They came back to her now. Ash reminded her of one of those men. Like a rabbit caught in the headlights, meekly resigned to being punished for their misdeeds, waiting for the embarrassment to be over. She wished she had been more sensitive.

Su Qin felt like her legs wouldn't carry her. For the first time, it occurred to her to leave the neighbourhood committee. She was no longer willing to represent public morality and bully strangers by prying into their private lives when she herself had failed so miserably.

Ash slowed his pace, but Su Qin still lagged behind. He looked back, and in that second he suddenly saw how his mother had changed. He had always remembered her as moody and temperamental, but now she had become a frail old woman who needed to be helped along. She looked dazed and unfocussed, walking unsteadily, as if something infinitely heavy was weighing her down. Strangely, it was the sight of her droopy breasts and saggy belly that tugged at Ash's heartstrings for the very first time. It was a peculiar feeling, one that he had longed for as a child but never had. For some reason, he craved a lollipop. He popped his fingers in his mouth and sucked them, but was dismayed to find that they were not as chubby and satisfying as they used to be.

Su Qin caught up with him. She barely came up to his shoulders, but she reached up and pulled his fingers out of his mouth. She had calmed down by now and was determined that she would do what she could to help. He was still her son, she owed him that. There were lots of things that were too late to remedy, but at the very least, she could protect her son's privacy. She knew all about how to do that.

She fussed over him, taking his luggage – an oversized zip-bag which seemed to weigh almost nothing. Casually, she asked what was in it. Ash thought for a while, as though he was searching for the right way to phrase his answer. Finally he said, "Second-hand kids' clothes. They're not mine but they belong to me."

Su Qin pressed her lips tightly together, afraid that she might let an unkind remark slip out. She immediately decided that she would never raise the topic again. Or anything related to it, for that matter. She was going to allow him absolute privacy.

Ash looked at his mother, who had lapsed into an awkward silence. It was a common misunderstanding, he'd come across it a lot. Just as they were arriving at the apartment, he asked her hesitantly, "Um, do you think I look like . . . ?" (When he figured people had misunderstood, he always wanted to check what exactly they were feeling. Did he or did he not look like . . . ?)

Su Qin looked around at the passers-by – a hodgepodge of grown-ups and children – pottering past. She did not know what to say. Why does he insist on talking about it now? she wondered. She began to panic. Her public moral responsibilities ticked away like an alarm clock, but she forced herself to push them to the back of her mind.

"Oh, you mean that?" she finally said, sounding ever-so broad-minded. "Don't worry about it, I often come across them at work! It's fine! Everyone's an individual."

Ash was so disappointed he almost laughed. She had given the same answer as everyone else. They all thought he was.

In fact, he had no idea if he was or not.

He didn't know whether to laugh or cry. It was as if all the people in the world were standing in a queue, men (or those who identified as men) on one side, women (and those who identified as women) on the other, all moving slowly along in a crowd. The trouble was, he didn't know which lane he belonged in. He had crossed back and forth between the two for ages, but was still unsure. After so many years in the South, it only got more confusing.

"I've got all my exercise books in this bag. Would you like to see them?" Ash said as he unpacked.

He wanted to talk to his mother. He wanted to start with Lao Shan and give her all the details. Or with the boy's clothes in his bag. Or to go back in time, to his rhapsodic image of the relationship between Victor and Marina.

Su Qin was still stubbornly acting like an enlightened parent.

"Are they your diaries? Then I certainly can't read them! It's okay, Ash, you don't need to say anything. Whatever you've done or are going to do, I support you unconditionally! You're my son, and I will always be here for you."

She sounded like she was delivering a diplomatic communiqué. Then she rushed off to get some food ready, as if, right then and there, that was the only thing that mattered.

Ash realised that his mother was actually afraid, the way she had always feared breaking the rules, flouting social conventions. She had always been afraid of herself and Marina, and now she was afraid of him. Forget it, he told himself. He shouldn't drag her into his struggles. He carefully stacked the exercise books and stuffed them under the bed together with the old clothes, which was where he used to keep them in the South. He felt dismayed. He seemed to have brought his problems with him. Was coming back home going to be any help at all?

At dinner, Ash changed the subject to something his mother might find more palatable.

"When will Marina be back? I haven't met my brother-in-law yet. We can have a big family dinner!"

Despite everything else, his feelings about meals hadn't changed: the more the merrier. But his mother looked more and more enigmatic, humming and hawing uncomfortably.

"She hasn't been back for a while. We didn't talk properly when she did come home. I don't know if you knew, but it seems like she was going out with Victor before she got married."

Ash gasped in surprise. Had those wicked seeds he had planted really germinated?

But his mother nailed that topic almost as soon as she brought it up, and broached another with unnaturally good cheer.

"Your brother-in-law, he's a fine man. So good-mannered, and quick-thinking. And seems very well-behaved. He's a very hard worker and his company's grown quite big."

8

AFTER SU QIN gave up her job with the neighbourhood committee, she went to see Ding Bogang one last time – just for her own satisfaction. Quite what satisfaction she was looking for she didn't know.

She took him a bottle and some food. She had not forgotten Ding Bogang's flamboyant way of cooking up a storm, and knew just where to find his greasy maroon-coloured apron – exactly where it had always been. While Ding Bogang looked at the same photos over and over again, she retreated into the kitchen.

She filled Ding Bogang's cup, but he quailed away from her, apparently bewildered at this woman who had taken over his house. Even more surprising, she poured a full glass for herself too, and sat down to drink with him.

She took a gulp. It was revolting. To think that Ding Bogang had been drinking the same stuff for decades, and still drank it to this day! She used her chopsticks to place lots of choice morsels in his bowl, and then it was time to deliver the brutal truth.

"You must remember my Marina. Well, she dragged her heels for ages and finally married a man with a really good job, but she's gone cold on him! She's become so completely fake I can't get an honest word out of her. Do you have any idea why? Of course you don't, you old pisshead. Well, let me tell you, she was messing around with your son. It was me who put a stop to that. That was why I broke up with you so suddenly."

Ding Bogang's hand jerked and he spilled his drink down his front. He looked down and smiled, completely unconcerned.

"Ai-ya! Pearl will give me a telling-off when she comes back. But every time she does that, she buys me another bottle afterwards."

"Don't change the subject. I'll wash it for you before I go. Let me finish what I was saying," she said impatiently. Su Qin was determined to get everything off her chest, and she certainly had a lot to air: Ash's return, Pearl and Heipi, and Victor, the prodigious son, and that glass workshop of his. She talked so long that all the dishes on the table had gone cold and were practically congealed by the time she finished and her voice was beginning to sound like a bat flying round and round inside a cave.

"You're better off than all of us," she sighed. "You're in blissful ignorance."

She felt quite envious.

Ding Bogang listened and drank, nodded wisely, then, still listening and drinking, he took a pack of cards, laid them out on the table and played a round of solitaire. From start to finish, he did not say a word.

Well, at least she had got it all off her chest. She stared blankly at the table, noticing that two of the dishes hadn't been touched. Ding Bogang got up and moved slowly to the window. With his back to Su Qin, he hummed a few bars of an old workers' song.

Then he turned back, and beckoned mysteriously to her. He pointed his chin towards a newly-built high-rise block of apartments outside the window. It was a severe, sparsely-lit structure that almost blocked out the view completely. Then he jerked his chin again and again and exclaimed, "Look at all these fine buildings! Over there is the substation and galvanised iron warehouse, and that's the auditorium and health centre and staff canteen for the alkylbenzene factory workers. And over there, that's the chimney of the cement factory, and the big red brick water tower. Just beyond them you can see the flame from the petrochemical factory!"

Su Qin stood there patiently, trying her best to see what was no longer there. Suddenly, she realised that Ding Bogang had taken her hand and was stroking it gently. It was a gesture so full of understanding and comfort. Everything suddenly seemed clear.

Startled, she tried to search his eyes, but the moment had passed and he was acting daft again.

"Look, look outside!" he exclaimed. "I stand here every night, and the more I look at it, the more I like it. Nothing's changed."

Hot tears running down her cheeks, Su Qin held his rough, unfamiliar hand in hers. She knew now that she would never come back. She would never speak to him again. She still nurtured a sense of personal morality, like a dull ache inside her. Forlorn as she was, she was still determined to remain loyal to her late husband, even though the restraints she imposed on herself meant she would never find happiness again.

9

S HE KEPT HER WORD. It was not until six months later when Ding Bogang died that Su Qin returned to that crumbling old flat. No one seemed to know what to do, though their disorganised bumbling was entirely in keeping with the death of a man whose brain had been pickled in alcohol. For some reason, Victor had not yet turned up. Although Heipi was there, he was busy making phone calls about his scrap business. Pearl was trying to do practical things but had no idea where to start. Weeping and wailing was a lot easier.

After Su Qin arrived, everything went much more smoothly. She doled out the tasks: buying food and cooking lunch, greeting the odd neighbour or two who came to offer condolences, settling the hospital bill, getting a photo of Ding Bogang enlarged for the memorial table, throwing out his old clothes and informing former workmates of his death. It was only when the time came to decide what to do with Ding Bogang's ashes that his son turned up. Victor had scratches all over his face and wore a dazed expression. Su Qin had been ready to drop her previous prejudice against him but now she was annoyed. His dad had died! What was he playing at?

Heipi suggested they buy a cemetery plot. He was willing to foot the bill, he said, stammering as he confessed that he'd always wanted to find a way to thank his father-in-law for setting him on the road to success. He would be happy to fork out some of his fortune to see the old man laid to rest properly. But at that point, Victor, who had been kneeling upright and rigid as a sleepwalker all this time, suddenly spoke up. He was vehemently against it. They had to find a place that was guaranteed never to be demolished, and until they did, no one was allowed to touch his father's ashes. He had promised his dad that he would never let him suffer the same fate as his poor mother, whose bones were scattered who knew where. Victor got very emotional as he remembered his father's battle against the relocation of his mother's grave. He burst into hysterical laughter, reducing Heipi to shocked silence and making Pearl weep even harder.

"Dad's dead, who'll take us to see Mum at Qing Ming?" she wailed. The old rubbish dump had been transformed into a giant building site, festooned with scaffolding, but even at his most drink-sodden, Ding Bogang always knew where their mother lay. He used to wander around, his eyes darting here and there, taking a few steps then coming to a sudden halt, before pointing confidently with his toe.

"She's right here. We can't do the food offerings anymore, but let's light some joss paper. No need to make a fuss."

Su Qin felt bad listening to all this and patted Pearl on the shoulder. She felt that she was the only adult left in both families.

As night came, in the room full of joss paper and the flickering light of candles, even their grief was exhausted. Pearl kept yawning. She drooped sideways, and soon was emitting impressive snores. Heipi took her place and kept watch for the first half of the night, while Victor snatched a bit of sleep and then took over.

Su Qin kept to the cramped living room. She sat rather stiffly where Ding Bogang used to sit when he drank, staring at the empty dining table and the cracks in its surface. A soundtrack of occasions long past echoed in her ears: the banging of pots and pans, the clattering of bowls and chopsticks, and dishes being put on the table. She sat there for as long as it would have taken for a meal, then got up and stood at the window where Ding Bogang used to stand staring out. The last time she had seen him, he had pointed out landmarks to her, reliving the past in front of her eyes. In his deluded vision, the demolished chimney, the disassembled warehouse and the long-gone factories had all reappeared, along with the auditorium, health clinic and staff canteen, while the great torch burned day and night as fiercely as before.

Heipi had been looking at Su Qin, and finally understood that this neighbourhood committee business had been about his father-in-law all along. He tried to lighten up and relax, but he was quite wary of her. After all, she had seen him naked! Finally, he approached hesitantly and offered her a seat.

Su Qin turned away from the window. Her gloom was replaced by a condescending expression. She spent the rest of the night of the vigil talking to Heipi about Pearl's belly.

There was no way of easing into it gently. It would always sound like a lesson, a warning, like an edict from an elder citizen. She spoke with the authoritative voice of Pearl's long-dead mother and newly-deceased father, and of herself, too, even though she did not know how she fitted into all this. She had no intention of making any accusations about Heipi's private life, all she was concerned with was Pearl's belly and the contribution he should be making to it. A man's seed and his energy was limited. If he expended it all outside of home, he had less for his wife, and of poorer quality too. That would make it very hard for Pearl to get pregnant.

"Listen up," she commanded him. "Everything hinges on you doing your bit and how much you do. If there's a problem, you'll be to blame."

She addressed Heipi in the tone of a former senior figure in the neighbourhood committee. Heipi was incensed. Why did he have to listen to this preaching again? And what made him even angrier was that he found himself nodding sullenly, as if his late father-in-law was talking to him. It was weird. The old woman seemed to be half-man half-woman, definitely not all woman.

Heipi nodded again.

"You can rest assured, I'll do it, I'll do my bit to put something in Pearl's belly. I want a son more than anyone! If anything happens, you'll be the first to know. I'll be coming right over to thank you."

At quarter past one in the morning, Victor took over from Heipi.

He knelt down in the sitting room, ignoring Su Qin. Su Qin looked him over, turned and went into the kitchen. Within a few minutes, she brought out a bowl of egg-fried rice, fragrant and golden. Victor took it, noticing to his surprise that she had sprinkled chopped spring onion on top. He helped himself to a mouthful. The familiar taste overwhelmed him and he could almost believe that the old man had come back to life and was hiding out in the kitchen!

Su Qin sat down next to him, feeding the brazier with joss money. She looked at the picture of Ding Bogang. No one knew when it had been taken, but he looked quite young. He didn't have a red nose and he wasn't bald yet. In fact, he didn't look bad at all. Leaning over the brazier, Su Qin rubbed her hands together, making her palms rustle like a breeze.

"When I think about your father, and about his life, there's one thing I feel bad about. I let him, and you, down. Back then, when he asked me to find you a job . . . It was all my fault, I couldn't do it, I could have asked someone, but . . . You might not understand, but in those days, I would rather have died than gone public about my relationship with your dad."

Su Qin was surprised to find herself so apologetic, especially to Victor. It seemed like he found it strange too. With his mouth full of fried rice, he mumbled, "Forget it. If it hadn't been for that job opening, I would never have known I liked glass."

He took a few more bites and wiped his lips.

"As for those Wednesday nights, we should have known better."

Su Qin shook her head.

"Let's not bring that up again. I just want to ask one thing. When you quit your job and set up your glass workshop, did that have anything to do with Marina getting married? It's okay whatever you say, I just want everyone to be happy."

Victor interrupted as if he couldn't bear to listen to any more.

"You don't need to worry. But, yes, you're right."

He smiled suddenly and pointed to the scratch on his cheek.

"Actually, I have a girlfriend. We almost got our rocks off last night. Look, she scratched me!"

Su Qin looked away. This was the last thing she expected Victor to say. So, when Ding Bogang died, that was what his son was doing? No wonder he'd arrived late this morning, no wonder he spent so long kneeling in front of his father's body. She didn't know whether to be angry or feel sorry for him.

Victor went on with a faint smile.

"You know why I said 'almost'? Because I couldn't go any further. Ever since that night when you gave Marina two slaps across the face, I've been bewitched. I don't fancy other women. You'll probably find that hard to believe."

"No, I believe you," Su Qin replied quietly. She avoided looking at Ding Bogang's picture.

"But you don't know that she and I carried on seeing each other until she got married."

"Yes, I knew that."

"Did Marina tell you?"

"I saw your father. He was holding the photo Marina took of you."

Victor looked up in surprise, as if he was seeing Su Qin for the first time. He ran his tongue over his teeth, gave a tight little cough, and finally said, "Then can I ask you how Marina's been in the past few years? I don't have any reason for asking, I'd just like to know."

Su Qin's expression was unreadable. After some minutes' thought, she made up her mind that she didn't want to tell him anything about Marina. She couldn't risk anything starting again. She fed the brazier with joss paper again and avoided answering.

Finally, she said, "Ding Bogang was right when he said you were a good boy."

Victor suddenly seemed to understand something. To Su Qin's surprise, she saw silent tears rolling down his cheeks. He was still stuffing egg-fried rice into his mouth.

10

FOR THE ALKYLBENZENE factory residents, the end was approaching. When this sweltering summer was over, the buildings would be pulled down. In the factory zone, demolition had become as catching as an infectious disease. No one could avoid it. Now, it had spread to the alkylbenzene factory where Su Qin lived. In the alley outside the window, the crashing and banging went on all day long.

Ash stood looking out and sighed.

"It's a good thing I came back. It'll probably be my last time here."

Su Qin felt extremely unsettled. Finally she understood Ding Bogang's panic when he thought he would have no proper resting place.

"The old pisshead got it right. There really is no place that's safe," she said.

"There's no need to panic," Ash told her. "For you old folk, moving house is like peeling off a layer of skin. But people can live anywhere nowadays."

He turned on his laptop and showed her a pink and blue retail website.

"Look at my online store. It doesn't matter where I am – here or in the South, or anywhere on earth – it's still the same. This address never changes. Just one tap and it comes on. It's always there, and it's always busy."

Ash was now completely immersed in building his online business. He threw himself into the work, pouring with sweat like a farmer working the rich, dark earth. He had started small, but now business was booming and he could hardly keep up with this new crop of customers. In less than a year, he had updated and upgraded his laptop four times. He now had six online mailboxes, and his blog had ninety-five links. He had started four chat groups and joined more than thirty other groups. He had seven bank accounts. He had even created a special encrypted file where he stored his various passwords.

Su Qin peered over his shoulder at the laptop screen and nodded unconditional approval. Since the evening when she got it all off her chest to Ding Bogang just before he died, she had felt her own situation to be hopeless. She had decided to live for the moment. Ash's online shop had become her consuming interest, and she had taken over buying wholesale supplies and making all the Korean hair accessories. Just occasionally, she would think sadly to herself that she couldn't see anything changing for Ash. He would be like this until the day she died and for many years after – a lone figure in front of his laptop.

The afternoon that Marina came home, the weather was very strange. They had half an hour of sweltering heat followed by half an hour of torrential rain.

Instead of coming in through the front door, she walked down the alley until she got to the back window, as if she were just passing by. She was holding her umbrella to one side so that it concealed the upper half of her body. She stared silently through the window, its rusty mesh dripping with rainwater. The rain coursed down like a curtain, framing her face as if she were on a miniature darkened stage, playing the young woman she had once been but was now parted from forever.

Ash saw her there, but was involved with a buyer who was querying the size of a shawl, so he could only call to her through the mesh. Su Qin flung down the work she had been holding and hurried out of the main door clutching the old umbrella, the one with a broken spoke. She couldn't believe her eyes. Her son had returned, and here was her daughter too! There was something to be said for demolition, after all.

Marina didn't move. She stood there gazing into the street, her mother standing beside her. For a long time, there was only the sound of rain hitting the surrounding roofs and concrete paving and rushing into the sewers.

Su Qin beamed and said quite naturally, "Just imagine how many times we've ridden our bikes down this alley. The happiest time for me was when you received your admission letter from the university. I kept getting off the bike to tell people. It was a big day for our family."

Marina couldn't take her mother's evasiveness any longer. She burst out, "Haven't you noticed? I'm pregnant! Almost six months along."

Su Qin was momentarily lost for words. Then she blurted, "Er, well, of course I noticed but I thought you didn't want to tell me. I thought that must be the reason why you didn't want to come home, so I decided not to mention it. But now you've told me, I think it's great! Huang Xin must be happy. You've been married for four years."

"I haven't told him. We . . . Actually, we split up last month. I moved out and I'm renting an apartment somewhere else."

Su Qin swallowed hard. She told herself to stay calm, not to be angry with Marina. She'd always been like this: making sudden announcements about getting married, being pregnant, and now the separation. It was all her business, no one else's, of course. Looking on the bright side, her daughter had at least come to tell her. All the same, she felt the urge to give her a good shake and plead with her.

What's up with you? she wanted to yell. I'm your mother, talk to me, don't be like this! If something's wrong with your relationship, do you really have to split up? Believe me, it's no fun separating and getting divorced! Marina, please, please, talk to me, maybe we can still fix things!

But she didn't say any of that. She acted very calm.

"Oh, what a shame, your first baby."

She was testing the waters, desperate to know what Marina was planning.

Marina didn't answer, she just smiled. Then, for some reason, she folded her umbrella and let the rain pour down over her bare head. Su Qin was startled. She tried to angle her broken umbrella so that it covered Marina as well. They were standing shoulder to shoulder now.

But Marina pushed the umbrella away. She lifted her face and closed her eyes, as if she was basking in the sunshine instead of allowing the rain to run down her cheeks.

"Don't cover me, I just wanted to try how it feels standing out in the storm without an umbrella. The worst that can happen is that I get soaked, and maybe catch a cold and have to stay in bed for a few days."

Su Qin's face wore an anxious smile but she obeyed. For the sake of this all-too-infrequent opportunity to talk, she collapsed her umbrella too and stood in the rain.

After a while, she said carefully, "I've always used an umbrella in the rain. It's quite nice standing like this for a while, but I don't like having wet hair."

She reached out as if to touch her daughter's belly. Suddenly, she longed for this tiny infant with its uncertain future. She imagined a baby in the family. How happy she would be. She hadn't held a baby for years.

Marina laughed and interrupted her train of thought.

"Don't take it so literally. What I mean is having a father, or not, is like having an umbrella on a rainy day – or not. It's no big deal. With no umbrella, you get wet clothes and maybe a few sniffles. Dad died, but Ash and I are both fine! The baby in my belly isn't afraid of the rain. I want her to get a bit wet, get her prepared!"

"What do you mean? Your baby isn't going to have a father? So you're definitely going to have it?"

Su Qin didn't know whether she was happy or sad, but in any case, she didn't dare express an opinion.

"Yes. I made up my mind a little while ago. I'll have this baby and I'll be a single parent! That would be pretty awesome, don't you think?"

Marina wiped the rain off her face, the raindrops splashing onto her wrist. Her gesture was unimaginably languid and poetic.

"Let's not discuss the specifics," she said, "this is what I've decided."

Su Qin rubbed her hands together as if they were cold. Had her daughter gone crazy? But she pressed the pause button in her mind and forced herself not to think. Fine, she would just echo Marina.

"Sure, sure, that's a good decision. And besides, I can help you with the baby."

Marina looked at her and sighed contentedly. Then she looked up at the sky.

"This rain is so nice! Give me a few more minutes. Anyway, it's raining everywhere, in front, behind, wherever we walk."

Ash, who had been waiting in the flat, finally ran outside to look for them. Some way off, he could see them through the downpour, their faces blurred, floating above the streams of water. How happy they looked! He gaped at them in surprise. It was the kind of touching family scene that had seemed so unattainable in his childhood. As if he was still a kid, Ash ran out and joined them.

~

Su Qin heard an ambulance approaching, its siren blaring. The crowd around her gave a collective sigh and moved away, but she was engulfed in her memories, her eyes half-closed. There was Ash running towards them, beaming with joy. And there was Marina waving at her brother, then grabbing his arm, so that they both ended up standing in a puddle. This was Marina's goodbye – goodbye to their old home and goodbye to all the problems they had had. Nothing bad was going to happen to any of them from now on.

Maybe it was Ash's arrival that triggered Su Qin's long-suppressed resentment. She looked at her two children. There they were in the rain, without umbrellas. She thought of Marina's metaphor. Was having, or not having, a father really the same as being in the rain with or without an umbrella? Just look at them dancing around without a care in the world. She was furious with them!

She could see their future clearly. There was a big red cross over both of them: one, a divorced, single mother; the other, forever marginalised and alone. They were really two of a kind, destined always to be gossiped about, always fighting against public morals. Why did they have to be like this? It was unbearable. Moral standards were like a rope, always had been. She didn't mind if it strangled her, but she didn't want them to be strangled too. Su Qin heard herself yelling hoarsely, leaping at Marina like a wounded mother beast.

"You're so selfish, do you know that? Don't you ever think about other people? About Huang Xin? Or me? Have you given a thought to the baby you're carrying? So you think you're going to be a mother now, but do you have any idea what that means? A mother's only wish is for her child to have a good life. What right do you have to deprive this baby of its father and a decent home and condemn it to a life of suffering? Let me tell you, you don't deserve to have a child, because you don't know how to be a mother! Have you ever treated me as a mother? Have you ever treated Ash as a brother? Have you ever taken care of him? Look at you! Look at the two of you! I just don't know what to do with you."

Marina slowly wiped the rain off her face. She and Ash shared a look. Then she said, "Yes, you're right to have a go at me. I always thought you'd want me to stay with Huang Xin for the sake of my baby. But what do you think that would mean for me? I hate the way you say you want me to have a good life. I'm always worrying about you in everything I do, and I don't want to! You can't imagine how much I hate living like this."

"Ha! You've got a good life and you hate living like this? I guess you're planning to go back to Victor, right? Great, you can come and go as you please, since you don't think anyone else has any feelings!"

"Oh, thanks for that brilliant idea! I might just go ahead and do it! After all, he's the only man I ever think about day and night!"

Marina knew exactly how to wind her mother up. She didn't go into the house and instead turned on her heel and left. Ash ran to the umbrella, picked it up off the ground and handed it to her. Marina stopped and waved, perhaps to the house or perhaps to her mother and brother.

Su Qin followed them, wild with fury.

"You think you're so clever! You try showing your belly to Victor when it's a bit bigger. You mark my words, you'll be sorry when that baby's born. You don't have the first idea what being a mother means."

But Marina quickened her pace and didn't look back.

Su Qin was about to go on, but Ash stopped her.

"You've been too hard on her, you know," he said. "The more you've tried to stop her, the more she's fought back."

Su Qin waved her arms in the air, her voice filled with despair as she tried to reason with the logic of a child.

"She agreed, you know, then she hooked me in! I kept my word, so why didn't she?"

The rain showed no signs of stopping and Ash tried to persuade his mother to go indoors.

"She and Victor, it's been one misunderstanding after another, right from the start, but they are serious about each other," he said, but he looked even gloomier than Su Qin.

Su Qin paid no attention. She didn't know what to think. Then she shuddered, looked at Ash and shook her head in infinite misery.

"It's all gone wrong, my whole life has gone wrong, right up to today. What's the Almighty going to hand out to me next?"

Weeks later, Su Qin was on the street again, eyes half-closed. If only she'd been able to keep her thoughts to herself, she and Marina wouldn't have had that big row. She knew it was that argument that had brought Marina back to Crossroads again, heavily-pregnant as she was, and that had led to her lying in the road now.

Two emergency workers lifted Marina out of her arms, and someone shouted frantically, "She's miscarrying! She needs a doctor!"

Su Qin slumped in the puddle of Marina's blood. She pummelled her own menopausal flesh – the flab that had once pulsed with sinful oestrogen – and wished she was dead! She missed her husband, and Ding Bogang, and even his wife Huang Mingxiu, whom she had never met. All the dead and buried were innocent, all the living had sinned.

V

The Glass House

1

VICTOR COULD NEVER have said for sure which he loved more: glass or Marina. Not that there was any competition. Together, they gave his life substance, colour and meaning. But, in idle moments, he liked to ponder the question. He would light a cigarette and take his time, mulling it over in the swirls of smoke.

2

H E HAD KNOWN Marina for longer. But it certainly hadn't been love at first sight – no one falls in love at first sight with the daughter of their future stepmother. And Marina had such a long face. She never smiled, and she blanked him from the first time she'd come to their door and through all of those dinners. She didn't look at him, and he didn't look at her. But he sensed her opinion of him. She looked down her nose at him, the way the lead role sneers at an extra. It said to him something like, "What a loser, what a dork." That was what he felt, anyway.

Not that he let that get him down.

Victor was very fond of the factory zone. During the last two years in particular, he felt he fitted quite well into its nooks and crannies. He had no grand ambitions nor felt the need to stand out in the crowd – he could not comprehend why people craved these things. It was ironic really, given his name. Victor – as in victory, success, achievement. It might as well have been emblazoned on his forehead given the number of times he heard his name every day. Shouted or muttered, it never failed to make his stomach turn. Some people just aren't successful, and he was one of them.

Yes, Crossroads was a great place. Located in the stretch between the alkylbenzene factory, the thermal power plant, the plastics factory and the electron factory, it was the heart of the community, connecting all the warehouses and factories. It was to the factory zone what Manhattan is to New York and the Champs Élysées to Paris. People from all over the factory zone went there for entertainment and shopping.

And it was no wonder. Just look at the names: the two-storey hotel painted pink on the outside was "The Da-ge-da" (after the first generation mobile phones), the karaoke hall festooned with lightbulbs and paper flowers was "The Bund" (after the Shanghai waterfront), the shop selling soup-filled dumplings and hearty rice dishes was "The Lion Building" (after the famous fighting scene in *The Water Margin*), the photography studio where people went for portraits was "Around the World Photography", the sales department for the PVC and aluminium doors and windows was "Genesis", and so on.

Victor often hung about Crossroads, counting the fifteen-tonne lorries that filled the air with exhaust fumes and took up most of the road, leaving motorbikes, tricycles, bicycles and cars fighting for space in their wake, while the shops on either side of the road shone with glee – more wheels meant more business. Their owners revelled in the number of buckets of foul water they tossed into the road, it showed that business was booming. Apart from the factory employees and their families, there were outsiders dodging the puddles too, from other regions and speaking with different accents. Sometimes a man would get cross with a woman, and the woman would get cross with a child, and the child would kick a plastic bottle at a scrawny stray dog . . . Victor could spend hours leaning against a lamp post, watching vignettes like this unfold.

As he watched all those sweaty, frowning people on the street, he would think of Marina and her smile, of that time they went to the cemetery at Qing Ming, during that animated conversation about the dead when she had smiled for the first time. That smile! He felt drunk on it. His elation lasted until the early hours of the morning, but even when he came down to earth with a bump, he dreamed of making her smile again. That would be amazing.

There was something toxic about this fantasy though. He'd enjoyed being unemployed, but now felt frustrated, even more so knowing that Dad had tried to get him a job through Su Qin. So he'd decided to do it himself. He saw a scruffy advert with the corner torn off. Of course, apprenticeship wages were pitiful, but at least they were enough for him to get a foot in the door. And he soon became a champion snooker player. As a new kid on the block, you had to do something to stand out. And say what you like about gambling, you had to admit that snooker was a big deal in Crossroads.

The snooker tables in Crossroads were a scene of vice, all right! The light bulbs strung overhead produced a dim light that gave the impression of an underground casino, the green baize was bobbly, and the ends of the cues were covered in bite marks and spit and who knew what else. Then there was the man in charge who always had a toothpick between his teeth. He challenged any men who were passing, luring them into his underworld with cries of "Three-fifty a game! Three-fifty a game! Winner gets a free game!"

Young lads of Victor's age were easily tempted to stop and prove how tough, and lucky, they were. They'd jiggle a roll of banknotes out of the back pocket of their skintight jeans, grip the cue between their fingers and channel all their aggression into the game.

Victor was not aggressive, but he could ace the table. When he played, the cue was like an extended finger and the balls behaved as though he had bribed them, scattering and rolling precisely and obediently into the pockets. He would settle up and walk away, his pockets stuffed with rolls of grubby notes, patting his backside and laughing to himself. It gave him a sense of achievement to earn so much with so little effort.

Within a fortnight, Victor had been well and truly baptised into Crossroads, and was showing a different side of himself. He assumed a devil-may-care attitude, started wolf-whistling, and for no particular reason, would crack his knuckles and pick fights with people.

3

IT WAS AROUND THEN that he began to fall in love with glass. Instead of rushing back to his stuffy little den after dinner on Saturday, Victor started to talk about glass. At last, he had things to say.

"Do you know what glass is?" he began, narrowing his eyes into slits and looking just like his late mother. He rattled off the chemical compounds with confidence: "CaO, Na_2O, SiO_2, that's sodium phosphate, calcium silicate and silicon dioxide."

Ash and Pearl stared at him, wide-eyed. Marina was probably the only one who could understand those chemical compounds, but as usual her head was buried in the book she'd brought with her.

Then he changed tack and began to wax lyrical: "You know, glass isn't like water, or oil. It's really funny, it doesn't have a definite boiling point or freezing point, it just has a long melting process. Once it reaches 600 degrees, it becomes malleable and you can pull it into threads. And it's still like that at 1300 degrees, so soft and smooth you can make it into any shape you like – round, square, fan-shaped . . . It will do what you want! It reminds me of taffy candy."

"Huh!" Pearl scoffed. If only the things he made were edible.

"Ouch! Everyone knows body heat's thirty-seven degrees, and I know what one hundred degrees feels like from when I got scalded," said Ash, rubbing his arm. He hung on Victor's every word. "But I can't imagine 600 degrees! 1300 degrees!"

He made a hissing sound, as though someone was about to pour 1300-degree treacly glass down his throat.

Then Victor delved into why glass was so important. As he saw it, glass was the fourth most important thing after air, water and sunlight.

"Think about it for a moment. There's the soya sauce and sesame oil bottles in the kitchen. Then there's the vase, clock face and radio dial in the sitting room, and the watches on our wrists. If you look up, you'll see the light bulbs we turn on every day. And if you look outside, you'll see glass in the windows of buildings, and in cars, and traffic lights. And think about all the bottles for medicine and saline drip and the thermometer when you are ill. Honestly, if there was no glass, the world would come to a stop."

You couldn't argue with him. Glass really was the most important thing in the world.

Pearl was fired up too. Her eyes darted about, spotting glass everywhere.

"The ink bottle, glasses, photo frame, marbles, the bottle of Yanghe, the bottle of nail polish . . ."

"That's right," interrupted Victor. "But have you ever wondered why it is that glass is so important?"

He glanced around at the others.

Ding Bogang was slumped in his chair like a dirty overcoat, drunk and out for the count. Su Qin was in the safe haven of the kitchen, tackling the endless washing-up. Ash was too slow on the uptake to catch a fart, and Pearl was even slower. Victor had thrown the question out to Marina but it had fallen on deaf ears. Could anyone really sit there, completely motionless, reading like she did?

"Well, spit it out then!" Pearl urged him. She was so proud of her brother.

"I've been giving it a lot of thought and I think I've finally found the answer, although it might not be right, of course," Victor rubbed his hands together and narrowed his eyes in that restrained way that academics have.

"The reason why glass is so important is because it's transparent," he explained, leaning back in his chair.

His audience responded with varying degrees of disappointment. Was that it?

Victor remained very calm, as though he had anticipated such a response.

"I know it might not make sense to you now, but one day, when you're older, think it over when you have time. The amazing thing about being transparent is that it keeps things apart. You can see everything clearly, but you can never touch. Really, it's amazing when you think about it! Is there anything that can compare with glass?"

The rhetorical question hovered in the air, and after a long silence, Victor concluded with a flourish: "And so I believe that at the highest level, human relationships are just like glass."

Four years later, when Marina and Victor were meeting in secret, Marina randomly brought up that conversation and repeated Victor's lofty theory about glass word for word. He wished she was making fun of him, but no, her tone of voice was too serious for that. She stared at him intently, as if belatedly agreeing that their relationship was indeed like glass: they could see each other, but never touch.

Although he'd long since given up glassblowing at the factory, Victor was still devoted to glass. Pretending he'd forgotten all about it, he shook his head and laughed casually. But he was well aware that he had never, ever regretted this glass-like relationship. He was delighted to learn that Marina had been listening to him back then. All that nonsense had been for her ears anyway. All his efforts to impress her with his conversation, erudition and gift of the gab had a single aim – he had been desperate to make her smile!

Victor preferred not to mention the physical process of glassblowing. He acted as though he wasn't a factory worker at all, just someone who had dropped into the workshop to research and think through some abstract questions about glass. Actually, that was typical of the men in the factory zone who seldom talked about their work. These men found nothing particularly interesting about blowers, high-temperature furnaces, agitators, rotating shafts, traction frames, cooling tanks, bodies reeking of rubber and iron, beetroot-red, oil-slicked faces . . .

But Ash thought Victor was an inspiring and engaging speaker who just needed to be prompted, so he pressed him eagerly for more technical details. Victor glanced at Marina, saw she was concentrating on her book, and answered quietly and simply.

"Each person has a furnace and a glassblowing pipe. You guide the glass into the mould, then keep twisting the pipe as you blow into it."

"But if the molten glass is 600 degrees, or 1300 degrees, how do you guys deal with the heat?" Ash was still trying to understand.

Victor shot another glance at Marina before responding.

"We stand back from the furnace. And, well, we're all men, so we take our shirts off and work bare-chested. Anyway, just imagine us as human robots, because that's more or less what it's like," Victor shrugged, bringing the conversation to an end.

Then Marina, who had been sitting as still as a statue, suddenly looked up from her book and glanced at him. That floored him.

He knew that Marina had seen through him, that in spite of its magnificence, glass was simply glass, and there was nothing noble about his bare chest dripping with greasy sweat. He'd found himself a really shit job, and no matter how much he waxed lyrical about glass, there was no hiding that.

After an initial embarrassment, Victor felt a sense of relief – she understood him, and that was the best thing ever!

"Hey, Marina! At last you've looked up at my brother! I've been waiting for you to do that all evening!" Pearl roared with laughter, slapped her thigh and squinted at Victor, as if to congratulate him for getting the statue to move.

Marina bit her lip in embarrassment. It would be a very long time before she looked him in the eye again.

Not that there'd be many more of those awkward evenings when he felt they were cooped up like a chicken and a rabbit in the same cage. On the pretext that Marina had to prepare for the onslaught of the gaokao exam, Auntie Su simply stopped bringing her round for dinner. Victor had a vague feeling that it might have had something to do with that time he'd taken them to the night market. But he didn't want to explain. What good would it do? Nothing had happened, and nothing ever would.

He had never imagined that Ash might get involved.

4

THE RELATIONSHIP BETWEEN Victor and Ash, if you could even call it that, started with the Wednesday Alliance and their excursion to the night market together. You couldn't say they were close, but Victor had noticed the fat boy following him around like a little puppy, keen and bright-eyed but too shy to speak. What did he want? And what did he make of their parents getting together, and then splitting up?

Pearl had stopped coming to the Saturday dinners as well. She had started her traineeship and had asked to do overtime on Saturdays. After dinner, Victor and Ash sat there in silence. It was so boring.

Victor lit a cigarette and blew a smoke ring.

"Don't just sit there eating, say something, huh?"

Ash froze. A peculiar expression crossed his face, and all his fat and flesh seemed suddenly to contract under his skin. He glanced over at the kitchen but didn't say a word.

Victor was curious now – after all, this boy was Marina's little brother.

"Shall we go to my room?"

You'd let me into your room? Ash couldn't have been more surprised. His fat face turned bright red. He nodded, but no sound came from his throat.

Victor's bedroom was actually the glassed-in balcony. There was a very narrow bed and a very small desk, but no space for a chair. Above the bed was a false ceiling, like the ones you find in old arcade-style architecture. The windows that opened into the street had been papered over with the factory newspaper, blocking out the light that was supposed to flood into the room. When you stepped inside, it felt as though the whole world had shrunk and was pressing down on you.

Victor loved his little den. He stood there, completely at ease, with his head almost touching the ceiling. The gap was so close that it looked as though the ceiling was balancing on his head. He noticed Ash's surprise and respect and said, "Take a seat. You know, since my mum died, you're the first person who's come in here! You were about to say something just now, weren't you?"

Ash gazed around the room and gradually relaxed. He cleared his throat to ground himself.

"Yes, there's something I've been wanting to tell you, but I didn't know whether I should or not. Do you know, my sister . . . She really enjoyed it when you took her to Crossroads and gave her the little torch. She treasures it. She keeps it by her pillow and holds it at night when she can't sleep."

Ash spoke earnestly, and what he said wasn't too far from the truth. If it was dark when she got up in the night to go to the toilet, she always reached for the torch.

"What?"

Victor couldn't believe it.

"She likes me? But you saw how miserable she looked that day! Actually," he couldn't help boasting now, "I've got enough money to buy half that street, you know!"

"Oh, she's always like that, completely the opposite of how she looks on the outside. Honestly, she really likes you!"

Ash was being honest, at least for the first part, which was one hundred percent true.

She's completely the opposite on the inside? Well, that's unexpected, Victor thought to himself. Perhaps this was the key to getting through to Marina. After that, when they met in secret, and even long after they had stopped meeting, Victor would call on these words to get him through his distress.

"But she's such a good student, and I'm just . . ." he said out loud.

He still felt he was no match for her.

"Geez! You really don't know how to read girls, do you? The gifted boring ones, especially the ones who get good grades, love bad boys! Because they daren't be bad themselves. Just think back to the girls in your class at school."

Ash may only have been thirteen and a half, but he seemed to know what he was talking about, and what he said made sense.

"Has she said anything else about me?"

At that point, Victor was still sceptical. Rationally, he knew he needed more evidence, but Ash's words had boosted his confidence and he'd never felt so good!

"She thinks you're nice and tall, and she likes the way you walk. She likes the smell of your cigarettes! And that when you get into the ins and outs of glass you're like a real scholar or philosopher."

(It didn't matter whether Marina had actually said any of this, Ash could talk about Victor's good points forever!)

Victor was completely still. He felt as if an expensive mantle had been draped around his shoulders, promoting him up the ranks. That person who blew glass for a living wasn't the real him at all. Marina thought he was a philosopher!

Ash continued to add fuel to the fire, and was starting to express his own feelings too: "And you make her feel safe. She remembers that time we went to the cemetery, and you walked in front and looked after us both."

Really? She still remembers! My God, that was a year and a half ago! Victor didn't know what to say. There was evidence! It was true! Then, in an instant that belief, that happy, floating feeling was gone, replaced by a melancholy that weighed heavily down on him. It was a moment of self-realisation.

"Ok, that's enough," he said to Ash. "I'm very grateful to her. If only I was still a child prodigy, if only!"

He lit another cigarette, but compared to just a few minutes earlier, he seemed stiff and awkward.

Ash knew he had to put the brakes on.

"Sorry, I'm out of line," he said hurriedly. "If Marina ever finds out, she'll be furious with me!"

"Don't worry, I won't say anything! I know it can never happen for real! I promise I won't say a word!"

Ash was silent. His heart felt fluttery, and he tried to reassure himself: It doesn't matter. You weren't really out of order. Who knows, it might be exactly what Marina is thinking.

Ash's gaze came to rest on the factory newspaper pasted over the window. The paper itself was old and yellowed, but the headlines and subheadings were still clearly visible:

"Special" Party Membership Subscription

Extra Shifts and Extra Hours for National Day: Keep the Flames Burning, Keep Production High

Chairman of the Trade Union Zhang Dingpei's May 1st Visit to Old Workers

The Sweet Smell of Plum Blossom After the Bitterness of Winter – Report on the Young Workers' Martial Arts Competition

Ash found himself reading them silently, as though they might chase away the little lies that were fluttering about the room like butterflies.

He heard Victor mumbling.

"Er, if she . . . if she says anything about me, anything at all, you tell me, okay? I'd like that. She'll be going to university soon, won't she? Will you let me know how she gets on? I mean, my life here's so boring! It's nice to hear some interesting news."

"Of course! I'll say lots of nice things about you to her as well!" Ash promised wholeheartedly.

It would be no trouble at all. The situation had turned out exactly as he'd planned – he'd found Victor's weak point and the two of them had bonded.

"Right then," Victor said, filling the awkward silence that stretched between them. "If there's anything you need, you only have to ask. I've got my wages and my winnings from playing snooker."

"I just want you to be my big brother, to protect me forever, and be nice to me."

The words he had wanted to say for so long came tumbling out, spraying Victor's face with fine droplets.

Victor was taken aback. He didn't know what to say to this confession, and, after a brief pause, grabbed another cigarette, lit it and thrust it at Ash.

"Here, take this. Go on! Don't be a big fat girl about it. We're brothers, right?"

Ash took the cigarette shyly but happily. Of course, he choked on it, and his eyes started watering. They sat in silence for a while, until Victor had an idea and started grinning again.

"Come on, I'll show you some of my things."

He reached up and deftly removed one of the ceiling panels, then felt around in the space. He took out a cloth bundle, then reached in again and took out another. He did this several times, until he had half a dozen bundles laid out on the bed. They had all faded so much that the printed patterns were hard to make out, but they were all very clean. Victor stared at them, taking a moment to appreciate the sight of them on his bed, then, smiling to himself, set to and opened them.

They were full of clothes. Kids' clothes.

Ash almost cried out, he was so startled. He suddenly needed to pee.

Very gently, Victor opened up a side-fastening sweater printed with the character "福", happiness, within a circle.

"This was the first thing I ever wore! Isn't it lovely?"

Then there was a cream-coloured one-piece, a stripy blue vest with open-crotch trousers and a couple of bibs.

He opened the second bundle, which contained clothes for a toddler: dungarees, a woolly hat, and a padded cotton jacket with "祖国花朵", Flower of the Homeland, embroidered on the front.

Another bundle. And another. Then Victor dived under the bed and took out some more bundles.

Victor's cramped den was soon piled high with clothes, and in those mounds of fabric you could see a little boy's life: from crawling, to sitting, to walking, to running. There was no escaping the soft, cloying breath of childhood that enveloped them. Ash started trembling uncontrollably and his willy went stiff. He felt both terror and pleasure and a wonderful warm rush of happiness. He imagined himself in these old clothes of Victor's, shrinking back in time from ten years old to seven or eight, then to four or five. Victor had kept and looked after these clothes very carefully. How Ash wished they were his!

Whatever Victor was saying, Ash didn't hear a word until Victor suddenly shook his shoulders and said, "Hey!"

"Uh?" Ash pulled himself together.

The bedside lamp illuminated only one half of Victor's face, and Ash couldn't see his expression properly.

"Did you hear what I said?" asked Vic. "My mum saved them for me. She was convinced I'd be successful, someone important. Every now and then, I take them out and look at them. When I open them up, I feel like I've got my old self back. Can you believe I was once a child prodigy? I could count at one, knew pi at two, recite Tang poetry at three, read the newspaper at four. In third grade, I could read fourth grade books. In first year at high school, I could do second year homework! Don't believe me? Each item of clothing is evidence! Honestly, I was brilliant, like your sister. I was expected to go to university and have an amazing future."

Ash said nothing, holding in his sadness. He knew that Victor had flunked his exams the year his mother had died.

After a while, Victor started to pack up his "child prodigy" clothes. He did so as patiently and methodically as he had unpacked them, carefully folding each garment on its original creases, just as he had done many times before, then arranged them in piles. The packing up was just like the unpacking in reverse, as if he had pressed rewind on a video. Finally, all the small bundles were tied up again and each one was returned to its original place in the false ceiling or under the bed.

The room was restored to how it was before.

Perhaps now would be a good time to tell you what happened to those children's clothes.

About eight years later, when Victor reached the watershed age of thirty, before quitting his job and opening The Glass House, he spent several days going through his "child prodigy" clothes, as though bidding farewell to his old life. He'd originally intended to throw the lot out, but found he couldn't bring himself to do so. Instinctively, he decided to give them to Ash, the only one who appreciated how much they meant to him. So before he could have second thoughts, he dialled the parcel collection number. Ten minutes later a gum-chewing courier arrived and carelessly stuffed the faded bundles into cardboard boxes, making some tacky jokes as he worked. Victor flew into a rage, demanded an apology and very nearly started a fight. The courier buttoned his lips until he was safely out of the door. Then he exploded.

"Fuck! The factory zone never changes! What a weirdo!"

Far away in the South, Ash received an unexpected delivery. The doorbell buzzed, he signed for the boxes in some bewilderment and took them inside. As soon as he'd opened the first one, he ran straight out, calling out to the courier who was just about to speed off.

"Thank you! You have no idea how much this means to me! Can you give me your boss's number, so I can tell him how amazing you are! And recommend you get a bonus!"

But that wasn't the end of the story. Two years later, Ash took all the clothes and his own stack of exercise books back to the factory zone. Not long after that, he found a good home for them: a baby girl, who wouldn't care that they were boy's clothes – not that Ash had ever considered that they were gendered. The lucky little girl's birth was reported with absolute precision in all the newspapers the following day: 2:42pm on 13th April 2006.

5

A FTER THE BREAKUP, Ding Bogang turned to drink even more than before, breaking his record again and again. How many times at dinner had Victor reached with his chopsticks for a morsel of food, only to see his father's head crane forward, tilt to one side and the other as if he was doing exercises, and then land with a thud on the table?

Victor would remove Dad's bowl and chopsticks, clear away the bottle and cup and carry on eating as he stared at the top of Dad's shiny bald head. He understood why Dad drank himself to oblivion: because of that Su Qin woman, because of his glassblowing job and because of the reforms in the factory. The winds were changing, and this was the only way he knew how to cope. If those bouts of drunkenness before he fell asleep were the only time he was at peace, why shouldn't Victor let him have them? When he saw the top of his father's head, he stopped feeling so annoyed, and instead felt sorry for him. His father had nothing and was stuck in a rut. He never expected that his father might one day lash out in a drunken frenzy and attack him.

Victor couldn't remember the exact details of that first attack, because there had been so many since then. But he wasn't going to make Dad pay for it. Better to forgive and forget, so he didn't lash out at anybody else, right? In any case, it was the alcohol. That and old age creeping up on him.

What he did remember was that the first attack had led to him meeting Marina in the middle of the night. The thrilling randomness of that encounter, like a crack of lighting, had lit the torch of love that would burn his entire life. For that reason, Victor had always been grateful that his father beat the hell out of him and wanted him to keep on doing it.

Victor had left in a hurry that night, like a man on the run. He didn't stop to wash his face or change his clothes, but slammed the door on the way out, leapt on his bike and headed straight for Crossroads. He knew that the night market had just started, and that it would swallow up the beating he had endured like a stinking, bubbling swamp.

He went straight to the familiar snooker table. Standing in the dim glow of the yellow light bulb, he pressed his hand to his aching jaw and cheeks and stared dully at the coloured balls on the table. Their fate would soon be in his hands: they would be hit, knocked about, sent rolling across the table into the designated black holes. No one in Crossroads would bat an eyelid at his two black eyes and bloody nose. There wouldn't even be a "Hey man, what happened?"

That was the good thing about Crossroads. No one was interested in touchy-feely stuff, thank goodness.

Victor played at all the snooker tables in Crossroads, filling his pockets with cash. But eventually the crowd started to thin, and it began to feel cold and desolate. Crossroads was not like the big city at night. Its rhythms were those of the manual labourers, who liked to jump into bed early in the comfort of their own homes.

But Victor didn't want to go home. He liked the street best at this time. He wanted to stay on this deserted road for as long as possible.

He squatted on the kerb. The kerb was a good place, where you could see all kinds of things, like broken bikes, litter bins, electricity posts, vomit, dog shit, old newspapers . . . He could sit there all night if he wanted to and no one would pay any attention to him. Victor squatted there quietly, disappearing into the side of the road.

The only problem was the terrible stench. All the dregs of the day ended up there, with the mess of emissions from car exhausts, animals and humans. But Victor didn't care, he wanted to sink into this fetid air. He could think better that way.

In the previous two weeks, Ash had told him a lot about Marina. She had asked him what Vic's room was like, which sports he'd been good at in school, she'd written his name on a piece of paper and said the chemical formula for glass in her sleep.

"Oh yes, I'm sorry," Ash said. "Please don't be angry with me, but she kept asking, and I ran out of things to say, and I told her about your bundles of clothes. But guess what, she teared up, and when I asked why, she ignored me."

It was classic, so textbook, so perfect that he didn't dare to believe it. On the other hand, he couldn't bring himself to think it was all made up either. That would be so humiliating. He tried to figure out what Ash was up to, but why would the fat boy go to all the trouble of making it up? And it sounded so vivid, so natural. It couldn't be fake. And yet, could he really believe there might be anything between him and Marina? It was just . . . Oh, forget it, stop thinking these crazy thoughts.

But why not hope for the best? Maybe it was meant to happen, in which case he should just enjoy it. He was beginning to feel rather sentimental about things when he was brought back down to earth by his father's beating. It taught him a lesson – that he didn't deserve to have things go well.

Victor smoked as he mulled things over, his cigarette flickering like semaphore in a dark sea.

It was this flickering light that Marina saw that night, that drew her to him, that marked the start of their love affair with all its twists and turns, in which every member of their almost-family played a part: Ash with his enthusiastic encouragement, Su Qin with her determination to prevent it, the violent backdrop unwittingly created by Ding Bogang, and Pearl's belief in her ability to make things happen. All of them played a part, but none of them were the vital key to their relationship. When it comes to love, self-hypnosis is the deciding factor.

That evening, Marina, who was in the last term of her final year at school, had been on her way back from an evening class. It was only a two-hour class and she should have been home already, but the chain on her bike had snapped as she approached Crossroads. She pushed it along, scanning both sides of the increasingly deserted street for a bike repair stall, not that she was likely to find one at that hour. It was a nuisance but she was not overly fussed, at least it gave her a break from the relentless schoolwork. She was quietly enjoying the night, the street, a few lines of poetry floating through her mind, snatches of a pop song drifting past her ears, her dress billowing in the night breeze when the tip of Victor's lonely cigarette came into view, flickering like a firefly, and behind it, Victor's gaunt profile.

Victor was staring at the ground, absorbed in thought, when he suddenly noticed a pair of pretty leather shoes and half a bicycle chain on the ground in front of him. He stopped smoking, but didn't look up. The shoes had a tiny flower on each side of the strap, one of them missing a petal. He had often seen them on the shoe rack at home on Saturdays. He couldn't believe he was looking at them now, nor did he want to be seen by their owner in the present circumstances. He took another drag of his cigarette and closed his eyes. Dammit, he must be dreaming.

But he wasn't. The next time he ventured to open his eyes, he found himself looking straight into her eyes. She was squatting on the grimy kerb with him.

He hadn't seen her at a Saturday dinner for six months.

Victor knew that his face was black and blue and covered with lumps and bumps. What was he supposed to say? That he'd been beaten up by his drunken father, and that he was okay with it? Or perhaps he should let her assume he'd been in a fight? Things were not looking good. She didn't need to ask Ash nosy questions, she could see for herself what a state he was in. She could see he was a good-for-nothing piece of shit.

She was staring at him closely. In her eyes, he read shock, anger, confusion and a determination to haul him out of the gutter. Victor made himself look away. He was no match for those eyes.

Later, thinking back on their chance meeting, Marina would acknowledge that seeing Victor in that dire state had given her an almost irresistible urge to save him. But the timing was not right. In a fortnight she would be sitting the gaokao exam, and if she reached out to him now, she might end up in the gutter with him. Perhaps, after the exams . . . Marina promised herself vaguely in the darkness.

The animation drained from Marina's face. She pursed her lips and remained there with Victor, neither of them saying a word. They squatted, in silence, as though nothing needed saying, as though everything was natural and calm, as though they had done this a hundred times before.

Victor reached the end of his cigarette, but was still taking drags off it, eyes down, as though he wanted to stay in a tobacco haze forever. Marina suddenly reached out, took the cigarette from him, threw it on the ground, then stood up and stubbed it out with her pretty shoe. She shook her bike, which made the broken chain rattle.

Victor got to his feet, all the while trying to avoid her eyes. It had been a good night. He had been battered and dejected, but she had bumped into him and witnessed it. It had turned out well.

Victor picked up his bike, and with Marina sitting behind him, set off steering his bike with one hand and pushing her bike by the handlebars with the other. His sore, aching body was now fired with energy. As he worked his wrists and feet, he could feel the tension in his muscles. Two bikes and two people wobbled their way towards Marina's home.

Perhaps because they were both on the same bike, or because the atmosphere was too intense, or too relaxed, Victor did not say a word to Marina that night, not even when Su Qin came out and slapped her twice across the face and she moved closer and put her arm through his.

The next time they met was at the farewell dinner for the two families. Victor whistled to the new waxbill he had bought and listened to Marina and Pearl's boring conversation about girls and the humanities. Again, he and Marina did not say a word to each other. He was not sad or despairing, but calm and hopeful.

6

Not long after that, Victor was forced to leave his beloved glass behind. It turned out to be a stroke of luck, removing him from the human-flesh steamer that was the glassblowing workshop. He was temporarily transferred to the union, although he had next to no status there and simply did odd jobs like handing out application forms for early retirement and redundancy agreements. But it was an office job. How he got the promotion without any qualifications or connections was anyone's guess.

It would be five years before Victor himself knew the truth. When Ding Bogang was sinking into the swamp of amnesia and the dust was settling on the reforms in the factory zone, Victor handed in his notice. The vice-chairman of the union had burst out laughing, moving his frozen shoulder until his neck cracked loudly.

"I'm sure you know why we selected you for this post."

Victor shook his head. Since his first day at the factory he'd only spoken when he had to.

"Because you don't speak! Squeeze all the air out of you and you still wouldn't fart! You know, handing out forms was a killer. Those old guys were built like tanks, and when a group of them got together, it was too much for us office types. So, we had to find someone who could stand up to them, a youngster who could hold his tongue and stand in the frontline. We looked all over the factory and found you. We were reliably informed that your old man beats you when he's drunk, right? If I'm not mistaken, he hits you every couple of days or so, and lays into you good and proper once a week. Your neighbours on both sides have complained. It was good news for us because it meant you could put up with anything. We couldn't think of anyone more suitable. So you should be grateful to your old man. If it wasn't for him, you wouldn't be sitting in this comfortable union office right now!"

Victor could feel a lump in his throat. So that's what happened. He remembered how thrilled his father had been about his promotion, convinced that his child prodigy son was going to play a key role at work now. It was just as well that he had lost his memory.

Victor's demeanour remained utterly respectful. He felt pain slice through him, but kept his face as still as a slow-moving river. After all, he'd had years of experience of petty humiliations in the union office.

The vice-chairman kept laughing.

"Of course I shouldn't say things like this. But from the start, only a few people knew and they've all retired except me. I've kept it to myself, but every time I see you I want to laugh! I can't see the harm in telling you now, since you're giving in your notice."

The vice-chairman was enjoying himself enormously. It must really have been hard for him not being able to let the cat out of the bag all this time, Victor thought to himself.

Victor's job at the union had been awful, especially his first six months, when the "mobilisation period" reached its peak and it was more like going to the battle front than going to work. He was the human shield between the factory and the union. He had to deal with people's love for the factory zone, their hatred of the authorities, and the distress and helplessness caused by the changes. All these emotions came hurtling towards him, like the ocean waves crashing against the rocks. First, there was the shouting and swearing; they cursed his ancestors and forebears, his dead mother and his future children and grandchildren. Then there was the weeping and wailing, the women snivelling all over his clothes. As for the men, especially the older ones, their Adam's apples would convulse, they would screw up their faces and their eyes would bulge. Then they would hit him. Their blows would rain upon him and send him rolling across the floor. Going to work every day was like one round after another of bloody, painful street brawls.

But they had chosen exactly the right person for the job.

After work, Victor would go home to another nightmare. The first thing he saw was his father slumped in a chair and Pearl bustling around the house, pausing only to make flirty eyes at Heipi.

Victor would sit down, his body sore and swollen, feeling sick to the stomach. Heipi was attentive, and would offer him a cigarette, bring him some food and ask him about his day: which factory branch he'd been sent to hand out forms, which workshops were closing or merging and so on. Victor was too tired to talk, but made an effort for Pearl's sake. She needed a man if she was going to have a home and a family of her own, and anyway, even if this Heipi was as interesting as a lump of charcoal, she was obviously keen on him.

Fighting boredom as well as fatigue, Victor would sigh and answer Heipi's questions as patiently as he could. Heipi soaked up the details like a spy collecting intelligence. It mattered to him where Victor had been because retirement and redundancy forms meant a workshop or project was going to merge or close down, and that meant a new source of scrap.

It wasn't that Victor disliked Heipi, more that the thought of the man made him sad. It drove home the fact that he and Pearl had lost their chance of a better life – they could only be dragged down further into the mud. Victor had once known what elegance and beauty was. He had seen Marina's shoes with the little flowers and her apple-green top, and how she always had her head deep in her book. But that was a long time ago, a beautiful dream gone forever. The life he had now was barely worth living. Without Marina and glass, what else was there?

Victor became very thin. He was struggling with a single question: What made him human? Was it survival instincts like eating, drinking and sleeping? Or conscious likes and dislikes? If the former, then why did people have feelings and thoughts? If the latter, then his life as a walking corpse could be wiped out by a stroke then and there!

Wrapped up in his own thoughts, he didn't know that his loving sister Pearl had already been to see Marina and told her he loved her, and that she'd taken the initiative and given her a silk scarf supposedly from him. He didn't know that she'd run away, scared by her own recklessness and Marina's rejection.

If only Pearl had dared to look back that day, she would have seen Marina standing in the shade of the trees for a very long time. At the very moment she turned Pearl down, she was thinking of the promise she'd made to herself in the dark that evening when she had run into Victor, almost unrecognisable with his bloodied nose and swollen face, and squatted on the kerb with him. That passionate, emotional promise reached deep into her mind, urging her to go and see him. Why not? Not to help him or anything major, just to cheer him up, even if it was only to return the silk scarf that Pearl had brought her.

You see Pearl's silk scarf was a very intimate prop, and Pearl really was a matchmaker.

IT WAS DRIZZLING the day Marina went to return the silk scarf. She made her way through Crossroads with the same spring in her step that she had at the college, an umbrella half-covering her upper body. She walked the same stretch of road that she would walk eight years later on the day of the explosion, strolling past the tightly packed stalls: the bicycle repair stall, the hardware stall, the shaobing stall, the boiler room . . . She passed the newly-opened Luo's World Resources Company, where on the first floor, Heipi was inspecting the big ring in his hand, cheerfully getting ready to propose marriage that evening.

On either side of the street, people with nothing better to do were standing under shop awnings, taking shelter from the drizzle although they could hardly feel it. They had been watching scenes like this since they were little, and had seen them countless times before. It was what they did in the rain, in the snow, in gales and in the blazing sunshine; they stood by the side of the road and stared at the emptiness in front of them. The next time she saw such a scene, Marina would be celebrating: she had been accepted at college. She was leaving, and would never have to wade through this quagmire of poverty again.

Marina headed for the fourth turning, where she imagined she'd find Victor lording it over the snooker table, one shoulder higher than the other, one of the gang.

But the road before her destination was blocked by a group of people crowding around something. Another brawl! She tried to walk around it quickly, but the brawlers kept moving: middle-aged faces flashed into view and bobbed up and down, threatening fists were raised, all surrounding their target. Marina quickly lowered her umbrella to shield herself and spotted the very face she had come to see.

Victor was very different from how she'd imagined him. He looked pitiful, like a petty criminal, bent over awkwardly, clutching a folder to his chest with one hand and trying to protect his head with the other, standing there passively, his courage exhausted. Whenever fists landed on him, he grimaced, as if to say, "This isn't me, it's someone else."

It wasn't like him. The Victor she knew wouldn't have let people push him around. Marina listened to their shouting and swearing, and gradually realised what Pearl had called Victor's honourable promotion to the union office meant. He was the messenger of bad news, representing the evil that stamped its black seal on people's futures. Their attacks on him were outbursts of anger, a collective uproar, an essential but ineffective ritual. The rain drizzled on his attackers, leaving a fine mist on their faces and clothes, causing their hair to stick to their temples and leaving patches on their shoulders like pee stains. Their incoherent shouts and curses were drowned out by one another, making the scene seem like a mime. Such was Crossroads at the end of the century, and such was the humiliation and destruction of the factory zone.

Marina felt something stir deep inside her. Her distress transformed into a beautiful sweetness that coursed through her. How could she not love Victor? He was dear to her, she had to protect him at all costs.

She put up her umbrella again to shield herself, and to preserve that image.

She walked slowly to a different turning, which she knew Victor would have to take on his way home.

Many years later, after Marina had left the factory zone for the second time, after she was married and after he heard she was pregnant, Victor would try as hard as he could to forget that encounter on the corner of the street and the conversation they had in the rain. But he couldn't forget, no matter the passage of time.

That same evening, Heipi had asked Victor's father for his daughter's hand in marriage and whisked her away, and Ding Bogang had his first attack of amnesia. But Victor might as well have been a deaf-mute given his lack of emotional engagement. He didn't care. He impatiently closed his bedroom door, shutting his father out, holed up in his little den that was too small to swing a cat in, the film projector in his head switching between fast and slow, black and white and colour, zoom shot and aerial view.

In aerial view, as the angry and frustrated crowd finally dispersed, he saw himself as a scrawny chicken, cowering as he screwed the sodden forms into a ball and threw them away, before slowly setting off home.

Then his mind's eye zoomed in on Marina standing patiently at the turning. He tried to look away, but her image only grew larger. He could see she was watching him, and there was no mistaking her expression: she was waiting for him.

In an instant the scene switched to black and white. He thought he was losing his sight. He had never imagined he might see her again. His left arm started to burn in a worrying way, the same burning pain he had felt on that evening when his father had lashed out at him for the first time and Su Qin had hit Marina because of him. When Marina had held his arm tightly and he had blazed like the sun.

Victor still felt like the sun, but a sun that had never reached its zenith and was already setting in the dusk of evening.

The only people he met were senior workers as rugged as tree trunks, who attacked him and heaped scorn on him with a bitterness built up over a lifetime, putting him in an impossible position. But he had learned from experience, and gradually came to take it on the chin. Those wretched men's lives had taught him a basic truth: what makes you happy and what you desire are unattainable, and when it comes to other people, feelings, and dreams, you have to compromise and admit defeat, to be prepared to end up with nothing.

It was the same in the glass world, where you couldn't always achieve what you wanted; where compromising and admitting defeat were part of the process, and you had to be prepared to end up with nothing.

When his relationship with Marina was at its most honest and sincere, Victor finally asked the question he had never dared to ask: "What is it that you like about me?"

Marina thought it over and with a wry laugh, eventually replied, "Perhaps it's the feeling of defeat, the way your whole body withdraws, as though you can never have what you want. But I don't know why I like that about you. You know, I've always worshipped success and craved a better life. When I see you, I feel sad and uncomfortable, but at the same time, I feel everything else is fake and unreliable."

Victor had listened quietly, a chill stealing over the warmth in his heart. She had cared about him all these years, and there had been heartache, but because of his weaknesses, she could not go any further. Well, there was nothing he could do about it now. (Of course, this only occurred to him as an afterthought.)

Back on the corner of the street, his heart beating nineteen to the dozen, Victor tried to compose himself. He knew that he had to apply what he'd learned from life to his relationship with Marina. He was older than her and should be rational about it.

In fact, it was Marina who made the first move with a perfunctory greeting. He was completely in control of his emotions by the time he reached her. He smiled, and with total confidence, inquired about her life at university. He probed carefully, encouraging her to give as much detail as possible, as though he was transfixed by the university he had never stepped inside. He did his absolute best to give that impression, so that she would not have a chance to ask about his life.

Marina could hardly refuse to answer his questions. She was growing increasingly enthusiastic and animated as she spoke, until she started describing the ginkgo trees at the Institute of Literature. She stopped in mid-sentence and looked awkward, suddenly aware that she had been talking far too much – he was only asking about the stupid university, for heaven's sake! She stood there, blaming herself, staring sadly at Victor.

Victor looked at her umbrella. He knew it well, he had seen it in the crowd that evening as it lingered there for a while.

It seemed he was destined to meet her when he looked at his worst, like that time she'd seen him after his Dad's beating. It was a shame that friendly conversation had ended so abruptly. But years later, alone in The Glass House, wiping away invisible dust with a white cloth as he mulled over the past, Victor came to prefer those moments of silence together, especially the way that Marina had looked at him. If her eyes had come any closer, she would have found her home in his heart.

"I was so worried about you," Marina said suddenly, her eyes welling with tears of concern and embarrassment.

"Don't worry about me," said Victor. "As long as you're fine, that's okay. You've got to do it for me."

He looked down. Oh God, she was so close. If only he could stroke her wet hair!

"I have to do it for you?"

"Yes, since I can't do it for myself, I need you to do it for me. All of it – go to university for me, leave the factory zone for me, find a good job for me. Go and live the best life for me."

Victor started grinning again. It felt good to say these things. In fact, in a flash of memory, he thought of silly Pearl, his drunk dad, the fat boy Ash who had run off to the South on his own, and Auntie Su with her fake expression. He almost got carried away, wishing desperately that Marina could go and do everything for them – then at least then one of this sorry heap would have a hope of a bright future.

Marina's tears fell. Her ambition had always been to reach for the stars, and she was grateful for the validatory way he looked at her.

"Could I really do all this for you?"

Victor didn't answer. He looked at Marina. The intense emotion of having lost and then found her – but knowing deep down that he was destined to lose her again – was like a storm blustering in the dark.

Then the rain stopped. The fine mist that hung over them lifted and there was no reason for them to linger on the corner of the street. In the twilight, each went their own way with the calm satisfaction of having made a good agreement, one heading towards the alkylbenzene factory housing, the other towards the flats of the electron tube factory. The silk scarf, which was destined not to be used, lay silently in Marina's bag.

They didn't arrange to meet again. And it became a habit not to do so; arranging to meet seemed unnecessary and unnatural.

8

MARINA AND VICTOR'S four-year relationship was like a long-flowering plant, staying in bloom until the eve of her marriage. It began with secret liaisons in the rain-swept street. With caution and intent, they avoided busy places. It was a monotonous relationship, steeped in sadness.

On the one occasion when she'd asked him to bring some things to her at the teacher training college (she was busy doing practicals), the visit hadn't gone well.

It was Victor's problem, no one else's. Almost as soon as he left the factory zone, he felt out of place, and the closer he got to the city centre the worse it became. By the time he entered the main gates of the college, the feeling had become unbearable, and his traitorous mind persuaded him that Marina was probably feeling the same. He was wearing a T-shirt and jeans like everyone else, but believed that he looked like a workshop type. He might as well have been in overalls that hid the dirt, with metal shavings from the factory zone and phlegm from Crossroads on the soles of his shoes. He was convinced that the way he moved his hands and feet, the look in his eyes, the creases in his clothes and even the way he swallowed were absolute giveaways, that everyone could tell instantly that he was a worker from the factory zone: good at snooker and getting into fights, but otherwise useless, and absolutely undeserving of Marina.

For the entire half-day he was there he was fraught with tension. After managing a meal in the canteen, he had been relieved to step outside, but missed a step and tripped on the stairs. Marina had reached out to grab him, but had moved so quickly she had almost ended up in his arms. Victor felt her stiffen with annoyance and distress, and the intensity of her reaction caught them both off-guard. To cover her surprise, Marina hastily pointed to the sports track where some of the boys were having fun, shouting to each other as they threw a ball around. Victor turned to look at them with a forced smile.

Of course, the girls in Marina's dorm discussed her "brother", which was how she had introduced him. At university, girls always had brothers, cousins, family-friend-kind of brothers, brothers of classmates and any other kind of brother they could think of appearing out of nowhere. But everyone knew that they were brothers in name and not real brothers. One girl got as far as saying, "That brother of yours, sure, he's good looking, but . . ." then stopped, not daring to continue because the look on Marina's face said it all. When it came to Victor, Marina could deal with her own frustrations and impatience, but she would not hear others say a bad word about him. How could an outsider ever understand their difficult, shameful, ambiguous relationship as siblings in a part-time family in the murky atmosphere of the factory zone?

Eventually they left the college grounds. At the bus stop, waiting for the bus back to the factory zone, Victor started to loosen up. He squatted on the kerb, lit a cigarette, and finally felt the tension lift from his body. He cheerfully showed Marina the handful of cigarettes he kept on him.

Victor wasn't a sad case anymore. He had stopped brandishing redundancy forms at old and expendable workers and was now targeting middle management and above, still issuing forms, only this time they were share-application forms. It was done furtively and kept top secret, but it was pretty obvious what was going on: free cash. Those who took the forms didn't thank him, he was just the messenger. But they were decent to him. They'd toss him a cigarette and say, "Hey, young man, have a smoke!"

He'd have one in his mouth, one tucked behind each ear, another tucked in his jacket pocket and a couple between his finger and thumb. He was like a giant ashtray, and those middle management people who'd made a fortune on the sly kept loading him up with cigarettes. The human ash-tray smiled nicely and politely throughout. He'd had so many fists and feet in his face, and now he was being given cigarettes. The pleasure after the pain, hey! He hadn't had to buy cigarettes for weeks. And these days he smoked good brands: Zhonghua, Yunnan, Yuxi, Jin Nanjing, Furong Wang.

Victor was so relieved to be squatting and talking that he failed to notice the look in Marina's eyes. When the bus they were waiting for arrived, Marina climbed in without saying a word or waiting for Victor. Surprised, Victor extinguished his cigarette, carefully put away the part he hadn't smoked, then hauled Marina's big bag onto the bus. Marina squeezed her way to the back of the bus. But Victor was stuck at the front with Marina's big bag, and people were shouting at him because it was in the way. Marina stood at the back, her face looking both hard and fragile. She decided never to bring him into the city again. Her peers in this little district of the city had made her feel deeply upset and bitter. She didn't blame Victor for his lack of sophistication, but hated herself for feeling dissatisfied and demanding of him when they were obviously from the same social background.

That, of course, made her think about herself. In the past few years, she had turned her back on the factory zone (as she would continue to do for years to come) and striven for higher things. But throughout this slow process her attitude and self-confidence were not much stronger than his.

After that trip to the university, they only ever met in the factory zone.

They would weave their way through the hustle and bustle of Crossroads. Victor would lead her past the rundown shops and deep into the factory zone. They walked past the closed staff cinema and the abandoned swimming pool now full of old equipment to the back door of the storehouse and the heap of coal cinder between the cook house and the bath house, where, in the rough smell of old iron and the occasional seepage of steam, they could spend time together, relaxed and undisturbed.

After the final curtain fell on their liaisons, Victor picked over every meeting and every conversation. He was pleased with his ability to remember what they had talked about. Perhaps the child prodigy in him came into its own at times like these. All the same, he knew their prospects for the future were slimmer than slim. They were like friendly tourists sitting next to each other on a long journey, aware that as soon as they reach their destination, they will pick up their bags and go their separate ways.

Marina was very concerned about the beatings Victor received from his father. She would ask him to undo his shirt, and even when it was cold, she would make him undo his coat and unzip his wool sweater, so that she could see with her own eyes the bruises on his neck and the marks on his shoulder blades. Sometimes she gasped in horror and redoubled her efforts to give him good advice. And every time, Victor would do as she asked and silently undo his shirt or coat and then button up it again, listening carefully to her words of reassurance which were almost always the same. He didn't tell her that Dad wasn't as strong as he used to be, and that sometimes he had to take the initiative and provoke him first.

Sometimes, Victor would tell Marina about his waxbill. The little bird grew slowly, and when he watched it, he would feel as though time had stopped. It was almost human, sleeping during the day, and hopping about in its cage at night, as though staying up late to keep him company. Victor often had difficulty falling asleep, and when he saw the bird hopping about, he would turn onto his side and whistle to it quietly.

Once, Marina interrupted him and asked, "Do you whistle a tune or just random noises?"

Victor went quiet. He didn't want to tell her that he whistled the same thing every time: "Marina". Instead of answering, he whistled, very quietly. And Marina was like that little bird, staring at him avidly and listening intently.

At times like that, Victor would kill the moment by thinking about glass. And, as soon as he thought about glass, he would stop whistling, the sound fading away like a stone flung into the distance. He would casually change the subject to something mundane, like the kids in the factory zone when one of them did something bad. Marina didn't respond, just continued to stare at him. The way she looked at him was like a knife cutting into his heart. What was it that kept them apart? Why was he so weak and hopeless? It was like there was a pane of glass between them.

9

ONCE, MARINA HAD SUDDENLY suggested they go public about their meetings – but Victor knew that wasn't the real Marina speaking. She was in her final year at university and couldn't decide whether to go for a Masters or be assigned a teaching job in a school. She had picked up an old iron bar, getting rust all over her hand, which she had then carelessly wiped all over the other arm of her pristine white shirt. Bit by bit, as though clearing her throat, she spat out her complaints. Being at university wasn't all it was made out to be.

"I never get to host an event, or put on a show . . . I don't play any musical instruments, I'm no good at sport, and forget debating."

Marina gritted her lovely white teeth.

"Don't worry, just get the grades, and the rest will happen! You don't have to be good at everything!"

He was pleased she had voiced these concerns, because now, at last, he could reassure her, though he didn't feel it was as bad as she thought.

"Good grades?! That's so old-school! They're useless. At teacher training college, it's talent in the arts and all-round ability that counts! Otherwise you'll never make an impression or earn respect. I'm very worried about being assigned a job, because I don't think I'll make it to a top middle school. And if I have to go to a second or third rate school, then I'm finished. You have to jump through so many hoops to do a Masters, but I still think I'll try."

For Marina to reveal even the tiniest wobble about further education was unprecedented. She had always talked about doing a Masters or PhD as though it was as easy as pulling them out of a bag.

What could he say? Trying for a Masters wasn't like playing snooker at Crossroads. He couldn't help her at all, he could only watch her run around as fast as she could when she stepped into the ring. He continued smoking in silence. Then, he heard her say in a strange, angry tone that she wanted to take him to the girls' dorm and then home to see Su Qin. It was as though her dissatisfaction with reality was speaking. The girls in the dorm were such hypocrites, she exclaimed, and no different from her mother. And what right did her mother have to judge when she herself was in a relationship with Ding Bogang! They had to go public! How about it? Didn't he agree? Did he have the guts?

Victor had looked at her. Her face was bright red. If only he had been brave enough to take her in his arms and say, "Yes! Let's go and tell my dad, and your mum. Let's go and tell Crossroads and the whole world! And my little waxbill, who's listened to all my whistling about you!"

But he couldn't. From the outset, he had warned himself to remember those old workers who'd suffered so much and then ended up with nothing. He had to remember that life was cruel and respect that. She would do a Masters, and the two of them would grow further and further apart.

He started whistling. His tuneless, wordless whistling expressed what he couldn't say in words.

Marina understood. The force of her desperate outburst slowed, and she put on a smile and did her best to talk animatedly about coming second in the library's essay-writing competition – how the judges had cast their votes anonymously, how she'd been only two votes behind the winner and so on.

Victor immediately threw aside the cigarette he'd only just lit and clapped on behalf of an entire invisible audience. It might have sounded a bit hollow, but his enthusiasm was genuine and straight from the heart. He wanted her to be happy. She had no reason to be despondent, she was so hardworking.

The boiler room behind them shuddered as it belched out a plume of white smoke, and they could almost believe that they were about to set off on a magical journey on a steam train. Their mutual teary-eyed sadness allowed them both to feel they had the trust and support of the one they loved.

I have to leave this godforsaken place! I can't stand it here. Marina vowed to herself.

Of course. And I won't let you stay here. I can't stand the idea of you staying here like us. Victor declared silently in his turn.

"I can never be with you," Marina said without malice.

"You're right, and I would never agree to it. I would give my life to stop you," Victor answered firmly, as though singing a tragic aria.

Making these declarations made them feel more at ease, like kindred spirits. From that point on, the boundaries were clear, and it truly felt that there was a sheet of glass separating their thoughts.

On that occasion, they imagined for the first and only time what their separate futures would be like. In their make-believe scenario, Marina was married to an educated man like her father. They had a little girl, who was very close to Marina, and at weekends her little family of three would go to a restaurant and the cinema. Meanwhile, Victor was married to a feisty worker and had a chubby little boy who adored his father. Sketching out and constructing realistic scenes like these strengthened their resolve to remain separate, and allowed them to stagnate.

The most beautiful time of their lives passed by unfulfilled. She was twenty-six, he was twenty-nine.

Those four years were good, but not good enough. The time they shared was fulfilling but could never bring fulfilment, when it should have been enough to get them through the rest of their lives.

And so Victor waited in the good-humoured way that an indulgent guest enjoys good wine and food, knowing that at some point the last dish will come.

10

VICTOR HAD NO IDEA he was about to be served the last dish that day.

Marina had examined his wounds as usual. Ding Bogang had recently taken to pulling his hair and clawing at his skin, like women do, because it consumed less energy. As Marina carefully daubed his skin with the purple iodine that she had brought with her, she joked, "After this, you won't be scared of women doing this to you!"

But her spirits were low. Things had not been going well for her lately. Both her Masters application and job allocation had gone badly. She hadn't been accepted into the Masters program and had ended up being sent to a middle school between the factory zone and the city. It had a bad reputation, disruptive and precocious students, ignorant parents, witheringly dull colleagues, and poor accommodation for teaching and admin staff. While Marina could just about hold her head high in public, she'd already cracked in front of Victor and begged him to admit he despised her. Her once high-flying aspirations were now as limp as noodles.

She screwed the lid tightly on the bottle of purple iodine, but didn't put it back in her bag.

"Keep it. You'll have to do it yourself from now on."

Her eyes were cold, and she was looking the other way.

"Look, I did absolutely everything I could, and took every opportunity I could, and for what? To end up as mediocre as everyone else. It's a joke!

"Do you know what really gets me? The bell at the beginning and end of every lesson. Drrrr . . . Drrrrr . . . That electronic buzzing really gets on my nerves, like a reminder that my time's up! I know I've missed my chance, and there'll never be another opportunity. And you say I should wait and see? Do you still want me to struggle on – on your behalf? At the end of the day, you and me, we're the same, we're nothing!"

She looked at him as though those were her last words on the subject and she wanted a witness to her failure.

Victor avoided her aggressive look, and tried to pacify her.

"Look, whatever you say, you're as good as out of here, and better off than most people in the factory zone."

Why was she so disappointed? What did she really want? They would never be able to break through the barrier between them, but he loved her the way she was.

But Marina looked even gloomier, and Victor knew he had said the wrong thing.

"You know what they say, it takes ten years to grow a tree, and that a teacher takes a hundred years to grow a person. Teachers are the engineers of the soul."

It was stuff and nonsense, but Victor hoped that she hadn't heard it before.

"Forget it. The good thing is I have other options. Would you help me make a decision about something?"

Marina smiled suddenly and very beautifully. Over the next few nights, Victor revisited their conversations and realised that she had been leading up to this moment.

"Go on, I'm listening. Of course, I'll help you."

Victor's heart filled with joy. His greatest pleasure was to see Marina smile.

"Would you help me choose a husband? You know, I don't want to ask Mum because we always end up falling out, and Ash isn't around, but I need someone to help me weigh things up carefully."

"Do you . . . have someone in mind?" asked Victor, appalled. Every hair on his body stood on end. Of course, he would help! He was just surprised, that's all. He knew that she would get married sooner or later, and to somebody else. But it had still come as a surprise.

"Yes, there are several candidates. I've been taking it very seriously, all through my third and fourth year," Marina said with a wry smile. "In case you've forgotten, I'm quite good-looking! And it'll be better than struggling along alone like a headless fly. I couldn't bear that!"

Victor choked up. He suddenly felt deaf, blind and stupid. All the time they'd been meeting, she had been seeing other men as well, without saying a word, as if it was quite normal. But he had to pull himself together, he had no business being suspicious and jealous. He was just her big brother Vic, and he should be happy for her. Marrying a good man was important for Marina, especially with so much having not gone as she'd hoped.

"Are you angry?" Marina asked carefully, as she took her camera out of her checked canvas bag.

That was the day she had taken the photograph for him. It was their breakup photo, but Su Qin had immediately seen the love between them.

"No, no, I'm not angry," said Victor, even managing a little laugh. "I'm just trying to think what kind of person would suit you best."

"I don't care if they suit me or not, as long as they get me on the next rung of the ladder, that's the main thing," said Marina, speaking quietly and patiently.

"It's just marriage, you know, that's all," she said, pushing out her lip.

"I get it. I understand."

Victor quickly waved his hand to stop her from saying any more. The more trivial and ordinary she sounded, the more unbearable it was for him.

"Would you choose one for me, so I can make the decision today?"

Marina gave a detailed description of two candidates, listing their key points as if she was giving the dimensions and features of two pieces of furniture. One was an assistant professor of physics at the teacher training college. Once he got his certificate, he would apparently qualify for housing.

"He's been after me, just me and no one else, since we were students, and he's held out till now."

The other had studied industrial and civic architecture. Someone had introduced them, and they'd met a few times. He had been working in the Institute of Design but had quit to set up a small company with some friends, doing interior design and decorating. He earned a lot and liked to spend it too. He was local, and had a new-build in the city centre.

Victor peered at the very professional-looking camera next to Marina's hand, picked it up and examined the buttons on the top. He didn't know much about cameras, but was grateful to this one for providing a distraction as he listened to her descriptions of these two men who had appeared out of nowhere. He had a vivid picture of Marina starting a new life with either of them, and was devastated. It was like a meteorite had crashed to earth and he was about to fall into the massive hole that had opened beneath his feet.

"Are you listening?"

"Are there any more?"

Victor's tone of voice suggested they weren't entirely up to scratch. He sounded like a shopper pretending to pick and choose among the goods on display.

Marina blinked. She didn't answer immediately. Actually, the marriage route was not as easy as she made out. Although Su Qin had been chivvying her to get on with it, she had been desperate to put it off as long as possible. She had been quite satisfied with her liaisons in the dark with Victor while she waited to find someone she was truly interested in, but now she was afraid that if she left it any longer, there wouldn't be many options left and she'd be left on the shelf, which would be embarrassing. Not that she said any of this to Victor.

"More? I could tell you about all of them, but I don't want to send you to sleep. Anyway, they're all pretty much the same. So, if you could just choose one of these two!"

Marina tapped her fingernail on the metal shelf behind them. Tap, tap, tap. Tap, tap, tap. They were in the casting workshop, a tiny place that was just about still standing. It was where they came most often. It was cramped and basic, but had a kind of intimacy.

"Well, what about you? Are you leaning more towards one of them?" Victor said cautiously. He could hear his own voice, but it sounded as though it came from a tin can rather than his throat. It reminded him of the time that Marina had brought a personal stereo and they'd had fun making recordings. They'd recorded his voice and played it back. That was how his voice sounded now – awkward and distant.

"Me? You're asking me which one I like? Do you really have to ask? Do I have to say it out loud?" Marina responded instantly, almost under her breath, still absent-mindedly tapping her nails on the metal shelf. But they both knew what she had just said and there was a tenderness in the sting.

Those words made Victor's life worth living. The meteorite that had crashed moments before vanished, and the earth beneath his feet returned to its coma-like tranquillity. He swallowed the words whole. He wanted to take them home, chew them over slowly with the waxbill in his tiny bedroom, then keep them forever, so that he could savour that moment in the future whenever things were hard.

Marina took the camera from Victor, and took a few steps back. "Come on, let me take a photo of you."

Victor obediently leant against the rusty metal shelf and looked up at Marina. The photo was of him, alone, brimming with love and melancholy. He was facing the camera but not looking at it. He looked like it was the end of the world for him; he was shrouded in desolation, and so was Marina, in the shabby little world they inhabited.

"From where I'm standing, the one who quit and started his own design company is a better bet."

Victor moved out of the camera frame, but his voice still sounded as though it was coming out of a recorder.

He proceeded to give her brotherly advice, applying his limited experience to weighing up her options. He had spent many an hour in the union office going over the redundancy process with the workers, and had an odd respect for these big guys and the heroic way they had walked away from it all with a stamp of the feet and a wave of the hand. He often heard how well they had done afterwards: how they'd set up on their own, made a fortune, and had an income that was nothing short of jaw-dropping. They were truly amazing.

As for the assistant professor of physics, he would no doubt be very well-educated and have a high opinion of himself, with a crop of young women students hanging around him.

Without any hesitation, Marina forced a smile.

"All right, I'll do as you say."

11

ABOUT A MONTH LATER, Pearl took a bottle round to her father's and, on Su Qin's instructions, cheerfully presented him with Marina's wedding candy. She was also showing off the fact that she and Su Qin were still in touch. She liked to see herself as the family go-between.

"Mmmm," said Ding Bogang as he raised his cup, playfully unwrapped a candy, popped it in his mouth and took a swig of the fiery spirit. It must have produced a strange taste in his mouth, because he frowned and pulled a face at Pearl.

"Marina's wedding candy, hmm? Marina! What kind of a name is that! One of your work mates at the hotel, is she? She's taken her time, you got married years ago. Probably on the shelf and fed up with living on her own, hey?" said Dad, casting a sweeping glance at Victor.

Pearl passed some candy to Victor, watching his expression. He accepted happily, even taking two pieces.

"I'm doing you a favour, Pearl, you mustn't put on any more weight!"

"Hey, one of those was for Heipi."

But Victor had already shut the door behind him, as though he wanted to eat Marina's wedding candy in private.

In fact, he'd already had some the day before. But he was greedy for more, tossing them into his mouth like someone who's never tasted candy before.

The previous day, Marina had come straight to the point and said cheerily, "Huang Xin and I got our certificate. We're not going to have a wedding banquet, we're going on a honeymoon instead. As soon as his company's projects are settled in a couple of months' time, we'll go to Singapore, Malaysia and Thailand! Can you imagine, we'll be going abroad!"

"You'll be going abroad!" repeated Victor.

"But I didn't come to tell you about the honeymoon. I came to tell you that we can't see each other anymore. There's no point, you know that, it's just a waste."

She spoke with the steely determination of one of Chairman Mao's "Iron Girls". For the first time ever, her rational tone of voice repulsed him.

"What do you mean, it's a waste? A waste of what?" Victor forced himself to ask.

"It's a waste of . . ." Marina started, but didn't finish, or didn't want to pursue that line of thought. She looked calm and composed. "Anyway, we can't meet any more. I'll commit to that. Will you?"

Victor knew that Marina was someone who kept her word. She wouldn't come and see him again.

"Perhaps . . . Perhaps we could meet one last time," he began hesitantly. "I have a wedding present for you."

Victor put his hands in his pockets. He'd thought of this excuse spontaneously. Marina was being too abrupt. This wasn't the way to do it, not between the two of them. He didn't like this version of Marina, the one who had chosen a boyfriend, decided to get married, and never wanted to see him again. She had stabbed him so fast that there was no blood on the knife as she pulled it out.

"A present? Oh! Let me guess, it'll be something made of glass, right? And you'll tell me to look after it, and where to put it. And when Huang Xin asks about it, I'll have to tell him, and it'll take days to explain, and I'll have to start with my mum and your dad . . ."

Marina sounded very cold. She gave a frivolous laugh, as if she had already gone up the social ladder. She said she'd change, and she had. She had closed her heart and would never open it to him again.

Victor took his hands out of his pockets. He was annoyed that Marina had guessed it might be something made of glass. But she was spot on. He had been trying to think what to give her and he'd only thought of glass, nothing else – a framed mirror, an ornamental swan, a vase, a photo frame. But that was because glass was unique. Yes, it shattered when you dropped it, but at the end of the day, was there anything in the world that didn't break?

"Sure, why not," said Victor, holding in his pain and looking up at the sky. It was a nice day, not too hot or too cold. He could hear some people arguing heatedly nearby as they bargained over prices. It was good to hear them full of life.

"I mean, it's not as though we owe each other anything. We've known each other for years, and in future when we look back, we'll see they were good times. But from now on, we should go our own ways," Marina rummaged in her bag, took out a bag of pink wedding candy and tore it open. "Have one."

She unwrapped the candy and pushed it into his mouth with a little too much force. It was the most intimate thing she had done in all those years, and all thanks to her marriage to someone else. Victor tasted the candy carefully – he had never tasted anything sweeter, although accepting it now felt like acknowledging that everything else would always be out of reach.

But there was a question he needed to ask. It was one of the things that went round and round in his head at night when he couldn't sleep.

"Marina, can I ask you something? I mean, what if our families had never met, and we were simply friends or work colleagues, and if I'd gone to university as well. Imagine we hadn't met in Crossroads but, say, somewhere else, do you think we might have . . . What I mean is, if everything had been different, might we . . . ?"

Victor still had the candy in his mouth. He looked dazed and sounded muffled, and she couldn't make out what he was saying.

Marina didn't speak. There was a long pause then, as though someone jogged her arm, or jolted her hard, or shouted in her ear, she lurched towards him, and gently pressed her body against his.

In the lightning-fast kiss she gave him, the last of the candy in his mouth dissolved and its sweetness flooded over the bitter taste in their mouths.

That night, after Pearl had left with Heipi and Dad had finally settled, Victor got up before dawn. Still in his day clothes, he tiptoed across the room, picked up the birdcage, walked to Crossroads, where there was not a soul to be seen, and released the waxbill.

The little bird had been part of his life for eight years but looked exactly the same as the day Victor brought it home. It was surprised and excited by its new-found freedom, hopped about on the ground near him, then flew in small circles for a while. It looked at its tall, thin owner, cocked its head and sang its familiar song, quietly, tunelessly, wordlessly. Then it flapped its wings and took off, streaking briefly across the sky then disappearing like a flame thrown into the night.

As Victor watched it fly away, he decided to quit his job.

12

I N THE AUTUMN of that year, when Marina was taking honeymoon photos with Huang Xin in front of dazzling golden temples in Thailand, Victor threw himself into setting up The Glass House.

He rented a shopfront property at one end of Crossroads, took out all the money he had saved since starting work and built himself a shiny glass workshop. The structure had an invisible base, giving the illusion that it was suspended in mid-air and might disappear at any moment.

It was obvious that he had no talent for design (he was no Huang Xin), and that he had no idea about mechanics or architectural principles. But he didn't let that stop him. He pulled the original building apart entirely, right, left and centre, with the recklessness of an illiterate setting out to write a book. It drove him half-crazy. Finally, he managed a bizarre transformation: from the ashes of a dilapidated old shop rose a teetering glass edifice split across the middle.

The ground floor, the shop, was entirely constructed in glass: floor-to-ceiling glass doors and windows and glass bricks. Inside, everything from the shelves to the tables and chairs was made of transparent or semi-transparent material, as were the hundred or so items on display, creating layer upon layer of transparency. If you looked in from the street, you could see right through the multiple layers of The Glass House to the back alley.

Perched on top of the ground floor was a tiny upstairs space, a low-ceilinged, windowless room which provided his living area – an obvious replica of his glassed-in balcony. He spent his days downstairs in total transparency and climbed up to his dark den at night. Victor's new life began with his feet in the void.

Victor registered his business as glass, exclusively glass: tempered glass, frosted glass, sandblasted glass, patterned glass, wired glass, insulating glass, laminated glass, heat-bent glass, cellophane, and artworks made of glass. His passion for glass had been latent for years, as if his depression had suppressed it. Now that it had been released, it bubbled with fervour. His glass workshop stood out in in the very ordinary streets of Crossroads. It looked unreal.

The Glass House had another special feature: its sign. Shop signs can be subtle and mysterious, but this one was really in your face. It was an enormous mirror. On rainy days the water ran down it, and on fine days it would get covered in dust, but it always reflected, even blurrily, the electricity poles and trees.

"Such a huge mirror! What is it trying to say? It doesn't even have the shop's name on it!"

Everyone wondered the same thing.

Victor stroked his chin, looking bored.

"I couldn't think of a name. I was going to put a big piece of glass there, but it would break too easily, so I put the mirror there instead. At least mirrors are made of glass," he pursed his thin lips and refused to explain any further.

Eventually, people stopped caring about the name. The mirror was just a mirror, he could do as he pleased. They simply referred to his shop as The Glass House. It became a byword on Crossroads for someone or something that was romantic but impractical: "What on earth are you thinking? You're like The Glass House that Victor opened! Totally useless! Save yourself the trouble, hey?"

Of course, that wasn't how Marina saw it. Four years later, when Marina and her bump lumbered along the street on her way to The Glass House, she was full of fervent hope that there, with Victor, she would find a peace she had never known, a subtle yet solid feeling of comfort. Their lives together would be good, like ripe fruit full of juice.

13

VICTOR DIDN'T KNOW what Ding Bogang thought about him quitting his job and building The Glass House. By now his drinking and memory loss were off the scale and he was completely useless as a father. He never asked about or mentioned what his son was doing, or visited the shop. But every morning on his routine patrol through Crossroads, he went a little further than before, eventually walking past The Glass House, but without so much as a sideways glance at it.

When Victor couldn't sleep, he would come down early before opening time and sit at the back of the shop. Looking out through the glass windows and glass bricks, he would see his father walking past. The unkempt old man with the expressionless face seemed different somehow, brighter. Victor would watch him wearily and repeat the words that used to trip off his father's tongue, like the young idiot character in a Chinese comedy crosstalk: "My son, ah, he could count at one, use pi at two, recite Tang poems at three, read the newspaper at four! In third grade, he could read fourth-grade books, and at high school he could pass the second year exams in his first year!"

But he never went out and said hello, or took his father's arm. It just wasn't something he did. Besides, he knew that Pearl wouldn't be far behind, with that world-on-her-shoulders expression, following Dad wherever he went. Even when he was lying in the hospital emergency room, hooked up to the tubes and in a drunken stupor, even when he was taking his last breath, she was curled up in an armchair, snoring away, keeping him company to the end.

The night Ding Bogang died, as Victor later intimated to Su

Qin, he had almost bedded a woman. His unsuccessful efforts to produce sperm had sent him into a deep, sound sleep, oblivious that he had just lost the man who provided the sperm for his life.

I'll tell you how it came about. Remember the wordless shop sign in front of The Glass House? The big mirror that reflected passers-by, the green and brown leaves on the trees, autumn and winter without Marina, and time passing as fast as wild horses. Well, one day it reflected a woman. Life's like that, it brings you surprises, whether you want them or not.

There was a busy Five Yuan Shop opposite, and next door to that, a knock-off mobile phone shop and a sports shop selling famous brands at eye-watering prices. That was where she worked. You could tell at a glance she was probably from rural Henan or Anhui. The conventional view was that migrant girls were a step down from the people in the factory zone. Obviously, she had ambitions to make a better life for herself here in the factory zone, and she'd chosen an interesting way of doing it. Although there were plenty of mirrors at the sports shop, she'd started coming to look at herself in the big mirror at The Glass House during her lunchbreak.

She had a particular way of doing this. She started with her hair, stroking it this way and that way with her hands, twirling the ends or coiling it up on the top of her head. Then she looked at her face, at the corners of her eyes, the freckles on her cheeks, the blackheads on her nose, and her teeth, checking she didn't have any bits of food caught between them. Then she looked at her torso, from the side and the back, and finally at her feet and shoes. From his vantage point at the back of the shop, Victor could see very clearly that she had her eye on the main attraction. He felt sad that a new life was approaching so fast, and that he truly wasn't interested.

Then one day she appeared with a paper towel in her hand and started wiping the mirror. In fact, the first thing Victor did every morning when he opened up was to move the mirror outside and wipe it clean. But there she was outside the shop, wiping it vigorously.

At that point he was forced to come out and hold the mirror steady.

"Hey! Be careful!"

The girl's freckled face looked up, her small eyes smiling like little crescents.

"Be careful?"

Her intention was written all over her face.

Something stirred in Victor. It had been such a long time since a girl smiled at him – not since his breakup with Marina in 2002, three years earlier. But this smile brought back only too vividly another one, out in the cemetery at Qing Ming, that wonderful but tragic smile.

How could he erase her from his life, when she was the only thing that kept him going?

Victor turned brusque and said, "Don't wipe it again. It's wobbly."

The girl was taken aback for a moment, then began to chatter.

"It must be expensive. I've never in all my life seen a mirror this big. If you ask me, it's not only the biggest mirror in the whole of Crossroads and the whole of the factory zone, but also the biggest mirror in the whole city!"

She sounded as if she was making a point of using the "not only . . . but also" construction.

Victor didn't answer. He felt for this girl. She was just like Marina, trying to move up the ladder through marriage, even though they didn't love their partners.

Then she asked, "Was it expensive? How much was it?"

"Two months' wages for you," Victor answered reluctantly.

Without warning, she raised her leg and gave it a hard kick. In an instant Victor's enormous mirror shattered.

"Right then, I'll come and work here. Two months' hard graft and I'll pay you back!" she announced brightly.

Victor stood among the shards of glass, looking at her unhappily. It was all too obvious that she was looking for a good time. But she was the wrong girl, and she made him miss the right one even more.

"There's no need," he said dryly.

"No, no, I have to pay you back," the girl insisted, rubbing the freckles on her face. She smiled confidently.

She knew what she was doing. She was a migrant worker and she had her head screwed on. She honestly believed that in two months, maybe two weeks if she worked day and night, she could become a specialist in glass and lay the foundations to becoming the boss's wife. Imagine! A depressed boss and an energetic migrant worker in The Glass House that rose like a tower into the sky . . . Anything could happen! Everyone pictures their destiny in their own way, so why shouldn't she?

Not everyone wants to reinvent themselves and move on, so I'll tread lightly here. The main thing was that on the very night that Ding Bogang drank himself to eternal oblivion, this scheming girl stayed over. She used the wages Victor had given her to buy a mirror as big as the first one, and decided to give herself to Victor when she gave him the mirror.

If things had gone smoothly, she could have looked forward to tying the knot and the patter of tiny feet, which was exactly what Victor had envisioned with Marina. But it soon became apparent how absurd that idea was, and how painfully he missed his lost love.

At first, Victor was very co-operative. He took off his clothes and even felt a little aroused. But somehow his body was as numb as if it was anaesthetised. He couldn't even manage to hold her in his arms. In the end, he grabbed his clothes, abandoned the naked girl, fled downstairs and sat at the back of the glass shop.

He took a long look at his rumpled clothes and the swirling colours of the night, penetrating layer after layer of glass, shining on to his body. His life was utterly joyless. He was struck by a wave of sadness and contempt. How had he got into this mess? He thought about Marina and how courageously she had persevered, fulfilling what should have been both of their destinies, while he himself had stayed still. He should have been getting on with his own life and finding some long-term peace and stability.

Meanwhile, he had been climbing Mount Everest with his bare hands. Why not go with the flow, accept this freckled girl who'd looked in his mirror? He should move on with his life. He could picture it now, it was how everyone lived in Crossroads: he'd get fat and middle-aged, lose his hair, fight with his wife, yell at the brat, spend Sundays at the zoo with the brat . . . Actually, it wasn't a bad life. He was up for it.

But, as he wrestled with himself and tried to compromise, something became crystal clear. He was both proud and pained to discover that he couldn't do it. No one in the world could replace Marina. You could line up the most beautiful girls in the world, completely naked, and they wouldn't be worth a single hair from Marina's head. The impossibility of his relationship with Marina had basically destroyed the possibility of any other relationship. Of course, he was orchestrating his own self-destruction, like an ascetic monk weaving his own web.

He hated his lonely, miserable existence. The future looked bleak. It held nothing for him.

In the thin, early morning air, the thought of death glowed in the dark, a tiny flicker of flame. Surely, it would be better than the life he faced. Victor was shocked at the thought, but was about to consider it when he heard Pearl's voice outside, like a crackle of lightning in his ear: "Vic, you need to get to the hospital, Dad's dying."

Although Victor had been the first to hear the news from Pearl, he was the last to arrive. Blank-faced, he joined the shabby condolence ceremony, knelt in front of his father, his back straight, a lock of hair hanging loose and fresh red scratches on his face, looking appropriately distressed for the occasion.

Before leaving The Glass House, he had gone upstairs, shaken the girl awake and asked her not to come again. She had been furious and laid into him. Victor hadn't moved, or put up any resistance. He really didn't care, and he could use another beating, in tribute to his dad.

Screaming and swearing, the girl had clawed and bitten and

kicked every which way. In that pathetic display of fists and feet, he realised for the first time how miserable his poor dad must have been. He had tried so hard to do right by Victor, but the confused old man didn't know how to. All he could do was shout and swear and go at him hammer and tongs in the unrealistic hope that the child prodigy potential would carry him on to a better life. Well, it was okay now. He would never kneel in front of his dad and beg him to box his ears again.

Victor closed his eyes, and in the darkness the girl's nips and pinches were magnified. As he felt the bruises blooming on his skin, he imagined the smell of alcohol and tried to evoke the pain he had felt at his father's hands.

14

A FTER MORE THAN a decade, it took a moment or two for Victor to recognise Ash.

The Glass House was not very welcoming, and seldom had any customers. The people in the factory zone were still not used to this big ice cube of a shop and felt that all those twinkling, immaculate objects were not for them. Victor wasn't fussed – he rather liked this boring life. The most significant thing he did each day was take a snow-white cloth and leisurely clean and polish every one of his precious glass objects. In any case, Dad was dead, and there was no one to take an interest in how or whether he developed his career, or to drown their sorrows and worries on his account. Except for Pearl, who occasionally dropped by and parroted the usual things about settling down, career and so on.

When Ash walked in, he went straight to the back of the shop. Victor assumed it was some passer-by from out of town drawn in by curiosity, and continued dusting an imitation-crystal basket of flowers that tended to attract dust in the crevices of its branches and leaves.

The customer stopped behind him, casting a small shadow over him. Victor looked around, and took a few seconds to recognise the tall, slim man.

Ash moved to the side, then took a few steps back and a few steps forward, looking around with both fear and satisfaction, his face filled with supreme respect.

"You really did build your own glass house! I can't believe it, it's amazing!"

He clasped his hands in front of his chest, as though overcome with emotion.

Victor looked at him. Marina's little brother. Marina, a name that could never be his and yet had hung over and destroyed his entire life. The old times hurtled towards him like a rollercoaster, bringing the same sorrow and joy they always did. Come on, you're in your thirties now, you need to grow out of this! he told himself. He beamed a welcome and fetched some glass cups to make tea.

Ash had one hand in his pocket, clenched around the scrappy note that Victor had tucked inside the parcel of old clothes. How many times had he read that note with its unremarkable message!

Ash: I'm sending these "child prodigy" clothes to you. Do what you like with them. Good luck.

– Vic

He had brought the note with him, as though it was an essential prop for his reunion with Victor. And all the way here he'd been preparing what he would say. Ten years and eight months ago! Do you remember? When we all broke up at your door? Our two families, the six of us, like a bunch of unfeeling ants all going their own way. He had been sure this would be a good opening, but Victor's lukewarm reception had dampened his enthusiasm.

Ash sat down and crossed his legs (not noticing that Victor averted his eyes when he did so), and started to speak in a voice that sounded as earnest and eager as when he was a young boy:

"You sent the packages to me two years ago, and I've kept them safe ever since. Whenever I rented a new place, I took them with me, still in their original wrapping. I've brought them all back with me this time, every piece is there. They're all still in good condition."

Victor nodded, but seemed reluctant to talk about it.

"I didn't mean to put you to so much trouble. Why did you bring them back? I'd forgotten all about them. I'm so busy with glass these days."

Ash was upset. Since stepping through the door, he'd pretended to be impressed, but in fact he felt empty inside. Victor was so different. He wasn't the guardian angel, the hot-blooded big brother Ash had often thought about in the South. He was so ordinary, there was a wasted air about him and he seemed to have shrunk as well. But he was only thirty-two, how could he have changed so much?

"Are you on your own? You're not married?"

Ash asked, though he knew the answer. It was like asking someone to confirm their name before you killed them.

Victor nodded. He didn't explain, but shook out the snow-white cloth he was holding and watched the dust swirl randomly in the light.

Ash crumpled up the note he was holding, then tried a couple of times to open it up in his pocket and smooth it flat. Finally, he summoned the courage to say, "I've come back because there's something I have to tell you, and Marina too. Back then, when I was playing go-between between the two of you, it was all a pack of lies. She never told me she loved you, those words about her feeling safe, finding you attractive and the little gifts, I made them all up."

Victor didn't respond. As was his habit, he put one hand over his eye. When the white cloth stopped moving, the dust mites continued to float in the light.

Ash went on determinedly.

"Then, when I saw you were up for it, I lied to her as well. I said you adored her. I spiced it up and told her how miserable you were, so that naturally she'd be interested in helping you. I only did it because I was young and lonely and wanted to make the two families closer and warmer. But it all fell apart, so all my efforts were for nothing. It's only recently that I learned you two were for real. Especially you! Marina's smart, she does what she needs to, and now she's pregnant. But look at you. I came here today to tell you not to take my messing around seriously, that it was all castles in the air and that you should get on with your own life."

"She's pregnant?"

It was the first real news Victor had of Marina since she got married. At the vigil for his father, Su Qin wouldn't tell him anything, but there had been something in her expression that he couldn't work out and it had sat like a stone in his heart. Now, Ash's news split that stone into little pieces. So Marina was going to have a baby.

Ash's own feelings had also split into many pieces – a mixture of guilt, disappointment and heartache. He thought for a moment, then tried to encourage Victor.

"Hey, you know when you used to love talking about the philosophy of glass and said how it was all fake and empty, well, you need to shatter those illusions! Otherwise I'm going to carry this guilt around with me for the rest of my life."

Victor snorted a laugh, and took his hand away from his eye.

"You're using glass to tell me how things really are! Well, let me tell you, I wasn't a fool back then. I knew that Marina would never have looked at a loser like me! But I wanted to believe it, because it felt so good, you know. Otherwise, my life was meaningless. And I'm sure you already know that we were together for a while, so there's no need to apologise. If you hadn't created the first half, we would never have had the second half. So, I'm grateful to you!" Victor said without any sarcasm. It was a properly sincere thank-you.

"But you . . . And now she's . . ."

Ash shook his head. Surely, Victor was missing the point. Marina was going to have a baby, and he was still being loyal to her? What was he playing at? Ash put the question another way, hoping to make Victor see sense: "What will Marina think when she learns I made it all up for both of you?"

Victor panicked. A layer of sweat appeared on his face.

"Ash, would you mind, for my sake, not mentioning this to Marina? Couldn't we just let her think it all happened naturally? Would you promise me that?"

Ash nodded. Since he'd been back, he'd seen Marina many times, but he'd been too scared to say anything. Given her temperament, he didn't know how she'd react. But he'd gone to Victor determined to confess everything he'd done. Now he could forget about telling her. He would make that promise to Vic. The way he was now, he'd have to be made of stone to refuse him.

There was something else bothering Ash as well. Was now the time to bring it up? There was another reason he'd come.

He opened his mouth a few times to speak, and eventually, unable to think of a more delicate way of putting it, said in an upbeat-text-message tone of voice, "I'm still single. Can't work out if I'm looking for a boyfriend or girlfriend. Any suggestions?"

He gave a little laugh to cover his nervousness.

"Hmm," said Victor, pouring and drinking more tea, stalling for time. He picked up a piece of pale glass jewellery and held it up to the light for a long time before passing it to Ash, showing him the glass flow and the shadows within. He was back on his old subject: how wonderful glass was, how it could solve and explain difficult questions. For example, the potential complications when you've fallen for someone or someone's fallen for you, the calculations people make in their relationships, the rules for making them work, the give and take. If you couldn't figure these out, you only had to think about glass and it would tell you. If something was beyond your dreams, if there was something between you, if the relationship was melting and changing shape, glass was absolutely qualified to give an opinion. Glass had a burning point of 1300 degrees, it had seventy-two transformations, it knew when to cave in and adapt, and if there really was no other way, it would give up and shatter. Victor's face lit up as he spoke, and his voice took on a missionary tone.

"That's why I've devoted myself to it all these years. Whatever problems you run into, think about glass and you'll feel so much better."

While he was talking, he stood up and dusted the glass from the front of the shop all the way to the back, as though in the time they had been talking another layer of dust had descended on the scene. In the late midday sun, the light catching and reflecting off every glass surface in the shop created thousands upon thousands of shafts of light.

Ash looked up and stared at the dust motes floating quietly in the rays of light. The man in front of him had held a special place in his heart when he was growing up. Ash had looked up to him, adored him as an older brother and admired the way he spoke so eloquently about glass. But now, there was a tragic sense of fate in the monotony of his movements as he dusted the shop. He could see that Vic would spend many more years, probably the rest of his life, whiling away the time in Crossroads. Ash felt a surge of joyful relief – whatever anyone might say about him, he had walked away from those paths, seen other lives.

"Have you never thought of doing something else? Like driving a cab? Or getting married?"

"Not really. Glass is the only thing I know anything about. Perhaps that sounds a bit pathetic," Victor laughed, "but maybe it isn't. I know they say more is better and change is good but to be honest, now I've known someone like Marina, there are no more girlfriends for me."

At that point Ash laughed too, though he felt a stab of distress.

"And, as for those kids' clothes, they're yours," Victor brought the conversation to a close. He sounded completely satisfied with this.

There was nothing more to say. So Ash said goodbye, wished Victor and his glass well, and left.

Ash didn't know that after he left the shop, Victor had stood and watched him walk down the road. When he was sure that Ash had gone far enough and would not come back, he turned around, brought the big mirror inside, hung up the "Closed" sign, climbed up to his dark room and crawled into bed, never mind that it was broad daylight.

At that point the pain he'd been suppressing burst through his entire body, and he felt as though he'd been run over by a juggernaut.

Truly, he was grateful to Ash. But he had lied just now – he had been so shocked and upset to learn it had all been a lie. Yes, he had wondered about it before. He had looked for evidence and details, but after thorough examination, had eliminated his doubts one by one and committed himself to believing this fantasy.

Their relationship had become true, but it no longer existed, and now he could no longer tell what was true and what was false. He felt utterly bereft. He couldn't accept it. The one beautiful emotion that had sustained him all these years was built on a lie.

His life was a joke. As for the only two things in his life, glass was empty and Marina wasn't real. It was a life worse than death.

See, there it was again, he was thinking about death. Remember the last time he thought about dying?

Many people have had times in their lives when they've thought about dying. When the difficulty has passed, most will persuade themselves to keep going. Like others before him, Victor had tried to blur the issue and trick himself into going on. But this time, when the thought of dying struck a second time, he experienced a curious thrill.

He lay in his dark den, savouring this peculiar pleasure.

15

THE PLEASURE LASTED until Pearl turned up.

It was a sultry day, and having run all the way, Pearl's face was bright red and her hair was plastered to her sweaty forehead. Victor looked at her round body on her average frame, and remembering the news that Ash had brought him, felt it was rather a coincidence that the two girls would be giving birth at more or less the same time.

He hardly had time to think about it before Pearl delivered her good news. She had run all the way to tell him that Marina was coming, that she was pregnant, that he had a ready-made family about to arrive. He glared at his ridiculous sister, wondering if anything she said would ever be true.

She jabbered on, her spit flying everywhere, about Marina being separated after four years of marriage and how she was pregnant. Every sentence was an exclamation: "You'll never believe it! Marina is desperate to get back together with you! Tomorrow, you mustn't put your foot in it! Imagine how hard it is for her, after four years! Throwing it all away!"

It was peaceful and quiet inside The Glass House and Pearl's voice echoed through the transparency. He couldn't understand what she was saying.

Victor put his hand to his face for a while, but at the same time was disgusted by his habitual response of passive acceptance. Yet, the disgust gave him strength, and he used that strength to shoot back at his sister.

"No, I won't let it happen."

Pearl had blown in like a gust of wind, a deadly wind that left

Victor feeling badly burned. His heart had shattered after Ash's visit, and he hadn't even begun to pick up the pieces when Pearl came with news that crushed his heart even more. He couldn't move, not even to close the shop and climb upstairs.

He could hear that the door was wide open and that things were stirring in the street. Spring was the loveliest season in this city. People were strolling past in the sunshine. There were students the same age as Marina when she was at college, women about the same age as Marina was now, women heavily pregnant and women old and hunched. He watched them pass by in a blur through his tears.

He was annoyed at not being able to see properly.

How could Marina do that? Had she no self-respect, no respect for him, or for life? They had made an agreement. An agreement that included Huang Xin, who'd been chosen with deliberation and desperation. Did she really want to come back here? To have a second marriage, dragging her kid with her, to be The Glass House boss's wife? To give that little baby the same life they'd had, playing in the dirt in Crossroads with everyone pointing at them. She needed to think it over in the cold light of day.

Victor wiped his eyes. He could see better now, and in the crowd on the street, he thought he could see Marina. She was looking back at him, biting her lip in defiance, challenging fate, despising convention in that way he had always found intoxicating. Victor laughed bitterly at himself over this illusion and felt ashamed of his indignation – what did it matter, as long as she wasn't afraid, as long as the two of them were together? There was nothing to be ashamed of, was there? It was love.

Victor closed his eyes and tried his best to feel proud of being part of her world, but instead he felt increasing disillusion. He didn't dare to imagine that kind of life. As if she would really come and be his loving wife! Like a painting you've known for years suddenly coming to life, the figures stepping out of their world into yours, it would be a kind of deception and treachery. No, happiness was not something to have and to hold, it was something to imagine and take comfort in. If he and Marina were together for real, there would be nothing to sustain them, life would come to an end.

It was contradictory. It didn't make sense. Victor realised that he was muttering to himself. A little embarrassed, he jumped to his feet and walked over to the door, leant against the frame and looked out onto the street.

He hadn't noticed it was getting late and that people had started to hurry back to their own little corners of the world. The owner of the shop next door was washing his hair, bare-shouldered, and his wife was scratching their itchy son. Victor greeted her, remarking that the eight-year-old seemed to have grown again and looked at least ten. As he mechanically mouthed these pleasantries, he felt his sadness grow. The three of them next door were the epitome of a robust happy family, and he could almost picture himself, Marina and their little one in an ordinary scene like that. And he didn't like it. He couldn't imagine it. That wasn't how he and Marina were.

He had said as much to Pearl, that he refused to accept it, that he wouldn't let it happen. If Marina really did come tomorrow, that's what he would say. Of course, she would be hurt, and perhaps think herself a fool, but he would stop her, no matter what.

Still leaning against the doorframe, Victor looked back inside. The colours of late afternoon and early evening filled The Glass House with layer upon layer of light, creating deep shadows across the shop. In the battle between orange and black, the space looked like a giant jewel with a desperate beauty swirling inside. Victor watched with rapt attention. He saw beautiful scenes like this every day, but this time he learned something new. He had stumbled across a simple explanation: his inability to accept Marina, his unwillingness to take her back, was his way of loving her. He could only love her through a sheet of glass, when they could never touch. It was the only way that made sense.

It was in that sudden moment of enlightenment that the thought of dying visited Victor for the third time. He reacted with shock, but gave his mind time to slowly catch up; he had to treat this old friend with the utmost care, in case it turned out to be his best option.

Victor thought it over carefully. His mind was full of anxiety for Marina. He felt a strange kind of sympathy and a concern for her life in the future, even imagining her in old age. It was so selfish of him to leave her all on her own.

He roamed around the glass workshop a few times and tried to pull himself together. There was still glass, wasn't there? And glass would never let him down.

But at precisely 2:42pm the next day, Victor's last and only reason for living disappeared. His Glass House perished. The walls and doors were absolutely, utterly, thoroughly, mercilessly blown to pieces, turned into murder weapons that would destroy its creator.

In the half-hour before it happened, time passed slowly for Victor. He went over and over his thoughts obsessively. He worried about not being able to break his ties with Marina, and he worried about being too brutal. If only there was a way he could stop her without hurting her. He wished he could die there and then, hurl his desperate but ever loyal heart into the road. She was coming. He could hear, smell and feel her with all of his senses: she was walking towards him, eagerly looking forward to picking the only sweet bunch of grapes on the heavily-laden branches of their past. Marina's ideas were so beautiful. His heart pounded in his chest so hard that every second of every minute hurt, and as he heard her coming closer and closer, he could do nothing but wait.

Thank goodness, at that very moment, his glass showed such understanding. His love for glass had not been in vain. As if it had entered into his mind and read his deepest thoughts, the sheets self-destructed, forming a massive sparkling cave and burying him deep within, cutting him off from the outside world.

In fact, he had only a few scratches, but the familiar thought of dying flashed through his mind one last time. As naturally as water flowing into the sea, his hand reached for a wedge-shaped piece of glass. This fragment stayed with him through his bloody last moments, and when Victor was about to lose consciousness, it lovingly reminded him to place the snow-white cloth over his wrist to hide this distressing detail.

VI

One-way Street

1

13TH April, 2:42pm. It's worth repeating the time because otherwise it would be as random as any other time. People are always doing random things at random times. Like, say, lighting up a cigarette.

There was a faint scrape of a thumb against the wheel of a lighter as a passer-by in Crossroads got out a two-yuan lighter and flicked it at a Nanjing-brand cigarette. Then he crumpled the flattened pack in his pocket and thought, Damn, another pack almost gone. The lighter flame produced a small glint, like a firefly, seen by no one but God. And yet this firefly, with one flutter of its tiny wings, ignited the entire district of Crossroads. The result was an effortless, magnificent son et lumière show.

The explosion erupted from under the ground like an almighty dragon, accompanied by ear-splitting, earth-shattering sound effects. Leaves, windows, doors, roofs, abandoned newsstands, billboards adorned with liquor adverts, bicycle sheds, old sofas, refrigerators with last night's leftovers stacked inside, motorcycles with gloves hanging from the handlebars, tailors' dummies – everything that can leave the ground did so. Some things soared skywards and disappeared into the far reaches of the universe, never to be seen again, others hovered just above the ground, or were torn to shreds, or spurted pink juice, or left a trail of fluffy white feathers behind them.

Most astonishingly, people who happened to be walking by or hanging around parked vans or cars were tossed like crumpled balls of newspaper into the gutter (this included some real tough guys). When they wriggled out, they were covered in blood and screaming incoherently for help. The sky produced an appropriate backdrop: a gigantic plume of grey smoke with streaks of orange soared up then slowly spread and morphed into splendidly-contoured shapes bathed in vivid blocks of colour. Who would have thought that poor old Crossroads would ever enjoy such a moment of glory, so full of passion, so very post-modern! It was probably the only climax it had ever had in its life.

Marina, eight months pregnant by now, timed her arrival to perfection and thus had the good fortune to be able to share this pitiless chemical blast with the residents of Crossroads. The end of her silk scarf flew into the air and was sliced neatly in half by a rogue tree branch. Immediately after, the branch about-faced and jabbed Marina in one cheek, creating a rather abstract, jagged blood-red pattern across her face.

If she had not spent so much time searching for the scarf Pearl had given her all those years ago before she left for The Glass House, Marina would have already arrived and been with Victor. But Marina's rhythm and her logic were understandably off-kilter that day. She was consumed by the need to tie that scarf around her neck. She had to find it. Besides, she had not seen Vic for so many years, what difference did it make if she was a few minutes late? He didn't even know she was coming. She let herself revel in these last few moments of darkness in her life, secure in the knowledge that, very soon, everything would be transformed.

She searched through all her cupboards and drawers and finally found the scarf among some moth-balled sweaters, still in its wrapping paper, along with some long-forgotten college notebooks. With no great haste, she even opened one or two notebooks, leafed through and read a few lines, before unwrapping the scarf and smoothing it with her hand. It was extremely creased and could do with being ironed, she thought.

If she really had ironed it, then the wheel of fate would have spun once more and landed on another number, and the silk scarf could have adorned her neck for many more years. But Marina dismissed the idea. She scolded herself for dawdling. She was like an old woman who had never been out of the house in her life. Get a move on, she told herself, go and meet him.

And so the long-anticipated moment approached. She was exactly on time to meet her destiny.

Marina was so big by now that she was unsteady on her feet, like an old ship wallowing on its journey. Her thoughts and feelings were in turmoil, oscillating between past and present. She stroked her belly and looked at her reflection as she passed the shop windows. She felt like she was carrying not just her baby in her belly, but also the thirty years of her life so far. She felt like a snail, weighed down with the past, her shoes claggy with accumulated sadness. Every step she took became slower and more hesitant. Her heart pounded as she wondered: Is it really possible to turn back the clock?

2

AFTER SHE DISCOVERED she was pregnant and while she was still trying to decide whether to keep the baby or not, Marina had attended a lecture by a certain esteemed Professor Zhou, entitled "Analysis of Social Classes in China". The professor was a small, slight man with a southern accent, light-coloured spectacle frames and confidence-inspiring white hair. Marina had to slip out in the middle of the lecture because she was overcome with emotion. The professor's gentle demeanour and his compassionate tone made her very sad, his words a keen reminder that up until now she had been a loser. She wondered if he was picking her out individually, or was she just one among many sorry examples? All these years, she had put so much effort into breaking away from the class she had been born into and climbing up in society that in the process she had trampled underfoot the last remnants of tenderness she held for her past and refused to follow her heart's desires.

Of course, the desire for a better life, even a life of luxury, was universal, like the stubbornness to the point of stupidity shared by all the inhabitants of Crossroads – including Ding Bogang, with his bulbous red nose. Why else would he have named his son Victor and clung so stubbornly to the story about him being a child prodigy? There was Heipi, too. He was always telling Pearl nonsense about his plans to establish a noble dynasty. And none were more ambitious than Marina's own erstwhile husband Huang Xin and his friends, with their schemes to grow small companies into large ones, to rise up in the ranks and become ever richer.

Whether they were still in the mire, or already scaling the social ladder, people pursued the same simple goals almost without exception, as united as soldiers goose-stepping on military parade: bigger, better, more. Even though social difference was the chief cause of resentment and misery in the world, "Bigger, Better, More" still rang loudly in everyone's ears.

Marina always remembered an image from her childhood: the big shiny downtown shopping centres, her mother running cautious fingers over the glass countertops displaying goods for sale. Su Qin never wanted to shop in Crossroads. She preferred to cart her children across town to department stores in the city-centre, even if it was for something as small as a raincoat or gloves. The three of them, her mother, her brother and herself, made a good team, intently comparing the merits of different outlets. She saw the anticipation and pride on her mother's face as she pointed out the immaculate roads lined with plane trees, the polite and well-dressed pedestrians and the expensive white goods stores, as if the intimidating prices were admirable, sending a message to them that, "Look, this is where the upper class live, this is where we should be living!"

As for Marina, the luxury and elegance she saw as she grew up – in films, novels, poems, pop songs, and news reports – all made an even deeper impression on her. She realised, sadly, that it was the same old issue everywhere; not only in Chinese suburbs like Crossroads, but wherever people live. In New York, the centre of the world, the Upper East Side of Manhattan was an address fit for legislators, while Brooklyn was for the failing artist. As for Queens, it was only first-generation immigrants who were happy to acknowledge that place as home, while Hell's Kitchen had such a poor reputation that even stray dogs were ashamed to admit they hung out there, although a dessert in any of its restaurants would feed a family in Pyongyang for a week. Anyway, wherever people were from, East or West, pure stock or mixed race, Shanghai or the provinces, they were all snobs. The examples were endless. But one should not mock such arrogance; everyone had it, even those on the bottom rung of society.

Marina had never denied that her hatred for her humble origins arose from those visits downtown. It grew so intense that it made her teeth chatter. The factory zone, her obese brother, her fornicating mother, her drunken almost-stepfather, her almost-stepbrother and sister. She hated all this vulgarity! She felt like she had vicious barbs all over her body that she couldn't control. If only she could puncture her own despair.

She focussed her fury on her mother.

There was one night in the dormitory of her university when the subject of mothers came up. The girls spilled out their feelings, psychoanalysing their mothers' influence over them, recounting with detail the inevitable confrontations, their toxic adolescence, the hypocritical tears and eventual forgiveness. Their voices rose and fell theatrically, some of them actually choking with sobs. Only Marina kept silent. She wasn't going to share honestly with outsiders. She could not even be honest with herself.

All these years, there had been a lot of misunderstandings and competition between her and her mother, and perhaps she had lost her temper more than she should have. She really cared about her mother, but she was angry. The fact was that she had no objection to her mother finding a new partner. But why did she, such a beautiful, clean woman, have to go and choose a lout like Ding Bogang and act so sneakily about their affair? She had dragged all their reputations through the mud – their late father's, her own, the whole family's. Marina was furious, and that made her develop a cold, calculated reverence for cleanliness and correctness. She felt she could rely on no one but herself. She had to be ruthlessly ambitious, she had to struggle towards her goal, however distant, and leave this godforsaken factory zone behind forever, even if the road ahead was long and weary and ultimately led to failure.

It was Ash who had given her the strange idea of using Victor to get at her mother. She would never forget the calculating look in her little brother's eyes as he slumped back on the cushions, patting his soft chest and prattling away.

"You're not to tell anyone," he said, "But Victor is really funny. He's got the weirdest collection of old clothes, from when he was a kid, he's kept every single one. And you know they say he was a child prodigy. Don't you think that's strange?"

Then he added, as if this was weirdest thing of all: "And he really, really likes you!"

Ash sucked in his breath for greater effect.

"Likes me? Why? That's so weird!"

Marina made a show of sorting her books out but raised her eyebrows, to show Ash that she was listening. What was her fat-boy brother up to?

"Really, it's the truth! He said you were the most intelligent girl he'd ever met, so calm, such potential. And by the way, he also said . . ."

He paused, racking his brains for the thing most likely to appeal to Marina.

Ash was making mischief. Actually, he had no need to pick his words so carefully. No matter what he said, Marina would have believed him. She might even have let drop a few words for Ash to pass back to Vic. Marina found herself perversely excited, and curious. Perhaps she was tired of trying to behave correctly all the time and wanted to test if there was any chemistry between them. He was an unlikely match: an apprentice glass-blower who couldn't even hold his chopsticks properly, going nowhere in life and, worst of all, was the son of Over There.

Of course, Victor was a bit different, definitely worth messing with. But the key thing was her mother's overreaction. She was deeply shocked. Marina found that the abuse her beloved mother yelled at her added a certain piquancy, but was nonetheless surprised at what happened next. After two slaps on her daughter's face and a pinky-promise, her mother had broken it off with Ding Bogang. Just like that! She was shocked. For the first time, she realised just how wired-up her mother was, and how determined she was to lunge recklessly at a phantom threat. In fact, Ding Bogang wasn't that bad, and Marina had never wanted them to split up. So, from that point on, her dominant feeling toward Su Qin was that she owed her something.

True, she promised Su Qin at the time that she would stay away from Victor, but whenever there was a promise, there was always the temptation to break it. One reason being that Victor genuinely intrigued her, the other that her mother regarded him as absolutely the wrong choice.

Marina had succeeded in hauling herself out of the quagmire of the factory zone and was looking at a rosy future, so why would she want to go and look up Victor again? Obviously, thanking him for the silk scarf was only a pretext, and doing something to help "poor Victor" even more so. Her most fundamental motivation was buried deep inside her, like a tightly-wrapped cabbage heart: she liked the feeling that she was transgressing, knowing she should not do something but doing it anyway.

She could not have foreseen that this transgression would plunge her back into Crossroads, into Victor, binding her to him in an agonising loneliness that she could not put into words. She had begun to feel a depth of tenderness that she had never felt before. It made her feel disorientated.

And so something changed in Marina's feelings for Victor. Now it was she who needed him. Even though she could have had so many men who had better prospects than Victor, she always felt she had to stand on tiptoe and brim with energy when she was with any of them – and that was exhausting. Or maybe her origins in the factory zone had left an indelible mark on her, making her uncomfortable in wider society. With higher-class people, she felt mediocre. She shrank into herself like a hedgehog. It was only when she was hanging round the scrubby far side of the factory zone with Victor that she could allow the stiffened arches of her feet to relax. She could forget her origins and her burning need to get ahead, she could confess to all kinds of wild desires that were never going to happen. How happy it made her to have a friend like Vic, to feel so comfortable with him, to forget her driving ambitions and just to hang out with him and poke gentle fun at everyone and everything in the factory zone. When they were together, Marina felt as if they were floating on a great white cloud in a still, pure realm far beyond civilization.

And who is to say whether their easy friendship was not also laced with an underlying hint of passion?

Time and again, she would gaze at Victor's calm profile, the faint scar on his chin and the livid skin beneath the roots of his hair. As she watched him leisurely smoke a cigarette, puffing out a thin white stream of smoke, she would fall into a trance. He felt like family. She might also drift into a daydream in which Ding Bogang was with her mother, and Victor with her.

There was one occasion when Marina tried to make that happen.

"Actually, we're kind of a family, brother and sister," she had said to Victor. "You're just my big brother, right?"

Apart from when the two families first met, when her mother had ordered her to call him "brother", she had never called him that again. But now she liked the sound of it. It sounded like they were brother and sister, but also like lovers, a kind of incestuous intimacy – she felt quite emotional.

Victor looked away, apparently uncomfortable.

Marina repeated softly, "You're my brother. Kiss me, lovely brother."

He put his hands over his face. But the emotion she saw there told her that he really liked her calling him "lovely brother" like that. She longed for him to put his arms around her. She hesitated, then made her decision. She stepped towards him until she was so close that she could feel his breath on her skin. And there she halted, rooted to the spot. She knew that once she had crossed the line, there was no way back. At times like this, she was shocked at her own forwardness, by her appalling ruthlessness, which rendered her impervious to all tenderness and intimacy. She was actually afraid of herself.

After a moment or two, she pulled herself together and said slowly, as if she had suddenly remembered, "You know what, I'm twenty-six years old. You're twenty-nine. It's probably time to move on."

Soon after that, Marina decided to get married. She did it at lightning speed, thus avoiding all unnecessary hesitations and explanations, especially to her mother. She knew her mother would be polite but leave a lot unsaid and she didn't want that. It was only marriage, for heaven's sake.

As she made her lonely way up in society, Marina trained herself to become hard. One of the things she believed was that romantic love was both random and difficult to achieve. It did not improve one's quality of life, and could even be an obstacle in her climb to the top. In contrast, marriage was the sensible option, a useful threshold to be crossed. She was convinced that she was not the only one who believed this. How many people in the world could swear that their marriage had been built purely on romantic love? Wasn't marrying up in the world something everyone wanted?

So one day, in the workshop filled with discarded patterns and dyes, next to the boiler house with its belching steam, she asked Victor, without preamble, to choose her a husband. One was much the same as another, after all. She did, however, hope for a bit of time. She imagined time falling like layers of dust, sympathetically covering and sealing off everything between Victor and herself.

3

IT MUST BE SAID that Victor made a good choice for her.

Huang Xin certainly lived up to expectations. He and Marina shared the values of their generation. They married, and by the time they had marched forward together for four or five years, they had made notable progress: Marina had a job in a very good high school, Huang Xin's company had landed a major deal with the government, they moved to a modern duplex apartment as well as buying a semi-detached villa in the southern outskirts of the city. They were also considering a second car. When they met up with their friends (mostly doctors, prosecutors, CEOs and the like), the talk was all about who had the best tennis coach and the most trouble-free financial investments, how to find the best organic grocery shops and the food to be had at a particular Italian restaurant. On the surface, they had built successful lives for themselves. Yet Marina felt a dull ache, like a blunt knife cutting into her flesh, a looming shadow, as if a cancer was remorselessly eating away at her insides.

Once, she went with Huang Xin to a dinner party organised by the Young Entrepreneurs Association or some such organisation. The guests were bright and talented, the elite of the business world. As the meal progressed, Marina watched these self-confident, wonderfully amusing people circulating around the room, drinking toasts and hobnobbing and schmoozing each other. It was a seamless exercise in expanding their business networks, each of them aiming to build a thriving and enviable power base for themselves. That was the men. The womenfolk, meanwhile, talked about skincare products, luxury goods, their children's overseas study trips and other inconsequential topics, dropping in the occasional mention of some noteworthy achievement of their own or their husband's. It was all so familiar. It reeked of family aspirations, a heady smell that clung to the skin. And although the occasional guest became flustered, generally speaking the atmosphere was like a potent aphrodisiac; the men and the women radiated love for all and sundry.

Marina pushed the morsels of food around her tiny bowl, thinking glumly that this was a banquet of desires, oozing wealth and good cheer, staged in a blaze of lights and flowers, the tables covered with lights, glasses, ice cubes, saucers filled with condiments, bottles of wine, dishes of beautiful food . . . everything one could possibly imagine. While elsewhere, in dim rooms with flickering light bulbs, the potato-eater families sat together, silently chewing on their defeat and their hunger, tolerating each other's self-loathing and trying to keep each other warm.

Was there something wrong with her? She wondered. No, of course not. But she could not stop her thoughts ricocheting around like ping-pong balls. Her head hurt and her appetite had deserted her.

On the way home, Huang Xin totted up all the business cards he had collected during the evening. He was planning a selective little gathering the next week (he wanted to strike while the iron was hot), in the hopes that it would lead to more government-led deals for his company.

Marina drove, staring woodenly over the steering wheel, apparently in agreement with her husband. The scenes outside the car window flashed by: a pedestrian crossing illuminated by street lights, eddies of dust swirling in the night breeze, someone jogging along while pushing a bicycle, two migrant workers laughing and munching on kebabs, a skinny woman with a bulging laundry bag thrown over her shoulder. For some reason, she was suddenly overwhelmed with misery. She felt like a complete impostor. She should not have been swanning along in her car, she should have been slogging along the road on her own two feet.

This wasn't the first time it happened. Sometimes, when Marina was with Huang Xin and their friends, a dizzy, floaty feeling would come over her. She would pinch herself when no one was looking, casting panicked looks at the other faces in the room. Did they know she was a fraud? She had no emotional connection to Huang Xin. She could be the wife of any of the men here: she could walk with them into any of the five-star residential communities, under the rows of grey roofs and into spacious apartments, with their intercoms at the front doors and their identically-positioned TV and sofa, bed facing the same way, the toilet with same diameter of soil pipe. She could take off the same six-centimetre high heels as their wives, open the latest issue of the city's illustrated magazine, drink the same brand of milk and then spend much the same night with much the same man.

Why did she feel like she was losing her mind? She hoped that her rebellious streak had not reared its ugly head. She had left her humble origins so long ago, climbed so high, trained herself to be unemotional. Why was she spiralling down into this vortex of nostalgia, why was she so wrapped up in memories of Crossroads? She seemed unable to extricate herself and put those years behind her – the narrow-minded individuals who were out for anything they could get, the scars from her adolescence, the clambering and scrambling she'd had to do to get up the ladder and everything else she had turned her back on – none of it had gone away.

Stop it, stop it! Get a grip! She told herself that she just needed to give herself a good slap around the face. What she had to do right now was keep that serene smile firmly in place and pretend to be content, to keep moving forward and leave the past behind.

True, she sometimes resented her mother, as if it were her fault she was here, although that did not make much sense. She wanted to get out of Crossroads to have a better life in the city, didn't she? Still, she went back to the factory zone and to her mother's place less and less often to avoid talking to her. She was terrified of letting slip the dangerous thoughts that haunted her and could not bear to keep pretending to be vital and energetic.

Early one morning, Marina lay on her side in the darkness. She opened her eyes wide and stared at the man next to her, but all she could see was Crossroads, the suburb on the northern outskirts of the city with its dim streetlights, the dark corners where the amber glow could not reach, and that other man, also sleepless in a corner. Her dark, pinpoint pupils spun like newly-fired glass. They were appallingly hot, and she felt like there was a space inside them expanding and struggling to burst free that could not be opened up. Unbeknownst to her, the man lying next to her had also opened his eyes and was staring at her in bewilderment. She focussed and recognised him as Huang Xin, her husband, but ignored him and carried on with her cold, shadowy thoughts.

Huang Xin rolled towards her. His face was full of goodwill. If only Marina could fake it just a little, everything could be made whole again. No! Once again, she felt that wilful, steely determination in her heart. She would not pretend. She would let things break down, she refused to respond. She did not love him at all, she never had.

What was she going to do?

She seemed to come to a decision, her mind turning abruptly in another direction and conjuring up the image of a poisonous, coloured mushroom.

In the dim morning light, suddenly energised, she rolled agilely on top of Huang Xin, physically, violently, acting out her resolve. As she rode him, she stared sightlessly down at him, at his increasingly confused tremors, at the day that was to come. And so it began, that morning, with a fierce, frigid sexual act, with newly-legitimised sperm. That floating life was the gateway to the next phase, when Marina would become a stern, middle-class mother, tasked with the lengthy mission of bringing up the child, moving forward, eyes closed and thick-skinned, passing on the baton of this "good life" to the next generation, moving up the social pyramid in pursuit of yet more earthly possessions, more wealth, climbing higher and higher in society. Marina was completely cynical about it. She did not want this baby out of any kind of love: romantic love, sexual love, maternal love or any other kind. She just wanted to use it as a rope, as one more weapon in her armoury, to pull her upwards.

A month later, she realised that she had made a mistake, but she had thrown away her oars and could not sail back to shore. Every organ in her body felt nauseous in a way that had nothing to do with morning sickness. It was as if she could have vomited her entire body into a rubbish bin at any moment. Looking as white as a sheet, she went to the clinic determined to make an appointment for an abortion. As she waited, shivering, she suddenly heard a joyful shout. Someone was calling her name, the exact same voice that had shouted to her on campus at her teacher training college years before.

4

A S A FOURTH-YEAR STUDENT at university, Marina had taken an optional course in administration. The lecturer was a fiery speaker, who liked to quote from popular books to encourage his students during class. Marina made sure to read all those books, cover to cover, and took their teachings to heart. She became convinced that the only worthwhile thing for a human being to do in life was to succeed, everything else was valueless. It made her less inclined to be a teacher and she thought of switching to a profession that called for innovation, somewhere she could explore her potential and be a manager or a director.

Back then, management was a hot topic, with best-sellers that had titles like *How to Manage Your Own Company* or *Five Ways to be a Better Manager* on sale in airports and bookstores and featured in lectures and newspapers. Marina and her friends, like her peers in her generation, seemed to be obsessed with personal achievement and material success. It was only recently that it suddenly occurred to Marina that the lecturer was in fact mediocre and lazy, and spent most of his time flirting with the female students, telling them how to make their thighs look sexy (clench their knees together, and have a gap only two fingers' width between their thighs, no wider or narrower). But this did not make her despise the professor. On the contrary, she was somehow relieved to realise that the popular goal of "success" had a comical side.

The reason for mentioning this lecturer is because Marina remembered him presenting the Ishikawa, or fish bone, cause-and-effect diagram in class. Starting from the left, he drew the causes as branches on the blackboard, each one marked with a label in a small box. On the right-hand side was a big box, the effect. Marina smiled derisively to herself as she recalled this demonstration chart drawn with coloured chalk on the blackboard. It was outdated now, this management method, and she had never used it to analyse a project or a case. But maybe she should use it to analyse herself? How was she supposed to get to the last big box? Was it by hefting her great bulk over to Victor's house?

The Ishikawa diagram could also be drawn in reverse. There was the long, thin fish bone of her marriage to Huang Xin – collaborative, exemplary in social terms, but the atmosphere between them was tense at the best of times (although it is fair to say that Huang Xin was not at fault here).

The second fish bone, a very soft one, was Pearl. With someone like Pearl, Marina could not talk much about financial speculation. Compared with Marina's elegant friends, Pearl was dim: her IQ, her emotional intelligence, her understanding of finance and all other aspects of the world was low-to-moderate. She was a nobody, and Marina could safely ignore her. Yet there she was, in the gynaecology clinic, a vulgar fertility goddess, descending on Marina as she grappled with her fate in that gloomy waiting room, hauling her out into the open.

It was not a good time, but that didn't stop her. She was so loud! She told Marina all about Ding Bogang's memory loss, boasted about how Heipi stank of rubbish all the time, gave Marina a glimpse of her flaccid, empty belly, then shrilly exclaimed that Marina was going to have a baby. Marina could not help sighing at Pearl's simple-minded optimism and compared it to her own inner turmoil. People who had nothing were never afraid of losing because they had nothing to lose. She felt she wasn't even worth one of Pearl's toes. What was she afraid of? Why didn't she just leave Huang Xin? Let go of this life of excess, this hypocritical marriage. Run away!

As for the baby, she put her hand a little to the left of her naval, rested it there for a couple of minutes and patted her belly gently.

The baby inside moved a little. Lovingly, trustingly. Pearl was right: this little life was family.

It was Ash who could take credit for the third fish bone. He and Marina had met several times after he came back from the South.

They talked about Ding Bogang, although neither of them had been there when he died. They talked about the delicious aromas that used to waft from his kitchen and the thick gobs of grease that always seemed on the verge of dripping down the walls, the mesh screen he had cleverly made for their window from factory offcuts, the bicycle and the English-Chinese dictionary he had tried to bribe them with. And of course, they told each other stories about how he had lost his memory in his later years. They also talked about the care their mother had taken in arranging Ding Bogang's funeral, acknowledging, uneasily but with a degree of affection, that their mother had felt more for Ding Bogang than they could ever understand. But that was all water under the bridge. Both siblings fell silent for a while, mentally reevaluating the relationship between Ding Bogang and Su Qin.

On one particular day, however, Marina sensed that Ash actually wanted to talk about something else. He looked oddly furtive, a look she was familiar with.

"Come on, spit it out," she urged him. "It can't be that bad, can it?"

Her bump wasn't that big yet but sitting up was uncomfortable, so she was half-lying on the sofa and could see Ash's large bag which he had dragged along with him on his two previous visits as well.

Ash flashed a sunny smile at his sister and rubbed his chin. Then he admitted, "It's about Victor. You know I made it all up before. But now, when I think about it, I can see you knew all along. You beat me at my own game, didn't you?"

Marina shook her head and did not answer. So that was what he wanted to talk about. But it was all so long ago, it meant nothing now. Besides, didn't love always begin with making up things, misunderstandings, self-deception and cheating?

"The good thing is, you're clear-headed and you're tough. You were right to marry Huang Xin."

Ash sounded as old and wise as he always did. But then he went on: "So why are you acting like this now, what's all this about you two splitting up? And Mum tells me you were seeing Victor for a while before you got married. You should sort yourself out, do you hear me?"

Ash looked around the flat in annoyance.

Marina waved him away. She didn't want to hear this. Her present situation had nothing to do with Victor. She had to admit, though, that she was surprised. How did her mother know that she had been spending time with him? Why hadn't she said anything? It made her even more reluctant to go home.

Ash pressed his lips together and hummed and hawed a few times. Then he said a little awkwardly, "By the way, did Mum ever say anything to you about me?"

"She hasn't had the chance. You know I haven't been back for a long time. Speaking of, don't tell her about what's happening to me. She'll worry."

"I think she'll be more worried about me. I'm in a big mess right now. I'll tell you about Lao Shan."

Actually, Ash didn't know much about Lao Shan – where he had come from or where he was going to. He might have been ten years or thirty years older than Ash, he really had no idea. There were some people in this world whose age and occupation were not important. What counted was that he could control the air, the people and the things around him.

Ash had met Lao Shan when he was twenty years old. Fresh out of college, he had been given a job in the local mapping bureau, where he had a desk in the north-facing draughtsman's office for two years. The scale rulers and the precise positioning of rivers and roads made him feel utterly trapped, like a tiny pebble thrown into this unknown city, destined to be grown over by moss. He'd tried hard to find a girlfriend but honestly, women disgusted him. He could not forget how they used to grope and pet him, tutting over this poor, fatherless boy. That included his mother and sister. The fishy smell of their periods had permeated his teenage years and he loathed it. As for the men, they were even worse, with their lewd talk about the opposite sex. It reminded him of the hand in the window, and the lingering fear it had inspired.

Down in the South, fat, fair-skinned Ash stood out among the dark-skinned, wiry southern males. He used to look around him in confusion, like a migrant bird blown off course. Stranded amid the ebb and flow of the crowds, he cut such a submissive figure that he inevitably drew the unwelcome attention of the local toughs.

The first time they met, Lao Shan had jerked his chin at Ash but spoken with curious gentleness.

"Come with me," he commanded, and led him away from the main street to where a Passat was parked. Lao Shan was a skinny man with an educated air, who wore two delicate strings of gleaming beads around his wrists.

He was apparently in no hurry to talk to Ash, and concentrated on driving. Ash sat silently, occasionally casting sideways glances at him, but mostly peered outside at the blaze of lights from the city's buildings. He felt anesthetised somehow – he could not bring himself to exert any willpower or even think for himself. He would just do whatever this man beside him told him to do. He already felt dependent on him. From now on, there was no need to worry about anything. He imagined that this was the river that he was destined to go down. Ash closed his eyes, perfectly at ease.

Later, the psychologists kept urging him to recall that day, to face up to Lao Shan's unfathomable gaze. He had to admit that it was weird, the way he had let himself be befriended so casually.

The psychologists, twirling their pens and trying to be patient, apparently found it as hard to believe as he did.

"There must be other details. Think! Think hard!" they insisted.

Ash had remained silent. Every counselling session got stuck at this point, as he tried unsuccessfully to work his way back to that moment when, without a second's hesitation, he had gone along with Lao Shan. But Ash was happy to tell his shrink what happened next.

Lao Shan took him into a room filled with an enormous sofa and an equally large bed and turned on a small lamp which lit up in a reddish-purple hue. It shone on their faces and bodies, faint but alluring, accentuating the dips and bulges in their flesh. Lao Shan explained to Ash that he used to do photography and had always liked darkroom light bulbs.

"Look, it's like we're swimming in these colours," Lao Shan said quietly, stroking Ash's neck.

When he got to this part of the story, Ash looked his shrink in the eyes and spoke slowly to make his point.

"But I couldn't do it. I fled like a scalded cat. I just could not do it with him."

He saw, to his satisfaction, that the psychologist was bewildered. It was at this point that Ash usually repeated the same plea he had made when he was booking an appointment: "But I hate women's bodies too. I just want you to tell me what's wrong with me."

Lao Shan had tried a few more times and each time Ash rejected him. Lao Shan had even patted his sofa cushions, saying, "Look how big and soft they are! Imagine how much rolling around we could do."

On the last occasion, as Ash was leaving, Lao Shan took out a bank card and tapped Ash on his chubby buttocks with it.

"Take this and pay for an appointment with a shrink. Then come back to me when you're sorted. I've got a thing about you, and I never misjudge anyone," he said with bravado.

But Ash deleted Lao Shan from his phone. What do I do next? he asked himself, Which side am I on?

He liked Lao Shan, but hated him too, because Ash had thought he could see a way forward and now Lao Shan had blocked it for him.

Soon after his last meeting with Lao Shan, a shrink had actually called him and, with great seriousness, invited him to make an appointment. Ash stammered but felt he could not refuse because Lao Shan's name was dropped into the conversation. Fine, fine, he would give in. But once he went, dammit, he found himself enjoying the sessions, they gave him something to do. He treated his psychological problems as seriously as his work, and enjoyed being forced to interrogate his feelings. Without mincing words, it was like being forced to take a shit. He would go red in the face, straining, and then strain some more as, little by little, he forced his feelings out.

They really knew how to analyse you, these shrinks. He had no idea that he had so much stuff bottled up, or that he had grown up so damaged. He really had been a poor little boy. He had not only gone without a father's love, but his mother didn't love him either. No one did. He had never experienced a loving family, or lasting friendship, or sibling love. He had never felt safe and secure. He needed someone to care for him! Ash listened as the psychologist started by speaking in deadpan tones, so earnest, so logical and scientific. But then the conversation would become confusing, and the man or woman would get defensive, and when that happened, Ash knew it was time to move on. He would find another doctor and start over, digging and poking into the layers of emotion that had yet to be uncovered.

After a while, as he went from psychologist to psychologist, he became known for being undiagnosable. But he was also a model patient, beloved by all the clinics. It was his classic symptoms, his cherry-red face as he eagerly dug into his memories of the most trivial cock-ups, his familiarity and cooperation with all the reasoning processes, his willingness to try all the new tests coming from the West, his promptness in paying his bills. As time went by, the spewing and excreting actually seemed to have a physical effect: Ash's fat began to melt away and he lost weight. It was like he was going through puberty for a second time, getting taller as he got thinner, his eyes emerging from their fleshy folds and his chin acquiring definition. By now, his clothes hung so loosely on him, he looked like a starving artist.

The malicious thought occurred to him that if Lao Shan saw the results, he might regret leaving his bank card with him.

Ash's last shrink was an ugly, scrawny woman with a mouth full of nicotine-stained teeth, but with unassailable self-confidence. She threw him a big pile of pornographic pictures, like vocab cards, and made him classify them into race, skin colour, hair styles, peculiarities of the fingers and organs and sexual positions. She fixed Ash with a merciless glare, recording how long he paused on each card. She kept taking off and putting on her wide-rimmed glasses, asking strange questions: "What do you feel? Are you tense? Dry mouth? Spittle? Which one do you hate the most? If you were looking for a film star to go around with you, who would you want to be with you? Look at this one, does it get you excited, or does it disgust you?"

Ash did not like her approach. He felt disorientated, and the sessions left him mentally and physically drained. How he longed to be back with those early psychologists. This woman was ugly and difficult!

Finally, she threw her stub of a pencil down and announced authoritatively, "The fact is, you're just a homosexual stuck at the oral fixation stage. Your aversion to both homosexuality and heterosexuality comes from conscious inertia, but the body of an adult has its own independent processes. So, currently, your physical development and needs have caught up with you, but your psychological desires are still stuck in the past. Do you see? So take your time and at some point, maybe soon, when they're synchronised, you will come back to the normal world again."

She had a large metal ball on her desk table densely covered with symbols, which she was slowly rotating. Suddenly, she paused and shot him a sly look.

"But young man, that's not the most important thing. This ball tells me that deep inside you, you're carrying a big burden. Did you ever mess up in a major way? Were the consequences serious? You need to get that sorted out before you can emerge from your oral fixation. Let's talk about that the next time we meet!"

Ash walked out of the clinic, waxen-faced, the humid air clinging like a shroud to his body. He did not want to see this woman again. He was scared of the metal ball, of the way she had spun it and saw something to tell him off about. He didn't like it one bit. All these psychologists thought he was deficient, everyone despised him, no one really cared about him. But this woman had put her finger on something and he did not like it.

That night, Ash's bed felt like a ship being tossed in the ocean waves.

In the past few years, various bits of news from home had reached him: the restructuring and layoffs in the factory zone, the neighbourhood committees, Marina's marriage, Heipi the King of Scrap, Ding Bogang's memory loss, Vic's glass workshop and so on. Some things left him cold but there were two pieces of news that really troubled him – Victor leaving his job to set up on his own, and Marina's breakneck decision to get married. Ash was as sensitive as he had always been, and the fact that these two events occurred almost simultaneously made him extremely uneasy. They felt perilously close together. Of course, he could have continued to bury his head deep in the South, pretending that it was none of his business. But that wretched woman psychologist had triggered something in Ash and he could ignore it no longer, as though he'd been woken by a blinding light shining into his eyes in the middle of the night. A memory hit him like a ton of bricks.

When he woke up in the morning, he found he had fallen out of bed and had one leg resting on some packages under the bed. They were the kids' clothes Victor had sent him before he opened his glass business. He felt pain in his toes where they pressed on the bag and deliberately pressed harder, making them hurt more. Inside, he felt deeply confused. Was this what that old witch had foretold?

Should he go home, so he could try and recalibrate himself?

There was one thing he could not leave behind when he left. He dragged the case from under the bed and pulled out the exercise books. He'd kept them with him for ten years or more, and the pages were limp and yellowed. His vision suddenly blurred and he found he lacked the courage to read them. They felt like a great jumble of his past. He hurriedly bundled them together, grimacing and sucking in his breath as he did so.

He packed them, together with Victor's old clothes, into the biggest zipper bag he had.

Now, telling all of this to Marina left Ash dry in the mouth from talking. As if these exercise books were crucial evidence, he got them out of the bag by the sofa and, with fingers that were stiff and unwieldy, pushed them towards Marina.

It was the middle of the night, half the city's lights had been turned off and the streets were silent and dark. It was impossible to tell which year or month they were in. Marina was exhausted, barely able to sit upright. She pressed her hand into her aching back and, through her tears, she began to read: about the factory zone air, his vulva sketch, the hand coming through her window, Saturday's silent but satisfying dinners.

She felt terribly sorry for her brother. Why had it never occurred to her that Ash had set her up with Victor for a reason? Poor kid! Of the six of them, only he, the most vulnerable, had genuinely loved them and nurtured high hopes for both sides of the family. She felt so guilty. If only she could turn back time, if only she had paid a little more attention to Ash and acted like a real sister, even if it was just to boss him around, his life today would be different. At least he would not have unquestioningly jumped into an older man's car.

She remembered one Wednesday when Ash had suddenly woken her up in the middle of the night clinging to the edge of her bed. Shaking like a leaf and wiping tears from his eyes, he told her he'd had a bad dream. In the dream, someone told him to shout "Dad" and he had tried with all his might, pouring with sweat, opening and closing his lips, but no sound came out. It was like a foreign language that he couldn't get his tongue around. It was horrible. After all, he'd had a father and had shouted his name countless times, hadn't he? What was a dad? Why didn't he know?

"You don't know? It doesn't matter! Just shout!"

The stranger in his dream gave a harsh laugh that felt like a slap in the face.

Ash had sobbed as if his heart was broken. He huddled next to her in his quilt and begged her to talk about his father.

Marina remembered adjusting the shade of the bedside lamp so that it shone on the ceiling, making the small room look quite strange. She looked at the circle of light and said smugly, "Oh, you're much too young to remember. He was in the hospital for over a year before he died, so of course you don't remember him. I'm telling you, I'm the only one in our family who really thinks about him, all the time! All these years, I've never forgotten him. Even when we go Over There, I take my dad with me in my heart. I tell him everything I see, all my thoughts!"

Ash was impressed by his sister's words. A little tentatively, as if he was asking about a neighbour who had just moved in, he asked, "So, what was he really like?"

"Well, he had shiny black leather shoes. He spoke Russian and he taught me how to roll my tongue around the sounds to get them right. It was hard, but I learned it. He could use a sewing machine, and he got hold of a sewing pattern and made me a pink ski jacket, the first one in our school. He used to play the mouth organ. He played it to me at bedtime, and he played it more and more quietly till I fell asleep. And his favourite thing to do after dinner was to take us for a walk and tell jokes."

Marina seemed to have a never-ending stock of stories about their dad, ready to pluck out at random.

"Did Dad love me?" Ash asked cautiously.

"Huh, don't be silly, you didn't even understand the jokes, you didn't know which bits to laugh at!"

She looked back now, as a cold-blooded observer, and was very aware that in these cheery stories, there was a lot that she had made up, or at least embellished. She had taken liberties. It was her way of owning her father and mourning him alone. She added elegant touches and intimate details, all in aid of giving meaning and depth to her lonely quest. She had been smug, and enjoyed being cruel. She had stared at Ash, who remembered nothing, enjoying his alienation and misery. Who knows, maybe it was her indifference that had pushed her brother almost over the edge.

She did not want to admit it, but she had been brutal, hard, self-righteous and self-centred, not just to Ash and not just on those occasions. She had acted as if other people's feelings were meaningless, as if they were inanimate objects that experienced nothing. Her struggles and her achievements, they were the only things that mattered. Maybe she even blamed their father for dying young, for shirking his responsibilities. If she had had a father who protected and loved her, even sometimes spoiled her, surely she would never have grown up so cold and flinty, punishing everyone around her, and herself too. It was terrible. And now, was it all too late? If only she had nothing to her name, she could vanish into the crowd. All she wanted was to be a person who could cry, who was in touch with her feelings.

Marina stacked the exercise books into a neat, orderly pile and said, "Listen, kid, that business you talked about, it's nothing, nothing at all. It's just a matter of adjusting. I'll stick with you. I'm more off-kilter than you are and I need to do some adjusting too. Don't worry, I'm on your side no matter what. You just wait and see, I'll turn over a new leaf and be a great sister to you from now on."

Ash clasped his hands and looked down. He appeared not to care. He stuffed the exercise books back into the bag, and put on his grown-up voice again.

"Come home and stay for a bit. Tell Mum what's been going on with you. We can't both turn our backs on her. Plus, our old apartment is going to be demolished next month."

Marina reached out across her enormous bump and gave her brother an affectionate hug, like she should have when he was still eight years old and their father had just died. Ash felt hot tears falling down the back of his neck. Marina was murmuring something.

"I hope you understand why I left Huang Xin. I'm like you, looking for myself. Hopefully it's not too late for me. I really, genuinely want to be a good daughter, a good sister to you, and soon, a good mother too."

"Not a good wife?" Ash shot back.

Marina checked herself for a moment then gave a hesitant, dreamy smile.

"That depends if I get the chance."

For a long time after Ash had left, Marina stood at the window looking out at the city where the lights were gradually turning on and the skyline was taking shape, watching a flock of early-rising birds go by. She felt a sudden stirring of emotion. She really was determined to go back to Crossroads and sort out everything she had left behind. She even thought that would be the fairest thing for Huang Xin. What he needed was a decent, good-hearted woman for a wife, not her.

Just now, the fish bones in the Ishikawa diagram were pointing her only towards leaving Huang Xin and becoming a single mother. But she was still worried about how she would live, and dreaded her mother's reaction. She did not want to move too far too fast or cross the line with Victor, not just yet.

A month later, the fourth fish bone jabbed her and drew blood. It was her farewell to their old home in the rainstorm.

She had still not turned into a good daughter. It may have had something to do with the weather. The rainstorm fuelled their anger, drowned out their good sense and extinguished the increasingly burdensome love between mother and daughter. She met her mother for just half an hour, but they fought for twenty minutes of it, most fiercely about Victor.

After that, Marina turned around and walked quickly away in the rain, ignoring Ash's desperate calls. The further she went, the more she had misgivings about her angry outburst. Even if she was willing to break the promise she had made to her mother, even if Victor did take her in, it was a crazy plan. But really, it was the weird weather that was to blame. The rainstorm overhead made her blood surge. She felt that magical energy from the past flooding back again, along with the lightning strike of passion. Everything was possible – love and friendship, even, she fantasised, being a good wife to Victor. She made up her mind to take herself and her bump to Victor and accept what came – whether he turned his back or embraced her. She would take what fate meted out, no matter how challenging.

Her decision may have been reckless, but at least she had Pearl to back her up. Pearl had an even more exaggerated, albeit fake, bump to contend with. Marina pictured the pair of them making a pact like two intrepid warriors, holding their bellies, real and fake, primed to go off like bombs, setting off to search for Heipi and Victor, ready to mend fences and embrace their loves. Everything was guiding them along the fish bones towards a resolution.

5

ONE OF THE CONSEQUENCES of the blast was the huge heaps of broken glass. These mountains of debris were comprised of shards from floor-to-ceiling windows, glassed-in balconies, sliding bathroom doors, TV screens, bottles of wine, glass-topped dining tables, large vases, fruit dishes and fish tanks. For a week afterwards, the whole of Crossroads was filled with people enthusiastically wielding brooms and shovels. They cleared the glass as casually as they swept up the debris of firecrackers on Chinese New Year, gossiping animatedly all the while.

There were endless conversations to be had about the damage caused by the explosion, about the real number of casualties as compared with the number published in the media (especially if someone knew one of the victims), about the investigation into the cause of the accident, about how much would be paid out in compensation (the estimates inflated as the speakers got more and more animated) and about some minor official who had been scapegoated and was going to lose her job. The locals, young and old, began to bandy around media buzzwords like "propylene gas leaks", "multiple subcontracting of demolition works" and "lack of drawings for underground pipelines" as familiarly as they talked about the cucumbers and bitter melons in their shopping baskets.

The rows of buildings that lined the street nearest the epicentre had all their glass doors and windows blown out. The occupants now found themselves exposed to view, as if they were on a stage for all to see. They almost looked naked. You could stand down below in the street and watch them folding their underwear in their rooms, chopping meat and bones in their grease-smeared kitchens and tying up bundles of old newspapers on their balconies. It was very entertaining.

As for the underground pipes that were the cause of the accident, it was almost a matter of pride to point out how uniquely well-supplied the factory zone had been. Such a plethora of pipes, intricately entangled, as complex in their layout as a hand-knitted woollen sweater. Those pipes had been servicing the entire community, kept busy carrying ethylene, propylene, chlorine, windscreen washer fluid and solvents, supplying natural gas or diesel, emitting methanol, xylene and waste gas, oil and wastewater. In other locations, underground pipes were limited to supplying water, telephone cables and gas, but not Crossroads. Anything and everything you could imagine went along those pipes.

As for the guys who had installed pipes, they had been onto a cushy number. They had been able to install several tons of pipes in one go, and even if they had to pay out the local officials, they had still done extremely well out of their contracts. The locals didn't hold it against them. Who'd be stupid enough to miss out on a chance like that? So the only person left to blame was the man reckless enough to light a cigarette while walking through Crossroads. People sucked in their breath as they imagined him being blown to bits. Of course, at the forefront of their minds was how much would be paid out in compensation.

According to rumours, each square metre of glass would be compensated at over a hundred yuan. That was more than the market rate, so it was definitely a good deal. Further rumours went that some particularly opportunistic folk were quickly smashing old windows and doors that had actually survived the explosion unscathed in order to put in claims.

"There's one guy who's going to make a fortune – Victor, with his Glass House. He had glass from front to back, inside and out! He'll be able to retire on it. He won't have to open more than a few times a year!"

"But haven't you heard? The poor lad didn't make it. His whole workshop exploded. I mean, it was right at the end of the street, right by the main pipe that was leaking. Poor guy, he died a bachelor too!"

While the shards of glass in Crossroads danced and crunched under people's brooms, Marina was dancing in an abyss. For five whole days, she hovered between life and death, lying in her hospital bed, her left cheek adorned with that petal-like red slash.

She had passed out for an instant at the moment of the explosion, before her brain calmly resumed its imaginings. She had to move on! It wouldn't be easy but, come what may, she had to get to Victor.

She saw herself lumbering along until she got to The Glass House. Then, suddenly timid, she came to a halt. She had stopped at the large mirror by the door and looked at her reflection, patting her hair and the silk scarf around her neck. For some reason the woman in the mirror looked a little sad and unconfident, so Marina smiled encouragingly at her. She would walk in and embrace him tightly. They had never hugged properly before. This time she had to do it properly, squeeze him tight till his ribs cracked, cling to him like she was drowning. She would whisper into his ear, whisper the most loving words she could think of, spill out all the love and longing that she had suppressed all these years.

Marina sucked in her belly. It was a surprising reminder that she was about to have a baby. She was so big, she looked like a balloon-seller. The balloons really got in the way, she seemed to have them all over her. They were ugly, and were going to make it difficult to embrace anyone. Exasperated, she almost cried in frustration. If only she were the slender girl she had once been, if only she could turn the clock back to when she was twenty-two, or even younger, in her first year at university, her best time.

In the end, Marina saw herself calmly and quietly pushing open the glass door. It felt like she was coming home. She remembered her meetings with Victor before she was married and how they had always tried to be calm and restrained, like they could preserve the moment if they trod cautiously through the river of time.

The moment her hand touched the door handle and she was about to push it, something clicked and the door opened automatically. She stepped inside and found herself on a white sandy beach. The blue skies overhead were intermittently shrouded in fog. There was no one around. Why wasn't he here? He should have been waiting for her. She had come with such expectations and expended such effort to get here. She didn't want to wait a second longer. Had she got the time wrong? Or was he avoiding her?

Marina felt desolate. She walked further and further into the empty space. As she looked around, she suddenly thought of her father's small niche in the columbarium (Number 64503, Room 8, Floor 5, Runyang District) she used to visit. So many dead people there, she knew them all by name. Then she thought of Ding Bogang's wife's lonely, overgrown grave, where she had hung back in fear. She felt like it was nodding and greeting her. Victor had taken her and Ash on a walk through the cemetery under the warm spring sunshine over the fresh green grass that carpeted the graves. Why was she thinking of that now? Was she approaching death herself? It felt very familiar and peaceful.

She was not afraid of death, never had been. Death was not disappearing, it was just moving somewhere else while sleeping in the hearts of loved ones, just as her father slept in her heart, and his "Beloved Wife, Huang Xiuming" slept in Ding Bogang's heart. Even the loneliest of souls had a place in someone's heart. But before she died, there was one thing she had to do: she had to see Victor again, even if it was just to say a few words.

She turned a corner, and the empty beach suddenly became Crossroads. It was very crowded, not with people but with fragments of memory, jostling her as they rushed past, nearly knocking her off her feet: her and Victor's first meeting in the Dings' living room fourteen years ago, the way they avoided each other's eyes at the dinner table on Saturdays, the way his slender eyes narrowed as he recited a string of chemical terms to do with glass-making, the green torch he insisted on buying her, Crossroads in the drizzle, dozens of fists landing on him as he protected his head with his hands and did not resist, her bewilderment at the teacher training college, her checking his bruises in the depths of the abandoned factory, him choosing a husband for her . . . And the very last image, the wedding candy dissolving in their mouths.

Through the bars of light and shadow, the details hurtled past her, brushing against her skin.

"Wait!" she cried, "Wait, please!"

She was left with memories as empty as a destitute family's food cupboard. There was nothing to grab hold of, they were mere illusions. Marina groped around her, trying to hold on to these moments, begging them to stay for a while. But they slipped away mischievously, heartlessly.

She ran on, begging, searching, until at last she saw Victor, bathed in a sepia-coloured light like an old photograph. He looked as laidback as ever, crouched on the edge of the pavement at the corner, a cigarette in his hand, eyes narrowed as he puffed on it. Yet she could hardly make out that dear face. It was as if she was looking at him through a fog. Fine white silk trailed over him, curling and rippling around his silhouette the way a drop of black ink sinks and dissolves in water. Then he was gone, taking with him her goodbyes and her prayers.

Marina stopped and stood still. She wanted to stay there forever, asleep between the fog and the water.

6

Marina was still in a coma. The doctors' prognosis was bleak. They said that it was as if the patient had lost the will to live. The family had not been allowed to see the premature baby girl and knew little about how she was doing. The nurses rushed in and out of Marina's room, avoiding their questions. Pearl came to the hospital every day for news. Her face was puffy and she looked unkempt and slovenly. She dragged her feet as if she were shackled and tended to shrink into a corner if she saw anyone, even Su Qin. The two of them sometimes came across each other in the observation room, but Pearl kept her distance and only answered direct questions with a grunt.

Luckily, Su Qin found things to keep her busy after the accident. She always brought two plastic bags with her and clucked over them like a mother hen, even at Marina's bedside. They contained the beads she needed to sew onto the Korean hair accessories, and as soon as she sat down, she would start work, her two hands moving like a machine, her face expressionless, concentrating as if she had a deadline to meet in an hour's time. She did not talk much to Pearl and did not appear to notice the latter's uncharacteristic shyness, or her characteristically bulging (but completely empty) belly.

One day, however, after the doctor had left the room, Pearl suddenly muttered to Su Qin, "If she does wake up, what will we do?"

She sounded as if she wanted Marina to stay in a coma.

Su Qin was studying a crystal flower under the light, scrutinising it for defects and deciding whether it was worth adding to the hair clip she was working on. She made no attempt to respond.

Pearl moved closer to Su Qin, her head bowed, picked up a nursing pillow they had prepared for the baby and held it over her mouth and chin. Speaking in a strangled voice, Pearl tearfully confessed, "Auntie Su, I've been scared to say this up till now, but what if Marina wakes up? I really don't know what to tell her. All this is because of Heipi, and my bump. My bump . . ."

She trailed off, wringing her hands like a prisoner in court.

"Why don't I tell you about it first, as a sort of trial run?"

Su Qin gave Pearl a bemused look. Then she shifted her gaze to Marina's flattened abdomen and stiffened involuntarily. Marina remained unconscious, her face as pale as marble, impervious to every sensation and feeling. Su Qin, however, shushed Pearl, picked up her bags and gently steered her into the corridor.

They headed to the fire escape, where Pearl clumsily sat down on the stairs. She began to stammer out her story, her voice echoing in the narrow space. The sequence of events was a bit muddled and certain unnecessary details crept in.

The morning of Heipi's disappearance, Pearl had been woken by her husband's mobile phone. She shouted for him and realised he wasn't home. She remembered that she had confessed to him the day before that she was not actually pregnant. Ignoring the pang of regret she felt at this, Pearl answered the phone.

The call was from the guys at the demolition site. They appeared to be taking it in turns to talk. In deafening yells, they told Pearl they needed the drawings for the underground pipework. Five minutes later, they called again, with the same message. They told her that the demolition was urgent, they had a deadline, a buyer had been found for the pipes, a good price agreed and a truck would be collecting them that afternoon. Heipi's job had to be completed by noon, come what may!

Pearl dealt with the callers with great patience. She sounded like a very polite but thoroughly incompetent temp.

"I'm not Heipi, I'm his wife," she told them. "Who are you? I see. The project has been transferred to you? I'm sorry, I didn't know.

My Heipi, I mean, my boss, he wouldn't have the drawings, would he? We were commissioned by another company. Of course, our Heipi would have given them to you if he had them. What would we keep the drawings for? We can't eat them or wear them, can we? Or make money out of them!"

Eventually the men hung up, but until then Pearl kept on performing these verbal gymnastics. To her way of thinking, the more polite she was, the less angry Heipi would be. He might even come home. He might be standing outside the door listening at this very moment. This was his home, after all. It wasn't like the old days when he used to go and doss down in a rundown hotel and get drunk.

"Auntie Su," Pearl said seriously. "Do you know about the Walk-on-Water shoes? No? Never mind, Marina knows. We can talk about them later. I've searched all over the house and they're missing. The thing is, with the explosion . . . Forget it, I don't want to talk about that. I want to tell you about the demolition job."

At this point, she skipped backwards in time by about a month.

Heipi had received a big job. It had been subcontracted to him and what he took on was only a part of it, but it was the biggest slice of any cake he had had since he started in this business.

He rented two hydraulic presses and three forklift trucks, and hired a dozen strong workers to do the heavy lifting. They worked around the clock, swarming over the newly-abandoned buildings like ants, collecting steel bars and wire, PVC pipes, electrical cables and equipment, switches and plugs, door handles, wooden doors and windows, chairs and stools, beams, concrete piers and undamaged bricks. Most valuable of all was the maze of underground pipework. There were top-quality cast-iron pipes, and the elbows were copper – it was a gold-mine, as Ding Bogang would have put it. Heipi was over the moon.

Pearl's belly was at its most pregnant around then, thanks to the combined efforts of such nourishing dishes as pork chops, beef, fried eggs and leek pasties, along with the way she carried it out and proud with absolute confidence. It was like an insurance policy for her future happiness. Heipi gloated at the sight.

He was so chuffed that he put on a real performance for Pearl's bump, addressing it through her jumper and jacket.

"You know what, sonny?" he'd boasted, "This is one big deal your daddy's landed, son, and I'm only telling you, no one else. It's the biggest plant in the whole of the factory zone, and there's loads to reclaim. It's the alkylbenzene plant, you wouldn't understand what that is, but it doesn't matter. You'll never need to understand, kiddo, because your daddy's gonna tear it up and tear it down and there'll be nothing left! We're gonna make a fortune out of this job! Enough to send you to a bilingual kindergarten! Son, I just need you to grow up good and strong, so when I'm done with this job, you'll be ready to spend the money!"

Pearl went around with her nose in the air like a queen, as proud as could be, ignoring Heipi yacking on to her bump below. She wasn't worried about the emptiness of her belly, she believed in Marina and even more so in herself. After all, the two of them were discussing it, weren't they? Their combined efforts would solve all these troublesome problems, no sweat.

Pearl now leapt forward in time, to the night before the accident when she and Marina had made an agreement.

"It was getting dark, and I –"

She abruptly cut herself off. Was she going to talk about going to Victor's workshop to report the happy event? She hadn't thought that through, especially whether or not to tell Marina, so she skipped over it. It was getting dark and she hurried home, she said instead.

She had a shower and dressed, choosing the baggiest top she had. Then she hoisted up the hem and showed off her dome-like belly to Heipi. Her plump whiteness, which had never seen the light of day, was a stark contrast to her husband, who was dark-skinned and skinny from his work at the construction site.

"Come here, feel my bump," she commanded him. Remarkably,

this was the first time she had said that since she announced her pregnancy. Her belly had always been off-limits to Heipi – the nearest he ever got to it had been through three layers of clothing.

Heipi was delighted, but restrained himself and pulled her top down.

"Come on, don't scare our son. You always said my smell would scare him! Besides, what's there to feel?"

And he took a few steps back.

Pearl pulled her hem up again, imploring Heipi with her eyes.

"Take a good look! You think I look pregnant? Have you ever seen an eight-month pregnant belly?"

"No, I haven't. But I know some women are small and you're fat, so it doesn't show that much. I know that!"

And with that he pulled her top down again.

Pearl gave up. It was time to be blunt.

"Now listen to me, Heipi. I got it wrong. I'm not pregnant. All that's in my big belly is my guts and fat. It's called phantom pregnancy, or if you want the long name, hysterical abdominal distention syndrome. You can ask the doctor, it's a proper illness. You want a baby so badly that your belly gets bigger."

She flashed her empty belly at him again.

Heipi frowned, considering, then laughed.

"Really! What's this all about? I know I've been mean to you lately, but I'm just busy with that big job, getting more money for our son. I give you my word as your husband that I haven't been to any hookers. I've been absolutely faithful to you and to our son. Stop messing around, just say what you want! Is it money?"

"I'm not messing around. I really don't have a baby in my belly. I just wanted to make you happy," Pearl whispered. She gripped the edge of the table tightly so she wouldn't go down so fast if Heipi whacked her.

He stared at her. His weathered face, like old bark, slowly took on a dark, stubborn expression.

"It can't be true! You remember when we went to thank Auntie

Su, how happy we were that day, and how happy she was too! And your dad, you remember I went to pour wine on his grave and tell him he was going to have a grandchild. How could you let them down like that? And look at me, look at my hands, they're ingrained with dirt. Smell the smell on me!"

Heipi spluttered, close to tears.

"You listen to me, in another month, you've got to give me a baby! All my mates know, all my family back home have been told, all the shops around here, they all know that Heipi's going to be a father. You can't take that away! I'll never be able to hold up my head in Crossroads again!"

"I told you, I was lying to you!" Pearl insisted, getting impatient. Why hasn't he beaten me up yet? she thought, I'd rather have a good, honest beating and get it over with. She suddenly grasped the threadbare rayon top she was wearing and ripped it from neck to hem with all her might. Her great white belly loomed over the torn fabric, which dangled at her waist as if it was a new fashion trend.

"Don't worry, I'll do the embarrassing bits," she assured him. "Tomorrow I'll go and tell everyone we know that I made a mistake. Auntie Su, Vic, even my dad in his grave. It's fine, everyone knows what I'm like, they won't laugh."

Heipi took another step back and, from where he stood, sorrowfully reached out both hands to Pearl's belly. He looked like he was holding an unborn baby in mid-air.

"Pearl, we've been married for six years and in all that time you never got pregnant. I gave up, I would have stuck to betting and visiting hookers. It was you and that Auntie Su of yours who ganged up on me. You got my hopes up again. What were you thinking?"

A spasm of anguish crossed his face.

"I don't understand how you could lie about something as big as having a baby! That's a whopper of a mistake you made!"

Suddenly he was sobbing. His wits seemed to have deserted him as rivers of tears poured down his face, like the first time Pearl met him in the early hours of the morning in his hotel room. But this time the air was thick with grief and heartache rather than embarrassment.

"But I have to believe you, I want to believe you!" he wailed. "The more I believe, the happier I am! And you know why? Because you see, I can't believe you'd mess with me like that. You're not lying to me, you're messing with me, you're not treating me like a human being, you're crushing my heart underfoot, you're twisting it round and round! You're the one person who wouldn't do that to me, Pearl, you know what a hard life I've had."

His nose twitched and he took a breath and said more calmly, "You should have thought of this when you first dreamed up the idea, wife of mine! What are we going to do now? You've torn me apart. You've made me not want to see you anymore, and not want to earn money, either. And I worked so hard for Luo's World Resources, so we could eat and live well!"

Pearl was gripping the table so hard that her hands were sore. To be honest, she was pleased. She felt that things were going well. Finally, Heipi was figuring things out. Besides, what difference was there between lying and messing with someone? It wasn't like she'd done it out of malice, after all.

Later that night, she heard him on the phone. It sounded as if he was passing on some work to someone. He sounded impatient, but although she was curious, she didn't dare eavesdrop. She didn't know anything about the scrap trade anyway. Later on, in the small hours of the night, Heipi went out. He wasn't trying to be quiet. He walked around the flat for a bit and even went up into the loft, and then he was gone. Pearl was vaguely aware of his to-ing and fro-ing, and it occurred to her that he must have been so angry that he had gone to look for a hooker. She thought about getting up, but what could she say if she did? There was nothing to say. These days, they had nothing to talk about but the baby, and now there was no baby. Moreover, without her bargaining chip, she was hardly in a position to stop him going out for a bit of fun. That night she slept like a log, better than in a very long time. Telling the truth really was the best sleeping pill.

Back in the hospital, Pearl confessed all of her sins to Su Qin: "So, you see, Auntie Su, if I hadn't slept so soundly that night, if I'd talked to him about this a day later or a day earlier, things wouldn't have turned out like this."

She spread both her hands flat on her thighs and smoothed the creases in her trousers until she was satisfied. She picked up the bag she had been using as a chair cushion and fished out a creased envelope. She extracted a thin piece of paper, a sheet torn from medical records, and began to read aloud, stumbling over the words.

"I got the hospital to examine me and there's a problem: non-attachment of the uterine wall."

She held it out, staring intently at Su Qin like she had just presented damning evidence and was waiting to be charged with a crime. She looked like she really wanted a death sentence.

Su Qin, who had been so tense and aloof and busy these last few days, suddenly softened. Pearl's arrival and confession had triggered a cathartic release in her, akin to the resolution in *Crime and Punishment*. She threw down the Korean hair accessories she still had in her hands, scrambled over to take Pearl's hand and gently pressed her mountainous belly. A profusion of apologies spilled from her lips.

"Pearl, you mustn't think that, it's my fault! It's all my fault! I'm just a useless old woman. You know, I ruined both my children. And I really thought I could help you. I never imagined you wouldn't be able to get pregnant. I thought I was so clever, jumping in feet first, I wanted to teach Heipi a lesson . . . But you ended up riding a tiger you couldn't get off! And your brother, if only I'd found a job for him, he would never have set up that ridiculous glass workshop. I really let your father down, I'm so sorry! I never got anything right. You can't imagine how I feel right now, Pearl!"

Su Qin made it sound as if everything that had happened in the past was entirely her fault, like she had let everyone down. Her voice sounded old and weak and her lips were flecked with spittle.

7

MARINA MADE A huge effort to open her eyes. She felt as if the immense weight of an iron fence was being prised off her. Her head was spinning and her ears were roaring. She shut her eyes and tried again. This time, the world was askew, a heap of blurry images seen from faraway, through layers of dirty glass. For a moment she thought the stubbly-chinned male face floating in front of her was her husband, Huang Xin.

She remembered that the night before she set off for Vic's glass workshop, after she said goodbye to Pearl, she had spent a whole three hours in her room composing a long email to Huang Xin. She had even kept a copy on her hard drive. It was really a letter to herself, detailing her selfish, callous behaviour and confessing all the mistakes she had made in her emotional relationships. She had written about her dead father and about Pearl, and when she started on Victor, she found she couldn't stem the flow of words that streamed out of her, and the letter just kept going on and on. And yet it read clumsily, as if she was writing in a foreign language. She thought to herself that this was the first time that she had dug up her past and told her husband of four years anything about it. It was something that Huang Xin was certainly not going to welcome.

All the same, with the passage of time, he would surely come to understand in the end. Or perhaps he already did. Perhaps he had understood all those months ago, on the morning when she had conceived. In his heart of hearts, he must have known that their marriage was not good enough, even though it was not particularly bad either. Besides, by the time he got back, everything would look brighter. (He was away at a meeting bidding on a contract and then going to visit some nearby projects and would not be home for at least ten days, after which he would have time to peruse his personal emails. The good thing with emails was that everyone could take whatever time they needed to process things.)

Her baby! Where was her baby? Marina suddenly panicked. She remembered telling Huang Xin about the baby at the end of her email. She could have not told him, but she thought that even if they divorced, he had a right to know. With a great effort, feeling as if her arms were tied down, she pushed her hand down towards her belly, which she found, to her horror, was as flat as a pancake.

She opened her mouth, trying with all her might to scream, though the only sound that came out was a rustling as faint as the flapping of a butterfly's wings.

"What's that?" the stubbly-chinned man said as he leaned closer to her pillow. His voice wheezed like a broken trombone and Marina found it hard to make out the words.

"Hang on a minute," he said hesitantly. His eyes glowed like the light bulb hanging from the ceiling, like coloured reflections in a basin of water. She had seen them before, far back in the distant past. It was Ash.

She made an effort to reach out to her beloved brother but he was so far away. At last she reached him, and even though her arms were leaden and aching, she felt straightaway that there was something different about him. It was not just the extra chin and straggly whiskers. His eyes looked different, his hands were stronger than that evening not so long ago when they had hugged each other.

Yes, Ash had changed.

After the explosion, he had been through a lot. The women (Pearl and his mother, that is) were more frail and unreliable than he had expected. They seemed paralyzed, sitting slumped over on the floor, going over and over what had happened, their regrets and their remorse, refusing to eat or sleep. They were in pieces, unable to take anything in. He knew he could not expect any real help from that quarter.

It was down to Ash to take over. He dealt with Victor's funeral, clearing The Glass House, agreeing the care plan for the baby, talking to the doctors, signing documents, nodding in acknowledgement of trite expressions of sympathy, answering the same old questions from the investigating authorities, confirming dry and boring numbers with the compensation team and so on. Then in the evenings, he came to replace Su Qin and Pearl at the hospital so they could get some sleep. There he sat at Marina's bedside, drifting in and out of a doze, listening to her breathing and wondering at the numbness inside him. He felt like a stone. He had not shed a single tear yet.

He would love to have cried. He remembered the feeling of having eyes full of tears. When he cried, even though his mother and his sister hated him doing so, he felt the world was a gentler place. But right now, he couldn't figure out how to cry, or what about. He sat by Marina's bed, still trying to think it through and staring at his feet which seemed like they belonged to a stranger.

In the moments prior to the explosion, his feet had been resting inelegantly on his computer table, the keyboard balancing on his knees, as he argued back and forth with a couple of bargain hunters on the phone. Then the pungent smell that had permeated the whole of Crossroads reached him, and in the violent explosion that followed, his monitor shook violently and went black. Horrified, he dropped the keyboard and crouched on all fours like an alert dog, then hurriedly pulled the pile of exercise books from under his bed and cradled them in his arms. He couldn't let anything happen to them, come what may. The terrifying thought that this might be the end of the world brought tears to his eyes, but he felt some small comfort as well. At least he had got his secrets off his chest.

He spotted Victor's clothes under the bed too. The sight of the bags sent a chill down his spine and made him pull himself together. Before he knew he had moved out from his hiding place, his feet were carrying him out of the door as fast as they could. His legs carried him past scenes that he could make no sense of, past the panicking crowds, past the Korean hair accessories that were raining down on them. He had never imagined that he was such a tough, powerful runner. Finally, his feet took him into the ruins of the glass workshop, where they waded and kicked through the rubble like a duck wading through deep water. The Glass House had been a magnificent edifice, so transparent it looked like an empty, floating frame. Now, it was cloudy with shards of glass, most of it piled up in heaps that seemed to claw at Ash as if they were trying to drown him and mercilessly tore his trousers and shoes to ribbons.

He spotted Victor at the back of the shop, lying underneath remnants of the glass bricks that he used to keep immaculate. They were spattered crimson with blood. Victor was only wearing a vest and his upper body looked fit and muscular, the way it had looked on their trip to the cemetery all those years ago. That day, Ash remembered, Vic had taken off his jacket and shovelled the dirt vigorously onto the grass growing on top of the grave.

Ash suddenly noticed a red-stained rag draped over Victor's left wrist. He hesitated, then slowly shifted his gaze to Victor's right hand. In his palm lay a triangular piece of glass, obtuse angle pointed downwards while one sharp corner stuck up proudly, like the red-crowned crane, thickly clotted with a layer of blood.

In the days that followed, as he made all the necessary arrangements, a separate corner of Ash's mind forced itself to go over and over this last image of Victor. In his head, Victor had fused with his glass. (Of course, that couldn't be true, he must have been imagining it.) Meanwhile, his mother and Pearl's muffled sobs and self-recrimination buzzed in his ears like annoying insects. He put on a pretence of keeping busy, running back and forth, rushing in and out of the ward. Only he knew that his feet had not stopped trembling. It took all his self-control to keep his mouth shut and to swallow back the words that burned there like hot peppers. About Victor's death . . . he heard himself say to Su Qin and Pearl.

No! He told himself he had to keep quiet. It would be unfair to tell them, and what was the point? Besides, he did not know if he dared to admit that he was the trigger for all that had happened. It was in his exercise books, written when he was so lonely, that Victor and Marina had, step by step, made their relationship real. He'd caused it all.

No, stop! He told himself firmly. He did not want to be like Su Qin and Pearl with their never-ending tears. At the very least, Ash did not want to let himself cry or talk to anyone, especially Marina, until he had figured things out properly. He had to decide what to say first, if Marina woke up.

He was confused when he heard her first words, until he remembered that Marina had given birth, so the first thing she would ask for when she woke up was the baby. It was wonderful, but when Ash picked the infant up and held her high above him to show her off, he relinquished his chance to get a word in with her mother first.

That baby certainly had a will to live. She had been expelled into the world on a brutally cold street corner in Crossroads, when her mother went into shock and her womb into premature labour. Out she came, along with amniotic fluid and sticky blood, landing unceremoniously on the side of the road. She had sustained abrasions on her back, pulled a muscle in her left leg and developed an infected airway. The medic (who was decidedly not a gynaecologist) was so nervous that he tied the umbilical cord in an unsightly knot, and the baby was probably so upset by this that she kept her eyes tightly shut. When the breathing tube was inserted and again when it was removed, she almost didn't make it. But in the end she had hung on, and by the sixth day, she was finally clenching her fists and yelling in a strong, angry voice.

The nurses, Su Qin, Pearl and Ash took turns rocking and feeding her, crooning to her when she got distressed. It was all to no avail, she just wouldn't stop crying, so the doctor agreed to put her in her mother's arms, even though Marina was still unconscious. The baby girl gurgled triumphantly and some mysterious instinct guided her to turn her mouth and latch onto Marina's nipple. At that very moment, with great difficulty, Marina fluttered her eyelids, sighed softly and in her dream stepped away from the desolate, lonely shore where she had been stranded.

Marina gazed at her baby. Her face was as clear and pure as a little Bodhisattva. But soon, she too would grow up in a ruthless world. She would fall fleetingly in love, would wallow in giddy bubbles, enraptured with all sorts of desires. What she was about to hand to her baby was a sweaty, sticky baton: questionable prospects, wobbly self-esteem, a mother who was probably even more temperamental than her grandmother, and, of course, filthy old Crossroads, which she would grow to love and hate. What goes around comes around. Birth and class, struggle and failure, these questions never went away.

Marina felt the sting of a branch whipping across her face. Su Qin was right. She was a mother now, and it changed everything. She was painfully aware that she, who had always fought her destiny fearlessly, was now bound helplessly to her child.

Marina saw a sparkly hair clip on the windowsill, its artificial glitter catching the sunlight, glowing like unshed tears. She was suddenly filled with admiration for her mother. She had fought (and stumbled) to uphold her right to her own private morality. She hadn't done so badly, Marina could learn from her. Besides, she had already been out in the rainstorm with her baby, she could survive all that life threw at her. If the Jews, some of the world's most downtrodden but tenacious people, could say, "ein ma la'asot", "there's nothing to be done", and "ihye beseder", "it'll be alright", then so could she. Marina pressed an awkward kiss on her baby girl's head, then spent a long time gently stroking her sparse hair. She asked for a mirror and looked at her left cheek, at the raised scar in the shape of an upside-down Greek gamma, "γ". The scar was disfiguring, but she touched it and actually kind of liked it, though she didn't think it was deep or ugly enough for a punishment.

Ash waited in silence. He felt as though this was the perfect lead in. Now he could talk about the accident; in fact, it would be perverse to hold back. But Marina remained impassive, perhaps even intent on keeping him at arm's length. She was completely absorbed by the physical presence of the infant in her arms.

It wasn't until Ash was about to leave that Marina casually said, "Can you get something for me from home? There's something I need. Right above my bed, there's a little green torch. Can you bring it next time you come? I like to have it by my bed."

Ash stood quite still. He knew all about the green torch, but was surprised Marina still had it. Now that she had said that, he knew that nothing more needed to be said.

He did a quick calculation. It was thirteen years ago that the four of them had gone shopping together at the night market. In his memory, he could see them from a distance amid the poorly-dressed crowds, their images slightly smudged, like a cheap woodcut print. They had splashed out that evening: they had ice-cream and lamb kebabs, popped airguns and threw hoops. Pearl chose eye shadow and a belt. Ash picked out a Rubik's cube and peanuts. Victor insisted on buying Marina the little green torch. She'd gone red with embarrassment and tried to refuse it at first.

Ash nodded. He took the baby from Marina's arms. Her tiny body was warm and sweet, but suddenly felt immeasurably heavy. She pressed down on his arms until they trembled, and memories of another body flashed before his eyes. He remembered how he had put his arms around Victor, carefully covering his left wrist, and carried him out of the workshop and towards Crossroads. He'd carried him past the places where he'd played pool, bought cigarettes, gone to the night market and scuffled with his friends. Vic's body, once so sturdy and strong that it was an object of envy to Ash, now felt so light in his arms that it made his head swim.

Oh, baby! What is life? At last the tears came, and Ash's world became gentle and moist again. He felt overwhelmed with sadness that Victor, who had been so heavy in life, had died with such lightness; and the life of this baby, so light, would become so heavy. As Ash clung to the baby, a strange feeling surged through him. It was a timid but very precise desire to do all he could for this tiny creature, to ensure that she could have a decent life. He would act like a man. Fuck the shrinks.

Ash held the sleeping baby and breathed in her innocent fragrance.

"I've got something to tell you," he said to her tenderly. "I have a bag of kid's clothes. They're a bit old and they're for a boy, but you must wear them, you hear me?"

Outside, they heard Pearl shuffling towards the door and the rustle of Su Qin's plastic bags. As soon as they came through the door, Marina knew what would happen: there would be an outpouring of emotion, mutual consolation after the trauma they had all suffered, a fierce scramble to apportion blame, reiterated conjectures, comforting but useless.

"Dearest family," she wanted to say, "There really is no need for all these protestations. Love is always innocent. It can't be pinned down. We're not hothouse flowers, are we? Look at us, we all have ways of coping: there was Ding Bogang's wine-fuelled forgetfulness, Pearl's philosophy of foolishness, Ash's law of weakness and our mother's private way of virtue, and of course there was Vic's glass-blowing. So many strategies for stirring up grief and fermenting it until it turns into sweet syrup!"

Marina turned her head on the pillow. There was nothing there, but she could feel the invisible presence of the green torch quite distinctly. She hadn't had much need to use it over the years, but she had always made sure to replace the batteries inside and press the button to check that it still worked. It was cheap and shoddy and no longer as bright as it had been (it was from the night market, after all) but she took good care of it so it would always keep her company.

Outside the window, a few dreary grey clouds floated over the factory zone, like sheets of glass that needed a good clean.

She imagined Victor standing there, a white rag in his hand, unhurriedly, patiently, wiping clean the last mark he had left on this earth.

8

THE LAST TIME the two families met was on a scrubby patch of land on the banks of the Yangtze River.

Earlier that day, as a ship blew its siren in the distance, they had scattered Victor's ashes in the river, along with those of Ding Bogang – and Marina's father's ashes, which had been retrieved from the Shigang Ashes Storage Depot two years before.

It was Marina's idea to scatter the ashes in the Yangtze, that immensely long river whose turbid, flood-prone waters teemed with life and excrement. She was sure they would all have liked it. Even Ding Bogang could be reassured that his final resting place would never be pulled down or dug up.

Together, Pearl and Su Qin unwrapped the red silk bundles with clumsy fingers. Finally, their hands fell away and the three pieces of cloth and their contents tumbled into the rushing water and disappeared.

Ash peered after them. He had sneaked something else in too, along with his father, Ding Bogang and Victor: the ashes of his old exercise books.

Ash could not have told you why he decided to do this. The idea just came to him the evening before. He found a lighter but that did not seem dignified enough, so he looked for matches, fussing over the pattern on the matchbox and the length of the matches. He tried striking a few of them, almost playfully, to see what colour and shapes the flames made, before finally setting all the exercise books alight. They were just paper and had caught fire instantly.

The evening breeze had pushed in like a nosyparker, and the exercise books, ignorant of their impending demise, blithely fluttered their pages, flashing those familiar paragraphs at Ash once more, before the choking black smoke devoured them.

All those days and nights that he had committed to paper were gone in a flash. Ash held his breath as he carefully scooped up the warm ashes with his hands, feeling the breeze in his ears as the years of his childhood and youth flew by.

Su Qin came over and took the baby from Marina. She said to her daughter, rather obscurely, "I know you never got over losing your father, and neither did I. But when Ding Bogang came along, I liked him. Don't go blaming me, it's not a contradiction."

Marina's heart missed a beat. She knew that was true, but she also sensed her mother was leading up to something. And Su Qin did go on, groping for the right words.

"So what I'm trying to tell you is that there's no contradiction in your feelings for Victor and Huang Xin. Life moves on, and all that matters is that you're honest and sincere in what you do."

Marina nodded but said nothing. She was lost in thought, fascinated by the river currents before her.

Of course, Huang Xin had come back from his trip away as soon as he heard about the accident, and his anger, his fear for mother and daughter and his relief that they were both safe, reminded Marina of the times when they had been happy together, however short-lived. Or perhaps it was their baby that had softened her feelings. She had to admit that she quite liked it when Huang Xin picked up their little girl. Huang Xin mentioned her letter to him. He said he didn't really agree with it, but he appreciated it all the same, and in fact he was in the middle of writing a long reply. He looked carefully at her expression and asked if he could be the one to pick the little girl's name. He even offered to go with them to scatter the ashes. Marina had found it difficult to be nice, and in the end just allowed him to pick the name.

It was not that she wanted to reject Huang Xin's kindness outright, it was just that she was still feeling antagonistic. A bleak, cold wind was blasting through her body and she could not tell when she would ever thaw out and feel the warmth of spring in her heart. Besides, it was sad but true that Huang Xin really had no need to explain or justify himself. When it came to getting on in society, materialistic desires in and of themselves were not to be blamed. Quite the opposite, they were necessary to motivate people to work hard. This was common sense, as Marina well knew, just as she knew how proud and prejudiced she had always been.

She drank in the sight of the river. It was such a vast and mighty torrent, flowing all the way here from its source over a thousand miles away, regardless of what it carried along and what sank beneath its waters. It was neither proud nor self-abasing, as strong and generous as time itself, a worthy object of human worship. Marina wondered if she could emulate its boldness, lay past shadows to rest and continue to wrestle with fate. That was, after all, what Victor had wanted.

On the day that Marina regained consciousness, Pearl had dawdled until they were alone in the sickroom. Her eyes welled up and she stammered, "Marina, there's one more thing. After we said goodbye that day, I went to see my brother and told him what you were thinking. So he already knew how you felt before he died."

"And?" Marina had pushed herself upright in the bed. She felt as if a black veil was descending over her head, and an odd tingle ran through her body.

Pearl remembered the way Vic had covered his face with his hand, his desperate reply of, "I can't accept it. I can't let this happen."

She tensed, her heart thumping. She couldn't put it like that, could she? She looked away and made a show of playing with the baby's tiny fingers.

She tentatively began again: "He was thrilled, of course. He said he'd be delighted to welcome you and your baby."

But Pearl's skills at lying had all been used up on her fake pregnancy. Her little speech sounded as unconvincing as the clumsiest sort of after-dinner toast.

Marina took one look at Pearl's desperate expression and nodded as if in relief and gratitude. In fact, her head filled with the hissing of autumn cicadas, interspersed with the banging of a clapper from a dark alley.

Of course! She should have thought of that. There was no way that Victor would have let her turn the clock back. He would have stoutly defended the materialistic life she had chosen for herself and sternly demanded that she move forward and never look back. This was a fundamental principle of love, and it was also an instinct of the social class they both came from. He would have made this his parting gift to her.

Marina stopped herself from thinking any more. The river breeze was raw and slightly tangy. The old dark-green ship sounded its siren once more and drifted out of sight.

What was it Rilke wrote? It went something like this: "Our lives are wrapped around with hardship. To learn to live, to learn to love, is to take on all the hardships of this life, and then to find in them the presence of beauty and friendship, is to find the way out into the world."

Marina had copied this out when she was in college and happened to come across it again on that frantic, joyous morning when she was rummaging around for her silk scarf.

Yes, she had to learn to love. Victor was no longer around, but she would carry on alone battling angrily with her desires. You could not escape your fate. You were born within its confines, marked by it from birth, destined to trudge along the hard path of your life towards an end point that you knew was an illusion.

But there was nothing wrong with this, was there? This is what made life so strange, so heroic and so vibrant. Life was both honey and bile, and every bit of it had to be sipped carefully. Besides, it behoved them all to learn to love and to create love, because they were all living, breathing beings.

After they had scattered the ashes in the river they stood on the embankment for a long time, like tourists, until Ash suddenly came up with the idea that they should have a picnic right there.

Everyone agreed, and then divided up to go and buy some food. They may perhaps have been reminded of that day out on Qing Ming twelve years before, when all six of them had been as bright and lively as actors in a comedy. If they were to have another picnic, what better place than by the river? The houses where they used to live no longer existed. It was only in the here and now that the living and the dead could enjoy each other's company.

It was getting late, and their impromptu picnic was rather spartan – just sliced bread, cartons of milk and some fruit – and the tablecloth with its ugly pattern was a bit too small. But they didn't care. This picnic reminded them of a Saturday dinner, the table covered in colourful bowls and dishes under the warm yellow glow of the dim light bulb. It had been twelve years since the families officially split up, and this was their first reunion. They sat in the same places they had always done. Where Ding Bogang used to be, Pearl placed his green drinking cup (which she had not been able to bring herself to throw into the river earlier). Colourful balloons hung from the baby's Moses basket, which was set down, as was right and proper, in the place vacated by Victor.

Come to think of it, the small tablecloth would have been far too crowded if Huang Xin had been allowed to come – another reason for leaving him out this time.

Pearl suddenly gave a little cough, in place of tapping a wine glass with a fork like people do at a fancy dinner party. When she had everyone's attention, she looked at each of them in turn, and muttered awkwardly, "I'm all packed up to go off and look for Heipi. The police are giving me travel expenses. They say there are too many people they want to talk to and they can't follow them all up. Anyway, they say Heipi's just small fry. Don't worry about me. All I have to do is get a map of China and tick off the big cities, one by one. Anywhere there's a park with a lake, I'll ask around, he'll be in one of them wearing his Walk-on-Water shoes. I'm guessing he hasn't heard about the explosion yet."

Marina patted Pearl's broad shoulders and said with sincerity,

"Don't worry. Off you go, but don't be too long. This baby owes her life to you. You're my sister and her aunt, you have to look after us!"

Ash took a bite of the dry bread and chewed hard. This was the second time he had heard Marina call Pearl "sister". Image after image from all those years ago swam before his eyes: six people from two families, meeting for the first time in that long-demolished workers' housing block. At the time, it had felt like they were all jammed together on a puppet show stage, as rigid as tree stumps, standing awkwardly where they'd been told to, wholly unaware of what the future was to bring.

One of them threw some bread into the river, and hungry gulls swooped down to claim it. As twilight thickened, loosely covering them like a huge blanket, they sat close to one another, the expressions on their faces unreadable.